TZIPPY
THE THIEF

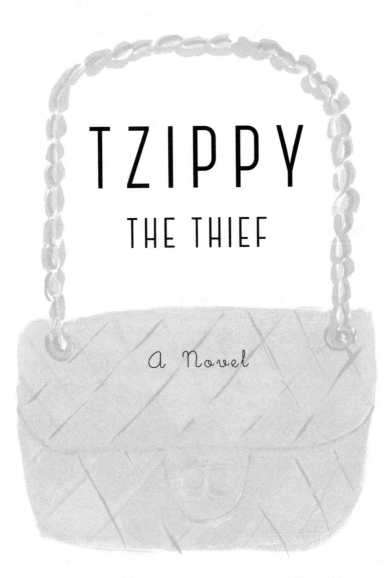

TZIPPY
THE THIEF

A Novel

PATRICIA STRIAR ROHNER

She Writes Press, a BookSparks imprint
A Division of SparkPointStudio, LLC.

Published 2016

Printed in the United States of America

Print ISBN: 978-1-63152-153-9
E-ISBN: 978-1-63152-154-6
Library of Congress Control Number: 2016941066

For information, address:
She Writes Press
1563 Solano Ave #546
Berkeley, CA 94707

Cover design © Julie Metz, Ltd./metzdesign.com
Cover photo © TK
Formatting by Katherine Lloyd/theDESKonline.com

She Writes Press is a division of SparkPoint Studio, LLC.

This book is dedicated to my friend, neighbor, and teacher, Mrs. Dorothy Nordmann. She told me never to stop writing and called me her "star." She believed in me and inspired me. I am forever grateful to her. May she rest in peace.

Chapter 1

Tzipora Finkel Bryer wiped her eyes. She was feeling weepy again. She put down the paper and slumped in the cane-backed chair in her bedroom, where she spent much of her time these days. Around her were the shades of silk her decorator had chosen—melon, lemon, and robin's egg blue—but tonight the pastels did not calm her; she felt particularly restless and nervous. She leaned her hands on the French provincial desk, usually reserved for paying bills, and looked at the brown spots on her wrinkled hands. They were indeed the hands of an old woman, and she knew it, though the engagement ring and wedding band her now-dead husband had given her fifty-five years before still sparkled on her finger.

Tzippy groaned and hit herself in the chest. She was suffering heartburn from the noodle kugel and herring with cream sauce. Earlier, she and Angie—her live-in maid of thirty-eight years, who did all the cooking, cleaning, and laundry—had eaten the rich fare Selma's daughter had served after the funeral, then driven home to her seaside apartment in Bal Harbour. Angie was already in bed. The only food that agreed with Tzippy these days was hot water and saltines. She coughed and spat incessantly, wadding up her soiled tissues and throwing them into a basket by her crumpled bed. She half wondered if she would even wake up the next morning.

She sighed and tried reading the paper again, her red half-glasses still perched on the bridge of her fine aquiline nose, but all she could think about was her dear friend Selma Grossman, her cherry wood casket being lowered into the rectangular grave. She shook her head, trying to dispel the image. Too many of her friends were dying. How long did she have?

Just twelve days earlier, Tzippy and her beau of three years, Stan, had celebrated New Year's Eve at the Fontainebleau Hotel's Y2K party, and the world hadn't ended. The year 2000 had started right on schedule; only Selma had died.

As a youngster, Tzippy had rarely thought about death. Once, a friend's father had fallen off his bike and died of a heart attack while riding in the park with his son. The incident had shocked Tzippy, had caused her little heart to flutter with disbelief. But mostly, she'd been safe from thoughts of her life ending. Of course, as a child she couldn't wait to be in the front of the line, waving her hand, beseeching the teacher to choose her. Her heart had brimmed with expectation. Now she prayed she wouldn't die on the toilet seat like Elvis Presley.

Poor Selma had died in her sleep. Half the synagogue had turned out for the funeral. Everyone had loved Selma, with her hearty laugh and generous spirit. For ten years, ever since her husband, Milt, had died, she had paid for the entire spread on Yom Kippur when the congregation broke its fast.

Tzippy had not been so extravagant with her money since Benny had passed—or at least she hadn't spent it frivolously on others. Tzippy didn't want to end up like Esther Berger, her old friend from West Belchertown, who had to live with her daughter, a girl with limited parenting and domestic skills and a cheap husband. No, Tzippy did not want to be at anyone's mercy.

There had been a good turnout for Selma at Mount Abrams Jewish Cemetery. Three of Selma's piano students had attended, young children looking scared and sad, standing off to the side, each holding the hand of a grown-up, probably one of their parents. Selma had taught them how to play and told them, "You need to bring music into the world." Tzippy shook her head in amazement, thinking about how her friend, eighty-five-year-old Selma, had given piano lessons right up to the end. She had to admit this giving spirit made her uncomfortable.

Rachel Levin had been there with her Hispanic driver. Since she'd had a stroke, she hadn't been able to get around alone. "I can't even put on my own pantyhose," she lamented. But she looked good, despite her troubles. Dr. Nathan and his new wife had also attended. He was a podiatrist, which had been his father's occupation. He came from Brooklyn, had gone to Brooklyn College on the GI Bill, and had a brother in the diamond business. The new wife was pretty and twenty years younger, which annoyed Tzippy. She resented men's having the advantage, trading their wives in like old cars. Still, she had managed to have her own way when she'd wanted it. She smiled, remembering Claude, her young lover. She liked being a rebel, still did.

Loyal, loving Stan had stood by her side at the gravesite and rubbed her arm when she wept as the rabbi finished his eulogy, extolling Selma's virtues and laying her to rest. Stan and Selma, they were the good ones. Tzippy's favorite sisters, Sophia and Julia, were buried at the cemetery, along with their husbands. Ben's golfing and gin rummy buddies, Milt Lieberman and Jerry Katz, were also interred there. It was like a small reunion park.

Now, she tried to think of cheerier things. She leafed through the January 2000 *Vogue* and admired the skinny models with their arched eyebrows and flawless complexions. There had been a time when she looked that attractive. Hadn't she caught her husband by wearing that wonderful French green chapeau with the sequined heart? Yes, she had been a looker.

Unable to concentrate, she put her magazine down on top of her unpaid bills and checkbook. Perhaps she'd feel better if she lay down. She turned up the air conditioner and looked out the window to the east, where the vast ocean crashed and rolled, making her feel small and insignificant. She admired the cherub-bedecked porcelain lamps with ivory shades on each of her night tables. Such pretty lighting, she mused. That decorator Arietta Flock sure had known her business.

She decided to undress and get into bed. With her pink night jacket covering her shoulders, the lamp still on, and her red half-glasses on her nose, she picked up the remote. She checked the TV for an old movie, maybe Clint Eastwood or Paul Newman— Tzippy appreciated a sexy man. She still had a good eye, even half-blind. But there was nothing.

In the morning, she would take a bath and then go to her appointment with Maria, her hairdresser. She needed to have her hair combed for the day and also to discuss a new style for her birthday party. Maybe she'd invest in another hairpiece to cover the bald spot on the back of her head—something fuller and with more blond highlights. On a pad, she wrote down the few errands she had to run. She had to go to Saks for the final fitting on her suit; she still didn't want to spend the money on the matching aubergine heels. Eggplant! Prada shoes were too damn expensive.

Just as she was calculating the cost of the entire birthday outfit, the phone rang. It was Shari, Tzippy's youngest and most challenging child, calling from Massachusetts.

"Mom, how are you? Did I call too late?" she said.

"Oh, sweetheart, it's good to hear your voice. No, I just got into bed to rest. It's been a tough day."

"What happened?"

"I went to Selma's funeral—Selma Grossman, you remember her—and it depressed me so. I can't stand all these people dying. I'll be next."

"Quit being morbid, will you?"

"Selma was a good woman. Her piano students were there. You should have heard what the rabbi said. What a mensch, he said. Everyone was crying. I wonder what they'll say when I die."

"They'll say you were a character, Mom. One of a kind. They'll say you drove me crazy but I loved you anyhow."

"Did I drive you crazy?"

"You know you did. I nearly starved myself to death because of you."

"Please stop saying that." *Enough with the needling*, Tzippy thought. When Shari had started her diet at age fifteen, Tzippy had been glad because she'd thought Shari could afford to drop five pounds. Looks had always been important to Tzippy, ever since her childhood, when her own mother had compared her and her sisters—all eight of them—and they'd fought over who was the slimmest and prettiest. But Shari had taken it to extremes and kept losing weight well after she needed to.

Tzippy didn't know Shari was having only an apple, a carrot, and a small carton of milk for lunch until the headmistress at the girls' school called to report her concerns. When poor, dead Selma Grossman had stopped her in the street one day and said, "What's the matter with Shari? She looks like she's just been released from Auschwitz," Tzippy shrank with shame. The remark haunted her to this day. Still, was it all her fault her daughter had tried to starve herself?

"I wish you didn't hold everything against me," Tzippy said.

"Okay, let's not review history. You're a tough old bird and will live to be a hundred. Is that better?"

"Please, Shari. Give me a break tonight."

"I still love you."

"That's my girl."

She heard a *smack* across the telephone wires as Shari blew her a kiss.

"But it *is* depressing, Shari."

"Mom, it's already Wednesday. In two days we'll be coming down to celebrate your eightieth birthday. You'll probably dance the night away and drink us all under the table."

"I doubt I'll drink *you* under the table."

"Probably not—I'll give you that. Still, you'll see another twenty years. Stop this."

"Okay, you're right. So, how is *your* life? How's your job at the Gap?"

"It's terrible. I hate it. I've told you. The help only works there to get the discount, they have so little motivation, and the district manager's a bitch. I stand on my feet all day, and I'm exhausted. Plus, I have to work on the weekends. The pay's mediocre. I can't put any money away."

"Oh, dear, I'm sorry. You've tried so many things. What else could you do?" Tzippy had heard the Gap saga before, but she still felt bad about Shari's poor luck. Shari had not moved up the corporate ladder like her other friends because she had lost focus partying, wasting time with guys who were beneath her, jumping from one career to another, fluctuating with unstable moods, starving, overindulging with booze, and hooking up with one-night stands. She had worked in real estate but had earned only $10,000 per year; had sold furniture, kitchenware, cheese, wine, and women's clothes; and had written a wine column for the local newspaper for free.

"I should have been a movie star and gotten rich and famous."

Benny had always said Shari could act, and she was pretty enough, but Tzippy reminded her, "It's a little late for that."

"I know, at forty-five, I've missed the boat. But I still look pretty good. I bought a new dress for your party. It's royal purple and has a plunging neckline. Quite sexy."

"I wish you had a boyfriend to show it off to. What happened to Ed?"

"I had to get rid of him. He flirted with everything in a skirt. I couldn't take it anymore. At the moment I'm between husbands, as you would say." It was a family joke. Shari had actually been married only once and engaged another time. Tzippy liked to say she was between husbands, instead of between boyfriends. It had a better ring.

"Maybe Brucie could fix you up with one of his cronies."

"My brother has enough on his plate at the moment," Shari said. "Business is bad. The banks are coming down on him."

"Yes, you're right. He's having a hard time."

"I wish Daddy were alive. He'd know what to do. I should have worked in the family business," Shari said.

"Well, you've gone from being a movie star to being a coat manufacturer all in one telephone conversation."

"Don't make fun of me, Mother. You always do that, and it makes me feel bad."

"I wasn't making fun; I was just joking."

Shari sighed. "Do you need anything special when I come?"

"No, just you and your famous pillow you always bring. And a box of those wonderful chocolates they sell on Arlington Street near that nice hotel."

"Okay, I'll get some. Now, Mom, go to sleep and quit worrying. We're going to dance and laugh and toast you all night long."

"Shari, thanks for being so nice to me, even if we have our rough patches. I love you."

"I love you, too."

Tzippy sighed and leaned back against her headboard, lined with miniature pillows that she and Angie had stolen from airplanes whenever they took a flight. Then she felt a cramp start to creep up her veiny right leg, viselike, making her foot curl. She couldn't control her toes; the cramp contorted them so they stuck together. Her body was betraying her, just like it would in the end. Paralyzed with pain, she yelled, "Angie," forcing out her maid's name in a low grunt.

When nothing happened, Tzippy began to panic. She picked up a spoon and banged it on her small night table, filled with medicines. "Angie," she howled. "Help me."

Wrinkled and sleepy, Angie appeared in her nightgown and robe, her hair all curled up in rags. "What's a matter, Mrs. B.?"

Tzippy stuck out her leg. "I have a terrible cramp. Oh, it's bad tonight," she whispered.

The large black woman bent down and began to massage Tzippy's leg. Then she kneaded her foot.

"Let me get the vinegar," Angie said, reaching for the glass bottle of clear liquid on the night table. "Hold still." She poured the white vinegar into the palms of her muscular hands and rubbed it all over Tzippy's leg and foot.

"The thigh, too," Tzippy said.

Angie continued to work on Tzippy's leg, which was thin-skinned and striated with veins from childbearing. Tzippy hated looking at her legs and often covered them with support hose. Angie massaged slowly, taking her time and gently relieving the torment.

"Oh, that's much better," Tzippy said, bending back into her pillows and sighing as the cramp gave way to luscious relief.

"That vinegar sure helps, doesn't it?"

"Yeah, I don't know why, but it works. Thank you, sweetie."

Tzippy watched as Angie rose, her girth making her slow to stand, and went into Tzippy's bathroom. For a moment, Tzippy was alone again, and she stretched her arms above her head. One of these days, she'd have to get to that yoga class they held at the community center. She'd been promising herself to go for over five years. Maybe it would keep her from dying. With new resolve, she decided to call in the morning.

From the bathroom came the clink of glass breaking and then a flood of perfume filled the room like a noxious cloud. It was one of the heavily floral scents that Tzippy no longer wore, and it pressed on her, as if to keep her from breathing. Then she heard dismayed humming from Angie and the rush of running water.

Angie emerged from the bathroom, flushed and bothered.

"What happened?" Tzippy asked.

"Oh, Mrs. B., I knocked over one of them little trial perfume bottles standing by the tub."

"What were you doing over there?"

"Nothing." Angie looked like she wanted to bolt from the room. "I broke it. I'm sorry."

"Are you okay?" Tzippy asked. "Did you cut yourself?"

"Oh, no," Angie said. "I'm fine. I loved that perfume."

"Well, it's about to suffocate me," Tzippy said. "Will you open the window?"

Angie hurried over and opened both windows to the south, the ones that looked down on the apartment's pool complex. A humid breeze blew in, and for once it was welcome.

"Thank you, Angie," Tzippy said. "I don't know what I'd do without you."

Angie looked relieved and said, "Sure looks like we're going steady."

Tzippy said, "I'm okay now. Go back to sleep."

Angie came over and gave her hand a squeeze. After she left, Tzippy leaned back on her pillows and sighed, grateful for her good fortune at having a live-in. She knew living with her children would be more excruciating than the cramps. In fact, thinking about their coming for her birthday party gave her angina. Sometimes Shari drank too much and fought with her brother, Brucie. The last time they'd had a party, Ike, Naomi's husband, had given an inebriated, run-on toast that embarrassed Tzippy. She'd always wanted everything perfect.

She had told herself over and over, *Try not to dwell on any more upsetting thoughts*. But she couldn't help it. The perfume still hung heavily in the air. What had Angie been doing over by the tub? She'd have to throw away all those little vials she'd pocketed; they were no use to her anymore. Suddenly, her head was spinning with chores. There was so much to think about.

Chapter 2

She awoke with unusual sprightliness, briefly forgetting the events of the previous day. Even through the gauzy drapes, she felt the welcome warmth of the morning and for the moment lay there, luxuriating in the pleasure of feeling the sun on her face. But when she pushed herself from the bed, her body complained and she had to rise bit by bit into a standing position. It was painful, but she pushed herself and quickly swallowed a pill. She took anti-anxiety meds to calm her down. She had started when Benny was screwing golden-haired Laura and Tzippy had panic attacks while driving with Claude, who became her Jamaican lover, and now Tzippy relied on the little white pills whenever she felt fearful or annoyed.

"Angie, where are you?" she called, like an abandoned child in her empty room.

Just then the phone rang.

"Hi, baby cakes," Stan said. As she pictured him, with his white hair and ruddy complexion, she calmed down. Perhaps he was wearing pajamas. Blue, like the color of the sky.

"Good morning, Stanley." Her voice sounded brittle and strained.

"What's wrong?"

"I just woke up. My body's not behaving."

"What hurts?"

"Everything."

"Give it time. Walk around, eat something." She could see

Stan with a barbell in one hand and the phone in the other. He tried to keep in good shape, worked hard at it.

Angie appeared at the door and put a cup of tea on the nightstand. Tzippy nodded curtly to her and waved her away. She didn't like other people overhearing her phone conversations.

"Pretty nice service they had for poor Selma," Stan said.

"Yes, it was. I'll miss her."

"She was a good egg."

"I wonder who'll do the Yom Kippur spread now that that sweet soul is gone."

"Maybe you," Stan said mischievously.

Tzippy felt a hot blush start at her breastbone. "I can't afford it."

"Baby cakes, you're loaded. Ben left you in good shape."

"I need my cash. You do it." He had no idea how much she loved having cash in the bank. It was her prime reason for renting, rather than buying.

"I'm not as flush as you," Stan said.

She remembered how he and Benny would argue about who would place the biggest bet on the underdog at the prize fights and Stan would say, "Ben, my boy, you're the leader of this pack—you go for it."

"How do you know?" Tzippy said sharply. "Have you looked at my bank account lately?" She hated when he talked about her money. Stan had never been as successful as Benny.

"I love you. Let's not argue."

"You're right," she said. Tzippy knew Stan was a decent, honorable, affectionate man and she loved him like a second husband, more easily and less intensely. Sometimes at dinner he kissed her lips and rubbed her thigh under the table. He hugged her while they cuddled on the yellow brocade sofa, fondled her breasts, and touched her crotch. Once, she and Stan had almost had sex on the yellow couch, but at the last second Tzippy had decided against it, fearing the sofa might stain. And something about doing it in her bedroom made her feel uncomfortable. So now she and Stan went away for weekends—to the gracious old hotels of Orchid Island and Palm Beach—to have sex. She undressed in unfamiliar bathrooms, turned the lights off, and climbed into bed so Stan didn't see anything she was embarrassed to show.

"Goldie sure was friendly to you yesterday," Tzippy commented.

"What are you talking about, baby cakes?"

"The way she batted her eyelashes at you when you were sitting on the sofa in Selma's daughter's den—that's what I mean."

"God, Tzippy. She's your cousin. The woman was just being nice."

"Nice, my ass. The way she cooed, 'Stanley, you're uncomfortable . . . Can I get you something?' Give me a break." Goldie was Tzippy's perennial rival, and still had good legs at eighty.

"I love it when women fight over me. What are you doing today?"

"I gotta get ready for the kids, my party."

"You free tonight? Let's go to the Fire Station."

Stan was such a sport, always taking her to the best restaurants and never once allowing her to pay a dime. "Fine. What time?"

"How's seven?"

"Perfect." She'd give Angie the night off so she could go visit her boyfriend, Jack.

Tzippy walked into her bathroom and washed her face and brushed her teeth. The smell from the broken perfume bottle hung in the air. She looked at the vials of different scents circling the tub. Some of them were in pretty containers, but she never used them. Might as well get rid of them. Maybe Angie would like a few, Tzippy thought, as she wrapped her hot-pink silk Nicole Miller bathrobe around her small frame. The robe had pictures of handbags scattered all over the fabric and made her look cheery and bright in the morning.

"Angie, how about a little breakfast?" Tzippy said as she entered the kitchen.

"Toast? Oatmeal? What you want?" Angie was busy wiping the counters and looked smart and efficient in her starched maid's uniform.

"I'll have some toast today."

Tzippy sat at the dining table, set down her list of errands, and looked at the newspaper.

"What we got to do before the party?" Angie asked.

"We have to go to Saks and get one last fitting for my outfit."

"Yes, we do."

"Are we all set for everything at the club?" Ocean Edge Country Club was a beautiful facility overlooking the Atlantic Ocean. She and Benny had loved it there; he used to play golf, get massages, and drink his Rob Roys at the bar with the boys, and Tzippy still had a social membership.

"Those girls of yours are running the whole shindig. They've picked the snacks, the food, the flowers, and the music. You're going to be happy," Angie said.

"How do you know all this?"

"When they call, they tell me things. Especially Shari, but Naomi, too. Don't you think we talk? I've known those girls all their lives, almost since they were babies. They've been worrying and fussing. Wait'll you see."

"I hope they're not spending too much money. It's only a birthday party, not a wedding."

"Now, you know you wouldn't like anything that was half-done, Mrs. B."

"You're right," she said. She picked up the paper and checked the obituaries to see the average age of the deceased, then said, "We need to go to the liquor store. You know Shari. She'll complain if we run out."

"She does enjoy her drink." Angie laughed, setting down the toast and jam.

"Naomi likes vodka. Brucie and Jill drink red wine. Let me write all this down," Tzippy said, as she added to her list.

"Ike likes his scotch."

Unlike many Jews, they were a family of drinkers. Shari, in addition to having an eating disorder, was an unacknowledged alcoholic. She had started her life as a boozer by drinking rye and ginger ale, and then had switched to rum and Diet Coke when Tzippy warned her that the sugar in the soda would make her either fat or sick. After Shari became a wino—red, white, whatever—she settled on Tanqueray on the rocks. The girl could be a happy drunk, dancing in the kitchen, but she could also turn mean, hissing at her brother or her mother. Eventually, she'd pass out, eyes closed, head sunk into the sofa pillows.

Tzippy never liked to drink alone but had spent many hours sipping scotch and popping pills during the years when Benny was on the road, sleeping with the golden-haired Laura. Brucie and his wife were tipplers, consuming a bottle of red wine every night. Tzippy's elder daughter, Naomi, sometimes imbibed in secret, pouring her vodka into plastic bottles when she traveled. Tzippy had once found a baby bottle filled with vodka in Naomi's handbag; it had fallen out as the handbag spilled, along with two tightly rolled joints, after Naomi had gone to the ladies' room. By that time, Naomi and Ike had been well past the baby stage. Tzippy had unscrewed the nipple and tasted the booze but never said a word. What was the point?

Of course, Ike often got drunk and talked too much. As a realtor, he was always selling something. He'd almost gone to jail once, for some sordid deal involving a payoff; the local paper had featured a picture of him receiving a roll of money. Fortunately, he knew the judge and got off. Tzippy tried not to dwell on the details.

"How about me?" Angie asked. "What am I going to wear to your party?"

Tzippy assessed her ample-breasted, wide-hipped employee. Angie had grown up poor in Mobile, Alabama, with a daddy who gambled and a mama who slaved away at Weenie's Dry Cleaner and Laundromat, a job that left her exhausted by the end of each day. As a young girl, Angie had spent hours watching clothes spin around and around under a sign that forbade bare feet, smoking, and overloading the washers and dryers.

She had been with the Bryers since 1962. She'd come to work for Tzippy when she was a mere nineteen years old and the children were thirteen, eleven, and seven. And when Ben had died, ten years ago, in 1990, Angie had packed up the New Jersey house and had come with Tzippy to live in her apartment in Bal Harbour.

Of course Angie would have to have something special to wear for the birthday party, and she would not be satisfied with an inexpensive frock. No, she'd want a designer-type dress with a coordinated hat or turban, big hoop earrings, and matching shoes.

"Oh, we'll find you something. We'll look after I'm done at Saks." Tzippy knew she'd spoiled Angie with Easter bonnets once a year and expensive birthday presents. Her pampering had started after some woman had tried to hire Angie while they were at the counter at Shupie's. That day, Tzippy had an appointment at the dentist across the street and decided to grab lunch because she felt faint with hunger. Angie was sitting right next to her at the counter, in her maid's uniform, obviously Tzippy's employee—anyone could see that.

"We'll go to Mrs. Maples'," Tzippy said. It was a store for plus-size women and sold the types of clothes Angie liked. "Don't worry."

Angie smiled as she set down a cup of tea, and Tzippy could tell she was pleased.

Now Angie asked, "Can I bring Jack to the party?"

"Oh, Angie, do we really need him?"

"Just asking, Mrs. B."

Tzippy felt so pressured by people. She had heard stories about Jack, things that didn't sound good. She'd heard he was a gambler, a risk taker. Some of the other women at the club talked about what their maids reported. However, she felt guilty saying no. Angie was fifty-seven, and maybe she felt she needed a companion at the party, someone to talk to and sit with besides the kids. And Jack made a nice appearance—a plus in Tzippy's eyes. He wasn't a bad-looking guy. Tall, well built, with just a slight potbelly, all his hair, gray temples—he'd probably been quite handsome as a younger man.

Just then, the phone rang and Angie answered.

"Mrs. Bryer's residence." She smiled at Tzippy. "Just a moment, please." She handed Tzippy the receiver and whispered, "It's the doctor's office."

"Yes?" Tzippy said.

"Good morning, Mrs. Bryer. I'm calling because Dr. Waterday would like you to come in and see him," reported the nurse.

"What's wrong?"

"I'm afraid I can't discuss the details over the phone, but the doctor wants to schedule a second mammogram."

"Why?"

"You'll have to talk to the doctor about that. Can you drop by?"

"I'm busy right now. Can it wait?"

"Let me ask the doctor and get back to you."

"Please, I'm in the middle of planning a party and a family visit." She hung up, both aggravated and nervous.

"What's a matter, Mrs. Bryer?" Angie asked, as she set a dish of blueberries on the table.

"Oh, Angie, I hope it's nothing. The doctor wants to see me. Say a prayer I'm okay."

Angie patted the old woman and said, "You'll be fine, Mrs. B. You're like a cat. You're not done yet."

"I hope you're right," Tzippy said, and half smiled at Angie. *There is no peace*, she thought. She didn't want to consider being sick and its possible consequences. *Please, God*, she prayed, *spare me*. All she wanted was to die in her sleep, like Selma.

Trying to distract herself, she ate her toast and again picked up the newspaper. An article entitled "Girls' Club Leader Found Dead" reported that Lydia Lopez, thirty-eight years old, had been found in her apartment. Tzippy stopped reading—she'd had enough of people dying—but then remembered that Stan went to the Boys' Club. She'd have to ask him about what he did there, exactly.

"Angie," she said, "I think I'll take a bath and get dressed. Then we'll go get my hair combed. I have to talk to Maria about my hairdo for the party."

"You be careful you don't break any perfume bottles, like I went and did," Angie said.

"Do you want any of those bottles before I throw them out?"

"Why, I don't mind having a few. Thank you," Angie said, looking both pleased and embarrassed.

"When we have more time, you'll have to choose the ones you want."

"Mrs. B., you're too good to me."

"Don't forget that when you're mad at me."

Angie let out her deep, hearty laugh, and Tzippy wondered how poor Esther Berger was doing with her daughter. Maybe she'd get a letter from her today. Yes, thank God she wasn't Esther.

They drove to Salon 29 on Harding, where Maria, one of Miami Beach's best hairdressers, worked her magic on the older women. Angie parked next to a row of lone men, the retired husbands, who sat smoking cigars in their long cars, listening to the radio, while their dyed-blond wives got their hair done. Inside, women wearing gold bangles and too much lipstick, their faces taut from plastic surgery, read fashion magazines and ate complimentary bagels while they waited their turn.

Despite the fact that it was midweek, Salon 29 bustled and buzzed. It was one of the beach's busiest hair studios, yet Maria always found a spot for Tzippy whenever she called. "Hello, doll," she yelled as Tzippy entered. Tzippy felt like a queen as she walked directly to Maria's chair, bypassing all the waiting women. Angie moved to the back of the shop, where she huddled with the other domestics.

"Let's see what we're going to do today," Maria said.

"Fix me up. I hate the way I look," Tzippy said. Staring into the mirror, she saw a small, old woman with coral lipstick on her mouth and two rouged cheeks, dressed in a pale aqua sweater, silk blouse and matching linen pants, pearl necklace and earrings framing her face. The air-conditioning was chilly; she pulled the cashmere more tightly around her and sat up straighter. She was getting old, but she always looked like a lady.

"What do you mean? You look beautiful," Maria said.

Tzippy was a realist and understood that growing older made glamour more difficult. As she spent increasing amounts of money on various cosmetics, Tzippy had become good friends with the makeup girl at the Estée Lauder counter at Saks.

Maria teased, combed, and attached the hairpiece to the back of Tzippy's head. When she was done, Tzippy beamed. Suddenly she was younger, perkier, and prettier. There was a suggestion of the old days when she and Ben used to dance at the club. She threw her head back and laughed. She loved remembering the past, when she had looked sexy and ravishing, coquettishly taking the cigarette from her scarlet lips after he'd lit it. In '44, when they were courting, Tzippy's hair had fallen over her eyes, Veronica Lake–style, and Ben had guided her elbow when they'd left a room.

"I think you're a genius," Tzippy said. Her hair, highlighted in gold tones, flipped up on the sides.

Tzippy extracted an envelope from her Chanel purse and showed Maria the photos she'd collected from *Vogue* and various other magazines. There were glossy shots of models with shiny hairdos and pouty lips. One was encased in gold veils. Another had a flower on her neck and was touching her face with her hand. A third photo was of a sultry, mysterious-looking Asian model. Sophisticated pictures of stylish women with perfectly coiffed hairdos and makeup came falling out of the thin white envelope.

"I've been collecting pictures to get ideas for the party. Do you see anything you like?" she asked Maria.

Maria smiled and said, "You've been busy." She studied the photos and pointed to a small picture of Jane Fonda with a gold and blond–streaked haircut styled in a puffy, feathery 'do. "We could do something like this, only more regal, add that new hairpiece we talked about, for more fullness in the back, since we'll cut it shorter. You like?"

"Oh, I think that's brilliant. You hit the nail on the head," said Tzippy, smiling and stuffing the photo collection back into the envelope. She placed a large tip in Maria's hand and paid the bill.

Then Tzippy and Angie drove to Saks for a final fitting of Tzippy's Armani pantsuit. The saleswoman again insisted that Tzippy buy the matching Prada shoes. "They absolutely make the outfit, Mrs. Bryer."

Tzippy reconsidered; after all, it was her party and she needed to look perfect. Angie stood nearby as Tzippy signed the charge.

Rolling her eyes to heaven, Angie shook her head and muttered, "My, oh my . . ." She stopped when Tzippy grimaced in her direction. Tzippy didn't need her maid's approval. *Perhaps there'll be no money left for the children after I get done shopping,* she said to herself. *The hell with it. It's my birthday, and I deserve it.*

Chapter 3

Mrs. Maples' Store for Large Women was located in a strip mall going north toward Hollywood. A large pink flamingo stood by the front door, and as the ladies entered, a bell rang. "God, that thing is noisy," Tzippy said.

Angie's face beamed with anticipation as she looked around. The shop was packed with cotton and synthetic dresses in colors called pink tutu, Caribbean blue, grasshopper green, and purple panache.

Tzippy touched the fabrics and dresses disdainfully and looked at the price tags. She raised her eyebrows in amazement. She could buy ten or twelve dresses for the price of those shoes, but, she reminded herself, they were special, and it was her birthday, and the shoes weren't made of cheap, flimsy material. Angie walked around and tried to find her size.

The woman who approached them was a wide-hipped forty-something with platinum hair. "May I help you, ladies?" she asked.

Angie opened her mouth to answer, but Tzippy took charge. "We're here to look at dresses," she said. "Something for a birthday celebration."

"Oh, I love a party. Whose?"

"Mine," said Tzippy.

"Is this dress for you?"

Tzippy laughed. "No, for Angie here."

"What would you like?" the saleswoman asked, turning to Angie. Angie took a dress off the rack, held it up to her large frame, and sashayed around.

"That one looks good," the saleswoman said.

Angie was aglow with excitement and said, "I want something flowing and bright. It's Mrs. B.'s party, and I have to look special." She giggled.

Tzippy sat down and waited for Angie to try on a few items.

"How I look, Mrs. B.?" Angie asked, as she strutted out of the dressing room in a long, flowing beige smock.

"Oh, I'm not sure that one does you justice," Tzippy said.

Angie spotted a wide-brimmed hat on a mannequin and plopped it on her head. "Is this any better?"

"Maybe, but go try on something with more color."

After the woman rehung several rejected dresses, she showed Angie a turquoise caftan with bugle beads. Baby pink Mardi Gras beads covered the matching turban. It was fabulous.

"Oh my, I do love this," Angie squealed, looking at Tzippy for approval.

"Wrap it up," Tzippy said. Angie gave the dress to the cashier, Tzippy paid, and then off they went to their car.

Angie sat behind the wheel of the Lincoln and asked, "Where to now, Mrs. B.?"

"I'm hungry. Let's go to Shupie's and sit at the counter, then swing by the liquor store."

After a quick lunch, the two women stopped at Mr. Ed's Liquor Mart. "I feel like becoming a boozer," Tzippy said as she walked up and down the aisle.

Angie, pushing the cart alongside Tzippy, smiled and raised her eyebrows, without saying a word.

Tzippy put a half-gallon of J&B scotch in the basket. "You think that's enough?"

"They all drink scotch," Angie said.

"You're right." She put a second bottle in the basket.

"Some party you're having," the salesman said, as they approached the register.

"It's my birthday," Tzippy said. "This is just for my apartment, so to speak."

"Gotta keep the guests happy," he said.

Angie laughed. "I'm doing a dance in her honor."

"Now, that's something. What kind of jig?" the salesman asked.

"It's an original."

Tzippy shook her head and smiled. "Please." She recalled the time Angie had danced and strutted at Naomi's Sweet Sixteen party, thirty-five years earlier. She had sung and swayed to the music, and Naomi's friends had laughed with delight. Tzippy was sure the kids had hired a piano player for her party, so maybe Angie would do a little one-step. "She's a great dancer," Tzippy said to the salesman.

"I bet she is."

Angie shimmied in front of the French wines, and customers clapped. Despite her girth, she was graceful and radiated joy when she danced.

"You're causing a scene," Tzippy said.

"No, it's good for business," the salesman said. "Don't worry."

Tzippy sighed. "Angie, you're too much."

Angie bent over and planted a kiss on Tzippy's cheek. "Just getting warmed up, Mrs. B."

On the car ride home, Tzippy took out her pad, placed her red half-glasses on the bridge of her nose, and started to add up all she'd spent. "I can't believe what this weekend is costing me," she groaned to Angie. "I just spent nearly seven hundred at the last two stores combined, the liquor mart and Mrs. Maples'. I tell you, I'm glad Benny isn't around to see this extravagance." She didn't mention that her shoes had cost considerably more all by themselves.

"Mrs. B., he'd want you to be happy. You know he would," Angie said.

"He'd tell me to slow down. He's dead and gone, and when my money runs out, there'll be no one else to replenish the supply." Tzippy secretly admitted to herself that she was a spender; that was the exact reason why she continued to rent in Florida.

"I wish I had a nice sugar daddy."

"Angie!"

They drove the rest of the way home in silence. Tzippy opened the window partway to catch the sea air. There was nothing like a cool breeze off the ocean. As she closed her eyes, she smiled, thinking of dear Benny up in heaven.

Later, after all the liquor had been stacked in the den or placed inside the bar with mixers and coasters and cocktail napkins, Tzippy lay down on her bed to rest before dinner with Stan. Just as Angie was about to go off to see Jack, she looked in on Tzippy and asked, "Anything else I need to do?"

"No, sweetie. You have a good time. I think we're in fine shape."

"I'm still planning on cooking the brisket and making the coleslaw Saturday morning. Maybe an apple pie."

"I love your deep-dish one."

"I'll pick up the apples I like. They sure make a difference."

"Thanks, Angie."

"And thank you again for the dress and everything."

"You're welcome. I love the turban on you. You go on, now. I'm going to take a nice, warm bath."

"Be careful, Mrs. B. We don't want you falling."

Undressing in front of the bathroom mirror while the tub was running, Tzippy examined herself. She sighed, trying to accept that she was no longer beautiful in the way she once had been. Her face had lost its prominent jaw, and her mouth its self-confidence. Her breasts hung like heavy sacks covering part of her wrinkled midsection. She had not nursed her children, but time had done its job. She had always been proud of her full breasts, but now she looked at them with disinterest. Her arms, once small and slender, had lost their muscle tone, and the folds of her skin made vertical ripples in her upper arm. Shaking them, trying to rid herself of their ugliness, she realized the soft skin would not obey. Her narrow hips were still as slight as a young girl's, but her bottom was flat as a pancake and unsexy, and her legs were streaked with blue veins even though they, too, were slim. Even her mons veneris, once covered with a full patch of dark hair, showed its age; the hair was sparse, fine, silver. Tzippy didn't like looking at herself anymore. Once a proud, exacting, and self-assured woman who had overseen the serving of hors d'oeuvres on silver platters and reigned over dinner parties, coiffed, high-heeled, and adorned with bright red lipstick, she now appeared flawed and bereft. She was all used up.

The emptiness she felt was more than physical; it was deeper and made her anxious, as if she were a child all alone in a large house. If only she could regain that exhilarating, powerful feeling of fullness she'd had in her prime. Perhaps it had been fleeting, self-admiring, and empty, just full of strut and brag.

Shaking her head, trying to dispel these uncomfortable thoughts, Tzippy turned off the faucet. Gently, she slid into the round tub full of sudsy water. The warmth soothed her, and she closed her eyes. When she opened them, she looked at the perfume vials surrounding the bathtub, noticed their shapes and their different heights. Something was different, she thought. There were fewer of them, less of a selection than she remembered. Strange, she thought. Perhaps she'd forgotten how many she had. She remembered that Angie had been in here and had broken a bottle, but there'd always been so many, collected from her myriad visits to fine shops. She knew she'd had one from that special store in Coral Gables. It had a long neck and a plump bottom with a top that resembled a knob. Where had it gone? As she washed her dry, tender skin, Tzippy thought she'd check with Angie later. No time now. It was already Thursday night, and the kids were coming the next day. The party was Saturday. She had to get ready for dinner tonight. She had no time for idle thoughts.

Stan came to pick Tzippy up for dinner at six-thirty.

"How you doing, baby cakes?" he asked, spreading his arms wide and doing a little soft-shoe shuffle. He looked dapper in a light blue sports jacket and white slacks.

"Oh, Stan, I've had a day. There's so much to do, you can't imagine."

"You look terrific. Turn around and show me."

She pirouetted in front of him and modeled her canary-yellow dress with the cape. Around her neck was the gold necklace he'd given her the month before for their third anniversary.

"You look pretty snappy yourself," he said. "The necklace looks swell, doesn't it?" he added.

"Yes, sweetheart. I love it." They'd celebrated that special weekend at the Breakers Hotel in Palm Beach. They had eaten at the hotel's five-star restaurant and enjoyed the pool, the cabana, and the piano bar; they'd had a glorious time. After they'd returned home, Tzippy had taken the gold necklace to the jeweler and gotten it appraised. To her astonishment, the jeweler had said, "There's a lot more gold in this than you realize."

"What do you mean?" she'd asked.

"It's worth fourteen thousand dollars." Tzippy had been speechless, impressed at how much Stan had spent on her.

"Well, I think we're one good-looking couple," Stan said now.

"Yes, we are. I like that tie."

"All for you, honey."

Off they went in Stan's old Cadillac. The fabric inside the roof was slightly frayed and hung down like a circus tent. The vehicle had been a sweetheart in its day, a striking, metallic-blue 1990 Eldorado, with gold spoke tires and a sporty but luxurious feel. Tzippy liked its size but was a bit embarrassed by its condition. Stan insisted the car was still in good shape and that the humidity from the Florida weather had caused the fabric to droop.

"It's pretty weird, the way it looks," Tzippy had said, rolling her eyes.

"Feels like a chuppah, don't you think?"

"Why don't you get yourself a new buggy?" she suggested now, not for the first time.

"When I'm ready, I will." Stan was frugal about himself and extravagant with the people he loved. He had a daughter, Evelene, on whom he lavished money and presents, as well as on his grandson, who had just earned his Ph.D. Stan had given the boy a trip to Europe as a graduation gift.

They drove up to the Fire Station, where Stan handed his keys to the valet and took Tzippy's arm. He'd reserved her favorite table, by the window overlooking the koi pond. Over drinks, she confided, "I'm very worried about the weekend, especially the dinner tomorrow night. What if the kids don't get along? You know how they are. Old fights, wounds; Shari and her big mouth. What should I do?"

Stan sipped his martini and stroked her hand. "Sweetheart, try not to get yourself all worked up. Sorry I won't be able to be there to support you at dinner, but I've got this golf banquet for the Men's League I can't miss."

"I understand, but it's easy for you to say," she said, as she sipped her glass of chardonnay. Unlike the rest of her family, now that she was older, all she really could tolerate was a little wine before dinner.

"You shouldn't let them get drunk. That's when things get out of hand."

"But if I don't have the booze, they get mad. They'll just go out and buy it themselves. You don't understand." She was embarrassed to tell him how much liquor she'd bought that morning.

"I understand plenty. Families are tough. Just don't put yourself in the middle. If they're going to go at it, stay out of it. Tzippy, my love, you can't stop them when they start squabbling. Maybe they need to get it all out of their system."

"You're probably right. I just can't help butting in."

"Baby cakes, your chance at mothering has pretty much come and gone. At this point in life, they're full-grown."

"That's the problem. I missed my opportunity when they were young." If only she hadn't spent their childhood popping pills, spending money, and shopping all the time.

"Quit beating yourself up. Let's go ahead and order. What do you want to eat? Have some stone crabs. You like them."

"I think I'll try the veal."

"Fine. I'm having a steak with béarnaise. I'm hungry tonight. I played a lousy round of golf with Fred Goldman. God, is he having money troubles."

"No kidding."

"Yeah, his wife is taking him to the cleaners in a nasty divorce. Didn't I tell you?"

"You must have. I just forget with everything else going on."

"I love you, baby cakes. You're the apple of my eye." He put his hand under Tzippy's yellow dress and rubbed her thigh.

Over warm rolls and butter, Tzippy told Stan about the newspaper article she'd read. "Some woman was killed who worked at the Girls' Club. Sounded awful. Girls' Club, Boys' Club . . . What kinds of things go on over there? Don't you go over to the Boys' Club from time to time?" She took the knife and spread the butter on a small piece of dark bread.

"Oh, I've been going there for years. It's a place for kids whose parents are either too busy or not up to the job."

"What do you do when you go?" she asked, trying to sound casual, removing a bit of crust from her pumpernickel.

"Talk to the boys, boys from broken homes. I like to give them advice, tell them to shape up and help their mother or go to school. A lot of them drop out when they're sixteen. Stuff like that."

"Does it help? Do they listen?" she asked.

"Sometimes they do, sometimes they don't. I like the kids, though, and it makes me feel like I'm doing something useful. You can't play golf and go to dinner and not try to do some good in life, baby cakes."

"You're such a decent man, Stanley," she said.

"Naw, I'm just being a person."

Later, on the way home, they stopped the big Cadillac under a streetlight at the end of a dead-end road. They enjoyed parking and making out; there was something romantic about kissing and petting in a parked car.

She let him fondle her breasts and put his hand inside her panty hose.

"You're getting me hard, baby cakes. Feel this," he said, as he moved her hand to his crotch.

"Oh, Stan, my, you're so big," Tzippy said, trying to flatter him.

"All for you."

They saw a light from behind and watched as a police car pulled onto the street. Tzippy immediately got nervous, imagining the officers' dark blue uniforms and holstered guns.

Stan took out his cigar and said, "Straighten out, honey."

"What does he want?" she asked, as she smoothed her yellow dress.

"Just checking—nothing much."

The cruiser stopped, and an officer got out. "Any problems?" he asked.

"No, Officer. We're just talking and enjoying the night," Stan said. He lit the cigar and exhaled.

The policeman looked inside. "You sure everything's okay?"

"The young lady and I are talking about getting married."

Tzippy smiled at the cop and said, "Yes, never too late, don't you think?" Stan had only suggested, never really asked. He was just playing with the cop. The truth was, Tzippy liked being Ben's widow. So many people had admired his rakish, slightly arrogant manner, and she didn't want to change her identity. As Benny's widow, she had cachet she would never have as Mrs. Fosberg. Still, Stan was a real romantic and she had to admit he treated her right.

"I think if you two nice people are in love, go for it."

"Thanks, Officer," Stan said.

"Have a good night," the cop said.

On their way back to Tzippy's place, the two of them sang an old favorite, "Blue Moon." Tzippy thought, *He is such a nice man. Maybe I would say yes, if he ever did ask.*

Stan wanted to stay over, but Tzippy insisted she had a doctor's appointment the next morning. She didn't tell him about the call from Dr. Waterday's office. No need to bring up possible problems this week. The kids were arriving. "And Shari's coming in tomorrow on the plane. Want to go with me to pick her up?"

"Sure. What time is the flight coming in?"

"Two-ten, I think. American."

"I'll get you at one so we have plenty of time."

On Friday, the airport was crowded and it was hard for Tzippy to walk too far, but she kept up and didn't complain. Every once in a while, she pretended to want to look at something in order to get Stan to stop so she could take a break and catch her breath. All those years of smoking! Her legs got tired, too.

When Shari got off the plane, she looked excited. Her large eyes were highlighted with black mascara. She stood five foot four and had remained as slim as a pipe cleaner, although she claimed she was no longer anorexic. She styled her hair short, and her high-boned cheeks were sunken and lined. Wearing tight jeans and high heels, she spoke rapidly and often sighed dramatically. Watching her approach, Tzippy got nervous; the girl always put her on the defensive, with her unexpected bursts of frank remarks.

"Mom, how are you? Stan, how nice to see you." She hugged them both, one after the other, and planted a kiss on each of their cheeks.

"How was the flight?" Stan asked.

"Oh, God, don't ask. A horrible man sat next to me and kept flirting. It was awful."

"Maybe he's single," Tzippy said.

"Oh, Mother, there you go again. He also was fat and had bad breath. Please."

Tzippy stared at Stan and said nothing.

"Look at you, Mom," Shari said. Tzippy was dressed in white silk pants and a pink cashmere sweater with white polka dots. "All decked out like a picture postcard."

"You know me."

"Your mother always looks great," Stan added. "Let's go get your bag."

"Are you hungry?" asked Tzippy. "Where's your pillow?"

"Oh, I figured I could live without my pillow for a few days," Shari said. "And no, I'm not hungry, but I sure would like some hooch."

Again, Tzippy glanced at Stan but did not respond. She said simply, "Your brother is due in later. He's coming with Jill."

"And Naomi? When are she and Ike getting here?"

"God knows. They had trouble with their new car. Ike bought a new sports car, and it broke down."

"Sounds like a lemon," Shari said.

"I think he got a deal on it."

"Some deal."

When they got back to the apartment, Angie hugged Shari and said, "You're as skinny as ever, child." Shari opened up the refrigerator and took out a bottle of wine but then put it back and poured herself a stiff gin instead. She grabbed her bag, drink in hand, and said, "Mom, I'm going downstairs to get settled. I'll see you in a bit." The apartment had guest rooms in the building, and Tzippy had reserved one for each of her children.

"Why are you rushing off?" Tzippy asked. "You just got here, for God's sake."

"I've got to freshen up, shower, relax, and make a few calls."

"Yes, of course," Tzippy said. "I'm being selfish. It's just so nice to see you." She went over and took Shari's face in her hands and kissed her on both cheeks.

Shari smiled and said, "Love you, too."

Their relationship had always straddled the line between adoration and repulsion. Tzippy knew she had treated her daughter as an experiment, in a way, making sure her last-born received all the lessons and attention that Tzippy herself had wanted as a girl. Ballet and piano lessons, horseback riding, tennis, ballroom dancing—Tzippy had pushed her to the limit. When, at nineteen, Shari had announced her engagement to a handsome rich kid Tzippy didn't particularly like, Tzippy had decided to throw the wedding of the century. She had insisted they buy the gown at Cynthia's, an exclusive boutique in New York where a white

Rolls Royce sat parked out front and uniformed maids served coffee in china cups and saucers.

Shari found a lovely Givenchy that cost $3,000, but Tzippy preferred a more costly frock, with seed pearls and diamonds, for $8,000. Shari balked. "You don't care about me," she said. "I'm just your pawn, your show-off piece. You keep robbing me of my chance to be me."

"How can you say that?" Tzippy said, stubbing out her cigarette. She was aware that the uniformed maids were all standing by, listening in. She bet they didn't usually get a show like this. Why did Shari always have to embarrass her?

"Because it's true," Shari said.

"Fine, be you. You never listen to me anyway." She finally gave in and let Shari have the less expensive dress, but she'd always regretted it.

After Shari went to her room, Stan said he was going home to take a nap. "Too much excitement around here for an old man, baby cakes." He kissed her on the cheek and left.

Tzippy put out candy and fruit in the living room and arranged flowers that had been delivered earlier in tall vases. The living room had pistachio-green walls and a portrait of her from the Israeli ball hung next to the marble fireplace. She had Angie move a few pieces of furniture and clean out a drawer in case the kids needed extra space.

She'd barely had a chance to sit down when she heard a knock on the door. Angie opened it to Brucie and his wife, Jill. Jill stood at least four inches taller than Bruce, statuesque and model-like in appearance. She was the type of woman people noticed in a crowd, because of both her height and her haunting beauty, her mass of long dark curls and wide dark eyes.

Bruce was a square, sturdy man of fifty-one, blond and blue-eyed. He had worn glasses from an early age. As the oldest of

Tzippy's children and the only boy, he enjoyed a preferential status. However, as the son of Ben Bryer, he suffered from an inferiority complex.

"Mom, how are you?" he said.

"Oh, Brucie, Jill, it's so good to see you. You look a little tired, Brucie."

"He's fine, except for stress at work," Jill said.

Jill's answering for Brucie annoyed Tzippy. "Is that so?" Tzippy stared at her son.

He changed the subject: "Is Bluebell here?" His sister's childhood nickname had stuck since the early days, when Shari used to wear a small bracelet of blue bells and everyone could hear her coming. She used to jump rope as a child and sing, "Bluebells, cockleshells, evie, ivy, over."

"She's already drinking," Tzippy said.

"Sounds like everything is normal, Mom," Bruce said.

Jill looked around and said, "Your place looks great," and then hugged her mother-in-law. Tzippy was fond of Jill, but she wished Bruce had a classier wife. He seemed happy with his trophy bride, but Tzippy knew Jill had grown up in a fourth-floor walk-up in a rough section of Boston. Her father had been a factory worker. None of those credentials impressed Tzippy. Besides that, Jill's diction often struck the wrong chord. Tzippy had determined long ago that someone should have given the girl elocution lessons.

"Angie, how are you? It's great to see you. I know you're cooking up some delicious dishes," Bruce said.

"Yes, you can be sure of that, Mr. Bruce. Good seeing you and your missus."

"I'm awfully thirsty. Got any beer?"

"Right here in the fridge," she answered.

"Do you want a snack?" asked Tzippy. "Dinner isn't till eight."

"What've you got?" Bruce liked to eat and had a bit of a paunch.

"Your favorite: sharp cheddar and pepperoni; some nice crackers. It won't be too much to ruin your appetite."

"Fine."

"Angie, would you give the kids a little something?"

After Jill and Brucie went downstairs to unpack, Tzippy decided to bathe and change. Tonight they were going to dinner at Valerie Rose, a favorite family place. They had a late reservation so Naomi and Ike could be there in plenty of time after their long trip from Connecticut. Valerie Rose was a steak-and-fish place, a lavish eatery with polished floors and twinkling Christmas lights.

When Naomi and Ike finally arrived, Tzippy said, "What a sight for sore eyes."

They were wearing disheveled clothes and told their story about the now-famous sports car and how they had been stranded on the side of the road.

"I think it was the fan belt," declared Ike, a tall, bespectacled, middle-aged man with a dashing mustache who loved fast cars, risky deals, and gambling—a recipe that gave Tzippy ulcers. But Naomi, patient and quiet, seemed able to deal with his nature. As a youngster and the middle child, she'd stayed in her room and kept to herself. Now, she wrote cookbooks, recipes with a dash of her personal life thrown in.

"We're going to jump into the shower and be back up," Naomi said.

"Need a drink?" Tzippy asked, trying to be hospitable.

"Later, thanks," Ike answered.

As they carried the bags downstairs to get settled, Tzippy's anxiety increased. Her body felt feverish, as it did at the start of a flu. And she couldn't do a thing about it.

Tzippy sat at the restaurant's glass-and-chrome bar, sipping chardonnay and eavesdropping on her children.

"What's happening with the coat business these days?" Ike asked Brucie, as they stood behind the women, who were sitting on the barstools.

"We're struggling; the banks are coming down on us. Short of money, bad cash-flow problems." The family-owned business, Coat Classics, which had provided US Army jackets and blankets during World War II and peacoats and stadium coats during the good days, was struggling to remain solvent. Then Bruce muttered, "Trouble meeting payroll. The competition overseas is killing us—places like India, Germany, and Lithuania. Cheap labor. We tried adding new items to diversify: throw pillows, bedspreads . . . You know, home decor is big. It's been tough."

"Do you think we'll go under?" asked Shari. Coat Classics had been run since its inception as an old-fashioned family business. It was good to its employees, sponsoring English-language classes for workers at the factory in Lowell, Massachusetts. Unlike most manufacturing companies, Coat Classics had not moved south for less costly labor. All the family members benefited from the business, receiving a monthly check for $200 and full health coverage.

At that, Tzippy turned around on her barstool and asked, "Brucie, didn't you say things were improving?" Three generations had lived off the proceeds.

"No, Mom, I didn't," he said. "I told you things *could* be better. Besides, that was last month, and things have gotten worse. I think I need more ice." He set the glass on the bar and motioned to the bartender.

Shari sat to the right of her mother, drinking a Tanqueray with a twist. "I'm glad Daddy's not alive to see what's become of his company," she said. "How long has it been? Brucie, you should know."

"Yes, ten years in October. You know that, Shari," Tzippy scolded, as Brucie scowled.

Then the hostess summoned the group to a large table in the back room.

"How about another round of drinks?" Ike suggested.

"I love the decor," Naomi said, admiring the velvet wallpaper and gold sconces on the walls. "It's like something out of a Victorian novel."

"Your father always liked this restaurant," Tzippy said.

"How much time are they giving you?" Ike asked Brucie.

"What do you mean?" Brucie asked.

"The bank."

"Did I say they were giving me time?" Brucie asked.

"I thought you said you were in arrears all over the place," Ike said.

Tzippy studied the menu. "I think I'll have the salmon."

"I have to have stone crabs," Jill said, as she tore a chunk of warm bread from the loaf that had been placed on the table. "Mom, look at that woman over there. Don't you just love her dress?"

"Where?" Tzippy asked.

"That blond woman with the backless peacock-blue dress. Isn't it great?"

"Oh, yes, definitely. You'd look good in it."

"Do you think?"

"Absolutely."

Shari took a gulp of her drink and said, "Daddy should have let women into the business." It had been a family rule that the women stayed at home and didn't have voting rights.

Ike said, "You know those old men, the patriarchal thinking. God, they'd be rolling over if they saw what was happening in America."

Naomi laughed good-naturedly. "Thank God for progress. Hear, hear," she said, lifting her glass and kissing her husband on the cheek.

43

Turning toward Bruce, Ike said, "I think you ought to sell the business and get out of it."

"That's a little hasty," Jill said. "Everything will be fine. Bruce is doing a wonderful job."

"Let's order," Tzippy said. "I'm starved."

Shari said, "For God's sake, Mom, we're talking."

"Don't start," Naomi said, eyeing the bread. "Leave it alone, Shari."

"Why not refresh our drinks?" Shari said. "I need another one."

"Shari, please don't drink too much," Tzippy said.

"Mother." Shari looked at her with an expression of impatience and then clinked the ice cubes in her glass. "Frankly, I think it's ridiculous that you don't have a few women in the business," she said to Brucie, who was sitting on her left. "Women buy most of the goddamn merchandise."

"Times change," Ike said.

"It's the way Daddy and your grandfather Zada wanted it," said Tzippy. She and Ben had lived in New Jersey so Ben could run the sales office in the garment district, but Brucie had put someone else there after Ben had died and stayed in Massachusetts, supervising the factory. Unfortunately, after 1990, woolen mills had become dinosaurs in the New England area.

"Shari and I have worked so hard on the party. Wait until you all see," Naomi said.

"The business was set up a certain way, and now isn't the time to change things," said Brucie.

"Maybe it would help save the bloody enterprise," Shari said. "It sure could use something to give it new life." She looked around the table for agreement.

"Ask the waitress for some more butter, please," said Tzippy. "This bread is wonderful, don't you think? Homemade."

"Let's take a vote on who thinks we should have women in the company," Shari said, raising her half-full glass.

Tzippy gave her daughter a swift kick with her Jimmy Choo shoe under the table, and then hissed, "Let's go to the ladies' room."

The two of them rose and went to the ornate restroom, where an attendant in a pink uniform sat next to a large dish filled with money. Pictures of old-fashioned young women with heads full of tousled brown hair decorated the dark red walls. Gold faucets and thick towels completed the decor.

"What are you doing? You're drinking too much and behaving badly," Tzippy scolded her daughter.

"Oh, for God's sake, Mother. There's nothing wrong with my bringing up a few points. You're such a nag." With that, Shari refreshed her lipstick, left the ladies' room, and returned to the table, with Tzippy in hot pursuit.

When they returned to the table, several appetizers were scattered for everyone to share: fried calamari, fresh shrimp, stuffed mushrooms. Everyone commented on the food's tastiness and ate with gusto. As the salads came, the small talk continued: Ike suggested going fishing the next day; Tzippy asked about Naomi's new cookbook. When the waiters served the sumptuous entrées—steaks, creamed vegetables, and hash browns—Tzippy tried to say nice things to Bruce, who looked wounded from the earlier conversation. He'd always been sensitive to criticism, and now, sure enough, as he had more to drink, he was becoming defensive, lecturing his sister about the family business.

"I don't need to be reminded how the coat business works," Shari said.

"I'm just trying to make you understand," he said, wiping his chin.

"You know, Brucie, you're not very smart. I could have done a way better job than you," Shari blurted out. "I have a head for business. But Daddy wouldn't hear of it and Mom kept trying to turn me into a lay-dee."

Tzippy stopped eating and held her breath. *This is all about me*, she thought, *and how I damaged my daughter.*

"Oh, you think so, Ms. Know-It-All?" Bruce said, his face turning the color of a ripe strawberry. "You think I ruined the company? Daddy had plenty of problems before he died. You have no idea. You're just a jealous little bitch. Why don't you shut up?"

"You gonna make me?" Shari prodded.

Brucie turned to her, put his two hands around her thin, pale forearm, and started to twist it in what they had called an Indian burn when they were kids.

"What the hell are you doing? That hurts, damn it," Shari howled. She beat her brother on the shoulder with her free fist and tried to yank her arm away, but Bruce wouldn't let go.

"Brucie!" Tzippy yelled.

"Hey, big boy, cool down," Ike said.

Jill whispered, "Bruce, you're embarrassing me. Stop."

But Bruce didn't let up. Contorting his face as he twisted his sister's arm, he looked driven. Tzippy hadn't seen him so angry in a long time; though he had a terrible temper, he had mostly been a quiet boy who avoided confrontation. Suddenly, Brucie released his grip on Shari's arm, rose from the table, and stomped out of the room.

No one said a word. Everyone looked at Shari, who said, "Did you see that? Did you see what he did? I divorced my fuckin' husband for less than that."

Tzippy sat stone still and said nothing.

Rolling her eyes, Naomi said, "I don't believe what I just saw. Jesus, Shari, don't ruin the party weekend."

"Thanks for helping," Shari said to everyone at the table.

"Let me go out and talk to him," Ike offered, rising from the table.

"You shouldn't have spoken to him like that," Tzippy said to Shari.

"What about *him*, for God's sake? So condescending and such a know-it-all."

"What a family," Jill said. "Your brother has worked so damn hard for all of you."

"He had no business doing that," Naomi said.

"I need a cigarette," said Shari. No one said a word as she lit up.

Tzippy wondered if the dinner was over or if she'd get to order a cup of something hot; she felt the need for a soothing drink. She coughed into a tissue and began to feel dizzy, then searched inside her Chanel bag for a tranquilizer and quickly swallowed the pill. She said to the waitress, "Please bring me a cup of tea with lemon."

"Are you all right, Mom?" Naomi asked.

"I'm fine," she lied. Maybe she would die in her sleep. That would be such a simple solution. She couldn't take all the fighting. Perhaps she should take a second pill.

The waitress set down the hot tea in front of Tzippy. "Is there anything else you need?"

"Yes, my dear, but I'm afraid it's not on the menu," Tzippy replied.

Chapter 4

The next morning, January 15, her eightieth birthday, Tzippy awoke depressed and anxious and reluctant to get out of bed. No one had said much on the ride home the night before. Sitting by the window of the cab, she'd watched the moving traffic and clutched her handbag. Naomi, Shari, and Ike had gone in one cab; Brucie had hailed another, since Angie had taken the car to prepare the food.

"I'm never speaking to her again," Brucie had said.

"She's your sister," Tzippy had said, letting an edge of irritation into her voice.

"And a bitch."

Squirming in the middle, Jill had looked fed up.

"I've had it," he'd continued. The flash of streetlights had made his receding hairline more prominent and caused his forehead to glisten in the dark. Seeing her reflection in the opposite glass, Tzippy had been thankful that the night concealed her despair.

Back in the apartment, she'd fallen into bed with the lights on.

"It's worse than I'd feared," she said when Stan called in the morning. "You had to have been there."

"Did you get in the middle?" Stan asked. "I told you not to get in the middle."

"No. I just tried to talk about pleasant things, but they started in about the business. Oh, it was awful. Brucie and Shari carried on like they were still kids."

"Now what?" Stan asked. "Is there anything I can do?"

"I have no idea. The party's tonight. I wish we weren't even having the damn thing."

"Don't say that, Tzippy. You were looking forward to it."

"Shari kept on about women in business. She said she was smarter than Brucie."

"What else?"

"Brucie twisted her arm and caused a scene. He says he's never talking to her again," she said. "I think I need a cup of tea."

"Was she drunk?"

"Sure, she had way too much to drink, but I couldn't slow her down. Believe me, I tried."

"I'm sure you did. She gets nasty when she's loaded."

"Oh, Stan, it was ugly. It still smarts for the girls that Ben didn't want them involved."

"Baby cakes, go have that tea. Fred's on the other line. I'll call you back."

"Thanks, Stanley."

"I love you."

"I'm glad someone does. Love you back."

Tzippy looked up at the ceiling in her bedroom, as if thanking God for Stan's support; then she went to the bathroom to wash up before putting the kettle on. The smell of perfume still permeated the air as she brushed her teeth and freshened up.

Angie called back and said, "I stayed at Jack's. I hope you don't mind. I'm going to Bella's. You okay?"

"Last night the kids fought. It wasn't a good night."

"Oh, I'm sorry, Mrs. B. Now, don't you go gettin' yourself all worked up. I'll be along. Take a nice bath. I'm doing the cooking today. Bella's kitchen is perfect for me. I'll bring the food. Don't forget, Marie's coming to do your hair." Bella, Angie's friend, was a caterer with a big kitchen and let Angie do heavy meal preparation there.

Tzippy couldn't get settled, but she went into the kitchen, filled up the teapot, and put it on the stove. Hostility and shame swirled inside her. All her life, she had tried to rise above. Sure, her parents had been immigrants, but look what a catch Benny had been, even if he'd treated her meanly at times. She was a woman who lived a certain life; she was someone above bickering, who gave beautiful dinner parties, shopped at the finest stores, and went to the best restaurants. She wasn't supposed to have children causing scenes and acting badly.

She looked around in desperation. Her apartment still gave her pleasure, with its well-selected items: the yellow brocade sofa, the armchair, the lamps with the cherubs. But despite her good fortune, her life felt empty. Her husband hadn't been faithful, and the children fought. She feared whatever was missing was a part of her; in spite of all her acquisitions, she had no peace. For a brief second, she understood that her life had been a waste. She felt flawed and deficient. *I will never be enough*, she thought. She had to fight against these feelings of low self-worth, but how? Where?

The teapot whistled, and she dropped a teabag into a cup, but she continued to obsess about her mistakes. She had never read stories to her children when they were young. The maids had done it. Who was she kidding? She'd been too busy being a fancy young lady to have any time simply to watch or enjoy the simple things, like strolling up the street with a child, gathering flowers and sticks together. Only with Claude had she slowed down. He had washed her hair, and she'd massaged his scalp, caressed his neck. She recalled the slipperiness of the soap, how his hands had gently washed her feet and thighs, and how they'd lain down on the freshly made bed and had cherished each other. She had felt contented then, but had she felt that way at her children's expense?

She took a pill to calm down and drank some tea. Although she wasn't hungry, she made herself some rye toast with jam. Sitting at a small kitchen table, she munched her breakfast until, finally, the Valium kicked in.

She felt calmer now but still pushed at by all those voices in her head. Whenever she'd felt like this, she'd bought something. Remembering that she needed some new pantyhose and a few gifts for the children, she decided to go out. She took a quick bath and dressed in a lightweight peach-colored jogging suit and white sneakers. A little makeup and coral lipstick, and she was done.

"I have to run over to the mall by way of the bank," she called down to the concierge. "Will you get me a cab?"

Just then, a knock startled her. She opened it to find her older daughter, sweaty and panting.

"Oh, Naomi," she said. "You surprised me!"

It was hot and humid, a Florida day before a rainstorm. Fields of clouds hung gray, heavy, and low in the sky. The humidity formed dampness on Tzippy's face. She withdrew $500 at First and Ocean and then asked the cabbie to drop her at Saks. Even though she had charge cards, she liked the feeling of having cash in her pocketbook. Her father, Bertram, had told her when they went antiquing together years before, "All you want is green dollars, and nothing else counts. No bartering, no checks, just money. You can't trust anything else." She called it her "walking-around money"; having it made her feel less nervous.

Tzippy strolled inside, enjoyed the air-conditioning. She took small steps in order to preserve her strength. Though the disappointment of the previous evening continued to disturb her, she looked around and admired the beautiful merchandise, all the large, expensive pocketbooks lined by color. The store was quiet; it had just opened for the day, and only a few people were inside. Stopping at counters, feigning interest, she rested, until she heard a familiar saleswoman's voice. "You're out mighty early, aren't you?"

Tzippy turned. "Oh!" she said. "Good morning, Molly. I needed a few things for my party." She walked toward the counter with the creams and lipsticks that she loved.

"I have a new color for you," Molly cooed. "Do you have a minute?"

"For you, I do."

Molly took out a gold lipstick case encrusted with stones and opened it to display a scarlet lipstick, perfect and glistening new. "It's our newest color, called Stay Scarlett."

"I like it."

"Here, let me put a little on you with the tester."

After applying some to Tzippy's lips, Molly placed a large, round mirror in front of her. Tzippy examined her mouth and proclaimed, "Very pretty. Do you think it's too bright, though?"

"No, no. It gives you life. Perks you right up."

"Maybe you're right."

"Why don't you buy one and use it for a while, see if you like it? I know you will."

Unable to say no to her friend, Tzippy agreed to the purchase. Then she added, "Why don't you give me three more? I'll give one to each of the girls. They'll be great gifts."

"Shall I put each one in a little gift bag?"

"Yes, that would be nice."

After waiting a few minutes while Molly did all the packaging and ringing up, Tzippy walked away from the counter; carrying a shopping bag with the new lipsticks and several free samples Molly had placed inside as extra goodies.

"Have a great party," Molly called out to her as she retreated.

Next, Tzippy stopped at the costume-jewelry counter, where she stalled, noticing a gray felt box on top of the glass, filled with different pins. She lifted up a gold brooch featuring a ballerina and admired it. The pin filled Tzippy's entire palm; the dancer's tiara was made of colored stones, and there were more gems on her tutu. Tzippy loved the way the dancer looked—free, strong, and vibrant.

She remembered when she was twelve and how she'd felt when she'd first seen the small carving at the antique show in Springfield she'd attended with her father. It was an ivory hand, graceful. The long, creamy, tapered fingers of a woman, raised up as if they wanted to grab something. The extending, the reaching, had resonated with her. She had stared at that beautiful thing and, without thinking, had grabbed it, her heart racing.

Now she turned the brooch of the dancer over in her hand and read the label. The price had been reduced from $399.00 to $329.00. She looked around the store and didn't see anyone nearby. She closed her hand over the pin and then slipped it into the outside pocket of her handbag. Then she walked slowly, opening her bag to get a tissue. As she began to cough into the tissue, she put the pin inside the pocketbook.

At the antique show years before, her father had been in a booth ahead of her, discussing a Royal Doulton figurine with a dealer. She'd watched him lift the porcelain boy holding a book and turn it upside down. Her mouth parched, her heart beating like rain pounding on a metal rooftop, Tzippy had slipped the ivory hand into the red handbag she'd been carrying.

She'd willed herself to be calm as she continued to follow Bertram around, listening as her father explained how to tell porcelain from pottery, the pale blueness in the white color, the delicate feel of the cup or the plate, the shimmer of the white in the light.

She'd never felt so fully alive. She had behaved like the eager student that she habitually was and followed whatever her father said. If she had been discovered, she would have said she'd put it in her pocketbook without thinking.

Now, in Saks Fifth Avenue, as she made her way toward the area where panty hose were sold, she took a deep breath and coughed into her tissue again. A tall, middle-aged man in an immaculately tailored suit followed her. As she selected the type of panty hose that she wanted from the rack, she felt the man's presence. Trying to act as normal as possible, Tzippy went to the nearest register to pay for her item.

"I'd like to charge this, please," Tzippy said to the saleswoman, handing over her Saks card.

The man in the tailored suit stood a few feet from her and said nothing.

Tzippy's heart started to beat more quickly, but she didn't want to show her fear. "Thank you so much," the saleswoman said.

"Yes, thank you." Tzippy began coughing into her tissue, feeling her face flush with discomfort.

The tall man in the suit approached her and said, "Is anything the matter, madam?"

"Oh, no, thank you. I'm fine." As fear spread over her, she lifted her head to conceal her anxiety. Taking a deep breath, she tried to keep from coughing again. She looked the man straight in the eye. After all, she was a wealthy woman, an independent woman, a woman of means.

"You seem agitated. Do you need a glass of water?"

"No, I'm fine. I cough all the time. Don't smoke, young man." She wagged her finger at him and spoke in her best manner, wishing she had worn something better, not this peach jogging suit.

"I'm afraid I need to speak with you, madam." Her heart felt as if it were in a vise. She felt faint, and her knees weakened. "Please come this way."

She needed to defend herself, stop this insanity. How dare he, she thought indignantly. Didn't he know who she was? He couldn't humiliate her like this. She was Mrs. Benjamin Bryer.

"Where are you taking me?" she asked, her voice rising. "Are you sure this is necessary?"

He was undeterred and insisted. "Yes. Please don't make a scene."

No, she didn't want a scene. No one should know what was happening to her. She followed him, the large shopping bag dangling from her wrist.

He brought her into a small office and asked her to sit down. She placed her Saks shopping bag on the floor beside her and her Chanel handbag on her lap. Another man, shorter but also in a fine suit, joined him. He said, "What are you shopping for today?"

"I needed some panty hose. A few gifts for my children." She tried to sound normal, casual.

"Your kids?"

"Yes, they're here for a family party."

"That's nice," the taller man said.

"Yes, my party—can you imagine? They're having a celebration for me." She was rambling.

"May I look inside your pocketbook, please?" the smaller detective asked.

"Perhaps I should call my lawyer first. I'm not sure he'd go along with this procedure. I'm sure you've heard of him—Mr. P. J. Popowitz."

The detectives did not seem impressed. "We can do this the easy way or we can do it the hard way," the smaller one said.

Handing over her purse, Tzippy swallowed.

He placed her beige Chanel bag on top of the desk. He took out her red Kate Spade wallet—stuffed with papers, cards, money, and change. He arranged her makeup items—lipstick, face powder, and small magnifying mirror—in a pile and laid down on the desk the red half glasses she used for close reading. Then he stuck his hand deeper inside and felt around. Finally, he pulled out the brooch with the sticker on the back, announcing the reduced price. The Saks Fifth Avenue label was clear as a bell.

She wanted that pin, was entitled to that pin. What was a little pin, on sale, for God's sake?

"Do you have a receipt for this brooch, ma'am?" the man asked.

"Do you have any idea how much money I spend in this store?" she asked. "Have you people any clue? Why, just this week I bought an Armani pantsuit and a pair of nine-hundred-and-ninety-five-dollar Prada shoes," she said, her voice rising, filling up with self-importance.

"I'm afraid we have to ask the police to take you downtown," the shorter detective said.

"What do you mean, downtown?" Her head was spinning. Humiliation filled her, causing her to sweat. She felt dampness between her legs. Did she have a pad on? Had she remembered to wear it?

"I don't feel well. May I have that glass of water now, please?"

"Certainly," said the taller detective.

She'd never gotten caught before. None of the items that she'd stolen over the years—the ivory hand, hotel towels, airline pillows, a gold watch, simple rings, a few pens, a small vase—had been discovered. It was her little game. What harm did it do to take a magazine from a doctor's office, an ashtray from a restaurant? She'd wanted things, needed to have them; it made her feel better, helped her exert power and control. Getting what she wanted filled up the emptiness inside her. How could she get caught now, on the day of her own birthday party? Not now. When she'd stolen the ivory hand that first time, she'd hid it under her mattress in her room, had kept it there for months, until her thirteenth birthday, when, on her special day, she'd told her sister Julia how she'd gotten it for cheap at the antique show. Julia had been impressed.

"You've got to be kidding me," Tzippy said. "It's just a pin, costume jewelry."

She sipped the tepid water from the paper cup that had been handed to her.

"Please, I'm very upset today. I must have put it in my bag by mistake." Her hand shaking, she set the cup down on the desk amid all her personal belongings, next to her green checkbook from First and Ocean Bank. "Let me buy it. It's just a trifle. That will clear this whole thing up."

"We're sure this isn't the first time you've taken things from our store," the shorter detective said.

"In fact, we know it isn't," said the taller one. "We've looked the other way before, madam."

Two local Bal Harbour policemen arrived and took her downtown in a patrol car. The cruiser was worn and smelled of use, like a New York taxicab. She needed another Valium, but she was afraid to take one out of her purse, now that her belongings had been reshuffled. Maybe they'd object. She didn't know what to do. Her hand sweating, her heart racing, she willed herself not to panic, not to lose control.

In the police station, a flat-roofed, redbrick building at the south end of town, the officer on duty took her name and other important information and booked her for shoplifting, and then a buxom female officer fingerprinted her.

Tzippy wanted to act like a haughty old matron and say, *I hope you understand what you're doing. I never . . . Wait until I report this to my attorney.* Instead, shame filled her pores and her tongue strangled her into silence. Without protesting, she allowed the policewoman to press each of her fingers onto the black pad. Then she wondered if this meant she was a felon.

"Do you want to call someone?" The policewoman looked like a pug dog, short and squat, with her badge pinned to her bosomy shirt pocket. She had brassy-colored hair, cut short and a little spiky.

"Call someone?"

"Yes, someone to come and get you."

She started to cough and asked if she could sit down. Whom could she call? Not the kids, not anyone important. She couldn't call Stan. He would be mortified if he knew she was a thief. All that goodwill she'd accumulated with him would be shattered, thrown to the wind like yesterday's newspaper.

Finally, she decided on Goldie, her cousin in Boca. Goldie had grown up next door to her; they were only three months apart in age and had been school chums.

"You won't believe where I am," she started.

"What's the matter? You sound terrible."

"I'm at the Bal Harbour police station. I need you to come get me."

"What are you talking about?" Tzippy heard a TV talk show on in the background: *The View*, one of Goldie's favorites.

"I have a small problem. I went to Saks for a few things. A misunderstanding . . . They arrested me for shoplifting."

"You're kidding, aren't you?"

"No."

"Did you really steal, Tzippy?"

"I took a dumb pin. Nothing. It was a mistake."

"Of course. Those jerks. Dumb cops. Don't they have anything else to do with their time? And the day of your party, no less." Goldie had a way of taking over. The kids used to call her the General.

"Will you come and get me? I need a ride home."

"I'll be there in thirty-five minutes. I'm your cousin, so I won't let you down," Goldie said.

"Thank you."

She hung up the phone, and the policewoman stared at her. "You'll need to wait by the cell," the cop said.

"By the cell?"

"Yes, over there." The straight-backed chair sat across from a large, empty cage with a dark metal door, nothing inside but a stainless-steel toilet seat sticking out from one side.

The policewoman ushered Tzippy over to the chair with her rough hands. Lowering herself onto it, Tzippy wondered, as she looked at the metal toilet attached to the cement wall, how many asses had sat on it. Mortification crept up her body in waves.

"I can't be here. I'm eighty years old," she cried. "What are you afraid of? Do you think I'm going to shoot up the place? Why can't I sit out in the front in a regular chair, like a human being?"

The policewoman walked away, head down, saying nothing.

"This is not right. How can you do this to me? My children are having a party for me tonight. You bastards," Tzippy sobbed.

She sat on the hard chair and clutched her stomach. Feeling cold, small, and humiliated, she sat and rocked like a baby in a crib. She kept rocking and swaying, hoping the minutes would pass quickly until Goldie came. *Hurry*, she thought. *Hurry and get me out of here.*

Finally, she stopped rocking and sat motionless, letting the emptiness of her location calm her. Sitting in the gray light, she could sense the vitality leeching from her body. Her legs felt weak. She counted the minutes and hummed and began to rock again.

When Goldie arrived, she entered the station with gusto and said indignantly, "How could you guys arrest a lady like this?" She stared at the cop on duty. Goldie was blond, frosted like Tzippy, fully made up, and wearing a black linen suit with silver flats. Her slim legs made her look younger than her eighty years. With her collagen-filled lips, she resembled a woman who had kissed a bee.

"God, look at you," Goldie said, as she spotted her cousin huddled in a ball on the chair.

After the cop told Tzippy to get up, she rushed to her cousin and stood as near as she could, craving Goldie's warmth and protection. The cop returned Tzippy's pocketbook and had her sign her name. There would be a court date. She would receive a letter. "Let's go," Tzippy cried, fearing further reprimands.

In Goldie's Cadillac, Tzippy blew her nose, coughed into a tissue, and berated herself for lifting the brooch. Then she murmured, "Thanks for coming."

"What were you thinking, Tzippy? Why did you snatch the damn pin?" Goldie looked at her as if she were seeing someone she'd never known before.

"It was an impulsive act," she said. "I'm under too much stress."

"I never thought I'd be picking you up at the police station. This is a first," Goldie said as she sped away. "We used to swipe candy from Whalen's drugstore when we were kids, but this is a bit much, Tzipora. Remember when we found five dollars on the floor of the drugstore and you wanted to keep it? I made you return it, and we never got it back. What a fool I was. Don't worry. What can they do to you? For God's sake, it was only a damn pin."

"That's what I thought," Tzippy agreed.

"You'd better call your lawyer. Just in case."

"Listen, don't say anything to anyone, okay? It's my party tonight. I don't want anyone to know yet. Okay?"

Goldie looked at her first cousin and sighed. "Mum's the word. I promise." They were silent for a while. Goldie hummed tunelessly while Tzippy stared out the window at a world that looked different to her now that she was a criminal. Finally, they arrived at Tzippy's building. Tzippy got out, and just as she was about to thank Goldie for her rescue, her cousin blew a kiss into the air with her bee-stung lips and sped away.

Chapter 5

Back home at the apartment, Tzippy tried to collect herself. Confused at her own behavior, even a bit shocked, and terrified that her friends and family would find out, she had an impulse to take the whole bottle of Valium. She'd heard of people who did such things. In fact, she'd read the articles avidly, wherever she'd found them. Shoplifting and suicide—what a combination. One woman had set herself on fire while waiting in the police station after she'd been arrested. A Montreal police officer had been put on leave; he had been reinstated but had killed himself when he'd done it again. All these years, and Tzippy had never managed to break the habit. She dreaded what would happen to her—the criminal record, the ban from the store, and the disrespect. She took one Valium out of the vial in her handbag, left the pocketbook distractedly on the living room side table, and answered the phone.

"Where the heck have you been?" Stan said. "I've been calling for hours. Christ, Tzippy, you ought to get a damn cell phone."

Tzippy squirmed at his anger. It wasn't like Stan. "I had to go out and pick up some panty hose. I didn't want to bother you."

"I've been worried about you, baby cakes. Why didn't you tell me you were going out?"

"It was last-minute."

"I could have taken you, though I have to admit I've been comforting Freddie. He thinks he's going to be broke after his wife is done with him. I told him to stay with the broad. It would make life easier."

"Are you sure he likes her well enough?" she said, relieved that he'd changed the subject and seemed calmer.

"Now, that's a good question. How much do you have to like someone to save five million bucks?"

"Oh, dear. That much? No kidding?"

"Yeah. What do you think he should do?"

"I'm not the right person to ask, Stan," she said, feeling like a fraud for giving him advice.

"You're a sensible woman. What do you think?"

"I think he should stay with her and get himself a girlfriend." She couldn't believe she'd said that and wondered what had come over her.

"I knew you were sensible, baby cakes."

She knew she was a thief—that's what she knew. It was her addiction, especially when she was agitated and needed to fill up the empty space in her chest where her shortcomings congregated. It had gotten worse after the episode many years ago when her brother Lenny had been visiting. He was a stand-up comic who'd been working in the Catskills, the star of the family, with his famous pals in show business and his blond, goyish girlfriends. Befriending both the malcontents and the millionaires, Lenny was an engaging fellow who knew how to connect with bombastic, narcissistic stars, insecure models, and pretty, young gay men.

Yet, despite all those connections, Lenny occasionally floundered. He'd never learned how to manage his money and sometimes stayed with the Bryers between gigs. Tzippy let him use the back bedroom, the one with the yellow walls and Venetian blinds.

As if it were yesterday, Tzippy could envision Shari standing at the top of the stairs. "If Uncle Lenny comes in my room one more time and bothers me, I'll tell Daddy." Shari pointed at her mother accusingly as Tzippy looked up from the bottom of the aqua-carpeted steps.

Determined and angry, the girl tried to catch her mother's eyes, but Tzippy looked past her. "Oh, sweetie," Tzippy said. "He's just being friendly. He loves you."

"He keeps touching me. It's creepy. He wants me to sit on his lap."

"Shari," Tzippy said. "You must be mistaken."

"No, I'm not," Shari insisted. "He can't keep his hands off me."

Shari was no more than eleven years old; she was wearing navy blue shorts and a T-shirt. Her young legs still had soft, dark hair on them; she hadn't even begun to menstruate. She was just a preteen kid, full of energy and puppy-dog spirit, cartwheeling and laughing in the backyard. She beseeched her mother to do something, in her earnest and confused way, but, although one of Tzippy's parents' boarders had fondled Tzippy in her youth, she still couldn't bring herself to believe anything bad about her revered brother. Lenny had introduced her to Judy Garland and Danny Kaye, real celebrities. He had introduced her to Ella Logan, the Broadway lead in *Finian's Rainbow*. How could Tzippy forget standing wrapped in a mink stole next to the diminutive singer with the small, round behind and the Irish brogue?

Shari sat down on the top step and stared out into space, and neither she nor Tzippy said another word. Tzippy shook her head absently; in that long silence, she knew her own selfishness and fear would keep her from talking to Lenny. Shari could go to her father, as she'd threatened, but nobody in the Bryer house talked about embarrassing subjects.

If Lenny ever did return to her room, Shari must have scared the hell out of him, because nothing more was said. Tzippy never uttered a syllable to Benny about the entire sordid incident and tried to forget her failure to stand up for her daughter, even as she watched Shari begin to slip away. She stopped doing cartwheels and laughed less; she became more moody and prickly and withdrawn. After that parental defeat, Tzippy's stealing escalated.

Oh, Tzippy didn't want to think of all that now. "Sweetheart," she told Stan, "I'll speak to you later. I have to get my hair fixed. Maria's coming over." The last thing she needed was for him to learn about her theft; she wouldn't be able to endure his disappointment in her. Not today—not any day.

"Are you okay?" he asked. "Your voice sounds shaky."

"No, yes. I guess I'm excited and nervous."

"Relax. This is your big night. Everyone loves you."

Tzippy didn't know what to say. Finally she sputtered, "I hope so."

"Baby cakes, wait'll you hear my toast tonight. I'm going to leave the crowd in tears."

"Please, Stan, don't overdo it. Keep it simple."

"Tzippy, my love, when was anything simple with you?"

Angie returned, loaded with food. Tzippy breathed more easily, seeing how efficient Angie was, carrying in her wonderful brisket and deep-dish apple pie. She put everything away, and the apartment filled with delicious aromas. They would have the kids for dinner tomorrow night. No one needed to know that Tzippy wasn't a fine member of the community or an ethical, good person. She loved her children and was an elegant hostess. Watching Angie's large body move around the small kitchen, fixing and fussing, quieted Tzippy's anxieties.

Then she took a bath so she'd be ready for her hairdo. She tried to steady her hand and apply her makeup but finally gave up in frustration. She took deep breaths until Angie came in with a cup of tea. "You want something to eat, Mrs. B.?"

"Just a few saltines. Would you put some snacks out for the kids in case they pop in before the party? There's strawberries, fresh melon, some cheeses we bought at Shupie's, a few olives. You know how to make it look delicious, Angie."

The phone rang again. This time it was Naomi. Tzippy was glad for the distraction. Her mind couldn't focus for long on any one subject.

"We had a great time fishing," Naomi said. "Ike caught a bluefish, and the captain went crazy—he said it was the biggest blue caught in the Miami area this year. Can you imagine?"

"You're kidding."

"No, I'm not. The captain called it in, and when we came ashore a crowd was waiting and a photographer from the Miami *Herald* took Ike's picture. What a riot."

"My goodness."

"He's going to get it stuffed and hang it on the wall," she reported.

"Have you heard from the others?"

No one had heard from Shari yet, and Brucie and Jill were playing tennis.

Maria arrived, wearing a white smock and looking professional, and led Tzippy into the bathroom, where she spread out her clean tools on the vanity table and covered Tzippy with a cape. "You look upset. Are you okay or just nervous?" Maria asked.

"Excited, I guess."

Maria clipped and combed, teased and sprayed. She cut Tzippy's hair on an angle, bending the scissors this way and that. She wielded the comb and the scissors expertly, the way an artist uses brushes and paints. When she was finished, she attached the hairpiece.

Even now, distraught and tired, Tzippy appreciated the woman's talent. Before her eyes, she'd turned into a younger, prettier version of herself. It amazed Tzippy that her appearance could be transformed so dramatically and that no one could tell that inside she was the same person: a woman of means, a stealer of goods.

"You're amazing," Tzippy said to Maria.

"You're a beautiful lady, and today is your party. We have to look good, no?"

"Mrs. B., the platter is on the dining table. I'm going to start getting ready, okay?" Angie called.

"Yes, go ahead."

Just then, Shari knocked on the bathroom door and peeked in. She said hello to Maria. "Mom, I like your hair," she said.

"Oh, sweetheart. How are you? How was your visit with your friend?"

"Great. After last night, I needed to do something stress-free. You remember Francesca Tyler, my old roommate? She's as big as a house but happy, with three kids and a husband. Lucky girl. I'm fine, looking forward to the party. We put a lot of effort into this shindig. Wait'll you see."

"Angie told me," Tzippy said. She tried to block out the night before at Valerie Rose's. "Shari, you look wonderful."

"Thanks. Glad you like." Shari turned and let her mother examine her dress—purple, sleek, short.

Tzippy noticed that her daughter was no longer young. Although her stomach was flat, there were lines on her forehead and her eyes crinkled when she smiled. All that booze didn't help either, Tzippy thought. There were no veins on Shari's legs, however, because she'd had no children. Naomi, after three kids, had veins.

Tzippy was the kind of woman who noticed all these imperfections, the one person in a room who would comment on a woman's thick ankles and lie to her daughter to make her feel better. She couldn't help herself.

"Let me do your makeup," Maria said, taking out her kit.

"Oh, Maria, would you?" Tzippy asked. "My hand was shaking earlier."

"I think I need a pre-party drink," Shari said.

Before Tzippy could object, Shari was walking around with a glass tinkling with ice, with two fingers of gin. She went out on the deck to smoke a cigarette and talk on her cell phone while Maria finished up with Tzippy.

"You look seventy, not eighty, today, my dear," said Maria.

"Let me pay you," Tzippy said. "You're a doll to come over; it saved me so much time and effort." She looked around for her Chanel bag and finally found it on the living room side table where she'd dropped it. She searched inside and couldn't find her wallet. What if she'd left it at the damn police station?

It was Shari who made the discovery. She'd gone to use the toilet and walked in on Angie dressing for the party. Shari should have used the powder room, not Angie's bathroom. It was a mistake. Tzippy heard the commotion.

"Oh, I'm sorry, I thought you were dressed," Shari said.

"No, it's okay. I'm done," Angie answered.

"What's my mother's wallet doing in your bathroom?" Tzippy heard Shari say.

"I have no idea," Angie said.

Shari took the wallet and returned it to Tzippy. "Why was this in the bathroom with Angie?" she asked.

Tzippy didn't understand. "Maybe I left it in there," she said, quickly taking it.

Maria put her suitcase with her supplies by the front door.

"Check your money, Mom," Shari said, ice cubes tinkling.

Tzippy did a fast count of the cash, and her heart sank. She said it was all there, despite what seemed to be the missing hundreds. Perhaps she'd miscounted or lost track because of the arrest. She was too stunned to reveal her shock to her daughter and too overwhelmed by the day's events.

Tzippy's mind spun with confusion. Had she dropped the money in Goldie's car, left it in the station, spent it and forgotten? She didn't understand. The idea that Angie would have taken her wallet and removed money seemed impossible. Tzippy began to cough in rapid, hacking heaves. "Please bring me my pills and a glass of water."

"Mrs. Bryer, I have to go," Maria said. "Are you going to be okay? Don't wreck your hair or your makeup, now."

"I don't feel very well all of a sudden. I'd lie down, but I don't want to ruin your beautiful work. Let me write you a check." She had to get rid of Maria so she could deal with this situation. "How much do I owe you?"

"Five hundred. Are you sure you're okay?"

"Yes. I'll rally." Tzippy didn't object to the extravagant amount and wrote the check from her First and Ocean account. She paid Angie an annual salary of $25,000, on top of room and board and extras, under the table, so Tzippy felt pleased with herself. The other Jewish ladies compensated well also, and she had to keep up.

After Maria left, Tzippy yelled. "Angie, come in here."

Angie stood by the bedroom door in her bright turquoise outfit, big and colorful. The turban sat perched on her head, her black hair framing her round face. Tzippy couldn't look at her and said, "Go sit down over there." She pointed to a chair by the bed.

Tzippy counted her money again and found that maybe as much as $350 was missing.

Now she couldn't help but stare at the maid, all bedecked in her finery. Angie had put on cheerful red lipstick, which made her full lips look puffy, like Goldie's. "What were you doing with my wallet?" she snapped.

"Mrs. Bryer, I don't know what you're talking about. You left the wallet in there yourself."

Shari stood by and watched.

"Angie," Tzippy said. "Don't lie to me."

"I ain't lying."

"I don't use that bathroom. I have my own," Tzippy said. "There's money missing. I know, because I took out five hundred dollars this morning." After all she had done for her—the caftan, the turban, the Easter hats.

Just then, Naomi and Ike entered the apartment.

"What's going on in here?" Ike asked, poking his head into the bedroom.

No one answered; the room was filled with silence.

"I'm so disappointed," Tzippy said, staring at her maid and companion. "And on my birthday."

Shari, intent on listening, stayed in the room and groaned. Ike persisted. "Is there anything I can do to help?"

Ignoring her son-in-law, Tzippy said, her voice almost a whisper, "Say something."

"You're accusing me of stealing, and I'm insulted, Mrs. B," Angie said stoutly.

Shari rolled her eyes and left to freshen her drink.

"Bring me a glass of wine, Shari," Tzippy said, then added out loud, though mostly to herself, "Maybe I'm losing my mind." She felt as if the walls were crumbling. Her life was falling apart: the theft in Saks; getting caught; now this. It was too much.

Tzippy heard Brucie and Jill enter the living room. Shari told her brother, "We have a new problem."

As if they'd never exchanged a harsh word, Bruce said, "Why? What's up?"

Then Angie spoke again: "You know how much you mean to me, Mrs. B. I think you're just excited because of your birthday and because the kids are here. We have a party to get to. Do you still want me to come?"

"I want some answers, Angie. I didn't buy that dress for nothing."

"Mom, are you okay?" Jill asked, as she entered Tzippy's bedroom. She was dressed in a form-fitting red sheath that showed off her long, lean figure, and Tzippy couldn't help exclaiming, "My, you do look festive."

"Thanks," Jill said, twirling around.

Tzippy shook her newly coiffed head, pondering the ridiculous coincidence. Two thieves under one roof. She sipped her wine, hoping it would make her feel better.

"Mom, I think we'd all better start getting over to the club," Ike said. "I'd take you in my white convertible, but I think you'd be more comfortable in the Lincoln."

"Angie can drive me." Tzippy thought she'd talk to her a little more, try to straighten things out.

"I'll go with you," Shari added.

Tzippy didn't object. The girls had worked hard on the party, and she didn't want to offend either one of them, but she was afraid the children would insist that she fire Angie. What would she do without her?

Then Tzippy heard Naomi say to Brucie, "Thank God Dad's not alive for all of this."

"If he were here, none of this would have happened," Brucie said.

"Please don't remind me of how things would be different," Naomi added.

Did the kids really believe that Tzippy had contributed to the family's falling apart?

"Let's go," Ike said, trying to round everyone up. "We have plenty of time to talk about this later. We're going to have a party."

Tzippy put on her new Armani outfit and matching Prada shoes and then left in the Lincoln with Angie driving and Shari in the backseat. No one said much; heaviness descended on the car. It was as if all three of them knew that the night was a fragile balloon that the slightest word would puncture.

They pulled into the long drive to the Ocean Edge Country

Club and came to a stop under the clubhouse's portico. When Tzippy entered the grillroom, where the party was to take place, she took a deep breath and reached inside for those reservoirs of strength that she'd always found in herself. She was a woman who prided herself on being able to rise to the occasion. The centerpieces gracing each table stunned her. She loved flowers, and the roses and peonies filled the room with color and a pleasant aroma. The girls had had the centerpieces done in large papier-mâché shoes in honor of Tzippy's love of footwear. The tablecloths were hot pink and trimmed with bling. Cousins and people she hadn't seen in a while milled about, greeting her with good wishes. The majordomo introduced himself to Brucie and shook his hand. Tzippy spotted Stan in a soft beige sport coat and green bow tie, looking fit and happy.

Still, as much as she wanted it to, the incident with the wallet wouldn't go away. Everybody seemed to be talking about it. Tzippy overheard Angie say to Brucie, "I think Shari got all excited about nothing. She was drinking."

Tzippy smiled and said, "Stan, would you be a dear and get me a glass of chardonnay?"

"Coming right up," he said.

People kept approaching her where she sat to wish her well, and Tzippy beamed at her guests, but through the buzz of conversation, she heard Brucie say, "Maybe it's just a big misunderstanding." *God,* she thought, *I wish it were.*

Angie took a sip of her cocktail and straightened her caftan. "I should say so," she said.

Then Jack came up between the two of them. "I wish none of this had happened," he huffed. Obviously, Angie had filled him in; she seemed thrilled that he was there, and she held his hand for support.

"You and me both," Brucie said.

Jack sat down and gestured for Angie to do the same. He

was a handsome man, Tzippy thought. Angie was lucky to have attracted him.

A waitress offered them a platter of stuffed mushrooms and then came toward Tzippy, who said, "Thanks. I think I will try one." The hors d'oeuvres looked delicious.

Finally, the headwaiter announced dinner. As all the guests found their seats, Shari and Naomi each took one of Tzippy's elbows and escorted her to her place at the head of the table. A piano player began playing "My Funny Valentine," the first on a list of Tzippy's favorite tunes. The waiters brought crisp salads, refilled water glasses, poured red and white wine, and took orders—each guest was offered a choice of filet mignon or salmon.

"Tzippy, my dear, everything is marvelous," Goldie cooed, approaching her cousin's table in a beige lace frock. She smiled and wished Tzippy happy birthday.

"Thanks again for everything," Tzippy said. She gave Goldie a brittle smile, wishing she'd go away. She didn't want to be reminded of earlier.

"It's quite a memorable time," Goldie said. "Those police, why don't they leave the old gals alone?" she whispered, then returned to her seat at another table.

"What's that?" asked Stan. He sipped on a martini with an olive.

"Goldie says I don't look a day over seventy. I have the best hairdresser," she lied.

As people ate and drank, Goldie got up and took the microphone to give a toast. She told the guests about the piano lessons Tzippy had taken in her youth. "Tzippy's parents put the piano in the bathtub because there was no place for the spinet anywhere else in the house. That didn't dissuade dear Tzippy, though. She practiced in the bathroom."

Everyone laughed and applauded.

Tzippy kissed her cousin and hugged her appreciatively. She

laughed at Stan's jokes and tried to behave normally. When he kissed her cheek and rubbed his hand up her leg underneath the table cloth, she said, "My oh my, Stanley, aren't you friendly tonight?"

"All for you, baby cakes, all for you."

Despite all the festivities and the toasts to "such a wonderful, funny lady," Tzippy couldn't stop thinking of the day's events. Two thieves in one house, two women lifting goods that didn't belong to them, two females hungering for something they couldn't find. She shook her head in wonder. Feeling hollow and vacant, she wanted to ask Angie, *You wouldn't steal from me, would you?* Her mind was unraveling.

Finally, the headwaiter asked if he could clear the dishes for dessert. The guests dispersed for cigarettes and bathroom breaks. Three waiters carried out a table, on top of which was a three-layered cake bedecked with candles, and everyone sang "Happy Birthday." Meanwhile other waiters were busy handing around trays filled with flutes of champagne.

Stan stood up to make a toast. "There aren't many ladies like Tzippy," he said. "She's one of a kind. I'm a very fortunate man to have her as my gal. She's funny and smart and looks great for her young age. I love you, Tzippy. May you live to be one hundred. Please go ahead and wear me out."

Everyone cheered.

⌢

The children stayed on to square up with Ocean Edge and have a nightcap, and on the way home—Angie driving the Lincoln, Tzippy in the passenger seat—she pushed Angie to explain what had happened and why she'd taken the money.

Angie said, "Mrs. Bryer, I've worked for you for how many years? Now, why would you ask me such a thing?"

"How can we stay together now?" Tzippy asked. In spite of

Angie's steadfast refusal to admit what she'd done, Tzippy knew the truth. But she also knew that she was used to Angie and Angie was used to her. Who else made such a wonderful brisket? Who else could knead her aching legs so well? "Do you dislike me that much?" Tzippy asked.

"I don't dislike you, Mrs. B."

"Then what? Are you envious?"

"It's an unfair world. You must know that . . ."

"But I pay you well."

"Yes, you do. You're better than most whites."

Tzippy had never heard Angie express herself with such bluntness. She was shocked at Angie's choice of words.

"Did you ever think maybe someone else took your money?"

"Who, then?" Tzippy asked.

"I don't know. I'm just saying."

"I'm too old for all this."

"There's been a lot of people coming and going in the apartment," Angie said. "You know that."

Tzippy thought about that last remark.

Angie added, "I'm not saying anything, but that Naomi's always been a strange one. You know it yourself."

What nerve, Tzippy thought. Naomi hadn't even come up to the apartment until after Shari had confronted Angie, and the only time she'd been there had been in the morning, after her run. Was it possible the money had been taken then? She thought about how the girl used to keep a huge collection of quarters under her bed, how she had snuck down the rope ladder to get out of the house as a teenager. Then there was the time she'd stolen her friend's transistor radio. "You're just saying that. Are you blaming Naomi?"

"There you go again, after all these years we've been together. I am not. I've always loved the girl."

Naomi had dropped out of college, smoked pot throughout

her early years, and even dated a guy who'd been in jail at one point. It was a miracle she'd fallen in love with Ike. His owning a Harley-Davidson had probably clinched the deal. Tzippy's head spun at Angie's brass in implicating Naomi in order to save her own hide. Angie, who had danced at Naomi's Sweet Sixteen party and had rolled up the girl's hair in rags when Naomi was a kid. She'd sewn Naomi's nametapes and painted her fingernails. Given her baths when she was a little one. Once, she'd even lanced a boil on the girl's bottom. Why, she'd taken care of Naomi as if she were Angie's own.

Sadness and fear filled Tzippy's heart. "I wish Benny were alive."

"That makes two of us."

"Benny was good to you, Angie." Tzippy remembered how he'd tipped her extra at the holidays, complimented her scrambled eggs, asked her to come with them on vacation, allowed her to drive his Oldsmobile, even let her take the girls with her to visit her friends. They'd had a nice rapport. *But*, Tzippy thought, *we were the rich Jewish employers. She was the domestic, the black maid on the number 20 bus coming to the suburbs every morning.*

The two women drove back to Bal Harbour in silence.

Chapter 6

The morning Tzippy woke after her eightieth-birthday party was a new hell. She twisted in the sheets, stared at the ceiling, and inventoried all the indignities her body was inflicting upon her. In addition to her physical difficulties, she felt emotionally overburdened—frightened, glum, and fed up. This last was a new one; to be so sated with life that she no longer cared was rather startling.

As she lay there, Tzippy allowed herself, for the first time, to really think about being a thief. Her head throbbed with an increasingly intense litany of self-criticism. She should have stopped this habit long ago, after the ivory hand; then it would have been only an aberration, and after a few years she'd have forgotten all about it and could have forgiven herself.

She should have moved on and had her life with Benny and the kids, her shopping, her affair with Claude. She should have forced herself to stop. She should have thrown Lenny out of her house; she should have protected her daughter. But then there was the whole story with Shari, the eating disorder and all the craziness. Without the stealing, she'd have had no obsessive emotional distraction, no shame or fear that she'd get caught. She wouldn't have had to justify all her pinching to herself. And she wouldn't have had to think about the items she'd squirreled away or had worn with nervousness, wondering if someone would comment on an unfamiliar watch or scarf.

Then there was the worst part. She had made her offspring accessories to theft, had used the children's innocence to camouflage her guilt. She'd taken Shari into the dressing room of Harding's, the local department store, when she was three years old, putting little outfits on the child, who thought she was dressing up as a princess. She had put Shari's regular clothes over a new outfit and then had walked her out breezily, explaining that they didn't want to dirty the new princess outfit and telling the saleswoman, "We'll be back later. I just remembered an appointment, and we must run." A common criminal pretending to be a fancy lady and using her very own daughter to hide the goods—the daughter she had later pushed and prodded and tried to polish into a young lady who'd turn out well.

Of course, Shari had been too young to understand what was happening at the time, but maybe on some level she'd known that her mother wasn't looking out for her best interests, a knowledge reinforced across the years. The image of eleven-year-old Shari protesting Uncle Lenny's advances shone in Tzippy's mind as she lay in bed. No wonder the girl disliked her so.

As her shame bore down on her, Tzippy wished she'd sought professional counseling to help her stop her addiction. If she had, she wouldn't be the woman she had become.

But all her life, Tzippy had been hoarding things and fussing over her possessions, even as a young girl. She'd traded her lunch for money so she'd have cash to buy pretty things for herself. She used to wrap up special purchases in tissue paper and place them under her bed: a thin lace collar, a delicate handkerchief, and a cameo pin for the neck of the shirtwaist. She had kept her starched white petticoat on a hanger on a nail in the back of the closet she'd shared with her sisters. She had put the straw hat she'd bought on sale, the one with the black ribbon headband and white gardenia, back there, too. To this day, she adored hats of all types. Hats and shoes. They completed an outfit. Wanting to be rich one day, she'd dreamed of nothing else. She wanted silver knives and forks, ironed tablecloths, napkins, marble bathtubs with lots of hot water.

Then she had married Ben and had never needed to pinch again; she'd had more than she needed. If only she hadn't stolen, taken what wasn't hers, then she would have been free to live her life, instead of being an agitated, unsure old lady with secrets about her silly capers, who couldn't tell her present boyfriend or her kids the truth. How could she remake herself so that she could feel better? How could she shed her sins and turn herself into someone she liked, who had ideals, who was charitable, not greedy? How could she rid herself of her selfishness?

The telephone rang as she placed her feet on the rug on her bedroom floor. Her son's confident, warm voice did little to comfort her. "Mom, how are you today?" Brucie asked.

"I'm feeling shaky," Tzippy said.

"We need to talk."

"Yes, I suppose we do." *What will I say to my children?* she wondered. *Do I need to tell them?* "I was hoping everyone would come here for dinner tonight. I've planned a nice meal before you leave."

"That's all fine and good, but what are you going to do about Angie?"

Instantly, Tzippy's thoughts flew to her other problem. "Oh, Brucie, not now. How can we even be sure Angie took the money? There must be another explanation."

"So, if not Angie, who?"

"I really don't know, but I'm not jumping to any conclusions."

"You can do whatever you want, but don't come crying to me if things get worse."

"Now, that's not a very caring attitude," Tzippy said. "I am your mother."

"Oh, I know . . . but you're not facing reality. For God's sake, Mom."

"I'm inviting Stan over for dinner tonight. He'll have a few good ideas."

Tzippy needed her children to calm down. She and Angie would work things out, come to some understanding.

"You know, I don't understand you," Brucie said. "You act like nothing happened. Are you sure you want Stan to know?"

"Yes, of course. He's a smart man. He'll know what to do. And maybe it's me. Maybe I'm losing my mind." There, she'd said it.

"Maybe we should give Angie a leave of absence, time off. A chance to think about things."

"How will I manage?" *I can't live alone.*

"There are plenty of nice women looking for work."

Tzippy said nothing but made little tsks of disapproval. She dreaded breaking in a different maid. On the other hand, she could hire someone younger for less money and train her the way she wanted. Hadn't her friend hired a Hispanic girl for cheap?

"Mom, I've had a hell of a few days, first with Shari, and now with Angie stealing. Let's talk to Angie and sort this out. I can't leave you down here with this mess. Dad wouldn't want me to, and you know it."

"Oh, Brucie," Tzippy wailed, "I told you I'm not feeling well. Can't we just have a nice meal? How about four o'clock? We'll have dinner at six. I'll tell Stan."

"Fine. Four p.m. it is. But understand that we *will* talk about this problem—*all* of us—before we eat. It has to be dealt with. Now, I'm going to play a few sets of tennis and take a swim. You should rest. You're probably exhausted. Not a bad party, though. What did you think?"

"You kids did a terrific job. It was lovely. Simply wonderful."

Tzippy washed up and stared at her drawn face in the mirror. Everything was moving too fast. She was so in need of comfort, and though it had been years, she thought of Claude, one of the few people who had given her the relief she needed in life. She recalled how Ben had hired him as a handyman-chauffeur, how handsome he'd been, this Jamaican, the color of cane juice. She had been so upset over Ben's affair with the golden-haired Laura, which had been going on for several years, and Claude had been polite and quiet and well mannered. One day in 1968, when she had been forty-eight years old, enraged and ashamed over Ben's infidelity, she had asked Claude to take her driving. Staring out the window at the passing trees, she had suddenly felt her heart begin to pound and she'd become flushed and faint. She'd told Claude she had a pain in her chest and had made him stop the Cadillac and come sit in the backseat with her. Just like that, she'd asked him, "Would you sit back here and hold my hand?"

This handsome man in his mid-thirties with light brown eyes had gotten out of the large car, sat his lanky frame in the beige leather seat, taken Tzippy's small, delicate hand in his own, and sat there while her panic subsided. Neither one of them had said a word until she'd gotten hold of herself.

After that, Tzippy started sitting in the front seat next to Claude. Sometimes when she became anxious, she'd touch his arm as he drove. When she thought of Ben's shtupping golden-haired Laura, she'd grab the hem of Claude's jacket and squeeze it tightly. Somehow his presence and calmness settled her, took away her fear. He never said anything, just kept driving.

Occasionally, the two of them sat on the screened porch on the white rocking chairs and drank freshly brewed tea. They gazed at the flowers in the rock garden and in the yard and discussed how the plantings looked. They watched the Italian gardeners manicure the lawns and clip the hedges, and calmly commented on the magenta azalea bushes. She never understood why Claude made her feel better. She just accepted it. Once, in the Cadillac, she asked him to stop and he bought steaming cups of coffee and fresh pastries from the German bakery, and the two of them found a secluded, grassy spot in Cameron Field. Then, with sugar-dusted lips, she kissed Claude for the first time.

Tzippy shook her head now, trying to dispel the image. She was a foolish woman for sure. This was no time to be reminiscing about her past lover. She had to go find Angie and talk to her. Perhaps she'd want to go to church and spend the day with Jack.

Tzippy walked into the kitchen, where Angie was making freshly squeezed orange juice, Tzippy's favorite.

"Thank you," Tzippy said, as Angie gave her a small glass. She sat down at the little corner table in the kitchen, sipping the cool juice. "We need to talk, Angie," she said. She felt the old anxiety, but there was no one to hold her hand.

"Yes, Mrs. B." Angie's voice was flat, taut.

"This is very awkward for me," Tzippy said, "but I was thinking, why don't you take the rest of the day off after you set the table and get everything ready for dinner tonight?"

"Who's going to serve supper and clean up?" Angie asked.

"I'll get the kids to do it. I need to spend some time alone with them and talk about what we should do."

"Uh-huh," Angie said. She started to hum.

"The whole situation with the missing money has upset me," Tzippy said. She stood and turned away. "Perhaps you should take a few weeks off, go on a vacation with Jack."

"Now, Mrs. B., who does you think I am, Mrs. Rockefeller?"

"I just need some time to consider what to do."

"You mean, if you're going to fire me?"

"Angie, damn it. Did you take my money or not? I can't keep a thief, can I?"

The irony of the situation made her entirely uncomfortable. She felt like a hypocrite, berating Angie after she herself had been arrested and fingerprinted at the police station. She, who had been sitting next to a jail cell, huddled in a ball of shame, was scolding Angie for taking her three hundred bucks.

"How you going to manage without me?"

"That's a good question." She started to cough and grabbed her tissue box. "Could you make me some tea, please?"

"Toast, too?"

"Sure."

Angie placed a white napkin, a knife, and a spoon in front of Tzippy.

"Why did you ruin everything?" Tzippy asked.

Angie was silent as she put the bread in the toaster and got the jam out of the refrigerator. The teakettle heated up, and steam began to shoot from the spout. "Why do you think?" she finally said. Her voice sounded tense and unhappy.

"Oh, Angie, stop this game."

"This ain't any game, Mrs. B."

"I'm too old for these problems."

"Here, eat something and drink your tea."

"Just take the day off so I can think."

"Whatever you say. You the boss."

After she set the table with Tzippy's fine china and showed Tzippy how to heat up both the brisket and the deep-dish apple pie, Angie left for the rest of the day. She looked mournful and weary as she told Tzippy she hoped the children enjoyed the dinner, and maybe even a bit miffed that she wouldn't be there to hear their compliments.

Tzippy strolled around the apartment and tidied up. Then, on impulse, she went into Angie's room. It was a small room with a large double bed that took up most of the space, along with a night table, a lamp, and a chest of drawers. The bed was covered with a tapestry print bedspread and was neat as a pin. Tzippy opened the drawers and peeked under stacks of Angie's carefully folded clothes; she even looked under the bed. She wasn't sure what she expected to find. Finally, in a corner of the closet, she saw a small box and opened it to find it filled with little perfume bottles. All the missing vials of perfume, including her favorite one, were standing like soldiers.

The phone rang, and Tzippy rushed to pick it up.

"Hello, yes."

"Baby cakes, that was one fine party last night."

"Oh, Stanley," Tzippy said. "I was going to call you. The kids did a great job, especially the girls. They worked hard, and it showed."

"Well, they love you, that's all. What's up for today?"

"Would you come over at four and help me figure out what to do? It's such a mess. I think Angie stole some of my money, and I know she's been taking perfume from me. I may have to let her go."

"You're kidding."

"I wish I was. I didn't mention it last night, with the party and everything. Shari found my wallet in Angie's bathroom—with some money missing. The kids and I need help with this one. Then stay for dinner. They're all leaving tomorrow."

"Of course I'll come. Are you okay? What are you going to do without her? I can't believe she's a thief."

The word struck Tzippy with a jolt. Coming from Stan's mouth, it sounded worse. "Now, please don't say that so fast."

"Well, what would you call her?"

"I don't know. Maybe it's a nervous habit."

"Oh, you *are* something. Whatever you say, baby cakes. She shouldn't be taking your stuff."

"It's a mess. I'm so distraught."

"Sweetheart, we'll figure this out. There are plenty of women looking for honest work."

"That's what Brucie said. It's such an adjustment, that's all."

"Listen, I already have a few ideas. Let's talk later, okay?"

"Fine. I think I'll go take a bath and relax. I don't feel well."

"Good idea. I'm going to play nine with Fred."

"I'll see you at four, okay?"

"I love you, baby cakes."

"I love you, too."

The kids seemed rejuvenated and rested when they arrived at the apartment. Brucie's cheeks were sunburned and he walked with a spring in his step after playing a few sets of tennis with Jill. She looked beautiful, her white piqué sundress showing off her tan and her lovely shape. Naomi and Ike, relaxed after sailing and sunning, giggled at each other's jokes. Tzippy was relieved to see them getting along. Ike had a habit of skirting the edges of the law, and it caused Naomi a lot of grief. They'd even separated for a while, which had worried her. Thank God only one daughter was divorced, not two—although Shari, despite the fact that she'd started drinking Tanqueray on the rocks the minute she'd arrived, seemed less wound up than usual. Perhaps getting away from her everyday life was doing her some good.

"Where's Stan?" asked Brucie, sitting down in the living room, getting right to business.

"He'll be here in a minute. He's never late," said Tzippy. She had napped and bathed and felt fresh in a matching cashmere twin set and slim pants, all in the shade of vanilla ice cream. Her hair was still in place from Maria's styling, and the hairpiece helped her feel attractive. "By the way, girls, you did a magnificent job planning the party. I want to thank you from the bottom of my heart. Everything was lovely. I especially adored those centerpieces in the shoes. Look, I brought one home," she said, pointing to a floral arrangement in a high button shoe on her coffee table.

Naomi and Shari grinned and looked at each other.

"Maybe we'll go into the party-planning business," Naomi joked.

Just then Stan came in, appearing fit and friendly. He was wearing a pistachio-green sport shirt, open at the neck, a cream-colored sport jacket, and gray slacks. "Sorry I'm late. The traffic got backed up. Some old guy put his foot on the gas, instead of the brake."

"No, kidding?" Ike exclaimed. "Anyone hurt?"

"No, but there was a pile-up. I bet they take his license away. Old fool could have killed someone."

Ike grinned at Brucie but said nothing.

"Okay," Brucie said. "We've got a situation here. What are we going to do?" He looked around at the assembled group, enjoying the role of paterfamilias. "I suppose you heard about the missing money, Stan?"

Stan nodded and appeared to be trying to look chagrined, but he seemed exceptionally happy and didn't quite manage. "Yeah," he said. "Who would have thunk it? Really. I can't believe Angie took it."

"Oh, she took it, all right," Shari said.

"We're pretty sure she did," Tzippy said. "I found some of my perfume bottles in a corner of her closet, stashed in a little box on the floor."

"I think you're going to have to let her go, Mom," Ike announced, with an attorney's confidence.

"That's what I've been telling her," Bruce said.

"God, Mom, I can't believe Angie would take your money after all these years," Naomi said. "She was always so nice to me."

"It doesn't make sense, does it?" Tzippy said. "It's most likely Jack's influence. I don't really care for him."

"She's probably been stealing from you for years," Shari said, sitting down in the yellow lounge chair by the sofa. Tzippy thought she looked tired.

"Please, I've been a mess all day," Tzippy said. "Would you bring me a glass of chardonnay, Shari?"

"I'll get it; don't bother," Naomi said.

"There's cheese and crackers on the table. Bring it over here for everyone, would you?" Tzippy instructed.

"I'll go fix myself a drink," Stan said, on his way to the bar in the den. "I know my way around," he said, laughing.

"You're going to have to find a new maid, Mom," Brucie said.

"But I'm not firing Angie so fast," Tzippy said. "Maybe I should give her a leave of absence." The thought of a new employee made her ill. She didn't like change.

"I have a great idea," Stan said, returning with a glass with two fingers of scotch, neat. Everyone looked up. "I know you kids are all worried about your mother." He sipped from his Scotch. He smiled slightly and sucked in his belly. He was in good shape for a man his age, eighty-two on his next birthday. He cleared his throat and waited a second before continuing. "I think I should marry your mother and move in here and take care of her. That way, we could get a woman to come in during the day to cook and clean, and I could take your mother to her appointments and stuff. Why look for a live-in, for God's sake? I love your mother. I'll marry her, and then you guys won't have to worry. What do you think?" He looked around the room at all the staring faces.

Tzippy felt the blood rise into her cheeks. This was his idea of a proposal? She'd known, of course, that marrying Stan was a possibility, but she hadn't imagined it would take this form.

"It's not what we think that counts, Stan. It's what my mother thinks," Shari said, rising to the occasion.

"Mom, you have to decide this one," Brucie said.

"I think it's a great idea," Naomi said.

"Me, too," Jill added.

"Wait a minute . . . let your mother speak," Ike said.

All eyes were on Tzippy. She didn't know what to say. Her mind quickly went over all the pieces of the puzzle. A man living in her apartment. She loved Stan. No big deal. Maybe he'd understand. He was such a good man. A prenup. No more Angie. "Well, I just don't know," she stammered, sipping her white wine. "Why, Stanley, do you really mean this?"

"Oh, baby cakes, at this stage in my life, I wouldn't say it if I didn't mean it." He grinned at the entire family.

It wasn't the most romantic moment she'd ever experienced, and Tzippy wasn't even sure she shouldn't be a bit offended—marriage to Stan as a solution to her sudden problem with Angie? But she also had a rush of gratitude. He could be goofy and awkward, unlike Bennie, who had been so suave, but he was the kinder man, the better man, and true blue.

"Why, yes. Let's do it," she said. She stood up, went over to Stan, and planted a kiss on his lips. All the children rose and hugged one another. They smiled and toasted and cheered, and Tzippy felt a new wave of goodwill fill their lives. No, they wouldn't have to worry about their mother. Dear Stanley Fosberg had saved the day.

She'd think about the theft at Saks later. And she needed to call her doctor back, but there was no need to mention that now, either. She had a wedding to plan. They'd all have to gather back here in a month, after she and Stan had written their prenup. She'd arrange a small ceremony right here in her apartment, with the rabbi who had buried poor Selma Grossman. Right here, in front of the yellow brocade sofa where she and Stan had almost done it, she, Tzipora Finkel Bryer, would marry Stan Fosberg at age eighty. Life was full of surprises. Wait until she told Goldie. Oh, glory days. She, not her cousin, was the one who'd gotten the guy.

Chapter 7

Five days after the party, Tzippy was still trying not to think about all the other problems pressing on her, or about all the reasons she could find not to take such a momentous step. Now was not the time for negativity! A lifestyle change was in order. Marrying Stan would make her stop the stealing, keep her from getting lonely, and give her a fresh focus. He'd be a positive influence, maybe show her how to get involved in the Girls' Club, like he was involved with the Boys' Club, and do some good with her life, instead of just spending money or stealing. Maybe he could help her become a mensch—an honorable, decent, compassionate person who did the right thing—and not some thieving, selfish woman.

She also needed to ask Ben for his blessing. Seeking his counsel, especially when life baffled her, was an old habit. She pictured him in his golf pants with his open-collared shirt, his Ben Hogan hat, his twinkling blue eyes, and smiled.

Ben, she thought, *what do you think? You've known Stan for years and like him. Remember how he brought you baby-blue pajamas from Neiman's when you were sick in the hospital after your bypass? He loved you like a brother, looked up to you, Benny. Stan is a good, decent man, not some crook.*

She imagined Ben nodding in agreement, and in that moment, she knew Stan's proposal was just what the doctor had ordered. For the first time since she had married Ben, Tzippy knew she didn't need his last name anymore—he was dead, and she wasn't. Life went on. She wasn't standing still. At eighty years old, she had no more time to waste.

Brucie, Shari, and Naomi were thrilled with their prospective stepfather. Stan's daughter, Evelene, seemed like a sensible, smart woman who approved of Tzippy. And Tzippy felt certain that members of Stan's family didn't get arrested for shoplifting or for stealing from their employers.

Fortunately, Angie's crime had become clearer to Tzippy because of a phone call she'd gotten from Shari from the Miami airport, two days after the party, as Shari waited to board her flight back to Boston.

"Mom, I have to tell you about something weird that happened at your party," Shari said. She sounded conspiratorial and pleased with herself.

"Yes?"

"After the cocktail hour, I needed a break from the noise, all the stress with me finding the wallet—you know. Well, I went outside to have a smoke. I walked out the front door of the clubhouse and lit up, and then I looked to my right and saw Angie and Jack over by the golf carts, talking." Shari's voice trembled with the import of what she was about to say. Then she continued, "Anyway, I saw Angie give Jack some cash. She handed him this wad of green bills, folded in her fingers, and he slipped it into his pants pocket."

"Really?" Now, *this* was interesting. Tzippy heard Shari take a drag of a cigarette over the phone.

"Yes, really. I can't be sure if it was your money, but why else would she be giving him cash in the middle of a birthday party? For God's sake, what's the urgency? She wanted to get rid of the incriminating evidence, that's what." Shari's voice was triumphant.

"Why didn't you tell me this sooner?"

"With all the partying, I just needed to slow down and go over the details in my mind before I was positive."

"Yes, yes, I understand," Tzippy said, though she didn't really. Being drunk had never stopped Shari before.

"I bet the only reason he's dating Angie is to get her to steal from you."

"That no-good lowlife. Well, thank you for telling me," Tzippy said. "That relieves my mind."

"Makes sense, doesn't it?"

"Yes, it certainly does."

Despite this new information, it hadn't been easy to let Angie go. After the kids had left and she'd had this talk with Shari, she had still waited until late afternoon Monday to tell Angie. Tzippy wasn't stupid enough to think she could just sail right through the breakup. She'd employed Angie for so many years that the parting felt like a divorce, and the two of them threw accusations and recriminations at each other right up until the end.

"What about the money you gave Jack outside the club?"

"How do you know about that?"

"A little birdie told me."

"That was cash I owed him. It has nothing to do with you."

"That is too convenient for me to believe, Angie," Tzippy said.

"And just how are you going to manage without me?" Angie asked, as she packed her suitcase in the small bedroom where Tzippy had found the perfume vials. Jack was coming over to get Angie, and then Tzippy would take a pill and go to sleep.

"Stan will take care of me," Tzippy said. She stood in the door-way of Angie's bedroom, overcome with weariness; she wanted to sit down on the double bed and rest. Her legs were weak.

"Oh, he's going to love getting up in the middle of the night to massage your little feet with vinegar," Angie said. "I'd like to see that."

"Why, he loves me very much," Tzippy said. "Of course he'll do that," though suddenly she was a little unsure.

"Humph," Angie said, and slammed her suitcase closed. She picked it up by the handle and swung it around like a weapon. "Mrs. B., you got trouble ahead—I can see it." She stared stonily at Tzippy. "And when you needs me again and calls, I just might not be available. I hope everything works out for you, but I have my doubts, you being the woman you are."

"What do you mean by that?" Tzippy asked.

"Well, I can't see you living with a new man," Angie said. "No, not at this stage of your life. You're too settled in your ways. You like to be the boss."

"What do you mean, 'like to be the boss'?" Tzippy asked.

"You know what I mean." Angie was wearing support hose pushed down around her ankles; they looked like a tan rope rolled into bunches.

"But that's not your concern now, is it?" Tzippy said tartly.

"No, not anymore. You're right about that." A tear fell onto Angie's cheek.

Tzippy almost teared up herself and said, *Oh, Angie, it's all right. I understand,* but she just looked at Angie, stricken with the thought of their lost intimacy. Who would lunch with her at Shupie's counter? Whom could she talk to about woman things?

Then, regaining her composure, she continued, "Just so you know, we're going to hire a gal to come in during the day."

"Are you sure you're going to be okay?" Angie asked. In spite of her hurt and anger, she looked concerned. She had a big hat-box in one hand—one of the numerous Easter bonnets Tzippy had given her through the years.

"I'll survive," Tzippy said. "But I'll miss you." She crossed her arms on her chest, trying to be stoic, while a wave of grief rose through her. "And to think you stole my money." Tzippy looked away so she wouldn't weep. "We could have gone on forever."

"Mrs. B., stop it. I didn't do nothing," Angie insisted, her mouth clenched tight.

"I can't believe this. What about those perfume bottles, then, hidden in the closet?"

"You gave them to me. You just don't remember."

"I said I was *going* to give them to you. I didn't know you'd been taking them all along. Were you taking one the night that bottle broke?"

At that, Angie went on the offensive. "What about all those little pillows you stole from the airplanes, Mrs. B.? Or the magazines from Dr. Waterday's office, or the towels off the cart in those hotels? Doesn't that make you a thief, too?"

"What do you mean, 'too'?" Tzippy asked sharply. "Is this a confession?" Tzippy's heart started to race, and she began coughing vigorously. "Anyway, Angie, don't turn this around on me. I'm your employer, and you're not supposed to steal my money!"

Angie hung her head and was silent.

In the end, however, Tzippy held the trump card. Jack came and carried out Angie's valises and boxes—two large, brown suitcases filled with the clothes and hats that Tzippy had bought her over the years. Her starched white uniforms lay folded neatly inside, in case she secured a position where she was required to wear them.

As Jack was about to leave Tzippy's apartment, he stood in the doorway and looked around, as if he'd forgotten something. Tzippy said nothing, just watched his eyes scan the open floor plan; the top of the refrigerator, where the Cuisinart was kept; and then over to the coffee table, where the floral arrangement in the high button shoe from the party still sat, alongside an encrusted Jay Strongwater picture frame and a pretty candy dish. He stared at Tzippy with dark eyes, then turned and left, not even bothering to close the door.

"How did it go?" Stan asked when he arrived the next morning. He carried a small black case, which he set down in the front hall.

"It was terrible, Stan. We were both so hurt. And then that Jack came by to pick her up. He stood in the doorway, looking like he was casing the place. I don't like him one bit. Oh, I'm so glad you're here."

"I don't envy you. The whole thing is too disappointing," he said, giving Tzippy a hug. "Why don't you change, and we'll go for a stroll and get some fresh air?"

"A stroll would be lovely. Can I get you something to drink, like iced tea?"

"Terrific."

She went into the kitchen and poured him a glass of tea, took it to him, and set it down next to him as he opened a magazine. "I'll go change," she said, her mind racing. She knew that Stan would be a good influence. They'd walk on the gravel path in front of the beach and feel the cool breeze. He would fix her. Her mother, Annabelle, used to say, "Go to the sea and be healed." Or was it her father, Bertram? She couldn't remember. So much she couldn't recall. She kept black-and-white pictures of her favorite scenes: her and her sisters at the Stork Club on Sophia's birthday; Ben in front of his new green Packard; her on her wedding day, with the big satin bow on the top of her head, waiting for Ben to take care of her.

Stan would take care of her now. Shari would come, and maybe they could have a few good talks. Tzippy wanted to clean up her life, try to make amends. And she didn't want to be ashamed of her beginnings anymore. Sure, her family had come from Eastern Europe. Many immigrants had. But she'd been embarrassed by their lack of status. In truth, they had been a hardworking group who had little choice. Weren't her father's love of art and beauty and her mother's tenacity worthy of admiration? Was it too late to change?

But first she had to get in touch with her lawyer, Pincus Jacob Popowitz, and get started on the prenup. He'd advise her on what to do, and Stan was a reasonable man. It wouldn't be too complicated, she thought. And she needed to talk to PJ about her arrest, but . . .

For the ceremony, she'd buy something at Neiman's, since she couldn't go back to Saks—a silk suit with a pillbox hat, a little Jackie O. outfit, classy and understated—and they'd "do the deal," as Selma Grossman used to say. *God, it's too bad she's not alive to witness me marrying Stan Fosberg,* Tzippy thought. She'd have gotten a big kick out of that.

After the ceremony, she'd tell Stan about the shoplifting and court date, explain it as a misunderstanding, an oversight on her part. She'd been stressed and overwrought and hadn't known what she was doing. He'd understand. What could they do to an old woman? And then there was Dr. Waterday. Nothing was ever simple. Stan would be there whatever happened. Tzippy was sure their marriage was the right decision.

"Do you want me to send over my girl? She could clean up Angie's room, throw in a load of wash, whatever you need her to do," Stan yelled from the living room.

"Oh, sweetheart, that would be great. What's her name, again?"

"Jocelyn Bell. She's a nice girl, will do whatever you tell her to do."

"Oh, thanks. Stan, I love you," she said, sticking her freshly made-up face, wafting Joy perfume, out the bedroom door.

"Baby cakes, this is the start of something big," he sang, and then reached inside his sport jacket for his phone to call his maid.

As Stan was talking on his cell, Tzippy, who had quickly dressed in light lavender pants and a matching cashmere sweater set, picked up the phone in her bedroom and called her lawyer. She had to make an appointment, get the marriage moving along. After all, how long could she endure having Shari with her? Shari was a rager. Shari would return and stay with her until the wedding. The entire visit could blow up within two days. But she was the only one of Tzippy's children who could get away and come live with her.

"Tzippy, how are you? Good to hear from you," PJ said. He had been Benny's longtime lawyer and was an old family friend. He'd attended all the children's weddings, had written Ben's will, and had helped with many business problems.

"Oh, I'm fine, just a little tired."

"What's happening?" PJ said. His father, Sy, had met Tzippy when she was a young bride. Sy Popowitz had impressed Tzippy with his warmth and class. He was a wealthy man with a summer home on the New England coast, a pristine white house with a wraparound porch and white wicker furniture. She'd sat on the open porch, drinking iced tea with freshly crushed mint, while Sy asked about Tzippy's background. She had been trying to make a good impression.

"I heard you were from the western part of Massachusetts," he said, his brilliant red hair blowing in the sea breeze.

"Yes, a little town out by Amherst."

"Pretty country. I used to date a gal from Smith before I fell in love with Letty, who was a Radcliffe girl."

"Yes, Ben told me she went to Radcliffe." Tzippy immediately envied both Letty and the Smith coed. While the wealthy, bright gals in her area had attended colleges like Smith and Mt. Holyoke, Tzippy had been employed after high school at Finkel's Furniture Emporium, her father's dusty furniture and antiques store, selling dark green brocade sofas to middle-aged women in overcoats and unattractive hats. Tzippy felt insecure, knowing she hadn't gone to college.

"Smith's a beautiful campus," Tzippy said. She and Julia and Sophia used to go over there and walk around. Smith girls were pug-nosed, smart overachievers who came from the right families. Despite her lack of a college education, Tzippy had made the most of herself and had dressed up every day she'd gone to work, in high heels with ankle straps, a shirtwaist with a cameo pin on the lace collar, seams straight on her hose, red lipstick and rouge. Tzippy had reminded herself that Ben Bryer had chosen Tzipora Finkel, Smith and Radcliffe girls be damned.

Now, on the phone with Sy's son, she hesitated to tell him her news. "I think I need a prenup," she started.

"What do you mean? Are you getting remarried, Tzippy?"

"Yes, as a matter of fact, I am."

"Well, this comes as a surprise. Who's the lucky man?"

"Stan Fosberg, a longtime friend of Ben's and mine. We've been dating quite a while."

"Well, that's terrific. An old friend who becomes a husband can be a fine thing."

No sooner had Tzippy finished her conversation with PJ than the telephone rang.

"Yes?" she said into the receiver.

"Mom, it's Shari. I had to call. There's been a crisis. Jill's left Brucie."

Tzippy felt as if someone had hit her between the eyes. "But they were just here," Tzippy said. "You've got to be kidding." She popped a pill, coughed into her tissues, and sipped some water. She hadn't eaten a thing all day, and she was beginning to feel faint. She wished she could lie down.

"Wait," she said. "Stan's here. Let me put him on to hear this." Tzippy went to the doorway and said, "Stan, Jill has left Brucie. Sweetheart, I need you to listen to this. Please pick up the phone."

With Stan on the extension and Tzippy on the bedroom phone, Shari continued. "He just called me. Jill thinks she's in love with a cardiologist and said she was leaving. She said the coat business is ruined and there isn't any money left. She didn't want anything except the baby-blue Porsche anyway. Then she drove off in it to go meet her doctor. Can you imagine?"

Tzippy sat down on her bed and sank into all the little airplane pillows that she and Angie had taken over the years. She just wanted to stretch out and feel their downy comfort for a moment.

"She just drove off in the Porsche?" Stan yelled. "Christ."

"How's poor Brucie?" Tzippy asked.

"He's a wreck. Just devastated," answered Shari.

"And the children?" Tzippy asked.

"Jill says they're grown up now and can come visit anytime," Shari said.

"I can't believe this is happening," Tzippy said.

"That girl has balls," Stan said.

"The doctor is some big shot, has three houses, a dead wife, and three grown kids," Shari continued. "Jill thinks she'll live the high life. She was his nurse. Don't you recall her talking about Dr. Blum?"

Tzippy couldn't remember and said nothing.

"Listen, I'm going over to see Brucie. It's less than an hour's drive. He sounded terrible on the phone. When I get back, I'll call and tell you more. Okay?" While Bruce had moved to Bayport, Massachusetts, to be near the coat factory, Shari had stayed in Boston after her divorce.

"Should I call him?"

"Sure, go ahead. He's your son. You can call anytime you want," Shari said.

"Let's talk about this first, Tzippy," Stan suggested. "Go over what you'll say."

"You know, I never liked that girl," said Tzippy.

"Yeah, I know. You were probably right."

"Too late now."

"He's not the first guy to fall for the wrong woman," Stan said. "Still they've been married a long time."

"Listen, I gotta go have a drink," Shari said. "This is all too much of a morning for me."

"I'll talk to you later," Tzippy said. "Be sure to call me after you see Bruce. I want to know what you think."

"Sure. Take care. Bye, Stan."

As Tzippy remained amid the chorus of small pillows, Stan came in and sat on the corner of the bed and just stared at her. "Wow," he said. "That came out of left field."

"Can you believe the nerve of that girl? If it hadn't been for Brucie, she'd still be a waitress at some low-class joint."

"Tzippy, let's go for a walk. Then I'll buy you a nice lunch down at the café. We'll sit outside and discuss what you want to say to Brucie. Come, you need a break."

Tzippy stood up, grabbed her bag and her red half-glasses, and then sat back down. Her heart was beating rapidly, and the thoughts flying through her head had the same slippery, elusive touch as the Chanel scarves she'd pinched over the years. She shook her head and gazed up at Stan, as though he could save her. As though he would.

Chapter 8

As they got off the elevator and walked out of the apartment complex, Tzippy and Stan left behind the opulent units and passed the swimming pool, guarded by a muscled attendant, and the chaise lounges, covered in long terry-cloth towels, and the water, both chlorinated and turquoise. They went through the gate that kept trespassers off the property at night and descended the stairs to the pebbled walking path set back from the vast ocean.

It was low tide, and an expanse of flat sand stretched to the water. Children and mothers collected seashells in bright pails. Joggers ran past them in sweaty T-shirts and rippling shorts, and other people strolled by, carrying coffee and daily newspapers, enjoying their first, fresh breeze of the day.

Tzippy breathed in the sea air and tried to calm down. The sky was lightly overcast, but she could feel the sun breaking through and trying to heat up the day. The susurrations coming from the ocean filled her with a sense of peace. She looked at the sand and the water and took Stan's hand, thankful that he'd insisted they go for a walk. Along the path were occasional wooden benches, but she walked on, full of energy from the fresh air. She noticed a few swimmers bobbing up and down in the ocean like seals. Licking her lips, Tzippy tried to summon the taste of sea salt. She couldn't recollect the last time she'd taken a swim in the Atlantic, but she recalled how much she used to like jumping in the waves, feeling the crash of water on her body. She spotted a boat out on the horizon and wondered where it was going.

Stan finally broke the silence. "Did you see that coming about Brucie and Jill?"

Tzippy shook her head. "I'm as surprised as you are, although I often wondered how long they'd last. She never married Brucie expecting to struggle in life."

"Yeah, she was a poor girl looking to upgrade."

"Bruce can be a bear when things aren't going well. He gets snappy and short-tempered. I know—I'm his mother. Maybe she got fed up."

"Sounds like she fell for the cardiologist. What's his name? Blum?"

"Some bigwig at the hospital, I guess. It makes sense, in a twisted way, if you forget that Brucie fixed her teeth and put her through school so she could make something of herself. Now she's an exquisite nurse and he's a widowed surgeon. They work in the same facility."

"Classic story."

"Just like in the soap operas." Thinking of Bruce and his trouble made Tzippy tired, and she asked Stan if they could stop and rest on a nearby bench. She looked up at him and asked, "What should I say to him when we talk?"

"Baby cakes, all he wants right now is your love and support. Just tell him how sorry you are and what a fool Jill is and how you're behind him in every way. She's an opportunist, and he never saw it."

"Should I say that word?"

"It's pretty obvious, isn't it?"

"It must kill him to see that now."

"Yup, you got that right." Stan stretched his legs out in front of him and inhaled deeply. "Sure feels wonderful out here, doesn't it?"

Tzippy kissed him on the cheek and smiled. "You're such a nice man."

He looked up at the sky and closed his eyes against the emerging sun, then asked, "So, how about some lunch? You must be starving."

Tzippy agreed, and they continued slowly down the path until they came to a large hotel on the strip. Stan took her hand and helped her ascend the few steps to the veranda. At the three different pools of varying sizes, children and their parents were splashing and enjoying the warm day. Several elderly men with gray chest hair and potbellies, wearing dark glasses and floppy hats, lay on chaise lounges, reading the newspaper and sneaking glances at sleek bimbos in skimpy bikinis.

Tzippy and Stan made their way to the café, where Stan asked, "Inside or out?"

"Let's sit outside today."

Tzippy ordered a spinach salad, and Stan got a club sandwich. As they sipped iced tea, they chattered away happily. Now that Tzippy had agreed to marry him, she detected an added coziness in their exchanges, and occasionally they looked at each other with the new intimacy reserved for the betrothed. Despite her troubles, she was excited and ate with a hearty appetite. *Just be in the moment,* she thought, as the turn-of-the-millennium gurus all seemed to be saying.

"Stan," she said, working up her nerve to broach a new subject. "Do you think I could go to the Girls' Club, like you go to the Boys' Club?"

"I don't see why not," he said, seeming delighted at the concept of her going. "It would do you good. Some of the clubs in the other areas are beginning to go coed. You should come."

"You think?"

"I love to go over and chat with the kids. They're great. Besides they need a little encouragement. Some of them really have rough lives."

"Should I just walk in and say I'd like to help?"

"Something like that," he said, taking a healthy bite of his sandwich. "I'll go with you the first time and give you some support, okay?"

Tzippy stabbed a piece of spinach and a slice of hard-boiled egg, covered with bacon bits, and popped it into her mouth. She felt better. But then she noticed that the vast patches of blue beginning to show in the sky were almost the color of Brucie's Porsche, and her good mood began to dissipate. She couldn't get over how her emotions roller-coastered from despair to hopefulness.

"How did you ever start going to the Boys' Club?" she asked, to take her mind off her bleak thoughts.

"I was a poor kid, lived with my uncle in the projects of Newark. You know all this. Anyway, after my parents were killed in that car accident, Uncle Louie took me in. Trouble was, he had a gambling problem and was never home. I hung around the pool parlor, where the Jews and the Italians were always placing bets. They used to ask me to take the money, the bills all crumpled up in a brown paper bag, and run it up three blocks to the bookie. I became a runner, they paid me well, and I loved being part of their gang. I'm lucky I didn't become a real crook. So now I feel bad for kids with tough home lives."

She had heard bits and pieces of Stan's story before, but this time, she felt somehow as if she were hearing it in a different way.

"Before I knew it," Stan continued, "I was in deep. As soon as I got my license, I started driving for one of the guys, a fellow named Izzy Solomon, a real scammer, always checking for a fast deal. Dogs, football, the track—anything was fair game. But I could see it wasn't much of a life—boring when it wasn't dangerous—so I got out as soon as I had a chance. A buddy of mine was selling paint, and we got into the paint business together and made a lot of money. Me and Johnny Bender and the paint business. I owe it all to him."

Tzippy smiled at her soon-to-be husband and said, "You're a good man, Stan, and I love you."

⌒

As they strolled back along the path to Tzippy's apartment, they began planning their wedding ceremony—whom they'd invite, where they'd go afterward.

"I have an appointment with PJ to discuss the prenup," Tzippy said.

"What are you going to put in it?"

"The usual stuff: keeping the money for the kids after I go, making sure they get what's left of what Benny left me."

"I'll do the same for Evelene and my grandson."

"Since you're going to move in with me, how about I put in something about your staying in the apartment as long as you want to, if I go first? Does that sound right?"

"Thanks, Tzippy. A guy needs a place to live."

"I guess that'll mean the kids can't use the place," she said, thinking out loud.

"It could be awkward. They can visit, use the rooms downstairs, but I'm not going anywhere."

"Oh, I'll explain it to them. They'll understand."

"I'll talk to my guy, too. Then we'll compare notes," Stan said.

When they got back to the apartment complex, Stan helped Tzippy up the stairs to the pool area. She was tired, but she said, "Let's stop by my mailbox before we go up."

The mailbox area was near the front door, and they had to pass several sitting areas, over-air-conditioned, decorated with large oil paintings, and stuffed with large club chairs. Tzippy took out her key and opened her mailbox, always jammed with junk, and quickly leafed through the contents to see what she could discard. Her heart pounded when she found a white envelope from the court, probably a summons to appear; they sure hadn't wasted any time setting that up. She stuffed the letter in among the other mail and walked to the elevator with Stan by her side. She'd need another pill, something to calm her down. How the hell was she going to break the news of her arrest to Stan?

After they entered her unit, she put her mail in her bedroom on her writing desk. On her way back to the living room, she noticed Stan's black toiletry bag on the foyer table.

"Stanley, what's this case?"

He laughed and said, "I'm a Boy Scout." He saluted her. "'Be prepared,' they always say. Just in case we have a late night. Does that bother you?"

"Oh, I don't know," she said. "You old fox." *I'm not ready for all these changes*, she thought. "It does seem silly to wait until we're married, but . . ."

"You need some more time?"

"Right now, I need a pill and a glass of water."

"Coming right up," Stan said.

"Stan, when did you say your girl was coming? This place could use a pickup. I want her to clean Angie's room especially."

Stan looked inside the bedroom that used to be Angie's and assessed the space. "You know, Tzippy, this would make a great office. I could set up a desk and a small twin bed in case I want to hang out and not disturb you."

"Stan, if that's what you'd like, go ahead and do it." She figured it would be a good idea to start getting him moved in, so he wouldn't think about bolting when he heard about her shoplifting. This way, he'd have roots, so to speak. "Why don't you put your nice leather chair and the matching ottoman in there? I want you to be comfortable and happy."

He handed her a small glass of water, and Tzippy took out

her vial of pills. "I just need to calm down a little. Everything is moving so fast. I want to be relaxed before I call Brucie," she explained, as she popped the medication into her mouth.

"Are you feeling okay?" He planted a kiss on the top of her head.

She smiled, thinking how comfortable they were together. *Now, nothing should mess this up*, she thought.

Chapter 9

Several weeks later, as they hurried out of the apartment on the way to the airport, Tzippy said, "I don't want to be late." It was the end of January, two weeks after her party.

"God forbid Shari gets mad," Stan said.

"You know how she is."

Now, Tzippy stood in the waiting area, wearing a white linen suit, very ladylike. Her red half-glasses were perched on her nose, and she thought she looked a bit like Nancy Reagan. But she kept coughing into a wad of tissues. She'd been so excited when Shari had decided to quit her job at the Gap and freed herself up for this time together. Whether Shari's motives were selfish or irresponsible, Tzippy didn't care right now; she was just relieved to be assured of female companionship now that Angie was gone. Besides, maybe this would be her last chance to make things right. Tzippy hoped they'd sleep together in her bed so they could talk late at night. Maybe they could have some good heart-to-hearts, patch things up. Maybe they could have their own private girls' club, the one Tzippy should have been having all along.

Shari hurried off the plane, clutching her own pillow, and kissed Tzippy on the cheek. "My, you look nice today, Mom. Mrs. Loel Guinness has nothing on you."

Tzippy laughed and accepted the compliment. Years before, Shari had discovered an article Tzippy had saved from the *New York Times*. Now yellow with age, the piece had been fawning in its coverage of Gloria Guinness, who had owned four homes and one yacht. According to the society reporter, Mrs. Lowell Guinness, the most elegant woman in the world, had evolved rules for successful dinner parties and wore only slim lines in order to look her best. Tzippy, forever searching for role models, had clipped out the article and tucked it in a drawer of her dressing table, where Shari had spotted it. Perhaps it was the fact that Gloria Guinness had started as a nightclub hostess and after four husbands had landed on the International Best-Dressed List in 1964 that had impressed Tzippy.

"Hi, kid," Stan said to Shari. "What's with the pillow?"

"I know, it's a bit much. Just indulge me. I prefer my own—that's all."

"Head for the baggage claim, ladies," Stan instructed, pushing them in the right direction. Tzippy walked slowly but tried to keep up.

Unable to wait for news, and because Shari had never called after she'd visited Brucie, Tzippy asked, "How was Brucie when you saw him last?"

"Oh, Mom, he's a mess."

"Tell me," she said.

As they stood in front of the revolving carousel and waited for Shari's bags, Shari said, "He's so unhappy, Mom. He just stood outside and chopped wood the entire time I was there yesterday."

"What do you mean, chopped wood?" Tzippy pictured him on the gravel driveway, the country road out front.

"Brucie had this whole pile of wood delivered to his house for his fireplace, and it just sat there in a heap, like a mini-lumberyard. He kept splitting the wood like a madman."

Shari's bags appeared then, and they made their way deep into the parking garage, where they found Tzippy's town car. Tzippy was glad to get in and sit down.

"Are you girls all set?" Stan asked. His bushy eyebrows rose like two half circles as he looked at Tzippy next to him and at Shari in the backseat.

Shari asked, "Do you mind if I smoke, if I open the window?"

Tzippy said, "Just blow the smoke outside. I hate the smell in the car."

Shari lit up, keeping the window fully open, and continued with her story. "So, Brucie just kept splitting the wood, stacking the pieces in a neat pile, and I sat on his porch, watching him. He wouldn't stop." She took a drag of her cigarette. "He split each piece on a tree stump. I didn't even know he knew how. His face was all red and sweaty, and his shirt was drenched. He took his glasses off, wiped them, and put them back on. I was afraid he'd have a coronary," she said, blowing smoke out into the air.

"My God, he's losing his mind," Tzippy said. "Stan, are you listening?"

"Let her talk," he said.

"His wood splitting went on for over an hour. I tried to talk to him, but he just grunted."

Stan asked, "Then what happened?"

Shari paused dramatically, enjoying her role. "He peered up and said, 'Listen, because I'll say this only once. Jill's a bitch, and she used me!'"

Tzippy stared at Stan.

"He also told me he'd lost his temper the day before and screamed at a girl at the Dunkin' Donuts drive-through window. He almost threw the coffee in her face but didn't."

Tzippy said, "My poor boy."

Stan said, "He could've gotten arrested."

At the word "arrested," Tzippy felt her heart calcify and started to cough. "Now, let's not get carried away," she said, squirming in her seat. She grabbed a wad of tissues.

"Finally, we went inside the house," Shari said, "but only because it had gotten dark. I begged him." Shari's voice grew shriller. "'For God's sake, Brucie,' I said, 'you can't see. You'll chop off a goddamn finger. Please, let's go inside.' So we did."

"Oh, Stan, maybe I should go up north and see him."

"He's a grown man, Tzippy, not a boy."

"What happened next?" Tzippy asked, turning to the back.

By then, Shari had finished smoking her cigarette. She closed the window and rearranged herself. "Oh, that air conditioning feels good," she said. "Where was I? Oh, yes, we went inside, and then it got worse."

"How could it?" Tzippy asked.

"Mom, he started crying. I felt so bad for him. There I was, cradling my brother in my arms, giving him handfuls of tissues to wipe his eyes. Me, his rotten sister, who has always been a thorn in his side."

"You did the right thing, Shari. That's how it can get with siblings sometimes. It's normal."

"Maybe it's normal, but it didn't feel right. I don't like it when men cry."

"Let me tell you," Stan said, "Sometimes we've got the right. How is he now?"

"I think he's better. I gave him a stiff drink and told him to take a shower and get a good night's sleep. I told him to call my shrink."

Tzippy asked, "Do you think he will?"

"He ought to. He sure needs someone to talk to. When I left, he was passed out on the leather couch."

"Where are his kids?" Tzippy asked.

"They're coming to see him next week."

Stan said, "I'm sure he can find his own shrink."

"You're right, absolutely," Shari said.

By then they were at Tzippy's. They all got out and left the car for the parking attendant, and Stan instructed a young bellman to carry up Shari's bags.

"Oh, I'm glad you're here," said Tzippy, putting her arm around her daughter's thin frame. "We'll have a nice visit."

"I'm glad I'm here, too, Mom. I need a rest."

"Sweetie, I'm sorry," Tzippy said. She hated that Shari's life seemed to be a series of calamities, that she'd been let down by people she'd trusted and rejected by those she'd desired.

Shari's smile was bright and brittle. "No matter."

"Poor Brucie," Tzippy said. "I feel terrible."

"I know, it's a bummer," Shari said.

"Do you want to get your mail?" Stan asked.

Tzippy hadn't told Stan about her court date yet. Now she'd have to tell Shari, too. And the damn doctor! "I arranged the date of my meeting with PJ so you'd be here. Around the first week of February, we're scheduled."

Shari asked, "You want me to go with you?"

"We'll all go out to lunch, although I may have to speak to PJ in private," she said, thinking more about her arrest than about the prenup.

Back in the apartment, Shari said, "Is it too early for a drink?"

"It's four o'clock in the afternoon. Go ahead," said Tzippy.

"Hi there," said a small, tan woman with a broad grin. She wore a pale pink maid's outfit with a white apron, scalloped around the edges.

"Oh, this is Jocelyn Bell." She whispered to Shari, "Stan's sharing his maid with me." Then she turned to Jocelyn. "This is my daughter, Shari," Tzippy said.

"Hello," Shari said. "I'm glad to meet you."

"Shari would like a drink," Tzippy said.

"Yes, a little Tanqueray on the rocks with a twist would be lovely."

Jocelyn asked, "How are you, Mr. Fosberg?"

"I'm just fine, Jocelyn, thank you," Stan said. "How about a nice cold beer for me?"

110

"My pleasure."

"Oh, maybe I'll have something, too. A glass of chardonnay, please," Tzippy said. "Are you hungry, Shari?"

"I'll wait for dinner."

"Where are we going tonight, Stan?"

"Whatever you girls like. Shari, what are you in the mood for?"

"I feel so bad about Brucie," Tzippy said. "Here we are, planning a leisurely dinner while he's miserable."

Stan said, "We gotta eat. How's the Dolphin?"

"Make us a reservation for seven-thirty, okay?" Tzippy said.

"Where do you want me to sleep, Mom?" Shari asked.

"Sleep with me so we can have some good talks," Tzippy said. She felt an urgent need to be closer to Shari and maybe get some support about the court appearance. "Will you mind my snoring?"

"I can live with it. Naomi hates it, but I can deal." Shari laughed.

Tzippy said, "Good" and squeezed Shari's shoulder. "Or there's Angie's old room, if you prefer."

"No, I'll bunk in with you. I can always move if the snoring gets to be too much."

"That's going to be my new office," Stan announced, walking toward Angie's old bedroom. "What do you think?"

"Perfect," said Shari. "The two lovebirds. It's great."

"What about Ike?" Tzippy blurted out. She couldn't stop thinking about her son. "They get along well, and Brucie needs a friend."

"I'll give him a call myself, if you think it will help," Stan said. "I guess I qualify." He had found his wife, Dolly, in bed with their next-door neighbor forty years earlier.

"Let me think about that," Tzippy said.

"I'm going out on the deck to have a cigar and make a few calls," Stan said. He gave Tzippy a quick kiss, took his beer, and closed the door to the balcony behind him.

"I can't believe you're getting married," said Shari.

"I can hardly believe it myself," Tzippy said.

She knew this time around she'd be a lot less nervous than she'd been with Benny. "You know," she said, "I was a wreck when I married your father." She remembered how she'd fussed over every detail of the wedding and then, after the ceremony, how scared she'd been. "I was very young and innocent back then."

"Did Daddy know you were nervous?"

"Oh, he figured it out." Tzippy laughed, thinking back. "Did I ever tell you about my wedding night?" She sat down on a yellow chair and put her glass of wine on the coffee table.

"You never told me anything about sex." Shari relaxed on the sofa, drink in hand.

"Well, it took three days to consummate our marriage," Tzippy confessed.

"No way!"

"I kept freezing up and saying I couldn't do it. Just like that, you're married and you're supposed to have sex. When I was a girl, only prostitutes had sex. I called my sister Esther twice for advice.'"

"What a riot. What did Daddy do?"

"What could he do? By the third day, he was angry. Esther told me to calm down and just do it, to quit acting like a prude. Finally, I told Ben about Mr. Murphy."

"Who was he?" Shari asked. She gulped her drink.

Tzippy couldn't believe she'd brought him up; now the floodgates were open. "He was an old man, one of the boarders my mother took in to help with expenses. He used to come in our bedroom and fondle me while Sophie and Julia slept in their double bed."

"I need another drink," Shari said, going to the kitchen. She quickly returned with a glass full of Tanqueray. "After what you went through, I can't believe you never rescued me from Uncle Lenny," she said.

Tzippy groaned, hanging her head in shame. "I couldn't; I was too embarrassed to discuss it, and he was my brother."

"I was your daughter. I took care of him, scared him off with a knife." Shari took a swig of her drink and said, "So, you never told your mother?"

"Oh, Shari, you didn't," Tzippy said, widening her eyes. "I wanted to tell my mother; I kept trying, but the words wouldn't come out. And I knew she needed the boarders' money."

"I wanted to tell Daddy, but I couldn't get the words out, either," Shari said, nodding. "Oh, fuck," she said, shaking her head as if she wanted bees to stop flying around her. "You were how old when you married Dad? It was an entirely new experience for you."

"Yes, of course. I was in my early twenties." Tzippy never gave an exact age. She had, in fact, been twenty-five. "Oh, Shari, I feel terrible about what happened with my brother. I failed you."

"Well, that's water over the dam," she said, shaking her head once more. "So, what happened? Finish your story."

"Well, when we finally had sex, your father was so thrilled I was a virgin that he went out and bought me two dozen long-stemmed red roses."

"I love that," Shari said.

"Yes, he scattered the roses all over the bed."

"Great story." Shari took another gulp of gin. "Mom, did I ever tell you what happened to me?"

"No, sweetheart. What?" Tzippy drank some of her chardonnay. Her mouth was dry from talking.

"I was so dumb about sex that I thought I had intercourse when I never really did," Shari said.

"What do you mean?"

"Do you remember Chuck Daniels, the tall, blond cutie from the high school football team? You didn't like him because he wasn't Jewish. Anyway, one night while you and Daddy were upstairs sleeping, we were fooling around on the couch in the den. I felt his penis near me, and he tried to enter me, but I told him not to, so he stopped. But I was sure I'd blown it. I mean, his penis came so close." Her voice was almost a whisper. "I figured I was no longer a virgin and that you'd kill me if you ever knew. I was riddled with guilt, stopped eating, the whole bit. Two years later, when I really did have intercourse, I realized my mistake. Can you imagine, all that time, tormenting myself?" Shari's face reflected her anguish.

Tzippy said, "My goodness." She started coughing and grabbed some tissues. *If only I'd talked to her.*

The phone rang in the background. She heard the maid answer and wanted to escape. "Who is it, Jocelyn?"

"Your cousin Goldie."

Tzippy hesitated, and Shari looked away warily. Tzippy called out, "Tell her I'll call her back." Then she said, "I should have explained things better. Maybe you wouldn't have starved yourself."

"Mom, you explained nothing. My shrink said that incident was just 'the straw that broke the camel's back.'"

Tzippy knew she was right. "I guess I was too shy to discuss it."

Shari emptied her drink. Tzippy sipped her wine. "What a pair we are!" Shari said.

The two women started laughing. Tzippy said, "Oh, dear God," and began coughing again.

"Isn't it strange, Mom—you starting a new marriage and Bruce ending his?" Shari said.

"Yes, life is funny and unpredictable."

"Were you happy when you were married to Daddy?"

"Why, yes and no. Nothing is perfect."

"Why not?"

"It's too long a story—another time."

"Tell me."

Tzippy searched her daughter's face and, wanting to continue their closeness, said, "He had a lady friend."

"I suspected."

"Her name was Laura. She was younger than me. A shiksa. I hated it."

"I'm sorry," Shari said. She actually looked sorry; for once, she didn't seem even slightly pleased at the knowledge that her mother's life had involved some unhappiness.

"It was a hard time."

"Tell me more."

"Not now. Later."

"You promise?"

"Yes, I promise. Let's concentrate on when to have this wedding. I was thinking the beginning of April."

But then, of course, thinking about the wedding reminded Tzippy about her court date. "Sooner, rather than later, I think," she continued. After she was married, she'd tell Stan. Why upset things now? When she saw PJ, she'd have to ask him if the court date could get postponed. A continuance. People did it all the time, didn't they?

Was she really such a bad person to keep all this to herself until after the ceremony? God, she didn't feel good about herself. Maybe she should see Rabbi Friedman. If she could just explain to him what had happened at Saks, she might feel better. She had to see him about the wedding ceremony anyway. But then, she was sure, he'd want her to confess to Stan before the ceremony.

Maybe she should see a rabbi she didn't know. Perhaps Goldie knew one up by Boca. She would ask when she called her back.

Shari asked, "Will you buy a new dress?"

Tzippy laughed. "Of course."

"And food? What time of day?"

"Five o'clock. Drinks and hors d'oeuvres. Then we can all go out to dinner somewhere nice."

"Sounds good to me. Thanks for sharing, Mom," Shari said, bending over and planting a kiss on her mother's cheek. "All this sex and wedding talk is making me thirsty. Just a splash more of gin, and then I'm going out to have a smoke."

Tzippy smiled at her daughter and said, "Tell Stan to come in when you go out."

Jocelyn came in, carrying a stack of freshly washed towels. "Is there anything you need me to do?" she asked.

"Make sure we have enough Tanqueray," Tzippy said. "Otherwise, let's order some more. I want Shari to have what she likes."

Suddenly she recalled Angie dancing in the liquor store when they'd bought all the booze before the party. Tzippy wondered how she was doing.

After she gave the matter some more thought, Tzippy decided to find a new rabbi to talk to, instead of going to see Rabbi Friedman. He had always intimidated her a bit, and anyway, she didn't need him to know her true self when he performed the ceremony. Goldie said her rabbi, Rabbi Hershberger, was a good man. According to Goldie, he came from a long line of rabbinical scholars and had been leading her temple for three years. The congregation loved him.

Tzippy's religious education had been traditional; she and her siblings had attended the Hebrew day school in Springfield, where old-fashioned rabbis had taught them Rashi, Torah, the Prophets, all in Hebrew, a language that Tzippy had never mastered because she had been too distracted thinking about how she wanted to be attending public school like the regular kids. She knew her parents wouldn't permit public school, let alone the private McBurtie School, which Tzippy secretly preferred. At McBurtie, the girls appeared refined and wore matching blazers. At Tzippy's Hebrew day school in the afternoons, middle-aged female teachers in sensible shoes taught arithmetic and English and American history, and the kids had recess on a cement playground out back. Many of the students came from very religious homes where the father was a rabbi or the son was preparing to be a rabbinical student.

Even though Tzippy resisted the training, some of it rubbed off and, consequently, she still knew about all the holidays and the traditions even though she didn't keep them anymore. Her parents' home had been kosher, and Tzippy remembered how her mother had soaked the dishes in the bathtub for three days before Passover. She recalled the oilcloth on their kitchen counters; the butcher who cut the meat and the poultry, his bloody apron and large hands; the yarmulkes all the boys wore; her uncle Louie wrapped in a prayer shawl and singing from the Torah on the high holidays.

Tzippy and Ben had been less religious with their own children. Brucie had had his bar mitzvah, but they hadn't bothered with the girls. Friday nights, Tzippy had served challah, over which Ben recited a prayer, and had had the maid prepare chicken soup. Sometimes she had lit the Sabbath candles, but not faithfully, though she had never smoked her Lucky Strikes on the Sabbath. Tzippy had dressed up in her finest on the high holidays and sat through the entire, lengthy service. For her, the best part had been Rabbi Friedman's sermons, which she often found inspiring and instructive. She'd wished to be a better person, even back then.

Rabbi Hershberger's office in Boca was in the back of the temple, a large building with modern stained-glass windows and a six-pointed star of David over the door. The office smelled of furniture polish; books about funerals, kabbalah, and the soul sat on the rabbi's desk. As she entered the sanctuary, Tzippy became solemn and hopeful.

"I heard you had a small problem to discuss," Rabbi Hershberger said. Tzippy looked squarely at him. He had kind eyes and a jut-jawed face with gray whiskers, even though he wasn't that old. As Goldie had reported, he and his wife had seven children, six of them girls. A photograph of them hung on the wall.

"I had this bad day at Saks," she started.

Rabbi Hershberger looked skeptical. He rubbed his jaw.

"I was under a lot of stress. My children had been fighting in a restaurant. It had gotten out of hand . . ." She explained about the brooch and the store detectives and the fingerprinting.

Rabbi Hershberger's face became distressed. "That was a very unpleasant experience for you, Mrs. Bryer."

"I felt so humiliated. It was awful." And then she explained about court. "I have to go before the judge. Plus, I'm to be married again. I'm afraid to tell my husband-to-be. Maybe I should wait to tell him."

"You must tell your future husband," the rabbi said. "You can't begin a marriage with a lie."

"Are you sure I couldn't wait until after the ceremony?"

"What are you afraid of, my dear?"

"I'm afraid he'll change his mind when he hears about my stealing."

"If he loves you, he'll stick by you, don't you think? Love demands that we be true to our spouse."

"Yes," Tzippy said. "He's a good man. But he thinks so highly of me. I'm afraid I'll disappoint him."

"Maybe you will," Rabbi Hershberger told her. "But don't start your marriage with guilt. You will feel badly. It will affect your sense of self-worth. You must align yourself with eternal values, not superficial ones—values such as love, charity, and justice. Those values live on. Come—let us pray."

He opened a black book and recited a Hebrew prayer. The rabbi was right, of course. She had been selfish to think any other way, but she'd been hoping for more lenient advice. She had to wonder if Stan would be as forgiving as the Lord.

The rabbi paused and said, "Let me tell you a story. Once, there was a man who died and found himself in a movie theater. He was thrilled, because he had spent a lot of time watching movies when he'd been alive, so he was glad to know that he would spend life after death in a theater. Then he saw an usher and said, 'What's showing?'

"The usher said, 'A double feature.'

"'Which movies?'

"'You'll see.'"

The rabbi paused and licked his lips, then continued, "A moment later, the screen lit up and the title of the first feature appeared: *How I Lived My Life*. The second movie of the double feature lit up: *How I Could Have Lived My Life*." Then the rabbi stared at Tzippy. "Now, my dear, what do you think?"

Tzippy stared at Rabbi Hershberger and wished he would take her in his large arms and hug her. She thought of her father and how much she had loved him. She remembered how she'd awakened him at night when she was small, after she'd had a bad dream, and gotten into bed with him. She recollected his strong arms and barrel chest and how instantly she'd felt safe when he put his arms around her.

Rabbi Hershberger didn't embrace her; instead, he simply opened the door of his study and let her out. "Go and be brave," he said.

Goldie was waiting in her car under the blue sky. "What did he say?" she asked.

"I have to tell Stan. Without question, I must confess."

Goldie said, "Will you be okay?"

"He's a wonderful person, a mensch. Maybe when I'm married to him, I won't want to steal."

"You think?"

"I hope. The other day, we took a walk by the ocean and it was lovely. Just the two of us walking, feeling the breeze. I can't remember ever doing that with Ben," she said, placing her fingers on the leather of the car door and feeling its smoothness.

"As we walked, something filled me with peace," she continued, watching the sun shining in the distance as they drove by. "Maybe he's what I need."

Goldie looked at her and said, "I hope it works out for you, Tzipora."

Tzippy smiled; grateful for Goldie's good wishes and wishing she didn't feel the little zing of satisfaction she got from realizing that her cousin was envious.

Chapter 10

Sleeping with Shari turned into an adventure. Since Benny had died, Tzippy had slept alone and gotten used to it. Now, she saw, that was about to change. She looked upon the time with Shari as practice for when Stan moved in for real. But it was hard. What if Stan hugged her at night and made her feel suffocated? She liked sleeping without anyone touching her, grabbing her breast. Some nights she liked the windows open, instead of having the air-conditioning on; others, she preferred the air-conditioning turned low so she could bundle up in the cool room. Would Stan be amenable? And what if he wanted to stay up late and watch television, when she enjoyed the quiet and liked to read until her eyelids closed? All these matters concerned her.

Most nights she and Shari cuddled and watched the *Late Show* before they went to sleep. When Tzippy snored, Shari shook her to make her stop. One night Tzippy woke, turned on the light by her bed, took out a magazine, and began reading, until Shari said, "It's the middle of the night. Jeez."

"I can't sleep."

The moon was bright, near full. Tzippy's bedroom looked pretty in the soft glow.

"How long will you be up?" Shari asked.

"A few minutes."

"Do you want some warm milk?" Shari asked.

"Hot water, tea."

Shari got up and looked through the sliders. "Look at all the stars, Mom."

"Oh, they're just magnificent. Like sparkling jewels," Tzippy said. As they stood gazing, Tzippy with her arm around her daughter, their two heads touching, she savored the moment.

They walked together to the small kitchen. Shari put on the teakettle and poured some skim milk into a saucepan to heat while Tzippy sat at the little table in the corner and waited to be served. There was an unspoken understanding in the family that the children would care for her in her old age and tend to her needs first.

They started to talk about the early years, when Bruce, Naomi, and Shari had been young.

"Remember when you took me to see *Oliver*?" Shari asked.

"Of course."

"It was the best, Oliver saying, 'Please, sir, I want some more.' I'll never forget it. I was ten years old."

When the teakettle whistled, she poured the hot water into a cup and placed a tea bag on a saucer for Tzippy. She didn't like her tea too strong. Then Shari made herself some cocoa. "Come, let's go back to bed," she said, carrying the two drinks.

"You wanted to become an actress after that," Tzippy said, as she followed Shari into the bedroom and got under the covers on her side. Tzippy remembered the awe on Shari's face, her absolute fascination with the world of the theater.

"I should have gone into acting, don't you think?" Shari sat with the covers pulled up around her thin frame and sipped her cocoa.

"Well, sweetie, you tried," Tzippy reminded her. Hadn't they spent tons of money on lessons during the junior high years? Tzippy recalled the teacher, Mrs. Lidlow, and the many scenes that Shari had memorized. The entire family had trucked down to Mrs. Lidlow's basement, where she put on her recitals, to watch Shari perform some monologue from *Our Town*—a young girl pleading with a nun, Shari dressed in black, looking like a beatnik.

"Do you think she has talent?" Tzippy had asked the stern-faced Mrs. Lidlow, who wore her glasses on the tip of her nose.

"Not enough to make it in the big time, I'm afraid," she'd answered. Another dream attempted and failed. But Shari hadn't seen it; she had continued to believe that her vocation lay in the theater, and Tzippy's heart had palpitated as she saw one more piece of evidence of her family's steadfast refusal to face facts. On the one hand, who was Mrs. Lidlow for Tzippy to have taken her word? She was no Stella Adler.

Was it after Mrs. Lidlow that Shari had had that incident with the football player and gone on her starvation diet? As a girl, Shari had looked young for her age. Tzippy recalled her in her Brownie uniform, selling cookies. She was the brunette, unlike Naomi, who had fine, fair hair that fell in wisps around her face. Shari had been lovely, with quick, darting eyes and lustrous skin, but somewhere in there she had lost faith in herself and tried to change. The dyed hair; the half-eaten meals of cottage cheese and melba toast; the way her clothes fell off her body, loose and shapeless; the cigarettes and the drinking and the desperate way she'd been with boys. Tzippy was to blame for all of it.

Then, around the age of thirty, the ever-youthful Shari had suddenly grown older. Maybe it was the drinking, maybe something else. Tzippy didn't know. Her skin had lost its shine; her eyes had become bloodshot. Allergies and rashes had come. Her gums had receded. She had refused to go to a doctor to be examined.

Shari put down her cocoa and stared at Tzippy. "Why do you think I got so messed up?"

Tzippy didn't want to answer. She had too much guilt. "Don't you have an opinion?"

"Yes, but I thought you knew. You're my mother."

"Maybe I pushed you."

"All I ever wanted was to please you."

Tzippy recalled how Shari had clung to her, done errands for her, performed for her. She had run to the store and bought Lucky Strikes, had fixed her cups of tea or Sanka, and had purchased Tzippy's favorite Hanes seamless, sandal-foot stockings on her birthday, sized properly. She'd even complied when Tzippy had instructed her to walk past a table of businessmen dining at a local restaurant to see if the men would turn to admire Shari.

"It's just that I wanted so much for you." Then she admitted the truth. "For me. As a child, I used to watch the McBurtie School girls with their blond hair and pug noses and longed to be one of them: privileged, refined, rich. I guess I thought I could live through you. It wasn't fair. I shouldn't have . . . I should have let you be you. I told myself they were all good things; why wouldn't you want them?"

Shari looked at her and remained silent.

Tzippy continued, "I was embarrassed by my Jewishness as a child, the strangeness. There was no Christmas, we had Sabbath on Saturday, not Sunday, and the food was cooked differently. No shellfish, no bacon. Once, I went to a Chinese restaurant with friends and ordered a grilled cheese sandwich. They called me the Kosher Kid. Why couldn't we be like the others, normal? Why did I have to be poor? Do you know I had to wear my clothes sometimes four and five days in a row to save my mama money on washing? It was all so humiliating." That was as much as she could bear to say.

Shari said, "I get it, Mom. But I don't think you ever understood what it did to me. I felt I was never good enough. I walked around berating myself. I couldn't get into the right college. I wasn't pretty enough, and when I said the wrong things, you kicked me under the table. You still do! Remember when you kicked me at the restaurant the night before the party?"

Tzippy had to admit it.

"Christ, I starved myself because I felt so guilty about not being a virgin . . . or at least that's what I thought, which is even more ridiculous. You wouldn't talk to me about sex, but you made such a big deal about how the most precious thing you brought Daddy was your virginity. I figured I was damaged goods."

Tzippy hung her head and reached for her pills. "Please," she said. "I'm an old woman."

But now that Shari was started, there was no stopping her. "Isn't it amazing," she said, her eyes flaring. "All those lessons you gave me—art, piano, dance, elocution, Hebrew—and I still fucked up my life. But I had plenty of help. Your own goddamn brother, fondling me right in our house. I scared him off, showed him the kitchen knife and told him I'd stab him. Ha ha ha." Shari hopped out of bed and began circling the bedroom like a lioness, proud of herself.

Tzippy started coughing and grabbed some tissues, the image of the carbon-steel blade with the brown wooden handle clear in her mind.

"Fuck it," Shari said, and went out onto the balcony to smoke. It was two in the morning, but she didn't seem to care. Tzippy hated the smell that clung to her even when she returned, but she still wanted Shari to spend time with her. She sensed the immense sadness cupped beneath her daughter's bony shoulders, delicate as an egg.

The next morning, they resumed their life without mentioning the night before. When Naomi called and asked how things were going, Tzippy said fine. Why not? What good would the truth do Naomi?

"I'm having a book signing at the library for my new book," Naomi announced.

"Oh, sweetheart, that's terrific."

"Ike's so proud."

"As he should be."

"He's giving one of my new cookbooks to each of his clients when they move into their new homes. Isn't that a good idea?"

"I love it."

Naomi paused. "He spoke to Brucie."

"How is he?" Tzippy asked.

"He's a mess."

"Still?"

"You should call him again. Ike's going to see him."

"Yes, I'm planning to," Tzippy said. She was pleased that Ike, who lived outside Hartford, could easily drive to see her son.

She and Shari discussed what Naomi had said about Brucie, and then Tzippy called him at his office to check on him. "Just wanted to see how you were doing, Brucie," Tzippy said, trying not to sound too distressed.

"I'm hanging in there," Brucie said. "That bitch. She's good and gone. You never liked her anyhow, Mom."

"I never said that, did I?"

"You didn't need to."

"I'm sorry nonetheless."

"I'll live. It's just bad right now."

"You were too good for her, Brucie."

"Thanks, but you sound like a typical Jewish mother."

Maybe she did, but she didn't care. She couldn't help herself. In fact, as she'd gotten older, she wished she'd been more like a typical Jewish mother than like the woman she'd been, all wrapped up in herself. When the call was over, Shari, who'd been listening in, said she'd done okay. She had kept it short and sweet. No need to carry on too much. It would only make things worse. It had been difficult, but she'd managed.

The next night, she woke up with a cramp in her foot and had to ask Shari to rub it.

"God, Mom, you've got to be kidding," Shari said, pulling herself out of bed. "What is it you want me to do?"

Tzippy instructed, "Rub that vinegar on my foot. It will help."

She stuck her contorted foot out in front of her. Shari picked up the bottle of vinegar, poured some into her hand, and began to rub Tzippy's foot. "This stuff stinks. How can you stand it?" Shari asked. After a few strokes, she said, "Is it helping?"

"A little." Tzippy missed her Angie, who had never complained about doing it. "It's okay. Never mind," she said, and pulled her foot in to her, rubbing it under the covers. Finally, when the cramp wouldn't subside, she got up while Shari sat on the other side of the bed and watched.

"Are you okay?" Shari asked, as Tzippy hobbled around. "Maybe you should wear socks."

"I'll live," Tzippy said. Wasn't that what Brucie had told her? Still, she felt weak and couldn't move much past the edge of the bed.

"Sit down," Shari said. "Let me try again."

She poured more vinegar onto her hands and rubbed Tzippy's foot again. This time she stayed with it, until the foot returned to its original shape.

"Better?" Shari asked.

"Yes, thank you."

They turned off the light and went to sleep.

Since Angie wasn't there, Shari drove to Neiman Marcus. Each time they came to a light, Tzippy pressed her feet on the floor.

To distract herself, she stared fixedly out the window. A Cadillac passed them. At the corner, someone waved from another car. Tzippy saw it was Claire Fisher, smoking a cigarette in the backseat of her chauffeured black town car. By then, Tzippy thought, Stan and Fred must have started their eighteen holes with the new vice president of something-or-other—a goy; then they were scheduled for massages. A Hispanic driver in a beige sedan moved in front of them. A powder-blue convertible turned into the parking lot before them, beneath a palm tree.

Tzippy felt nervous entering the store. It was her first time back shopping since her arrest. Looking around, she checked to see if anyone who looked like a store detective was milling around. Did they know about her here? She wondered if they passed the word from store to store of whom to watch. Perhaps they had people following her. She prayed they'd let her shop in peace.

She and Shari walked past the men's department, where the mannequins wore color-coordinated cable-knit sweaters, slacks, and socks. Tzippy saw a man watching her, but she couldn't be sure; she knew she'd never get over being arrested. And shopping at Neiman Marcus was like seeing an old love—familiar but sad because she couldn't go to her favorite store, Saks.

Finally, they arrived at the women's department, full of designer dresses and eyeless mannequins wearing Chanel suits. A red-lipsticked saleswoman approached and showed Tzippy some Nicole Miller dresses.

"Too youthful," Tzippy said. Then she added, "You'd look good in the Nicole Miller, Shari."

"We're here for you, Mom."

"Try it on."

"If you promise to keep looking for yourself."

"Of course. I won't forget about my own wedding." Then Tzippy spotted a Dior dress on a mannequin, deep red and draped over the shoulder. "What about this for you, Shari?"

"No," she said. "I think I like this Nicole Miller." She held a black dress with small polka dots and cap sleeves. "This is so cute, don't you think?"

"Yes, but this Dior is fabulous. Try them both on."

Shari checked the price on the two dresses. The Nicole Miller was $350, while the Dior was over $1,000. "Mother, this is far too expensive."

"Please try it on."

"I love the Nicole Miller. It's more me."

Tzippy reminded herself that it was Shari's decision, recalled how she had behaved about her wedding dress, and refrained from saying, *I'm paying.* Instead, she said, "Shari, get the dress you want the most."

In the end, they bought the Nicole Miller. "It will be perfect for the wedding," said Tzippy. "My treat. Do you have shoes? A bag?"

"Black is easy. Of course."

The dress made Shari look pretty and less gaunt. *If only she drank less*, Tzippy thought.

They looked for a suit for Tzippy, something understated. Tzippy had an idea in her head. "Something Jackie O., with a pillbox hat. What do you think?"

The saleswoman nodded and pursed her red lips. "Let me see what I have out back."

They settled on beige shantung silk with a knobby texture. The hat, in the same color, had a veil attached to it, though it covered Tzippy's nose, her best feature.

"You look fabulous," Shari said, as Tzippy stood on the platform in the dressing room so the seamstress could measure the correct hem length.

"Do you think I need gloves?" Tzippy asked.

"Not for the ceremony. Besides you'll need your hands free for the ring," the saleswoman said, smiling.

"What kind of shoes?" Tzippy asked. Everything had to be perfect. "A bag."

Perhaps she could get the entire ensemble right here in Neiman Marcus. She was tired now and wanted to wrap things up. She'd get the rest another time. "Shari, let's go for a bite afterward," she said, turning slowly so the seamstress could complete the pinning.

"Where?"

"Shupie's. It's my favorite. Angie and I used to go."

They sat at Shupie's counter after Neiman's. The aroma of freshly baked bread wafted through the store, and Tzippy looked around to see if anyone she knew was there. All of a sudden, she saw a large black woman sitting at the end of the counter and for a brief minute thought it was Angie. Was she working already for someone else? Tzippy put her glasses on and peered at the woman. No, she thought, breathing a sigh of relief, it wasn't Angie. Then she saw her old friend Lillian Stone from Boca, pushing a small basket of groceries, and Tzippy waved to her, making a mental note to call her and make a date. She said, "What do you want for lunch?"

They studied the menu and Shari said, "Everything looks tasty."

While Shari ate a Cobb salad, Tzippy didn't say a word. She could not remember the last time she'd seen her daughter consume anything as rich as bacon or blue cheese, and she didn't want to jinx the moment. She had a bowl of clam chowder to relax her stomach and felt better with a little food in her. The days when she could eat anything she liked were long gone. Everything distressed her now that she was older.

Stan always said she could stand to gain a few pounds. Tzippy realized she had lost some weight because of all the stress, and she wanted to look good, not gaunt, for her wedding. Maybe she should drink milk shakes at night. That wouldn't upset her stomach too much, she thought. Tomorrow they were going to see PJ, and she'd tell him about the shoplifting. She hadn't said a word yet to Stan.

Chapter 11

Pincus Jacob Popowitz's office was located in Palm Beach, not far from either Brown Brothers or Worth Avenue, two prestigious addresses Tzippy held in considerable esteem. PJ and his partners owned a three-story brick building that was painted white for the warm climate. Out front, an American flag hung limply in the heat; a security exchange office and a brokerage house flanked the building. The appointment was for 1:00 p.m. on Monday, February 7.

Tzippy arrived early, nervous and fidgety but trying to keep herself under control. She and Shari sat in the well-decorated, overly air-conditioned waiting room and lazily turned the pages of *Time* and *Forbes*. Shari crossed and re-crossed her legs and hummed under her breath.

PJ was punctual as he had ever been, and when the time came for their appointment, he stood up as the two women entered his office.

"How are you, Tzippy?" PJ said, wrapping his arms around her. "My, you look wonderful. You never seem to age. What's with you? How do you do it?"

"Take a closer look, but thank you anyhow," she said. "You look well yourself." Tzippy had dressed with care that morning in a stunning Chanel suit, suitable for Palm Beach, white with black piping, and had painted her lips fire-engine red.

PJ was a robust man of sixty with silver-gray hair and a jowly face. He radiated the air of someone who enjoyed a life of expensive lunches and recreational tennis. After he'd written Ben's will and gathered the Bryer family in the conference room after Ben's death to explain it, he'd been retained to look after Tzippy's future affairs.

"And how are you, Shari?" PJ said. Tzippy watched as his eyes appraised her. "What have you been up to lately?" He smiled, and his voice became silky.

"As my mother would say," she said, "I'm between husbands and almost between jobs."

Tzippy smiled a bit thinly.

PJ said, "Excellent." Tzippy wondered if PJ was dating the rich divorcees who lived in the mansions by the ocean. "Since my second divorce was finalized, I've been spending some time on my boat," he offered, pointing to a picture on the wall of a thirty-eight-foot Bertram with the name *Sweet Caroline* painted on the front. "It gives me perspective." Tzippy imagined him fishing, sunning, and drinking frozen margaritas.

"Does *Caroline* stand for somebody?" Shari asked, peering at the photo.

"I love the Red Sox, don't you? 'Sweet Caroline' is the song the fans sing at the seventh-inning stretch. Besides, it has snap."

"I like snap," Shari said, sitting down in one of the armchairs next to PJ's desk. "I don't know about the Red Sox, even though I live in the town. Daddy always loved the Yankees." Shari wore a red sheath that showed off her trim figure; she looked rested and healthy.

"Certainly, you're entitled to your ideas on whom to root for," he teased.

"Just because Daddy liked the Yankees doesn't mean I do. I'm still deciding on the Sox. They're a little unpredictable."

"Unpredictable is good, isn't it?"

Shari blinked coyly and smiled. Tzippy could see she was pleased with PJ's flirting.

"We may have to discuss this subject later, in private," PJ said.

Tzippy coughed, feeling ignored, and got down to business by saying, "I needed to see you because I'm getting remarried soon. Here's the financial information you requested," she said, handing him a large manila envelope.

"Yes, you said that on the phone. What a surprise."

Tzippy and PJ talked about the terms of the prenup and the different ways Tzippy could arrange things for the children.

"You also need to revise your will, Tzippy," PJ said. "And change any beneficiaries on your life insurance policy."

"I'm not leaving Stan money. He's got his own. Mine goes to the kids."

"Are you changing your name?"

"I'll be Mrs. Fosberg."

"That'll be strange, Mom," said Shari.

"You know you can't get married for thirty days after Stan signs the prenup," PJ said. "It's a state rule."

"I heard something like that."

"We don't want it to look like you're pressuring him into anything."

"He's all for it. In fact, he's on his way to his lawyer's today."

"Good. And what about the apartment?"

"He'll live in it if I go first. The children can stay in those guest rooms in the apartment complex when they visit, just like they do now from time to time. What do you think, Shari?"

"It seems fair."

PJ looked up at her and said, "There are other places to stay. It won't be too hard."

"I hope not," she said, not liking the implication of PJ and Shari together. She crossed her legs and admired them to distract herself. She still had slim ankles, and they looked nice in her high-heeled shoes.

"Are there any other matters you need to discuss today, Tzippy?"

"Yes, one, but it's more private. Shari, would you mind waiting outside for a few minutes?" Tzippy said.

Shari stared at her and frowned slightly. "No problem, Mom," she said. As she walked out of the office, she shimmied slightly; Tzippy watched PJ's eyes follow her.

Tzippy put her hands in her lap and tried to calm herself. Though talking to the rabbi had been difficult, this was even harder. "Could I have a glass of water?" she asked. She took a deep breath. She needed to release herself; the shame of her theft had closed her up, like a bug under a rock.

"Of course," he said, pouring some from a carafe.

"PJ, let me get right to the point. I was arrested for shoplifting at Saks," she said. She let the crimson in her cheeks run through her, and she licked her lips.

PJ's eyes grew larger; he shifted in his chair and cleared his voice and then, Tzippy thought, tried to look less shocked by picking up a pen and writing something on a yellow legal pad. Tzippy could tell he was being polite.

"When did this occur?"

"In January, about a month ago. Right before the birthday party the kids threw for me." Wondering why PJ hadn't been invited, she added, "It was a family party. I was extremely stressed; the kids had a big fight in the restaurant the night before. Brucie and Shari really went at it, and I didn't know what I was doing. I took this pin and stuck it in my bag without thinking." Stopping, she realized she wasn't telling the whole truth, but she couldn't contain herself. "These two detectives questioned me, and two Bal Harbour cops brought me to the station. It was awful."

"What were you thinking, Tzippy? Stealing from Saks Fifth Avenue?" PJ said, wiping his face with a handkerchief. Then he pulled himself together and continued, "Of course you were upset. The children were arguing. What kind of disagreement did they have?" PJ said, writing on the yellow pad.

"Brucie lost it. He twisted Shari's arm, hurt her. She started yelling in the restaurant. It was so embarrassing."

"Yes," he said, making notes on his pad.

"They were fighting about the coat business and how things had gone downhill since Ben died. Then Brucie's wife, Jill, left him. You have no idea, PJ." She thought she'd throw that in for good measure. She had to make him understand. The pressure in her head increased. Where were her pills?

"She left him? No kidding?"

"It's been a nightmare."

"I see. Such an embarrassing situation for you to be arrested." He dabbed his face again. "This is a difficult time for you," he said. "By the way, what did you say you took at Saks?"

"A brooch, a pin. Nothing major. Costume jewelry. It was on sale for around four hundred bucks. They made such a big deal about it, you'd think I robbed Fort Knox; they took me to the station in a police cruiser, for God's sake. I was frightened and made to wait right in front of a jail cell. Me. Can you imagine?" She trailed off and hung her head.

"It must have been terrible. You should have called me immediately."

Lifting her head, she said, "I should have, but I wasn't thinking." She knew why she hadn't called him: she'd been too ashamed.

"Have you gone before the judge?"

"No, but I'd like you to represent me when I go. Here's the letter. I was hoping you could get the date changed. Maybe to after the wedding."

PJ studied the letter and said he'd look into getting it moved. "Has Stan been supportive?"

"Funny you should ask. I'm unsure about when I should tell

him. Have you any advice?" He was a lawyer, not a rabbi, but he had a legitimate point of view.

"Let's get the date changed until after the ceremony, and then we'll decide. I wouldn't make a big deal. For goodness' sake, you were under a great deal of stress and it was a small item. I think I can make it go away. The judge we get will be crucial. Some of them are pretty old themselves and can be reasonable."

Tzippy smiled at her friend with appreciation and sighed. "Thank you, PJ—I don't know what I'd do without you."

He looked up at Tzippy and said, "Do you feel better now?"

"Yes." She sipped some water and cleared her throat.

"So! Can I take you two ladies to lunch? There's a fabulous little place that just opened down the street. Let's go."

Tzippy said, "I'd like to powder my nose first."

The well-appointed restaurant and bar were casual-chic. Many of the female patrons were blondes wearing pastel colors and carrying designer bags. The guests were eating stone crabs, Caesar salads, and sushi. Shari chatted away with PJ at the table. Sensing she could relax, Tzippy ordered a drink.

"Chardonnay," she said.

Shari asked for a gin and tonic and PJ for a martini. He also ordered a cheeseburger with sweet-potato fries, while Tzippy chose a Caesar salad with shrimp and Shari requested a grilled cheddar cheese sandwich with onion rings. Tzippy was pleased to see Shari ordering another calorie-rich meal so soon after the Cobb salad she'd had at Shupie's; she allowed herself to hope it was the beginning of an upswing, for Shari and for her. Now that PJ was handling her problem, Tzippy couldn't believe how much better she felt; she was like a young bride with slight shoulders, not an old one ready to cave in. Maybe she was old-fashioned, but having a smart, powerful man on her side was something she had always craved.

"I wish I had some legal problems for you to solve," Shari cooed to PJ, as they were about to leave.

PJ laughed. "Everyone has legal issues."

"You think?" Shari actually batted her eyelashes.

"Maybe we could go for a ride on my boat and discuss them," he said, smiling. "When are you free?"

Tzippy began to cough, placing a tissue against her mouth, as her good mood took a downturn.

"Why, anytime. At least, for thirty days," she said, glancing at Tzippy.

"The weather's supposed to be terrific this weekend. I'll call you at your mother's."

They said their good-byes, and when Tzippy got herself settled in the town car, she said, "When did you decide you were interested in PJ? You never told me."

"He's available and we know him. Why not?"

"Our family's employed PJ and his father's law firm for many years. You don't want to mess things up."

"And you mean?"

"We don't need problems."

"Mother, you worry too much," Shari said. "I think I'll buy a new bikini at that little shop we passed on the way."

Tzippy decided not to say anything more. Instead, she sat back and tried not to press her foot on the floor every time Shari braked.

"I can't stand that she's going on a date with him," Tzippy whispered into the phone to Stan the following Saturday.

"He usually goes for younger women," Stan said, "but what the hell."

"It's going to be trouble. I can feel it."

"Who knows? It might just be a one-time thing. All they're

doing is going off on his boat, and it's beautiful out. Try not to think about it."

Tzippy sighed and tried to believe Stan was right. Just then, Shari came into the bedroom in a new yellow bikini with brass buttons on the bust. "How do I look, Mom?" she asked.

"Gotta go, Stan. I'll call you later," Tzippy said, and hung up.

"Let me study you," she said, examining Shari. Her slim body was firm for a woman of forty-five, except for the declining muscles in her thighs. "Why, you look wonderful. Turn around. What are you going to put on after?"

Shari pulled a colorful shift from her straw bag.

"That's cute," Tzippy said.

"I can wear the same shoes," Shari said, as she pirouetted in high cork wedges.

"Now, please don't drink too much. I beg you."

"Okay, Mom," Shari said.

Tzippy added, "PJ will love your suit. Have you got plenty of sunscreen? Here, wear this," she offered. She walked into her large closet and came out with a straw hat with a yellow ribbon around the brim.

"That's perfect," Shari said, placing it on her head and checking herself in the mirror. "What do you think?"

"You look great," Tzippy said. "Wait. Here." She took a pair of gold hoop earrings out of her jewelry box. "These will go with your suit."

"Oh, thanks, Mom," Shari said, putting them on and admiring her image in the mirror. "Accessories by Tzipora Bryer. Well, I'm off. We're meeting in an hour." She kissed Tzippy on the cheek and left, swinging the large straw bag that held her change of clothes.

Jocelyn came into the room and set a cup of tea on Tzippy's table. She smiled and said, "Shari sure was excited, Mrs. B." Angie had called her by the same nickname. Once Tzippy was alone, she was surprised to find herself hoping Shari would have a genuinely good time on her date, even if it was with PJ. The poor girl had had a tough enough time with men already, not to mention jobs, eating, and drinking, and she deserved a break once in a while.

As Tzippy sat on the bed and sipped her tea, she again thought back on her life as a mother, searching for the moment when the threads had started to unravel. Perhaps there had not even been a single moment, but she kept looking for it. Was it because she hadn't confronted her own brother about his behavior with Shari? Was that the wrong decision from which everything had flowed? Or was it more complicated and insidious? Was Tzippy like Humpty Dumpty, broken and beyond repair, and thus incapable of keeping the things around her whole?

She called Stan back. "Shari just left, all excited and starry-eyed. What if this little fling goes south?" she said.

"I know you're worried, but what can you do? At least she's still optimistic. Time to think about something else. Sweetie, it's already ten in the morning."

"I need a change," Tzippy said. She couldn't put her finger on it, but she knew she was approaching a corner. She was eighty years old and needed to do something meaningful with her life. She felt a stirring inside her unlike any she'd known before.

Chapter 12

Late that evening, when Shari returned from her date, her hair was disheveled, her cheeks flushed. She seemed beside herself with excitement. In a high, breathless voice she said, "He's really nice, Mom," and then collapsed on the bed, flipping her wedges onto the carpet. She spread her arms. "I definitely like him."

Tzippy despaired at the expression on her daughter's face. She'd seen it before, a heartbreaking combination of optimism and naiveté, as though Shari believed that all her problems were now finally over and a new life was about to begin. Tzippy worried that Shari would behave in some irrational manner that would jeopardize the family's long relationship with PJ and his law firm. She wished they're weren't seeing each other, but she wanted to remain calm, so she said, in a controlled tone, "That's nice, sweetie. I'm glad you had a good time. What did you do?"

"Oh, we just sat on the boat in these big chairs and fished while I tried to get a good tan. It was so beautiful out. We sipped gin and tonics. PJ caught a few small fish, and I got a bite of a big dolphin, but it got away." She sat up and pointed at Tzippy. "Let me tell you, that was exciting." She flopped back down again. "He thought of everything! When we got hungry, he surprised me with shrimp and crab salad, crusty bread, and a bottle of chablis, in a big picnic basket. It was all so friendly and nice. PJ even kissed me and told me I was a great gal."

Tzippy gulped when she heard the two of them had kissed. Was it too late to stop this ball from rolling? She forced herself to recover. "He said you're a great gal? Well, you are, you know."

"We're going to a restaurant tomorrow night. It just opened down in South Beach."

Shari stood up and twirled around the bedroom like a starry-eyed teenager. Then she put Tzippy's hat on her head, the big, floppy straw hat with the yellow ribbons, and said into the mirror against the door, "Perhaps I'll become the next Mrs. Popowitz . . . What do you think, Mom?"

Tzippy couldn't find the words. She wished her daughter was less of a romantic and more sensible, but she didn't want to be unkind, so she simply stammered, "Oh, sweetheart, let's just take this one day at a time."

"I know . . . I'm being silly," Shari said, tossing the straw hat onto the bed. "It's such foolishness on my part. And who wants to be the third Mrs. Popowitz, anyway? Right?"

"Well, you have a point."

Shari threw herself back on the bed facedown and kicked like a child. "But if he asked me, I'd accept," she squealed into the pillow, trying to hide her words. She turned over and sat up.

Tzippy was beginning to get alarmed at how hyperactive Shari seemed. Her anxiety only increased as she thought about what a loose cannon Shari was, and how easily she could ruin Tzippy's relationship with PJ. The last thing Tzippy needed at this point in her life was to have to find a new lawyer.

"Oh, I'm crazy, I know it. It's terrible. One day at a time. Anyway, we're supposed to be planning *your* wedding, not mine," Shari said, laughing at herself.

"Well, we're not going to do anything tonight," Tzippy said, "except sleep."

"I don't know if I can," Shari said. "You know how what's-her-name sings 'I Could Have Danced All Night' in *My Fair*

Lady? That's how I feel. I'd better take a Xanax. Or do you have any sleeping pills?"

Tzippy did, but she didn't want Shari to know. "No, I haven't any sleeping pills. Now, let's both just calm down. Why don't we go out on the balcony?"

The cool air outside was soothing. They stood there for a long time and stared at the big, bright moon, as Shari smoked and sipped a Tanqueray on the rocks and Tzippy hummed an old tune.

Tzippy slept uneasily, and Shari, it seemed, from the looks of her the next morning, hardly slept at all. But she was bright and energetic and ready to get to work on Tzippy's wedding.

"Are you sure you're not too tired?" Tzippy asked.

"I'm fine, Mom. Never finer."

"Well, we have a ton of things to do," Tzippy said.

"Let me go shower and change, and we'll get going."

While Shari was in the shower, Tzippy decided to commune with her dead husband. Ben was irreplaceable, even though he had broken her heart—a natural-born leader and salesman. Right from the start, Tzippy had known he was going far.

Her own father, Bertram, had been a dreamer, an art lover, and a gentleman. He'd stayed far away from reality; too poetic to be practical even about the furniture he sold. But he'd told Tzippy that she was smart, one of the best things he'd ever said to her, and she planned to make a wise choice when she left his house, prepared to be the wife of a great man and to live off his reflected glory. When the time came, she knew what to do. Sitting at the bar with her mother, Tzippy looked fetching, a green beret pulled to one side and its sequined heart placed jauntily over one eye. And from the moment he spied her, Benny was determined, too. He had the maître d' take a drink to Tzippy's mother, and then he saundered over and introduced himself. Just like that. He said he wanted to meet her daughter. Such a go-getter, not afraid. Tzippy liked those traits.

She knew Ben would provide her with social status, the respect of others, financial security—in short, a comfort-filled life replete with silver tea sets. She learned early that Ben wanted his way—that he went out with the ladies and that he lied—but she endured this double standard because she wanted to be Mrs. Benjamin Bryer.

And right now, she needed Ben's advice about their daughter.

"What do you think, Ben?" she asked the silent room, resting her hands on her lap as she sat on the end of the bed. She pictured him today in a suit and tie, on his way to the office.

"You know I screwed up with her," she continued. "I know it."

She wondered what he'd say. She envisioned him puffing on his cigarette, smiling at her, exhaling smoke. He'd stare in silence and say nothing at first. Benny always thought before he spoke.

He'd probably say something like, "You've got a handful with her now. Thinking she's in love with P. J. Popowitz, that crook. Yeah, he's a good lawyer, but nothing will come of it—we know that. Can't you get her into some kind of therapy? She's a goddamn alcoholic, besides. Tzippy, do something. Now is the time, or she'll end up being some kind of old bag lady with a few bucks. A family joke."

She knew he was right. Hadn't Aunt Fanny come to the bar at the Dolphin Yacht Club with her own bottle of Jack Daniel's? She'd just set it on the teak bar and asked the bartender for a glass with some ice. Heaven forbid that was what became of Shari. Tzippy wasn't going to hesitate anymore. Stan would be supportive, but he didn't entirely get how sick Shari was, how fucked up Tzippy had made her. Only Ben knew—and he shared Tzippy's guilt because while he had been off gallivanting, he'd left the parenting to Tzippy and it had been a bloody joke.

Shari appeared, all wrapped up in a large terry-cloth robe, looking younger and more relaxed. They decided to go down to the party store on Harding Avenue and see about a few unnecessary but fun items, like cocktail napkins with Tzippy's and Stan's names on them, mints with the couple's initials.

Tzippy knew the saleswoman by name. She stared at the samples of different mints spread out in the glass case and asked Shari, "What color combination, do you think? I can't decide. Maybe white with silver initials."

Shari was examining the wedding invitations in a large leather-bound book. Without answering her mother, she asked the saleswoman, "What kind of invitations work best when there have been other marriages?"

"Shari, for goodness' sake, we're here to choose my candies. What are you thinking?" Tzippy asked.

"Oh, yes, Mother. I'm sorry . . . the mints. I don't know. White and silver are so traditional. Why not try something different, like yellow with blue initials? They'll match your decor."

"What do you think, Martha?" Tzippy asked the saleswoman.

"Either way is lovely. How about yellow with gold letters?"

Shari still had her face in the invitation samples.

"Shari, why did we come here today?" Tzippy scolded.

"Oh, I'm sorry, Mom."

"I think yellow mints with gold. They'll pick up the decor and still be wedding-like. Perfect, Martha," Tzippy decided. "And the napkins?"

"We'll do them in yellow with your names in gold. Everything will be coordinated," Martha said.

When they left the little shop, Tzippy was pleased but still annoyed by her daughter's obsession with PJ and the idea of their getting married.

⌒

Shari and PJ's dinner at the new restaurant in South Beach was followed by a spur-of-the moment surprise trip to Bimini. Tzippy worried the entire time they were away, but Shari called and sounded fine, just excited. When she started confiding in Tzippy about having sex on *Sweet Caroline*, Tzippy listened with discomfort and tried to be tactful. It was obvious Shari needed to talk about it, so Tzippy made herself listen. Hadn't Tzippy called up her own sister, Esther, on her wedding night when she was scared of having intercourse?

Shari gave her reports of bubble baths in the wee hours, of swimming across the bay to a deserted island and having sex there. Tzippy absorbed the information and attempted a calm demeanor, despite her apprehension. She popped a new kind of pill, Ativan, to quiet her nerves.

After she returned from Bimini, Shari was ecstatic. She started looking through bridal magazines and talking about where they could live after they were married. PJ had said how much he liked being with her and that he could get used to her company, which of course fed Shari's fantasy of marriage. Tzippy listened but tried to quell Shari's enthusiasm. She kept reminding Shari that it was she and Stan who were getting married, right this minute.

On the days when Shari was free, they continued crossing stuff off the long list Tzippy had made. Even while all this was going on, Tzippy remembered the promise to herself that she'd made the day Stan had taken her to the Boys' Club. But where to begin? Maybe all the problems had really started when Shari had stopped eating. At first, Tzippy thought about the subject of eating disorders as if it were a research project. How else could she learn about what she'd done to her daughter? She thought that perhaps she should buy index cards and put them in a gray metal box; she went to the library and took out three books. After she'd read them, she planned to follow up with articles, to ask questions. Was this how to do it? Or should she just go by the seat of her pants, by instinct, as she usually did?

She had two daughters but only one who suffered from a serious eating disorder. Why? How? The books said that Shari wanted to please her and didn't know how to think for herself. Had Tzippy's insistence on living a certain kind of life prevented Shari's development?

Maybe she needed to talk to others; she'd always been more of a talker than a reader. It was the middle of February when she looked through the Yellow Pages and found a listing for the Lakeville Eating Disorder Center. One afternoon, when Shari was away with PJ, she was free to call. She picked up the phone and dialed the number. Immediately, she began to sweat. What would she say? *I wrecked my kid. All by myself. Ruined her mind. She had a perfectly fine mind until I went to work on it.*

"Hello," Tzippy said. "May I speak to someone who's in charge?"

"Yes?" the woman answered. "This is Pam Warnick." Her voice was professional, older, and educated.

"Oh, hello," Tzippy started. "Really, I . . . I . . ." She took a deep breath. "I don't know how to begin. My name is Tzipora Bryer. I live in the area. I'm an older woman. Years ago, my daughter had anorexia. She's still not right, but she's better. Now she's an alcoholic. Oh, it's a long story."

"It's always a long story," Pam said.

"Yes," Tzippy said. "Yes, it is."

"Would you like to tell it to me?" Though Pam's voice wasn't exactly friendly, there was something about it that encouraged Tzippy, that made her believe that if she talked, the woman would listen.

"Well," Tzippy said, "I just called . . . I mean, I had no idea that . . ."

"What's your name, again?" Pam said. "Let me write it down."

Tzippy cleared her throat. She couldn't just hang up. "Bryer," she said. "Tzipora Bryer. That's *T-z-i-p-o-r-a*. It's an old-world name."

"It's lovely," the woman said. "And telephone number."

Tzippy gave it to her.

"Well, Mrs. Bryer."

Tzippy was suddenly flooded with inspiration. After all, she was a talker. "I don't suppose . . . I mean, I wouldn't want to intrude . . . but is there any way I could come in and meet you? Sit with you? Talk? It would be so much easier if I could look at you, if I weren't so . . ."

"Alone?" the woman said.

"Yes," Tzippy said. "Yes, that's it exactly. I need to . . . get involved. Be of some help. Please . . ." Tzippy's voice lost its strength, and she started to whisper. "I'm so tired."

"Of course you are," Pam Warnick said. "It's an exhausting illness. I'm free tomorrow afternoon. Say, two p.m.?"

Tzippy couldn't believe what was happening. She'd just dialed a phone number, and now she was going to sit and talk to a stranger? She didn't think so.

"Well," she said. "Tomorrow?"

"It won't get any easier, Mrs. Bryer. I promise you."

Tzippy took a deep breath. "Two o'clock?"

"When you get here, just tell the girl at the desk that I'm expecting you. I'll come down and get you in the lobby."

Tzippy hung up and decided she'd go alone to Lakeville, in a cab. Stan would be playing golf with Fred anyway. Shari had a date with PJ. It was perfect, really. She needed to think, and she had no idea how she'd feel afterward. She wanted time to process everything. She found a map in a drawer and tried to figure out how far away Lakeville was from Bal Harbour. She called Black and White Cab and arranged for a taxi to pick her up at twelve-thirty.

The next day, Tzippy lounged in her bathrobe all morning, waiting for Shari to leave. Really, it was infuriating how slowly time passed when she was waiting for something. Shari chattered mindlessly about the lunch she expected to have with PJ: where they might go after, what they might do. Finally, just when Tzippy thought she couldn't stand it a moment longer, Shari left. After a bath and a quick lunch, Tzippy dressed in a proper suit of cream-colored linen and put on light makeup with coral lipstick for color.

At 12:30 p.m., she was waiting in the lobby of her building. The cabbie followed the directions Pamela Warnick had given her; they drove by storefronts, sat in traffic, felt the heat. Tzippy patted her neck with a tissue. Her suit was getting wrinkled. The highway was busy.

"Major traffic jam," the driver said. "I'm going to put on the air."

"That's good," Tzippy said. Leaning back on the seat, she saw the clouds covering the blue sky—puffy, soft, white clouds. *Is that where heaven is?* she wondered, and hoped Ben was watching her go to Lakeville and approving.

Finally, the traffic eased and the cab picked up speed. The air-conditioning brought Tzippy some relief. She sat up straighter and found her strength. Would she be able to admit the truth to this woman? *Yes, I have to,* she thought. *Otherwise, what's the point?* She smiled to herself, pleased to be on her way and pleased with her decision.

Out of town, on Crestview Lane, Lakeville was a large building of yellow bricks with a gray awning coming out fifteen feet and held up by two long gray poles. Over an arched window, gold letters announced the clinic's name.

"You're here," the cab driver said, stopping in front.

"You'll wait?" she asked. The cabbie had a long braid with black elastic bands, spaced an inch apart, descending the length of it. He looked like a biker without his leather vest. "The guy on the phone said two-fifty for the whole thing. Didn't he tell you?" She didn't want to be left alone, just in case.

"Your money."

"Thanks," she said. She walked slowly down the path and entered the glass doors. At the front desk, she asked for Pamela Warnick. "She's expecting me."

Pam was a tall, nearly sixty-year-old woman with gray hair. She wore a light blue button-down shirt outside her skirt and resembled an aging coed. She motioned for Tzippy to take a seat in a wingback chair, and then she sat down.

Tzippy smiled nervously. "I'm not even sure why I'm here," she said.

"Yes, you are." Pam Warnick stared at Tzippy and then reached out across the desk. "I was in the same boat—I know," she said, stroking Tzippy's wrinkled hand.

At the woman's touch, Tzippy started to weep. Silent tears ran down her face; she could feel them ruining her makeup and smudging her mascara. She took a tissue out of her Chanel bag and dabbed her eyes, and then she began to cough. "This is harder than I thought."

"It's okay. If you're like me, you never thought you'd be in this situation. I assumed my daughter, Cynthia, would be a star—until she died of heart failure." Pam Warnick sat back and let out a sarcastic laugh, as tears formed in her eyes as well. "She struggled with anorexia and bulimia throughout her adolescence. After she died, I was so distraught I went back to school and got two degrees: a master's degree in social work and one in psychology. It was thirty years ago," Pam Warnick said. "Cindy died when she was just sixteen."

"Oh my God," Tzippy said. She couldn't stop staring at this woman, who had buried her child and looked almost haunted, yet sat so erect and tall in her seat. "How did you get through it?"

"I've had a lot of help. Dr. Karl Watkins focused his entire practice on treating eating disorders after his own niece died of one. He's been an enormous help. Without the grant money he got from various hospitals, I wouldn't be here today."

"Why do these girls get these diseases?" Tzippy asked.

"There are lots of different explanations, but the thread is constant: a dread of never doing well enough. My daughter thought I was always pushing her to be perfect, and she felt like she failed me."

"I gave my daughter everything," Tzippy said. "I thought I was doing a good thing."

"I'm sure you did, but giving things and providing love and acceptance are very different. Too often, we don't listen to our own children. We tell them what to do. I know—I did it myself, I'm ashamed to admit."

"I guess my husband and I just made a mess of things. I don't know about you, but my marriage wasn't good and I kept on denying it. Only today can I admit how much I hated myself, and how much my husband and I fell down on the job with Shari." Tzippy let out a deep breath of relief. She had finally told the truth.

"My marriage wasn't good, either, but I thought I knew more about child rearing than my husband did," Pam said, lifting her chin, giving off an air of superiority.

"What was your husband like?"

"He was a physicist, a scientist. Rigid, brilliant. He wanted his daughter to be a math genius."

"My husband was so different. He was a successful salesman; he had his own business and made a lot of money. I wanted Shari to have everything. My husband had a lover, and I stayed anyway. It was a big mistake. Shari was neglected, and I was miserable. I knew Ben wouldn't want to give me the money I'd want in a divorce, and I didn't want to be single, I guess. We shared in the guilt when Shari became anorexic. We knew we had damaged her."

"We're all different. One woman who comes to our support group tells about how her daughter hides in the bathroom and how her mother listens to her vomit every night. No one dares say a thing."

"They're scared of her."

"A man comes here and admits to making a big deal about his daughter's shape, admonishing her about being fat, even smacking her on her bottom when she gains the slightest bit of weight."

Tzippy hung her head and thought about how she'd stayed with Benny. Why hadn't she left? She could have insisted on a Park Avenue walk-up and stayed in town and had a nanny or Angie care for the children, but she'd stayed so she could keep her status. She hadn't wanted any gossip. Wasn't that what her mother had taught her, that any husband is better than no husband? And then she wondered whether, if she'd left, she would have been any better as a mother. It wasn't Ben's fault or his lover's fault that she had made mistakes with Shari; it was her fault.

"Are you okay?" Pam Warnick asked. "You look a little pale. Can I get you some water?"

"Yes, please, would you mind?" Tzippy felt faint, and her mouth was dry. She couldn't stop thinking about how she'd robbed them all of a normal life. *I am a thief*, she thought, and for an instant, a glimpse of the insidious ways in which thievery had nothing to do with brooches flashed before her.

"I think I need to go now," Tzippy said. "I have a cab waiting."

"I'm sorry for your distress. Sometimes the very beginning steps are the hardest."

"Perhaps I can come back when the support group meets."

"We'd be delighted to have you."

Tzippy stood up slowly. She felt dizzy.

"It was brave of you to come," Pam said, "but you should remember that even as you take care of yourself, you shouldn't forget your daughter. She's still with you, bless her heart."

As Tzippy left the air-conditioned clinic, she experienced the hot blast of Miami almost as a welcome hug. She spotted the waiting taxi and hurried to get in.

"That wasn't too long," the cabbie said.

"I couldn't stay any longer."

"That bad, huh?" He turned around to face her.

"Yes," she said. "That bad."

All the way back to her apartment in Bal Harbour, she prayed to God. *Thank you, Lord, for sparing my daughter from dying. I'm sorry I wasn't a better mother. Thank you for making me see myself.*

She sat in the back of the cab and prayed and coughed into her tissue. She was an old woman who had lived for eighty long years, and today, at Lakeview, she had learned something new. She tried to speak, to talk to the cabbie, but her throat closed. A solid lump of tears stayed inside her, and she leaned back against the seat and shut her eyes, taking deep breaths.

"You're here now," the cabbie said, swinging the braided pigtail around his neck. "Let me walk you upstairs," he offered. He came around and opened the door and took Tzippy's elbow in his hand and escorted her upstairs to her apartment. He walked slowly, accommodating her pace. When they reached her front door, she gave him her key and he opened it for her.

"Thank you for bringing me up," she said.

"I'm sorry you're so tired. Go inside and rest. Tomorrow you'll figure out what to do."

She smiled at the hippie driver and gave him an extra $30 when he took his hand away. "Thank you for being so kind."

She watched him walk down the corridor, his braid gently bouncing on his back, his worn leather vest open. He didn't even know her, yet he had taken pity on her. He had looked at her squarely and seen she needed help. He had been kind to a stranger. Shari was Tzippy's own flesh and blood, and yet, Tzippy realized, she'd never really seen her.

Chapter 13

It was morning, the sun was shining through the drapes, and the day felt young. Tzippy was sitting on the edge of her bed, enjoying her tea, when the phone rang.

"Hi, baby cakes. It's been two days, but I feel like it's been ages," Stan said.

"Oh, Stan, I've been so busy. What about you, sweetheart?"

"Me? Well, Fred and I golfed yesterday, but then he thought he had heatstroke in the middle of the ninth hole and we had to leave."

"You're kidding. Is he all right?" Tzippy didn't know Fred well, but any bad news about people her age filled her with dread.

Stan laughed. "They said he was dehydrated and needed to drink more water. He'll be fine for the tournament tomorrow. So, what's up with you?"

"I've been thinking more and more about Shari, and . . . well, she's still seeing PJ all hot and heavy. God, the girl keeps talking about marrying him. Can you imagine?"

"I'm not sure we could handle that. One at a time, don't you think?"

"The big thing is, yesterday I took a cab ride to an eating disorder clinic—all by myself—and met this woman, Pam, who runs the place. Her daughter died from what Shari had."

Stan was silent for just a moment. "Forgive me for butting in, but maybe this isn't the right time, with the wedding coming up and all."

"Oh, Stan, I have to fix things with Shari. I want to understand what went wrong. When she was really sick, I was afraid to get much information. I didn't want to know. I was like an ostrich. I know that sounds weak, but that's the truth. Now, I'm going to find out what I should have learned years ago and try to help her."

"Well, you know best," Stan said. "And you know I'll back you up, no matter what. So, when can we get together?"

Suddenly she heard the two little annoying beeps that told her someone else was trying to call. "Oh, Stan, the phone is clicking."

"Go ahead, call me back," Stan said. "Good-bye, sweetheart."

Tzippy hit the flash button and said hello.

"This is Pam Warnick, from Lakeville. We met yesterday." The voice was clipped and professional.

"Oh," Tzippy said. "Hello. I'm surprised to hear from you so soon." She took a sip of tea and tried not to cough.

"You gave me the impression yesterday that you wanted to 'get involved.' I just thought of something you could do, if you'd like."

"Yes."

"There's a young woman with severe anorexia who's had to be hospitalized. They're feeding her intravenously, and she's getting psychiatric counseling. Perhaps you could visit her. I know it would do her some good, and perhaps it might even help you."

"Visit her? A stranger? Won't she think that's odd?"

"It's called befriending. It's one of the services we provide. It makes the girls feel better."

"How would it help me?"

"Sometimes it's hard for us to see our own children clearly, and when we see someone we don't know who suffers from the same disease, it can give us insight."

"Oh, I see." *Befriending*, Tzippy thought. It sounded safe, being nice to someone. "I've never done this sort of thing, that's all."

"When a girl is in the hospital, she's so happy to have a visitor. Your daughter was never hospitalized?"

"No, no," she said quickly. Tzippy was sure she would have fallen apart if Shari had had to be hospitalized—in a regular hospital, much less a psychiatric facility. No one had suggested medical intervention. They'd just kept on putting up a good front. "Okay," Tzippy said. Suddenly she had the sensation of falling into a hole, like Alice going after the White Rabbit.

"Here's where you go. Have you got a pencil? St. Frances Hospital. The young woman's name is Nicole Spencer."

"When should I do this befriending?" Tzippy asked Pam Warnick.

"Whenever you can. Tomorrow would be great."

After she'd written down the name of the girl and had hung up the phone, she sat back and shook her head briefly, as if to clear it. Maybe she'd said yes too quickly—she should have taken time to think about it. After all, she'd met Pam Warnick only once, and besides, no one would know if Tzippy didn't go; no one was taking attendance. How odd of this woman to have called her out of the blue. Tzippy was eighty years old! Perhaps this was too much to ask of her. She wanted to do the right thing, but going to visit a starving girl she didn't know in a psychiatric hospital? Then again, she thought, it was a free country. Once she got there, she could always leave. And hadn't she asked for this? Wasn't this what she had gone looking for?

Shari was getting ready to go to the yacht show down on Collins Avenue with PJ, and she walked into Tzippy's bedroom in the midst of her mother's somber thoughts.

"What's up, Mom?" she asked. "You look so sad."

"Do I?" Tzippy asked. She glanced at herself in the mirror and saw that Shari was right. Her mouth was turned down, and the lines around it were deep and indented. She looked eighty-five today.

"Whom were you talking to?" Shari asked. "What's befriending?"

Tzippy wasn't ready to answer that question yet, and she knew the quickest way to distract Shari would be to compliment her on her appearance. She took in Shari's white linen pants and navy-and-white–striped shirt and said, "Any man would be proud to have you on his arm."

"You think I'm okay? I get so nervous, you'd think I was a teenager again."

"Heaven forbid," Tzippy said.

"What do you mean?"

"I don't know what's gotten into me," Tzippy said. She stood up and grabbed Shari and turned her toward the mirror. "Just see," she said. "So beautiful."

Shari turned and gave her mother a hug.

Tzippy was relieved when Shari left. She called Stan and told him of her plans to visit this strange girl.

"Her name's Nicole," Tzippy said. "She's in bad shape."

"Are you sure you'll be okay?" he asked.

"I'll be fine. I want to do this."

The day before, this entire experience had felt secretive and private, but now she was telling Stan, and soon enough, she'd tell Shari.

"When are you going?" Stan asked.

"The woman suggested tomorrow, but I don't know. Shari's out for the afternoon. Maybe I'll just go today."

"No time like the present," Stan said. "You want me to drive you?"

"No, thank you, sweetheart. I'm going to take a cab again."

Tzippy called the Black and White Cab number and asked for the same hippie driver she'd had before. After a bath, she dressed in a charcoal-gray suit and put on just a touch of makeup. When she went downstairs, the cabbie smiled in recognition.

"Hello there," he said, as he opened the back door to let her in.

After she settled in the seat, he bent down and said, "My name's Ringo, after my favorite drummer."

Tzippy laughed. "My name is Tzipora, but you can call me Tzippy."

"After the Road Runner, my favorite cartoon character," Ringo said.

Tzippy laughed again; she felt warmth toward this hippie driver, now that he had escorted her upstairs to her apartment the last time they'd met.

"Where are we headed today, Tzippy?"

She gave him the address of St. Frances, and he drove quickly down the freeway and made good time.

"You're here," Ringo said, stopping in front.

The hospital had an arched window featuring the name St. Frances in gold letters and a large cross, also in gold, next to its name. So goyishe! Feeling a bit nervous, Tzippy said, "You'll wait, won't you?"

"No problem."

She walked slowly, and when she entered the hospital, she asked at the admissions desk for Nicole Spencer. The eating-disorders wing was on the third floor. Nicole Spencer was in 302. That way to the elevator.

Tzippy stepped carefully across the threshold after the elevator doors parted. Nurses conferred at the station, a large vase of flowers on the counter in front of them. Several patients, thin girls in green johnnies, milled around. One had an IV attached to her arm and dragged the pole with her when she moved.

Nicole was on her back in bed when Tzippy peeked into

302. The sight of the young woman—who looked nothing like a young woman—stopped Tzippy in the doorway. Nicole's eyes were huge, her pale cheeks hollow. She resembled a monkey and was clearly wasting away. To Tzippy, this felt almost as bad as watching her father get buried. Shari had been this thin the day Selma Grossman had said Shari belonged in Auschwitz, but never as ghastly as Nicole.

"Hi," Tzippy said, trying to sound friendly.

"Hi," Nicole said.

"My name is Tzippy. Tzippy Bryer. Pam Warnick from Lakeville suggested that I come over to see you."

Tzippy moved cautiously to the foot of Nicole's bed. There were pictures on the wall, childlike drawings in all the colors of the rainbow. Neither woman seemed to know what to say. Finally, Tzippy asked, "How long have you been here?"

"Who's counting?" the girl said. "In this place, time just drags on and on."

Nicole had tubes in her arms and one small tube attached to the inside of her nose. Tzippy had never seen a tube attached to someone's nose. The girl looked near death.

"Before you were here, what did you do?"

"I was a nurse."

"A nurse?" Tzippy was incredulous. "Here?"

"No, at another hospital. Pretty crazy, huh?"

"How old are you?"

"Twenty-three."

"Really?" She looked like an adolescent.

"I should know better, I know."

"And the tubes?"

"Because I have to gain weight."

"You won't eat?"

"I'm too afraid to eat."

Tzippy could see that she had once been pretty and had large blue eyes. "Yes, of course." Tzippy noticed her thin hair, her dry skin, her colorless complexion, and the brown fuzz on her arms, like stovepipes. Tzippy's heart ached for the emaciated young woman. "What do you do all day?" she asked.

"I write poetry," Nicole announced. "Here," she said, clearly wanting to show off her writing. She pointed to some pages on the small table by the bed.

Tzippy picked up the paper and read the words.

No matter where I go or what I see,
I believe in love and goodness
I believe in kindness
If I am kind, I won't be selfish.
God will take care of me
Because he knows I need his help.

"It's lovely," Tzippy said. She didn't know what else to say. It wasn't poetry, but it was something. Here was a young woman, a nurse, who wouldn't eat of her own free will, who was hooked up to tubes in her nose, and she wrote about love and goodness. It was unfathomable that someone who clearly didn't love or understand how to be kind to herself would have anything positive to say on the subject.

Tzippy had to go. She needed some air. "I think I'll come another day, if you don't mind."

"Too scary for you, right? Why are you here?"

"My daughter had anorexia years ago. I thought I'd like to help out in some way."

"Is she okay now?"

"She's better."

"Maybe you should be thinking of her instead of helping me. But thanks for coming." Her teeth appeared too big for her small face.

Nicole's words stung, but Tzippy didn't flinch. "Are you sure you don't mind my leaving?"

160

"My show's coming on—*All My Children*. I love Erica."

"She's beautiful."

"Yes, she is."

"And Nicole—you were right. It *is* too scary."

They gave each other a small smile of recognition.

Tzippy headed toward the nurses' station and spotted a small bud vase on the corner, turquoise, with a pink rose in it. For just a moment, while the nurses were turned away, busy, she started to reach out and take it, as she'd done at Saks with the brooch. It would be easy—just put it in the palm of her hand and slip it in her Chanel bag. *No*, she thought. *I can't.* She wanted it as she had wanted the ivory hand, but instead she got on the elevator, let the floors fall away, and walked slowly into the sunshine.

My daughter could have been in a hospital like this, hooked up to tubes, starving to death, she thought. *What was I doing then? I was at the Vogue Shop, trying on clothes, spending Ben's money. We weren't paying attention. I was popping Librium, sipping scotch. What was I thinking?*

"I couldn't stay any longer," Tzippy said, as she slid into the backseat of the cab.

"A relative?" Ringo asked.

"It's complicated," Tzippy said.

She sat and coughed into a tissue. Taking deep breaths, trying to calm down, she took a pill out of the vial in her bag and placed it under her tongue. As the cab pulled off into the traffic, she closed her eyes and began to relax.

Back in her apartment, she got a cool washcloth and placed it over her eyes as she lay on the couch. Images of Nicole Spencer's face kept swimming up out of the blackness and being replaced with Shari's face.

There had been many difficult times with Shari: the shock of seeing the bald spot, the size of an egg, on the back of her head, and how Shari had had to go get needles in her scalp to make the hair grow back. The day her friend Stella had stopped her on the street and asked if something was wrong with Shari and Tzippy had cringed, the implications that she had neglected her daughter or denied her food too insulting to stomach. Yes, that had been one of those wretched moments she'd never forget. Then Shari's soon-to-be husband, Bud, had had the good sense to lie and say her name was Smith, so no one could identify her as the daughter of the event's chairman. Oh, these embarrassing and difficult moments went on and on.

Still, despite how precarious things had been, Shari had managed to stay just out of reach of medical and psychiatric establishments, always kept herself just above the functioning line. It was amazing: she had never passed out on the hockey field from lack of nourishment, never flunked out of school, never crawled under the bedsheets and stayed there in a darkened room. No, she had gotten up every day and gone into the world, and Tzippy and Ben had given her no quarter. At eleven or twelve, Shari had felt pressure to get into the right clique, the right clubs, the right high school, and then the right college. Naomi had kept to herself and stayed out of the fray, but Shari was jealous of her brother, thought he got more attention from Ben. She and Brucie were always fighting, yelling, pinching. Tzippy had sided with Brucie too much of the time, since he was the only son.

And then Tzippy recalled how she and Ben had taken Shari to the Dolphin Yacht Club for one of Ben's parties for "the boys"— the salesmen he occasionally treated to a weekend of lavish food and free drinks and young, available girls in order to guarantee their loyalty, in order to make sure they gave Ben generous orders for his coats.

The Dolphin Yacht Club was pristine and white, and all the expensive boats in southern Florida, where they had an apartment, were moored there. When Ben, Tzippy, and Shari entered the Dolphin, the music was loud and a crowd had gathered on the wooden dance floor. Older men in tuxedos and expensive haircuts were shaking their butts with girls the age of their daughters, blondes in long white dresses like debutantes. No one thought a thing was the matter. It was there that Tzippy had once spotted Bob Hope dancing cheek to cheek with a young starlet after a rendezvous in one of the yachts anchored outside.

"Let's get a table," Ben said.

Two of Ben's salesmen were staying for the weekend—John O'Hare, a pug-nosed Irish guy from Chicago, and Chuck Bodini, a long-limbed Italian who worked for the same chain of stores. Bodini was hiding in the corridor, but he didn't escape Tzippy's eye. In fact, Tzippy commented to Shari, "He's not fooling me. I know his wife. We had dinner in New York together. He's embarrassed to look at me."

John O'Hare was drunk and sloppy. His lady friend, clearly in her twenties, wore a too-tight white cocktail dress and fawned all over him. He sat next to Tzippy and spoke too loudly. Shari sat across the table in a green dress with a full skirt, an appropriate dress for a young teen. Benny kept standing and waving his arms, full of himself, as if he were leading a band or directing traffic, checking that everyone had enough to eat and drink.

When John O'Hare said, in a voice that boomed across the round table, "She's the best fuck I ever had," Shari looked at him and made a face of disgust and shock.

At the time, Tzippy thought that perhaps Shari found John O'Hare unattractive, wondered who would want to have sex with him. She was an adolescent and used to boys with thin bodies, used to movie stars in magazines, muscled and handsome. John O'Hare was soft, middle-aged, and sloppy. But now Tzippy knew that even then, Shari saw him for what he was: ugly and crude.

In spite of John's provocation that night, Tzippy kept her

composure and said, in her ladylike way, "Really, John, you should keep your voice down."

Shari shot her mother a puzzled look, as if she couldn't understand why Tzippy wasn't more offended, though she said nothing. But then O'Hare asked Tzippy for the name of her furrier in New York City so he could pick up something for his wife back in Chicago—maybe a chinchilla wrap, luxurious but small—to take her as a token from his three-day weekend of fucking.

"Arthur Kornberg," Tzippy said. "Just tell him I sent you. He'll take good care of you, John."

At that, Shari stood up so quickly that her chair shot out behind her. Her eyes opened wide, and she stared at her mother's face in disbelief. It was at that precise moment, Tzippy surmised, that Shari lost all faith in her parents and the type of upbringing they were providing for her. It was at that moment, Tzippy realized, that Shari knew how Tzippy and Ben had tried to fool their daughter into thinking she had been given the best of all childhoods, when in fact she had been used, was a witness to the sordidness of wealth, to opportunity, to the double standard, and to the low position of women. *That* was the straw that broke the camel's back; *that* was the moment when Shari gave up. And Tzippy knew it now better than she knew her own middle name.

Tzippy picked up the phone and called Stan. "Honey, would you come over? I really need to talk to you about Shari," she said.

"I'm surprised to hear from you so soon," said Stan.

"It was too upsetting. I couldn't stay there long."

"That bad, huh? Okay, baby cakes, I'll be right over," Stan said.

Tzippy hung up the phone and walked over to the glass sliders. Down below, she could see children and parents on the beach. She put on her glasses, went closer to the railing, and noticed one mother's slim legs and a child, a little girl around three years old, wearing a pink bikini. They were walking toward the water; the girl held a pail and shovel in one hand and had long brown hair and sturdy thighs. She looked content and well fed. The mother held the child's hand tightly, making sure the waves didn't wash her out or that she didn't run recklessly into the ocean. Tzippy saw how vigilant and protective the mother was, how she understood the maternal need to protect and shield. As the breeze from outside ruffled Tzippy's hair, tears crept down her wrinkled cheeks, stinging in the sun.

Chapter 14

W e need to go to the florist and see about some last-minute things," Tzippy said, scribbling on her pad as they drove down Collins Avenue. The street was filled with traffic, and the palm trees swayed in the winds off the ocean. Shari was at the wheel, tan and attractive, wearing a pair of large sunglasses and a candy-apple-red linen dress. She'd been with Tzippy for three weeks. It was now the twenty-first, and the wedding was just a little over a month away.

"What's wrong?" asked Shari. "Isn't the perfect Mr. Jason perfect?"

Tzippy pursed her lips. "I'm not sure there'll be enough foliage on the chuppah. The last time I went to a wedding he designed, the pink roses on the ends of the aisles looked sparse." Then Tzippy stopped talking and reminded herself that she had more urgent things to think about.

"Fine, Mom," Shari said. "You know best. But try to keep in mind how small this will be. It's only us."

"*Only* you?" Tzippy said. "Aren't you good enough?"

Shari smiled and kept her eyes on the traffic. "Maybe you should come back as a party planner in your next life," she said.

"And I want an arrangement of flowers in the foyer, something light, in white and yellow. I don't need a hairpiece, because of my pillbox, but maybe something for you two girls?"

"I don't think so," Shari said. "Who are you trying to impress? Please don't get carried away."

Tzippy hardly heard her. She couldn't help herself. She just liked things a certain way. "Boutonnieres for Stan and Fred, his best man."

"Well, that makes sense."

"And, of course, my bouquet. I'm bringing a picture from a magazine to show Jason. I want white roses and ivy." Tzippy patted her large purse, where she had stowed the photographs.

"Sounds lovely, Mom."

"But first we need to go look at our dresses, make sure everything is in order, pick out hose, a few accessories. What do you think?"

"Neiman's it is. Do you have any gum? I'm trying to cut down on the cigarettes. PJ doesn't like me smoking."

"Let me see," Tzippy said. She put her pad back and dug into her large Marc Jacobs bag, the only one big enough to fit all of her necessities. The trouble with big bags, she thought, was that you could never find a damn thing in them.

Shari pulled into the mall entryway and parked the car in the large lot. Although Tzippy didn't feel well, she was pushing herself because she had so much to do. She'd been up with cramps in her feet the night before, and her acid reflux was bothering her. Shari seemed tired, too, after all her late night dates with PJ. Even so, Tzippy and Shari both knew they had to get the wedding details taken care of, and when they entered Neiman's, the cool, expensive air of the store energized them; it purred as they strolled by all the mannequins wearing designer dresses.

While they walked, Tzippy continued to poke inside her handbag. "Let me look in there," Shari said, taking it.

"Be my guest," Tzippy said.

"God, what *isn't* in here?" Shari asked. She held up a blue-and-white container. "Why do you have a box of Band-Aids?"

"You never know when you might need one," Tzippy said. "Here, let me hold it while you look for gum."

"Mother, what's this?" Shari asked, as she waved a brochure from Lakeville Eating Disorder Center in the air.

Tzippy noticed several saleswomen in well-tailored suits look up. Shari was standing by a table where Jimmy Choos were perched on Lucite stands. "An eating disorder clinic?"

Trying not to get nervous, Tzippy whispered, "It's a place I visited. Why?"

"Do you have an eating disorder?"

"Don't be silly, Shari," Tzippy said. "Give me that." She reached for the brochure, but Shari held it away from her.

"I don't know. Seems a little fishy, that's all." Shari's face flushed pink, and the timbre of her voice rose. Several customers glanced over at the two of them. "Why would you go to an eating disorder clinic if you don't have an eating disorder?"

"For God's sake, lower your voice," Tzippy said. "Don't make a commotion."

"I want to know what you're up to," Shari said. "I was the one who was sick."

"Shari," Tzippy said. "I'm trying to learn things, to understand why you got this way."

"What way? What's the matter with me now?"

"Nothing," Tzippy said. "Nothing whatever. It's just . . . I'm trying to fix the past."

"All these years later?"

"Is there something you'd like me to show you, ladies?" a salesman asked, approaching the two of them. He was staring at Shari as if she were a dangerous animal.

"No, thank you. We're on our way to Dresses." Tzippy grabbed

her pocketbook from Shari and started to walk toward the department where they'd purchased their wedding outfits.

"Hey, I never got my gum," Shari said. She followed close
behind.

"Maybe I haven't got any," Tzippy said.

"What you haven't got," Shari said, "is common sense."

Tzippy halted in her tracks and turned around. "It's never too
late. I met a woman whose daughter passed away from bulimia
many years ago. She's in charge of the place."

"Oh, I get it. Are you thinking of running it with her? Mother
of the Year—that sort of thing?"

"Lower your voice, please. I'm trying to correct things now,
Shari."

"How? How will visiting a clinic correct things?"

"Do you need any help?" a saleswoman asked, holding a pink,
terry-cloth Juicy Couture sweatsuit.

"No, thank you," Shari said curtly. "Mother, talk to me. Correct what?"

"Oh, Shari, can't you see? This is about you!"

"No, it's not, Mother. It's never about me. It's always about
you."

"I don't know how to do it, but I'm trying to make it better," Tzippy said, turning toward her daughter. "I'm really trying.
I went to a hospital the other day and met a girl in there who was
all hooked up to tubes. The poor thing is starving herself."

"You did what? Went to a hospital and met a stranger? Who
is dying of anorexia?" Shari's speech elevated to a near shriek.

Tzippy knew she was in trouble, but she didn't know how to
backtrack. "It's called *befriending*," she said, with less confidence.
Suddenly, Tzippy wanted to sit down. She spotted a chair by a
fitting room and asked a saleswoman, "May I rest a minute? I feel
a little faint."

"Certainly—please. May I get you some water?"

"That would be lovely," Tzippy said, coughing into her tissues.

"I do not believe what I'm hearing," Shari said. She became increasingly agitated as she walked back and forth in front of her mother and then sat down next to her.

The saleswoman returned with bottled water. She gave one to Tzippy and then handed the other frostily to Shari.

"Miss," Shari said to the saleswoman, "too bad you don't have a bar for the customers."

"Shari," Tzippy said, "you're embarrassing me."

"*Embarrassing* you? Do you think that's the worst thing one person can do to another person? What is *befriending*?"

"It's just something people do to make the girls feel a little better. It's harmless, really."

"Befriending." Shari rolled her eyes toward the ceiling and sighed. "Now I've heard it all. Do you also be-starve and be-vomit?"

"Shari!"

"When I was seventeen years old and starving myself, my hair was falling out of my head and I had a bald spot on the back of my scalp the size of an orange. But you couldn't take the time to go with me to the doctor's office. Don't you remember? And *now* you have time to go over to some hospital and talk to a *stranger* who's hooked up to tubes?"

How could she forget? Tzippy coughed again and sipped her water. She remembered how Shari used to eat pieces of ex-lax as if it were chocolate candy. "Shari, please find my pills in my bag."

Shari dug into the pocketbook, retrieved the vial, and gave it to Tzippy. Then she put her hand farther into the bag and came up with a pack of sugarless gum. Quickly, she took off the red paper and popped two pieces into her mouth.

Miraculously, the gum seemed to calm her. She chewed silently for a minute or two, and when she resumed, her voice was quieter and more level. "Mother, I can't believe what you've been up to," she said.

"We can discuss this later," Tzippy said, finishing her water. "Let's just go and see about the dresses and then get out of here. I'm exhausted already."

As they started down the center aisle of the store, a tall, thin model, wearing a white dress with butterfly sleeves, passed them. The model stopped and pirouetted, lowering her mascara-heavy eyelashes, waiting for Tzippy to comment.

"Beautiful dress, but too much material for us. We're small-boned. Don't you think, Shari?"

"Don't change the subject," Shari hissed.

"I'm not changing the subject," Tzippy said. "The model is showing us her dress, for God's sake. Can't you be polite for one minute?"

The model smiled and turned on her heel and walked away down the long, carpeted walkway.

Spotting the saleswoman who had waited on them, Tzippy sang, "Minna, there you are. What a sight for sore eyes."

"Want to try on your things, ladies?" Minna asked, efficient as always. She had a pencil tucked behind her ear.

"Yes, we do," Tzippy said.

"About ten more days, and then the big event, right?" Minna said.

"You're absolutely correct," Tzippy said.

In the dressing room, Tzippy tried on her beige shantung silk suit and matching pillbox hat. A short, plump woman came in with a pincushion on her arm and started to adjust the skirt. Shari sat on the bench against the wall and chewed her gum. As Tzippy stood on the platform, she turned and admired herself in the mirror. "What do you think?"

"I think you ought to stay out of hospitals with strange girls and mind your own business," Shari said.

"I mean about the outfit, Shari. Can I have some attention here?"

"Turn, please," the dressmaker said, as she squatted on the floor.

Minna came into the dressing room and held the skirt of the suit together from the back. "I think we need to take it in a tad. It's still too wide on her. Mrs. Bryer's a small woman."

"Yes, yes," the seamstress agreed. "It's easy to do."

"I would like another fitting," Tzippy said.

"That's not a problem," Minna said, with mock surprise. "For you, on your wedding day? Don't insult me, please, Mrs. Bryer."

"Shari, try on your Nicole Miller one more time," Tzippy said.

While Minna went to retrieve the dress, Tzippy asked the seamstress, "What color nylons, do you think?"

"Natural. Nothing else would be correct."

"I may have lost weight since I bought the dress," Shari said. "Or I may have gained weight, with all the meals PJ has been feeding me."

"Well, which is it?" Tzippy asked.

"Oh, I just don't know," Shari said. "I'm so . . . *disordered.*"

"Here it is," Minna said, entering the dressing room. She held up the black dress with white polka dots.

Shari quickly slipped it on while Tzippy took off her suit. When Shari stood on the platform, she started to pull at the waist. "Oh, God, I've gotten fat," she moaned. "Look, it's tight, Mother—all those cocktails and late-night dinners. I hate the way I look."

"You're fine," Tzippy said.

"No, I'm not fine. I'm disgusting," Shari said. "See, I have a roll!" she shrieked, pulling at some extra flesh on her midsection.

"You look lovely. Minna, what do you think?" Tzippy asked desperately.

"I need the waistband let out a bit. Maybe move the button," Shari said to the seamstress. "I hate getting fatter. Oh, I hate myself."

Tzippy stared at Minna and then turned to her daughter, saying, "You'll go on a little diet for a few days and drop a pound or two. It's easy, sweetheart."

"Yes, you're right. I've done it a hundred times," Shari said. She paused and peered down at Tzippy from the platform. "Mom, I cannot believe you are talking with strangers about anorexia; it's been years since I was sick. I'm forty-five; I was fifteen then! Why are you discussing my illness with new people now?"

"Do you want us to leave?" Minna asked, taking the seamstress's hand.

"Please don't," Tzippy said, putting on her shoes. "We're pressed for time. Continue with the fitting. Shari, stop this."

Shari's face became scrunched; she appeared to be on the verge of tears.

"Come, they're under a lot of pressure. Come, Vivian," Minna said. She took the seamstress by her plump arm and led her out of the room, closing the louvered door behind them.

They didn't talk the whole way to the florist's, and when they finally got there, Tzippy tried to take care of business efficiently. Mr. Jason was a small man with chiseled features, a slim waist, and tapered pants. He had a habit of touching his index finger to his right cheekbone, as if making sure it was still there.

"I hope you're planning enough foliage on my chuppah, Jason. How about some white snapdragons?" Tzippy suggested. "And my bouquet," she said, pulling a photograph out of her large bag. "I want it to look like this one, please." Shari sulked behind a side column next to an arrangement of white mums, white lilies, and foliage.

"Don't disturb that, please," Mr. Jason said to Shari. "Yes, that is exactly what I was planning for the bouquet."

Then Shari got on her cell phone, talking to PJ, and Tzippy could hear her complaining. "I am so hurt. Well, wouldn't you be? She did hardly anything when I was starving myself. PJ, I weighed seventy-nine fuckin' pounds at the time. Oh, I shouldn't even be telling you all this shit."

"Shh . . . Shari, please keep your voice down," Tzippy said.

Shari was now walking around the shop. "PJ, I want your opinion about what she did," she said.

Mr. Jason rubbed his hands together, as if scrubbing off some unwanted substance. "Now, ladies," Mr. Jason said, "everyone gets nervous at about this time. Would you like a nice cup of tea? I can have my assistant get us all some."

Tzippy surveyed the scene: Shari on the phone with PJ behind the column of flowers, and Mr. Jason standing in front of her, rubbing his hands, worried about his floral arrangement. She had to get out of there before anything went wrong.

"Mr. Jason, we have to go. Boutonnieres, front-foyer flowers—please don't forget. I'm a wreck," Tzippy said. She coughed into a tissue and popped another pill. "Please, Shari, let's go. Now."

Shari shut her cell phone and reappeared from behind her column. "What's the problem, Mother?"

"The problem is that I am trying to plan my wedding and you were supposed to help me. Instead, you're making me ill with your dramatics," she said, her head spinning. Not only was Shari giving her grief, but she still had to tell Stan about the court date. She hadn't schlepped to Boca with Goldie to see that strange rabbi for no reason.

Tzippy walked out onto Harding Avenue and stood on the hot sidewalk while Shari went to retrieve the car. As exhausting as her new volunteer effort might prove, Tzippy knew there was no turning back.

When Shari pulled up, Mr. Jason stood in the doorway of his shop, still rubbing his hands together. "Mrs. Bryer," he said, "it will all work out." He lifted one of his hands in a gesture of farewell.

Tzippy bent down and got into the front seat of her town car. She pushed the button on the inside of the door and lowered her window. "Mr. Jason, say a prayer for me. Would you do that?" she called.

"For you, sweetheart, I will," he said, breaking into a grin.

"Thank you. You're a gentleman," Tzippy said, as she and Shari drove away.

Chapter 15

They drove home without speaking. Tzippy stared straight ahead, keeping her eyes blank as a doll's. At first the only noise was her incessant coughing and spitting into her tissues, but soon enough, Shari turned the radio on high and rocked her head to the music as if she were alone in the car. When Shari pulled up in front of the apartment, Tzippy got out and stood for a moment, blinking in the sun. Shari's linen dress was wrinkled into creased confusion, and her face bore a scowl of distress as she handed the keys to the valet. She lit up a cigarette and stood smoking after the town car moved away from the curb.

"I'm going inside to check my mail," Tzippy said. She opened the building's glass door and walked through the vestibule, where a majestic arrangement of mums, lilies, and snapdragons in a large brass vase stood on a round table. Tzippy was certain Mr. Jason would have approved.

Tzippy opened her mailbox and ruffled through her envelopes, discarding flyers and requests for money. A large blue envelope with a Vero Beach postmark stopped her short; it was addressed in scrawled blue ink in familiar handwriting that resembled a young elementary school student's. It was from Angela Summers. Angie. Tzippy felt her cheeks flush, and she inadvertently put her hand on her throat; her heart began to beat a bit more quickly, and she felt the need to sit down. Though the letter surprised her, she was more surprised by the emotion it engendered in her, and she resolved to refrain from opening it until she was upstairs.

Shari came in, and, though she still seemed peeved and put-upon, she nonetheless noticed the change in Tzippy's demeanor. "What's wrong, Mom?" she asked. "Bad news?"

Tzippy put her hand on Shari's sleeve and patted it.

"Nothing, dear," she said. "It must be the heat."

They walked together silently, farther down the corridor, and rode the elevator up to Tzippy's apartment. It was a healthy distance to her place, and by the time Tzippy made it to her front door, she was limp. Fortunately, Shari stayed quiet. Jocelyn Bell was inside, cooking in the small kitchen. The smell of home-made split-pea soup, one of Tzippy's favorites, wafted through the apartment. She couldn't help but think that if Angie had made the soup, it would have had kosher flanken rib bone in it and there would have been fresh challah on the side.

"Hello, Mrs. B. You look tired," Jocelyn said, coming into the living room. "Hello, Miss Shari." Shari smiled stiffly but didn't say a word.

"You got a few calls. Mr. Stan and Brucie phoned. May I get you ladies some hot tea?" Jocelyn asked.

"That would be perfect," Tzippy said.

Shari escaped to the deck, where she lit a cigarette and made another phone call. Tzippy could see her pacing back and forth, now talking in an annoyed voice, now gesticulating, now yelling into the phone.

"I must sit down," Tzippy said, and lowered herself into an armchair in the dining room. She rubbed her face with her delicate hands, hands covered with thin skin and brown spots; she massaged her eyes, patted her cheeks. Then she rummaged for her vial of pills and took another to calm down. It would be a long evening; she had to get her nerves under control.

Jocelyn put two glasses of iced tea and a small plate of apple strudel in front of her. "Does Miss Shari want her tea here?"

"Just set it there. She'll be in."

When Jocelyn returned to the kitchen, Tzippy took out the blue envelope and examined it. *Angie, dear Angie.* Tzippy missed her; there was no getting around the fact. She wondered whether all the images that crowded her mind—all those TV shows and matter-of-fact newspaper articles about blacks in South Florida who stole television sets and cars—had affected the way she'd treated Angie. Tzippy knew that Angie had begun her domestic work as a cook, earning $25 per week preparing lavish meals for a classy Jewish couple who had dinner parties. Trying to keep her head down, she had respected the rules of the white people's homes and worked hard, changed sheets and scrubbed bathrooms. Angie had confessed to being envious when the guests drove up in their shiny cars. Certainly, she had reason to be resentful, having grown up with Jim Crow laws, everything separate, having never been allowed on the white side. Tzippy had read about the partitions between blacks and whites in Southern restaurants, barbershops, residential buildings. There had been so many laws restricting them. She suddenly wondered whether Angie had stolen her money not because she needed it or wanted it but as a way of punishing Tzippy. Why hadn't she been more sensitive to Angie?

Tzippy opened the envelope carefully and inside found a large, white Hallmark card with a multicolored half circle—a rainbow—running from left to right. The fancy lettering sang out, *Thank you for being there.* A few small flowerpots with colorful buds and green leaves and two butterflies decorated the center of the card. Tzippy opened it and began to read the pre-printed message.

I just can't thank you enough for all you've done. You were the helping hand just when I needed it. You believed in me, and you gave me something very special—your time and loyalty—and I will always remember you for it.

Then, on the left side, there was a message written in Angie's hand.

Dear Mrs. Bryer,

I know you will be surprised by my letter, but I had to write. I have been a mess since you let me go. Maybe you won't care, but I want to apologize for taking your three hundred dollars. There ain't no excuses. I have no one else to blame but myself. Jack was a bad boyfriend. He and I are long over.

I've been working for a couple in Vero. They have a nice place on Orchid Island. I do the dishes and a little cooking, keep the rooms clean. Once in a while they have a party. I sure do miss you. If there was any way I could come back, I'd like to. I sure wish there was a way.

Love,

Angela Summers

Tzippy shook her head. The image of Angie squatting on her fat thighs, stooped over the bed, with her strong arms and round shoulders, massaging Tzippy's cramped feet in the middle of the night, brought tears to Tzippy's eyes. She slipped off her shoes and left them lying under the dining room table. She took a deep breath. Perhaps she'd take a bath, in hopes that the warm water would restore her strength and lift her mood. The last person she thought she'd be hearing from was Angie, her long-lost friend and employee. If only Angie were here to help her, to run her bath, to talk to her, everything would be better, wouldn't it? She'd know instinctively whether what Tzippy had tried to do with the clinic had been wrong or right. She'd know what to say to Shari to calm her down, to soothe her, to pull out the poisoned stinger.

Why had she taken that damn money? Tzippy had long suspected that Jack was no good. All those years she and Angie had been together, all those years . . .

Just then, Shari walked in from the deck and sat down. When she saw the strudel on the table, she practically shrieked. "Please, take that stuff away. It's too fattening."

Jocelyn hurried in from the kitchen to remove the offending dessert, then stood, holding the plate and looking down at the envelope in Tzippy's hand, as if she knew what it was. Tzippy shook her head, exasperated, and waited for Shari to calm down. "A piece wouldn't kill you," she said.

Evidently, Shari had been crying, and her nose was red. She had the Bryer nose, not the Finkel nose. Tzippy had always prided herself on the upturned tilt of her fine nose. Now that Shari was angry and tired, her nose, more Roman in shape than Tzippy's, seemed larger and less attractive. Then Tzippy reprimanded herself. Amid all that was going on, why was she dwelling on looks?

"Look at this," Tzippy said, waving the blue envelope at Shari. "A letter from Angie. Can you imagine? She wants to come back here and work."

"I can't believe she wrote you. What a riot," Shari said, raising her shoulders in disbelief.

Jocelyn took a step back as if she had just seen a snake. "What does she want, after what she went and did?" She looked like she might hurl the strudel on the floor. "I hope she knows she done ruined a good thing."

"Well, you can't fault her for trying," Tzippy said. "She was here a long time."

"My goodness," Jocelyn said. Now she held the plate of strudel close to her chest. "I hope she don't get any ideas."

Tzippy shook her head back and forth at Shari, showing her dislike at Jocelyn's moxie as the maid returned to the kitchen.

"She wrote to apologize," Tzippy told Shari. "You're free to read it." Tzippy held out the card, trying to be friendlier and bring them closer.

"I need something stronger than tea," Shari said. She jumped up and returned with a glass of ice-cold Tanqueray.

"Now, watch yourself," Tzippy said.

Shari took a sip. "What did she say?" she asked, examining the card.

"See for yourself. Go on, read it."

While Shari was examining Angie's card and message, the phone rang, and though Jocelyn darted into the room, Tzippy motioned her away. It was Brucie. *Poor, sweet bespectacled Brucie*, Tzippy thought. Maybe she should discuss the court business with him—he was Ben's substitute, after all—but now that Jill had left, he was distracted and not himself. She had to tell Stan and get it over with. Tzippy reassured herself that she was tougher than she realized.

"Brucie. How are you, sweetheart?"

"I'm struggling but hanging in. Business is still bad. Bank's up my ass. I'm working with my attorney on the divorce agreement. What about you?"

"Oh. Wedding details. Some new things I'm doing. And I just got a letter from Angie. She's admitted to taking the money. She's sorry and wants to be forgiven."

"Forgiving's easy," Brucie said. "But you're not taking her back, are you, Mom?"

"I don't know what to do. You know, she was very good to me in many ways."

"You were always a softie when it came to her. Do what you want, but don't come crying to me if she turns out bad."

"Brucie, don't say that."

"I just hate to see you hurt again. What does Shari think?"

"She's right here. Let me put the phone on speaker so we can talk. I'll let you ask her," Tzippy said. She pressed the button and heard an echoing hollowness.

"Hey there, big brother. How are you?" Shari said. Her voice was a little too loud, overcompensating. "Getting used to being single?"

"No, not really," Bruce said. His voice sounded as if he were at the end of a long, winding cave. "You were never good at it either. How's it going with PJ?"

"Pretty good. A little crazy," she said, smiling widely.

Tzippy suddenly felt left out. "She sees him practically every other night," she said. "You know, Brucie, the year Shari was born they made the movie *The Seven Year Itch* with Marilyn Monroe? Well, I think some of Marilyn's sex appeal has rubbed off on Shari!"

"Sounds serious," Brucie said, and made *woo-woo* noises.

"Oh, stop it," Shari said, blushing. "I like him well enough, but he's a lawyer, so I don't entirely trust him."

Tzippy looked up in surprise when she heard Shari say this first disparaging thing about her new beau.

"Be careful," Brucie said. "What do you think of this Angie business?"

"God, I don't know. I just heard about it a second ago. We've been fighting about other things." Shari looked at her mother and widened her eyes.

"Like what?"

"Oh, Mom's got this idea that she can fix what happened in the past between the two of us by going to some eating disorder clinic and visiting sick girls in the hospital. Can you imagine? At this point in time?"

"Listen," Tzippy butted in, "it's a wonderful clinic and this woman had a daughter who was ill, like Shari, but she died."

"I don't know what to say on that subject," Brucie said. "You guys always have a difficult time communicating. Maybe Mom wants to do better by you, Bluebell," he said. "You ought to give it a chance. It's never too late."

"Oh, you're a fine one to talk," Shari said. She stood and gestured with her gin. "You always take her side. I'm not too happy about the whole subject. In fact, I'm pissed. A little too late, in my opinion." She took a large swallow of gin. "And please remember I was the one who caught Angie with the cash. She's a thief, for goodness' sake! This isn't easy for me to say. Angie and I used to be real close." She shot Tzippy a look. "Our mother, however, will do exactly what she wants. Listen, I'm going to sign off and go have a cigarette. Here's Mom—you talk to her."

Shari went out onto the deck again.

"You see what's going on here?" Tzippy said, as she turned off the speakerphone and spoke to Bruce directly.

"Mom, hang in there."

"I'm serious about the eating disorder clinic. I'm going to go to a parents' group. In fact, I'm going to return to visit the girl in the hospital. I have to keep trying to fix things."

"Good for you. Shari's just being a pain in the ass, as usual."

"She's so difficult to be with now," she continued, keeping her voice low.

"Give her time."

"Brucie, you're such a dear. When will you be down for the wedding?"

"The day before. I have a lot of legal matters to attend to. Jill's lawyer and mine are butting heads, and I'm pretty upset. I haven't slept one full night in weeks."

"I thought all she wanted was the Porsche," Tzippy said.

"Right. That was for starters. Now it's china, silver, and stocks."

"I knew it was too easy." Her voice grew louder.

"She'd like me to sell the house and give her half."

"No!" she said.

"The damn problem is that she's entitled."

"I thought the cardiologist had three houses. Why does she need your house money?"

"She's no fool. She's hedging her bets."

"My, my, what a mess. I'm getting a click on the line. Let me go. We'll talk later."

"Love you, Mom."

"Love you, too."

Tzippy hit the flash button and heard Stan's soothing voice. "Hi, baby cakes, what's up?" he said, and then, after listening, added, "I see you have *tsuris*. Listen, why don't we have dinner and talk? Take Shari, too?"

"I doubt she'll want to come, but I'll ask her. What time?"

"Seven."

"Fine. Let me go. I have a lot to do before you come and pick me up."

As Tzippy hung up, Shari came in from the deck and announced, "PJ is coming over to get me and take me to dinner."

"Gosh, do I need some cocktail food?"

"No, we'll be leaving right away."

"Good. I'm going out with Stan."

In her bathroom, Tzippy turned on the Jacuzzi's faucet full blast and poured in vanilla-scented bath salts. As the wide tub filled with pale blue and pink bubbles, she sat down on the long vanity bench and stared at herself in the mirror. She shook her head, aggravated at the level of difficulty in her life, and then briskly rubbed cold cream over her makeup, grabbed a tissue, and wiped the residue from her face.

On the other side of the hall, Tzippy heard Shari enter the bathroom that had been Angie's, then turn on the shower. She also heard a wastebasket banging, the sound of something being thrown. Tzippy clutched herself and rocked with shame.

Then she took a pill and mixed the hot water with the cold until it was just the right temperature—a chore Angie had performed perfectly in the old days. She lowered herself into the tub and let the warm water soothe her as she watched the bubbles float around and felt the medication take effect. After a few minutes, she started to rehearse her speech to Stan.

"Stan, I have something to tell you. It's not awful, but I want you to know," she started.

"Stan, I hope you won't be upset with me. I'm embarrassed to tell you this," she uttered.

"Sweetie, I have a small matter to discuss. I hope you won't be shocked," she tried again.

It was useless. She would have to use her feminine charms and be direct, she decided. She dried herself off with her thick towels and rubbed Laura Mercier cream on her dry skin. How she hated the way her body had shriveled and lost its elasticity. No matter how many lotions she applied, her skin never returned to the suppleness of her middle years. It was a pity. As her dear friend, Selma, used to say, "After fifty, it's patch, patch, patch." Then she applied her makeup with care, rubbing foundation on her face and patting it with a small sponge, like the makeup girl at Neiman's had taught her to do. She'd learned how to camouflage the brown spots and give herself color on her cheeks without looking overdone. She finished with a little black mascara and some powder-pink lipstick, and when she examined herself in the mirror, she had to smile at her reflection. She put on a pretty blue cocktail dress with a sweetheart neckline. She wanted to look especially attractive; she hoped it would help when she told Stan about the arrest. She added diamond studs to her ears and scrutinized the results. *For an old bird*, she thought, *I still have style.*

Shari appeared in a black sheath, with pearls on her neck and wrist. One side of her hair was combed behind her ear. Her lips were coral. She was stunning, Tzippy thought; she nodded her approval. "You look lovely." Another rush of guilt flooded her, and she was glad when she heard a knock on her front door.

PJ wore an open-collared white linen shirt and black slacks. He appeared poised, rich, and handsome. "Hi there, ladies," he said, glancing around Tzippy's apartment. "I don't remember the last time I was here. Must have been a while. Very attractive place, Tzippy."

"Why, thank you, PJ. What have you been up to today?" Tzippy asked.

"Hi, sweetheart," PJ said, planting a kiss on Shari's cheek. "You look swell. I went out on my boat for a few hours. The bone fishing was terrific. It was a beautiful day to be on the water. I love seeing all the hotels along the beach when we come in, the jet planes overhead, the small boats passing by, the palm trees," he said, smiling at Tzippy. "How are you feeling?" he asked Shari.

"Still edgy."

"PJ, I'm just trying to repair old damage," Tzippy said.

"You ladies have a lot of history. Please, don't get me in the middle," PJ said.

Just then, Stan knocked on the door and Jocelyn let him in. He looked debonair in a pale yellow sport jacket and tan slacks. "Hi, everyone. Are you guys joining us?"

"No," Shari said. "I think my mother and I have seen enough of each other today. Why don't we go?" she said, turning to PJ.

"Have a drink first," Stan suggested. "I haven't seen PJ in ages. Stay and have a quick cocktail," he said, gesturing toward the couch.

"I'd love to," PJ said.

"No, I really want to go," Shari said.

"She's the boss," PJ said.

"Aw, come on, Shari. You have one, too. Be friendly," Stan said. He walked over to the bar and said, "What will you have, PJ?"

"Scotch, neat," PJ said quickly.

Tzippy watched Shari grimace and brought a coaster to put under PJ's drink.

"Shari, what about you? Tanqueray?" Stan asked.

"Sure. I'll have mine neat, too," she said, sitting on the yellow sofa.

"Tzippy, how about a glass of wine?" Stan said.

"Fine," she said. "Jocelyn, please bring some salted nuts."

"See, isn't this better?" Stan said, sitting on the chair by the yellow sofa with a drink in his hand. "PJ, how's the law business?"

"Oh, I'm busy as hell, Stan. There's no end to what people need to litigate," PJ said.

"Isn't it crazy how the world has become? Everyone is suing someone for something. The poor doctors are always in trouble," Stan said. "My pal Dr. Marlburg just got hit with a malpractice suit. He prescribed some meds for a man with arthritis, and the poor fellow developed colon cancer. What a bitch," Stan said. Tzippy put some cocktail napkins on the table and gave one to Shari.

"Stuff happens. What are you going to do? You have to be very careful nowadays," PJ said.

"You want me to serve some pea soup?" Jocelyn asked, as she set the bowl of mixed nuts on the coffee table.

"No, that won't be necessary. We'll have that tomorrow," said Tzippy.

"PJ, can we go now?" Shari said.

Tzippy pushed the mixed nuts toward PJ. She shifted her weight in the chair and leaned toward Stan.

"How's that prenup? Are the thirty days up yet?" Stan asked. He bit down on a chip of ice in his mouth. Tzippy hated when Stan did that, like a kid on the playground. She wished he would have the courage to say what was on his mind, which included resentment about her asking him to sign a prenup in the first place.

"Mother, make him stop talking."

"Stan, darling, the kids want to go to dinner," Tzippy said.

"The prenup's thirty days will be up when you two lovebirds tie the knot," PJ said.

"No one listens to me in this family," Shari said, banging down her emptied drink on the coffee table.

Tzippy flinched.

"What's the matter with you tonight, Shari?" Stan asked.

"What's the matter is that I've spent the whole day with my mother, who has been filling my head with some weird ideas she has about fixing the past."

"I think if your mother is trying to fix things, it sounds like a brave thing to do," Stan said.

"Well, good for you," Shari said. "What do you think?" she said, turning to PJ.

"I told you when I got here, I don't want to be put in the middle. But in general I've always thought your mother was a good soul," he said diplomatically.

"Oh, that's just great," Shari said. "Why do I ever expect support? Can we *please* go to dinner now?"

PJ got up from the sofa and put down his glass. "Tzippy, thanks for the drink. We're on our way to a new place in South Beach. Gotta go," he said. "Nice talking to you, Stan." He took Shari by the hand and led her to the door.

"Good night, you two," said Tzippy. "Have fun."

After they left, Stan turned to Tzippy and said, "What was that all about?"

"Oh, let's just go ourselves, and I'll tell you all about it as we drive," Tzippy said.

"Okay, baby cakes. You lead the way."

"Have a nice time," Jocelyn said.

"We'll have that pea soup tomorrow for lunch, Jocelyn. It does smell delicious," Tzippy said.

"I'm coming over for some, too," Stan said.

"You're very kind to say that, Mr. Stan," Jocelyn said, smiling. Tzippy closed the front door and hugged Stan's arm tight. He was a good man. The way he'd stood up for her had thrilled her. Maybe he wouldn't be too upset when she told him about the brooch.

Chapter 16

'm sorry," Tzippy said, as she and Stan drove away, "but I'm glad Shari and PJ are having dinner by themselves." She noticed the car's sagging roof lining, as she always did. She batted at it as if it were a live thing. She had never thought she would be riding in a car that looked like it suffered from Panama Canal humidity.

"Shari couldn't sit still just now," Stan said. "I guess I shouldn't have insisted they stay for a drink. What got into her?"

"She's all upset," Tzippy said. "She found out I went to that eating disorder clinic and visited the girl in the hospital, like I told you. That really set her off."

Stan took a deep breath. "Now, don't get me wrong," he said. "I should have mentioned this before, but how will visiting a strange girl help?"

Tzippy flashed him a look of annoyance. "I need to learn," she said. "I need to understand what I might have done that made Shari do the things she did."

"Why not ask her?" Stan said.

"Ask her?" Tzippy said. "What do you mean, 'ask her'?"

"At least she'll have an opinion," Stan said. "I noticed she's not too short on those. But maybe it's all too far in the past." He pulled into a line of traffic on the left.

"That's what Shari says," Tzippy told him. "But I think that's because it makes her so uncomfortable."

"Maybe you should have warned her before you went, given her a heads-up," Stan said diplomatically.

"Maybe I should have, but Shari makes me anxious and I was afraid of her reaction. It's a miracle she never went to a hospital. She was a mess as a teenager, all skin and bones. You should have seen the girl at St. Frances. She's twenty-three but looks like a child."

"Unbelievable. How come these girls do this to themselves? I don't get it."

"Neither do I, exactly. That's why I want to go to a support group."

"Why don't you take Shari along?"

"I just thought I'd go to a parents' group first. Get my sea legs."

"You'll need more than sea legs with her. More like mountain legs, if you ask me."

"Oh, Stan, it's been a day. On top of everything, I got a letter from Angie. I brought it to show you. She's very sorry about taking my money and wants to come back. She says Jack was a bad friend."

"Ha! I suspected he was a scammer. Where is she?"

"Up at Orchid Island, working for a couple."

"And she wants to return to little old Tzippy and not stay up there in that beautiful area? She must miss you. Aren't you afraid she'll steal again? Once a thief . . ."

Tzippy felt a pit in her stomach. "I think she learned her lesson," she said. "Nobody's perfect." Quietly, she opened the baby-blue silk purse that matched her dress and slipped out a small white pill from her vial inside, then put it on her tongue and swallowed.

"Where would we put her?" Stan said.

Tzippy glanced at him, but his face was expressionless and she couldn't tell whether he thought the whole thing with Angie was yet another one of her bad ideas.

"I know you were going to use the extra bedroom as your study," Tzippy said uncertainly. "Maybe I'm . . ."

Stan cut her off. "By the way, are we all set with the wedding?"

"I gave the rabbi our Hebrew names and told him no 'obeys' in the vows."

"That's my girl—we're a modern couple," he said.

Tzippy laughed and squeezed his hand.

"Well, we're here, baby cakes. Your favorite restaurant, just like you requested." It was called White Chateau and looked like an elegant old mansion with beautiful stained-glass windows. They stopped before the columns flanking the front door, and a young valet took the car keys while Tzippy clasped Stan's arm.

The night was balmy, with a slight breeze. Tzippy could feel the humidity, but it wasn't as heavy as it had been during the day. In fact, everything that had weighed on her earlier seemed easier to take. She took a deep breath and, miraculously, didn't cough; she felt fortunate that she was in Florida, not up north in the snow and cold.

"Did I tell you that you look particularly fetching tonight?" Stan asked, as they walked through the heavy ornate door.

"No, but thank you, honey," Tzippy said.

She sighed. Stan just made everything better, somehow; he helped her put things in perspective. She hoped her sweetheart neckline would keep him in a good mood.

The hostess, a young Jamaican woman dressed in a dark suit, led them to their table, the one in the corner that Tzippy liked so much. Round, with a small lamp with an antique shade, it felt intimate and safe. She sat across from Stan and, after the waitress brought their drinks, said, "I have to show you Angie's card." She took out the blue envelope. "It's the nicest note. Read it."

Stan sipped his dry martini and studied the envelope. "Her handwriting looks like a kid's, for God's sake."

"I know. I don't think she went too far in school."

He opened up the card and admired the design. "Attractive... nice inscription, too."

Tzippy gave him time to take it all in. She sipped her wine and waited for his responses.

"Well," he said, "she does sound like she wants to come back and feels really bad. I'm amazed."

"I do miss her," Tzippy said, "and she would be a great help to us."

Stan stared at her, with the smallest hint of a smile on his lips. "We'd have to get a larger place, one with three bedrooms, so I could have a study."

"Move into another place? All those boxes and packing—and the cost," Tzippy said.

"I'll pay the difference so we can be comfortable," he said. "Just be sure you can trust her before you make us move and rearrange ourselves, baby cakes."

Tzippy was filled with a rush of love and gratitude. "Stan, you are the sweetest man," she said. "I am so lucky."

"I've been telling you that for years. You just wouldn't listen."

The waitress came to the table and said, "Have you had a chance to look at the menu?"

"Give us another minute," Stan said. When the waitress left, he asked Tzippy, "What do you feel like having tonight?"

"Maybe some salmon."

"Let's split a Caesar, no anchovies." He pushed his lips together, then relaxed them. "What are we going to tell Jocelyn? She was my old maid, remember?"

"I'll just tell her that Angie wants another chance and I feel I have to give her that much," Tzippy said.

"Yeah," Stan said, "okay. But I'd better be there when you tell her. She has a temper on her."

The waitress reappeared and asked, "Ready now?"

"Tell the chef to please make my steak well done. No pink," he said, after he had given her the order. "And another martini." Tzippy was still nursing her first glass of chardonnay.

She noted, as she often had, how particular Stan was about the way he liked his food and drink. He had his rituals and allegiances and his strict moral code. Once again, she was struck with fear about the brooch, but she had promised herself that tonight would be the night to tell him, so she pushed herself to move forward.

"I have something else to tell you," she started, her voice scratchy.

Stan didn't seem to notice her trepidation. "Lay it on me, baby cakes," he said, arching his eyebrows.

"It's not a huge deal,' she said. "I mean, I hope you won't think it is."

She looked past him and suddenly wanted to leave the table and walk right out of the White Chateau and into the evening air.

"Tzippy," he said, "you okay?" He had dropped his comic manner and was staring at her intently. He pulled his chair closer to the table. The waitress breezed up with their fresh drinks. "There you go," he said.

"I mean, when you were a kid in Newark . . ." Tzippy said, staring in front of Stan's glass.

"Out with it," Stan said.

"I got caught taking something at Saks," she said.

A look of puzzlement crossed Stan's face. "Taking something?"

"A brooch," Tzippy said. "It was on sale."

"You got caught shoplifting?"

"Well, yes."

"Baby cakes, let me give you a tip from an old-timer: if you're going to pinch something, make sure it's full price."

"Stan, I wish you wouldn't joke around," Tzippy said, offended. "This is hard for me."

"Sorry," Stan said. He lifted his martini glass and took a large swallow. "Waitress," he called, flinging his arm in the air. The woman swooped down and bent over attentively. "Another one," he said. "Just like the other one."

"Now, don't drink too much, sweetheart," Tzippy said. "You know it makes you sleepy."

"Forgive me, baby cakes, but you dropped quite a bomb on me. I'd say the occasion warrants as many cocktails as I need, if I'm going to absorb this latest development."

"You're right, Stan. I'm being insensitive, and I apologize." She pushed and swirled the chardonnay in her glass. "You remember the night before my birthday party, when the kids and I all went to dinner?"

"Yeah, sure," he said. "Who can forget that brouhaha? Isn't that when Brucie gave poor Shari the old Indian burn?"

"Exactly. I was terribly shaken up by the whole episode."

"I can't blame you," he said. His third martini appeared, and he picked it up and sipped it.

"Well, this happened the next day. I've been meaning to tell you," she said, looking at Stan for a clue. "That whole fight with Brucie and Shari made me so distraught."

Stan nodded. "So you stole a pin at Saks and the store dicks saw you," he said.

There, she thought—he'd summed it up as bluntly as possible. Regret washed over her. As she sipped her wine, she willed herself to be braver. Rubbing her lips together, she said. "I think I'd like another glass of chardonnay, Stan."

He nodded, then asked, "So, what happened? I assume you're not telling me just because you want to confess, make a clean breast of it before the wedding." He stared meaningfully at her cleavage.

Tzippy didn't know how to respond. She had spent days worrying herself sick about telling Stan, and here he was, treating it all like a big joke.

She didn't want to go into the details: the store detectives, the police car, the fingerprints, and the chair next to the jail cell. Despite Stan's past, she couldn't say the words. She was a lady, and at her age, it was embarrassing.

"Yes, unfortunately, I have to go to court," she said lightly.

"No kidding?" Stan said. "They booked you for a dumb brooch? Those bastards!" Piano music drifted in the background. "My Funny Valentine." She and Ben had danced to that song long ago.

The wine was beginning to relax her, and she said, "The court date is after the wedding. PJ is taking care of all the legal matters." She waited to see what Stan would say next.

"I'm a little surprised by this news, Tzippy," Stan finally said.

"Yes, I'm sure you are." She sat up straighter and stuck out her breasts, exposing more cleavage in the sweetheart neckline.

"I mean, why'd you do it? You've got plenty of money."

She blushed hard and sat back in her chair. "I told you, I was upset," she said. "I didn't know what I was doing."

"Well, everyone makes mistakes," he said, nodding. "That's why there are erasers on pencils." Then, lifting what was left of his martini up in the air, Stan toasted, "To my bride, Tzippy the thief."

Tzippy squirmed in her seat, wishing Stan hadn't put it quite that way. "Oh, Stan," she said. Then she whispered, "Thanks for being understanding." A wave of relief washed over her. As she sipped her drink, she tried to regain her composure.

"That's okay," Stan said. "I'm feeling no pain."

Their Caesar salad arrived with a flourish of black pepper and fresh parmesan, as well as warm bread, soft and fresh, and butter in a small crock with parsley strewn on top. They sat in silence for a few minutes. When the waitress returned with their entrées, Stan sat back and rubbed his hands. "Now, this is more like it," he said. He cut into his steak with an industrial-size knife and shook his head as pink juice spread on his plate. He flagged the waitress. "Tell the chef he can do better," he insisted.

Tzippy had picked up a lemon wedge to squeeze over her salmon, when Stan said, "Isn't it funny, kind of, how you and Angie both took things?"

"I don't know if it's *funny*, exactly, but, yes, it is a strange coincidence. However, I would never steal from an employer or a personal friend of mine—that's the difference."

"You two are a pair—I'll give you that," he said, laughing. "It will be okay. I'll go with you and PJ to court. Don't worry, baby cakes," he said, draining his glass. It occurred to Tzippy that in court the judge would probably bring up the earlier times she'd been seen and not questioned. At some point, she'd have to tell Stan the whole sordid story, right from the beginning.

He reached out to her across the round table, and she took his hand. "Thank you, Stan, from the bottom of my heart," she said. "You always rise to the occasion."

"Oho!" Stan said, and wiggled his eyebrows at her. "Just you wait until later."

After coffee, they walked outside and waited for the Cadillac. The palm trees swayed slightly in the night air as Tzippy looked at the other couples in front of the White Chateau. Many of the women had blond hair and had spent so long in the sun that they resembled beef jerky. Tzippy *tsk*'d with distaste. The men, too, were tan but also often bald and a bit potbellied.

The valet came back with Stan's car, and they'd just pulled away when Stan said, "I have an announcement myself."

"What's that?"

"Freddy's got a buddy who sells Caddies, and I've decided to trade mine in and buy a new one in honor of our wedding. We can't be arriving at the Breakers in this old thing, as you would say. No, my bride will be driving up in style. A brand-new Caddy, shiny and bright, for you." He smiled and looked at Tzippy indulgently.

"Why, that's wonderful, Stan. I'm so pleased." *Thank God,* she thought. *I can stop riding under this shabby, sagging headliner once and for all.*

"I thought you'd be, baby cakes."

On their way home, Stan took Tzippy's hand and had her rub his crotch. She could feel his erection. He hummed along the way. "All for you, baby cakes," he said.

Tzippy was light-headed from the wine and from all the good news. Stan wasn't mad, Angie was coming home, and Stan was getting a new car. She was in a good mood as they approached the door, but her heart sank at the sound of loud voices inside.

She swung open the door and walked in. Shari stood in the living room with a glass of clear liquid in her hand. "You know, PJ, it's about simple respect. It's the *principle* of the thing," she said.

PJ's white linen shirt looked less crisp than it had earlier in the evening, and he scowled as he spoke. "God! How many times do I have to tell you?" he said. "I was just chatting."

"I thought you were better than that," Shari said.

"What's going on here?" Stan asked, as he and Tzippy entered the room.

PJ looked relieved to see them. "I'm glad you're back," he said. "Maybe you can talk some sense into her."

"Shari?" Tzippy said. "What's the matter?"

"Everything was fine," PJ said, "until I got a cell call and made the mistake of answering it." He sat down on the yellow sofa and put his elbows on his knees and his face in his hands.

"He took a phone call from some chick while he was out on a date with me. For God's sake, some people have absolutely no manners," Shari said. She stared at PJ with disdain.

Tzippy cleared her throat. Sweat was forming on PJ's upper lip.

Stan smiled and tried to lighten things up. He went to Shari and tried to touch her, but she flinched. "What happened? You were in the ladies' room and he took a call?"

PJ stood up. "That's exactly what happened, Stan." His voice was quiet and controlled.

Shari, who had looked beautiful earlier in the evening, now seemed worn out by anxiety; she had dark shadows under her eyes. "I'm not accustomed to coming back from the ladies' to find my date on the goddamn phone with another woman," she said. "It's unacceptable."

Tzippy understood her discomfort and even sympathized with her outburst—after all, who on Earth would want to come back from the restroom to find her boyfriend on the phone with some other woman? But she also wasn't surprised in the least; given PJ's track record. Nor did she want Shari to end up with him anyway. So she kept her mouth shut. All the while, Stan kept trying to smooth things over and make everyone happy, but the more he smiled, the more agitated Shari became.

"Maybe it was a business colleague who called," Tzippy said.

Shari sat down on the sofa, defeated. "You know, Mom, only you would say something as dumb as that. Clients or fellow attorneys don't call at eight o'clock on a Saturday night. Do you think I'm an idiot?" She paused and then answered her own question. "Yes, you do. All my life, you've thought that."

"Oh, sweetie," Tzippy said. She went to the sofa and sat beside her daughter and tried to put her arm around her, but Shari pulled away. "I absolutely do not think that, Shari, but let's talk about this in private." Tzippy briefly wondered why she wasn't being kinder and more supportive toward Shari. She could reprimand PJ; his behavior had been rude. He could have let the call go to voice mail and answered the woman tomorrow. What the hell was the rush? But then, scolding PJ wouldn't make things any easier on him and Shari—they all knew it.

"I have just about had it down here in Miami," Shari said, getting up off the yellow sofa. She walked to the coat closet, opened it, and took her suitcase down from the top shelf.

Tzippy went into the kitchen and started the coffeemaker. Stan was right. She put cups, a plate of cookies, and a few apple strudels on a tray and carried it back to the living room. A little sugar never hurt anyone.

Shari still had the suitcase and looked as though she might swing it if someone came too close. The she turned her back and disappeared into Tzippy's bedroom. She tried to close the door, but PJ had followed her and blocked it with his hand. He stood in the doorway and asked, "What's going on, Shari?"

"I'm leaving—that's what's going on," she said. From the living room, Tzippy could hear how shaky her voice sounded.

"Don't do this, Shari. You can't leave now," PJ said.

"And just why the hell not?"

"It's your mother's wedding, for starters. Because of us, for another reason. This is unexpected," PJ said. "It was just a stupid mistake. Old habits."

"All true," she said. "But I'm still sick of this scene."

She walked out the bedroom, carrying a pair of shoes.

"I feel bad, you acting like this," PJ said, following her.

"Listen, you and I are going nowhere," Shari said, turning to look at him. "I thought maybe something could develop, even marriage. What a fool I am."

"Marriage? Who said anything about marriage?" PJ said.

"*You* did, PJ. You've been telling me this whole time that you could see yourself with me in the long term."

PJ recoiled and said, "Whoa, Shari—don't be naive. For

one thing, I'm not marrying someone with an alcohol problem. You're a goddamn lush."

That was the last straw for Shari, and she burst into tears.

Tzippy flashed her eyes at Stan in dismay, but he merely motioned her to go get the coffee. She went into the kitchen and returned with the coffeepot, creamer, and a sugar bowl. Scattering spoons and napkins on the tablecloth, she said, "Let's have some coffee and clear our heads. It's late. This will help."

Reluctantly, Shari and PJ sat down at the table, along with Stan, as Tzippy filled cups for them. Then she sat at the head of the table and passed around the plate of desserts. "Here, have a sweet," she said to PJ.

"That apple strudel looks good. Where did you get it? My grandma used to make the best. God, I remember that from when I was a little boy," he said, picking up a piece and tasting it. "Not bad, but not my nana's."

"My grandmother made bow ties, *kickel,* light as air, covered with sugar. You couldn't eat just one. She made cookie jars full of them," Stan said.

"Why are we talking about food?" Shari asked, as she eyed the apple strudel on the plate.

"The boys were just trying to change the subject," Tzippy said. "Just trying to lighten things up."

"God!" Shari barked. "Listen, I really am leaving. Mom, I'm not going to sit around and watch you visit anorexics after you actively ignored me when I was sick. It's too much."

"Shari, my wedding is in a few weeks," Tzippy said.

"We want you to be here, sweetheart," Stan said. "Don't do this to your mother."

"What's your opinion, PJ? You're the lawyer," Shari said. Then she lifted a piece of strudel from the plate, broke it in half, and nibbled on one part. Tzippy watched her eat the pastry, but she said nothing.

PJ put down his coffee. "Of course you should stay," he said. "How many times does your mother get married?"

"Do you *want* me to stay?"

"With the eating thing, Shari, your mom is trying, and you ought to give her a chance."

"Trying?" Shari said. "You can say that again. She's the most goddamn trying person I know. Well, bully for you, siding with my mother. I don't care." She grabbed another piece of strudel, rose from the table, and returned to Tzippy's bedroom.

Stan got up and said, "Maybe we should leave the ladies alone, PJ. Come on—you and I ought to go. They need to talk."

PJ went to the bedroom door and said, "Shari, I'm leaving."

"Go. Do whatever. Go call your new girlfriend. I don't care," Shari said.

"Listen, this isn't the way I want to leave things between us," PJ said.

"Come on, guy. It's late," Stan said. "You'll talk tomorrow. Enough."

PJ reluctantly left with Stan prodding him from behind.

"I'll call you in the morning, baby cakes," Stan said, as he closed the door behind them.

From the bedroom came the sound of doors and drawers opening and closing. Tzippy cleared off the table and took another pill. God, she hoped she wouldn't get a cramp in her foot during the night while she was sleeping. She was on her own.

She was resting her feet when Shari went to the phone and called Delta to make a reservation.

"I'd like a nonstop flight, as early as possible," she said. Then she turned to Tzippy. "Mom, where did you put the strudel?" she asked.

"Shari," Tzippy said. "Don't."

"Don't what?" Shari said defiantly. "Don't eat any more? I thought you wanted me to eat more. Isn't that what mommies want for their anorexic daughters?" She turned and stalked to the kitchen, Tzippy following.

Tzippy watched as Shari found the strudel, picked up another piece, and raised it, as if daring Tzippy to take it away from her.

"That won't help anything," Tzippy said.

"Oh, yes, it will," Shari said. "It's like drinking. It makes me forget." She pushed the whole thing into her mouth until her cheeks were bulging and something like a smile played on her lips.

Tzippy shook her head, taking short breaths and snorting through her nose—unattractive, she knew, but she couldn't help it. She didn't know whether to cry or to hit Shari. "I'm going to bed," she finally announced.

"Good for you," Shari said. "Sleep. That's another thing that does it. Escape."

"Shari, I am an eighty-year-old woman, and I need my rest." Tzippy went into her bathroom and stared at herself in the mirror. *How could things have gotten so messed up so quickly?* She'd told Stan about the brooch, and the world hadn't ended; she and Stan were getting married; Angie was coming back. But now Shari—poor Shari.

She got undressed. She washed up, slipped into her bed, and lay there, listening. The apartment was silent. Maybe Shari had calmed down. But then Tzippy heard her walk right past the door and into Angie's old bathroom. Quickly, Tzippy sat up, got out of bed, and tiptoed after her. She heard the dead bolt turn dully in its cylinder, then water running, and then the unmistakable sound of vomiting.

Leaning against the bathroom door, she called, "Shari? What are you doing in there?"

The toilet flushed, but the water still ran. "Leave me alone," Shari said. "Go away."

"Shari, let me in," she said.

"No," Shari said. "Never, never, never, never, never."

Tzippy returned to her bed and turned out the light on her side. She couldn't take any more tonight. And all this time she'd thought Shari was better and all that needed to be fixed was the past. How long had this been going on? She hoped to God this was a onetime thing, triggered by Shari's profound upset that day.

Finally, Tzippy's bedroom door opened and Shari stood there for a moment. She looked smaller, more helpless, as though something other than food had been drained out of her. She came to the bed and slipped under the covers on the far side. After setting her alarm clock, she turned off the cherub-heavy lamp and whispered, "Good night" to Tzippy.

"I wish you weren't leaving, Shari," Tzippy said in the darkness.

"I wish a lot of things," Shari said, "but they never come true."

The alarm rang at 5:00 a.m., shocking Tzippy into wakefulness. The morning felt heavy and slow, but Tzippy got up with Shari, who quickly showered and then called downstairs for someone to get her a cab and come for her bags. Tzippy couldn't stop coughing into her tissues. She was so nervous that she took a pill right then.

The sun was barely up. She wrapped a bathrobe and then a pashmina around her for warmth, and asked Shari, "When will I see you next?"

"I don't know, Mom. I'm a mess. I can't stop thinking about PJ talking to some girl while he was out to dinner with me. And what's with all this eating disorder crap?"

"No, sweetie. You tell me."

"What do you mean?"

"I used to be a babe in the woods, but I've learned a few things. You throwing up last night . . ."

"Mom," Shari said. "Don't start."

"I want you to come back so we can go to support groups together. I want to work through this, with you. Enough of us stumbling around in the dark. We have lot of unfinished business."

A man came to the door and took Shari's bags and told her the cab was waiting.

"Thanks," Shari said. Then, after he left, she turned to Tzippy and said, "I feel so fat. All that strudel. I'm too messed up to work on anything at the moment."

"Oh, sweetheart. Please, let's not stop trying," Tzippy said, and took her daughter in her arms. "We'll do whatever we have to do," she said.

"I don't know, Mom. I'm not very strong," Shari started to cry. "And PJ is right: I *am* a goddamn lush. Why would anyone want to marry me?"

"Oh, dear," Tzippy said, dropping her arms. "Maybe you could stop—"

"I gotta go. I don't want to miss my plane. Have a nice wedding," she said, opening the door and lifting a small carry-on.

"What about your dress? I love that dress on you."

"Save it for me. I'll wear it for something else. Maybe I'll wear it to a support group."

Tzippy watched her walk down the corridor, carrying her bag, and as Shari turned the corner to the elevator, she stopped and gave a slight wave with her free hand. Tzippy stood in the hallway, an old lady in the early morning, and waved back, tears falling down her wrinkled cheeks. Before the sun was high over the vast ocean outside her apartment, before the bathers were lying out on their chaise lounges by the pool with its turquoise water, before the lifeguard was sitting high in his seat to guard the swimmers, Tzippy Bryer ached for her troubled daughter and bade her good-bye.

Chapter 17

The previous evening's close had been so unreal, and she had gotten so little sleep, that Tzippy felt as if she might have dreamed her daughter's precipitous departure and that when she returned to her bed, she'd find Shari still in it. But the bed was empty and Tzippy lay down with a groan. Recalling Shari's farewell wave in the corridor, she rested on the pillows and covered herself with a blanket. It felt safe there. And it felt good to be safe, and she wished for a release from all her responsibilities; she wished to be as blameless as a child in the womb or a fledgling in the nest. Her body felt heavy and her eyelids closed easily as she sank into the soft pillows, still wrapped in the pashmina.

When she woke two hours later, at 7:30 a.m., she felt somewhat better, though hardly renewed, and before she could stop them, a host of doubts and unwanted questions assailed her. Still spent and weary, with a cramp beginning to creep up her lower leg, she listened to the competing voices in her head.

You can do it. You'll be fine, said one voice. *You have hard work to do, and it won't be easy, but you have to keep pursuing your dreams. You're not afraid to do that, even if you're eighty.* The voice she heard was instructive and cheerful, urging her on; it sounded like her voice, but it seemed to come from somewhere outside her, some alternate Tzippy who was more optimistic, energetic, and restless. *You have a wedding to plan,* she said, closing her eyes and imagining herself walking down the aisle. *You can't fall down. Good works to perform.*

Then another voice, softer, whispered, *Why did you think you could do this? You're killing yourself with this whole Shari business. You ought to be lying on a chaise, reading a good book. At your age, for God's sake.*

Stop thinking negatively, the more positive voice said. *The court will go all right. Leave it to PJ. Stay optimistic. The wedding will be flawless, like you want. Stan is a wonderful guy. You and Shari will reach a new plateau. Maybe you can send Angie and Naomi to bring her here for the wedding. That would make things better. You are trying to be a better person. You will do philanthropic work.*

The list exhausted Tzippy, but she was determined and the voice rose in defiance. *You can do this, you want to do this, and you have promised yourself you will do this. Invest in yourself. Before you die.*

She decided to soak in the tub, to cleanse her body and soothe her aches, both in and out. She added a few drops of her favorite bubble bath and let the water, as hot as she could stand, froth it into foam. She eased in, and as she washed her body and rubbed her skin, she kept talking to herself, convincing herself that she was strong.

And then, the voice scolded, *you must call the doctor.* The voice surprised her; she hadn't even realized the issue had been poised in her unconscious, ready to leap. It had been well over a month since she'd gotten the call from Dr. Waterday's office. Hadn't she better make an appointment? She had put off that phone call, not wanting to deal with thoughts of sickness and possible death. She had her bucket list to finish, a long list of adventures she wanted to check off. Didn't she want to go to Israel and kiss the wall? Buy an original French chemise? Look at the statue of David in Florence one more time? *There will be no dancing once you're gone, Tzippy,* the voice said sadly. Smelling the scent of vanilla in her bathwater, she wiggled her toes. *But right now, you will regain your strength. You will refuse to buckle. You will give whatever you have to in order to live your life to the fullest while you can. Yes, yes, that's the spirit!*

By the time Tzippy finished her bath, Jocelyn had arrived to make her breakfast. The tea was hot and the toast was covered with raspberry jam, her favorite. While Tzippy ate at the dining room table, she opened the *Herald* and skimmed the news.

When she was finished, she went into her bedroom and, after making sure her door was locked, picked up the phone and called Angie's cell. Picturing Angie's squat and sturdy body, her fleshy cheeks and bright eyes, Tzippy smiled. Angie was a singer. As she made the beds, washed the clothes, cooked the food, she sang, high and booming. Even in the bathroom, when she took a pee, she kept on with her singing. She was a happy soul, thought Tzippy. She was filled with a great deal of love.

The phone rang several times, and Tzippy was afraid she was about to get Angie's voice mail, when the static stopped and she heard the familiar voice.

"Hello," Angie said, sounding as if she were wavering between annoyance and unease.

"Angie," Tzippy finally said, "this is Tzippy. I'm calling you because you wrote to me." She tried to be more formal than usual. "How are you?"

"I'm feeling fine, Mrs. B. How are you?"

"Tired, but okay."

"Oh, I'm glad you called me so soon. I was worried."

"Well, it was a nice card. I liked it and was surprised to receive it, to be honest," Tzippy said. She took a sip of water.

"I wanted to send you something special. You don't know how I've been suffering."

Tzippy didn't know what to say at first. How could she

reprimand Angie when she herself was going to court for theft? Finally, she answered, "We should talk in person, don't you think?"

"I'd like that, Mrs. B. Can we do that tomorrow?"

"Yes," Tzippy said, relieved that the next day was Jocelyn's day off, so she wouldn't have to finesse anything. "When can you get here?"

"I can catch a bus first thing. How's eleven sound? That will give me enough time to come down from Vero."

"Yes, eleven will work. Come to the condo so we can meet in private."

"Yes, Mrs. B. I'm really happy to hear from you," Angie said. A moment of silence passed, and then she said, "I've missed you."

Tzippy hadn't wanted to act too friendly, but she whispered, "I've missed you, too." The words just spilled out, like the contents of a purse.

"I know you have," Angie whispered back.

And then the line went dead. Tzippy sat on top of her bed and felt her strength return. This was what she was supposed to do: reunite with Angie. Then she recalled how Angie used to say, "Sure looks like we're going steady." The memory made Tzippy shake her head and smile.

Tzippy immediately called Stan and reported. "I called Angie. She's coming tomorrow. Shari left at the crack of dawn, and Jocelyn is here," she said, all in one breath.

"Well, you've been a busy bee."

"I have. I'll be exhausted by noon." She laughed. "What a night we had."

"PJ was complaining all the way down the elevator. 'Shari's overreacting, she's nuts, blah, blah.' I think he shouldn't have taken the damn call; that way, all the fuss could have been avoided. He plays too close to the edge, that guy."

"Well, now Shari's back home and will miss the wedding. It's a mess, Stan, let me tell you. After you and PJ left, she ate a lot of strudel—bam, bam, bam. Then she went to the john and made herself throw up. I was shocked. I thought all this was behind her, but she's still sick. They call it bingeing and purging."

"That girl needs some serious help. Why don't you get her into rehab?" Stan laughed, but of course, she knew, he was serious.

"Are you sure that's necessary? I thought she could come back and the two of us would go to support groups together," Tzippy said, coughing into a wad of tissues.

"Well, that's good for starters, but it might not solve everything the way an inpatient program could. Plus, how did you like PJ calling her a lush?"

"She called *herself* a lush this morning. Yes, something has to be done."

"Well, if you can't get her to commit to some kind of inpatient treatment, at least get her going to regular AA meetings."

She changed the subject. "Will you come over when I tell Jocelyn about Angie?"

"I said I would. No problem."

"And I need you to take me to the store to pick up my dress, after one more try-on, and Shari's, at some point," she said. "And then to the hairdresser's so I can have my hair combed," she added, hoping Maria could fit her in.

"Whatever you want, baby cakes."

"Thanks, Stan. You're a doll. I'm going to make a few calls now. Come over in an hour, okay?"

"You got it."

Feeling renewed and more confident, she called Dr. Waterday's office. "When was the last time you were in?" the nurse asked.

"It's been a while. I'm getting remarried, and I've been tied up with that."

"Well, a wedding will certainly take up your time. As I recall, the last time you were in the middle of a family party. You are one busy woman, Mrs. Bryer."

Before Tzippy hung up, she made an appointment to see Dr. Waterday at his office. She would just go and deal with whatever he told her. She'd take a cab. No need for Stan to get upset for nothing. Poor Stan—first the court, now the doctor. *It's a wonder he still wants to marry me,* Tzippy thought. *Haven't I heaped enough responsibility on him already? The least I can do before the wedding is make sure I get as many of my affairs as possible in order.*

God, I need a drink, she thought, then laughed to herself. In the old days, she'd have been sipping scotch by now, just as she and Claude used to sip after they made love. She pictured the firmness of his arms and shoulders. He had been an athlete, kept in shape, boxed at a local gym. His calves and thighs were firm; even his neck was thick. He drank only a little Scotch, just enough to keep Tzippy company. He didn't like a drinker, he once told Tzippy. God, what would he think of Shari?

Instead of drinking, she took a pill. Stan was coming over, and she wanted to be relaxed, not upset and all teary-eyed from memories. She picked up the phone and called Maria. She hated the way her baldness showed underneath her puffed-out hair. She might be an old woman, but she wasn't going to look like one, if she could avoid it.

The day went as planned. She and Stan ran her errands; Maria combed her hair while Stan waited in the car outside Salon 29 and listened to a ball game. She and Maria discussed her hairdo for the wedding. She wanted something regal, like she'd had for her party. She thought she'd wear the necklace that Stan had given her.

"You should come to my place a few hours beforehand to do my hair. I won't have time to come down here," Tzippy said, as Maria teased and fussed over her, securing the hairpiece in the back of her scalp to cover the thinning patch.

211

"No problem."

"How will I conceal this when I'm a married woman?" Tzippy asked.

"My darling," Maria said, waving her arm in the air. "At night you will go into the bathroom, remove the hairpiece, turn off the light, and then slip into bed. Your husband won't be thinking about your hair, I promise, and in the morning everyone's hair is messed. He'll never know."

"You're a clever duck," Tzippy said, laughing.

"It's my job to be," Maria said, as she vigorously sprayed the finished look in place.

The next morning Tzippy was up early, excited about her impending visit with Angie. Stan had warned her not to be too quick to forgive and not to be too friendly at first, but Tzippy was afraid she wouldn't be able to stop herself.

The night before, she'd lain awake, lonely, surprised at how used to Shari's presence in the bed she'd become. She had thought of her daughter, gone now, of her friend Angie, whom she would see soon, and of the history they shared: not only was her own life intertwined with Angie's, but Shari's was, too. That was when she'd reconsidered her idea of sending Angie and Naomi up north to get Shari.

"Let the woman prove herself, for God's sake," Stan had said the day before, and now, sure enough, Tzippy's plan would ensure that she did.

Stan was right, of course. Tzippy didn't want to be a fool and get robbed again, but she'd already decided that Angie's visit today was just a formality. She was eager for Angie's return, for things to be the way they used to be. When she thought about how long she'd known Angie, how many years Angie had worked for her, it seemed unlikely—nearly impossible—that Angie would make the same mistake twice.

While she waited, Tzippy put some fresh blueberry muffins from Shupie's on a dessert plate and set it next to the sugar bowl. She had to call Naomi and tell her about going to fetch Shari. *Naomi is a good girl; she'll help me,* she thought. She was about to sit down on the sofa, when she heard a knock on the door. Her heart pounding in anticipation, she opened it, and there stood Angie, big, tall, wide, and smiling. She looked just like the woman Tzippy remembered: dark, glistening skin; black hair framing a pie-shaped face; large, white teeth; stockings rolled just below her knees, sturdy and strong.

"Hi there, Mrs. B.," Angie said in her lilting voice. "Sure is good to see you."

"Yes, yes. Come in and let me close the door," Tzippy said, more excited than she wanted to be. They hugged tentatively, leaving a space between their bodies. She had missed Angie's singing, her support, her nighttime massages, and her devotion. And her cooking. But mostly, Tzippy had missed her friendship.

"Place looks good," Angie said, as she surveyed the familiar apartment.

Tzippy adjusted the brocade pillow with the tassels on the yellow sofa, patted the cushions, and said, "Come sit down." She couldn't recall whether she and Angie had ever sat on the sofa together before.

Tzippy asked, "How have you been doing up in Vero?"

"Oh, fine. Nice family. Husband's retired," Angie said. She picked up her delicate cup, which looked strange in her large, robust hands. "They entertain a lot and keep me busy. Their youngest son came home and stayed a few weeks. He's a nice young man, just out of graduate school. I don't know what he studied, though," she said, laughing at her oversight. She picked up a blueberry muffin and broke off a piece.

"What are we going to do?" Tzippy asked, as they stared at each other. "You wouldn't have written to me if you didn't want to come back to work."

"No," Angie said. "That's true."

"Angie, why did you take my money?"

A frown crossed Angie's face, as though she'd just experienced a sharp and unexpected pain. It was clear to Tzippy that she would rather talk about anything else, but she sighed and took a deep breath.

"Jack told me you were a rich old woman and wouldn't miss the money. He was messing with that skinny waitress at the Cotton Club, and I thought he would like me better if I did what he asked."

"He was a user," Tzippy said. It felt better to put the blame on him.

"I was a fool for Jack. A fool for love," Angie said. She turned her big hands up toward the ceiling in a gesture of helplessness.

"He was no good."

"Oh, I know that now. He left me high and dry. I messed up, Mrs. B., and I'm ashamed. That's all there is to it." Angie bent her head and shook her hair. "No one to blame but myself."

"I understand why someone would want a little something extra," Tzippy said, hesitantly. "Why someone might feel that they were . . . entitled."

"You do?" Angie said, her face a mask of disbelief.

"But it was so . . ." Tzippy was surprised to feel tears rolling down her cheeks. "It was so *personal*. It hurt me badly that you would steal from me. I didn't want to believe it."

Angie heaved herself up and went over to stand beside Tzippy. She put her arms around her, and Tzippy sank her face into Angie's shoulder. She smelled like Angie, and Tzippy suddenly felt all the barriers she'd erected to keep her feelings hidden being swept away. She sobbed as Angie held her. She cried for Angie and her attempts at love, for Shari and all her problems, for Brucie and his divorce, for all the pain and suffering in the world.

"Oh, sweetie," Angie whispered. "It wasn't about you, Lord

knows. Your money ain't you. I know I was wrong, but I sure didn't mean you no harm."

Slowly, Tzippy's sobs subsided, and for a moment she didn't know what to do. It felt good to be held not by a man, like Stan, but by another woman—a mother, a sister, a friend. Angie's warmth and goodness filled Tzippy's heart, and Tzippy knew she could bury herself in that love. Tzippy's own mother had been too busy scrubbing and cooking for her large brood to do much hugging. She used to push Tzippy away at times when young Tzippy had looked for affection. No wonder this felt so good. She lingered in Angie's big arm and large bosom, savoring the relief. Perhaps, she thought, it was as simple as this. Perhaps this was what Shari had needed all along.

Finally, Tzippy wiped her eyes, looked outside, and saw the blue sky. "Why don't we go outside and talk some more there?" she said.

When they'd settled on the chairs on the balcony and gazed over the pool and the ocean, Tzippy felt a new calm. What was the point of all this fighting, stealing, bickering?

"Angie, I want you to come back. You know it and I know it. But I have to trust you. I can't waste time worrying that you'll steal my money. It's not even about the money. It's about you and me. Do you understand?"

"Completely," Angie said, crossing her thick ankles. "I would never do that to you again."

"Next time, I'll call the police. No matter what I feel for you," Tzippy said.

"I understand."

Then Tzippy said something she hadn't expected to admit. "I'm no different from you in some respects. I took a brooch at Saks without paying, and I got caught." She waited for a response.

"No kidding," Angie said. She appeared both mystified and shocked.

"Yes. I'm not perfect, but I took from a store, not my employer who was good to me. There's a difference."

"You're right about that." Angie said. She looked out on the swimming pool below them and wiped her eyes with the back of her hand.

"Anyway, enough about that. You've already said you're sorry, and I accept your apology. I just wanted to make you aware of the distinction between what you did and what I did. Now, on to business: How much notice do you have to give?"

Angie looked at Tzippy and composed herself. "Well, I ought to give at least two weeks, but since it's you, you won't need a letter of reference."

"No, I won't," Tzippy said. "But two weeks ought to be fine. And then I have an errand I want you to do." Angie looked mystified, but Tzippy kept right on. "When you come back, I have a lot to do and we'll be busy. Stan and I are getting married on April second, and I'm on a mission to fix my relationship with Shari. I can't die leaving things like they are."

"You're not dying," Angie said.

"Well, I will be. Who knows when? I'm eighty."

"I want to help you, Mrs. B. I understand how important this is to you. I've known Shari since she was a young girl."

"She left in a huff because I went to the hospital and visited a sick young woman."

"Why she mad about that?" Angie asked, leaning back in her chair.

"The girl had problems with food, same as Shari. And Shari said I'm showing more interest in strangers than I did when she herself was sick." Tzippy stared out across the tops of the buildings, adrift in her pain.

"She doesn't mince any words, that one."

"You can say that again," Tzippy said. "But she's right, Angie. I messed up. I wasn't a good mother to her. That's a fact."

"Those are strong words, Mrs. B."

Tzippy felt a chill go through her, even though the sun was out. "I have to admit it. It's the only way to move on. Actually, I'm cherishing having another chance to get it right."

"What are you going to do?"

Tzippy took a deep breath. "The first thing is . . . I want you to fly up north, to go talk to Shari and get her to come back. To help her see that she and I need to fix our relationship."

"By myself?" Angie asked.

"I'm thinking with Naomi," Tzippy said. "I want you both to be my messengers. I know you can do it. I'd come with you, but I'd miss my own wedding."

"Maybe we can get her back before," Angie said. "I'd sure like to be there."

"She may listen to you two," Tzippy said. "She won't listen to me."

Angie threw her head back and laughed. "Oh, I don't know, but with Naomi's help, perhaps Shari will be swayed."

"No. You'll explain it to her like you did to me, and be honest. It's the only way we can make things better for all of us. Naomi has a healthy relationship with her sister. She will be convincing."

Angie nodded her head in agreement. As Tzippy gazed at her, she felt an unspoken understanding flowing between them. "All right, I'll help you," Angie finally said. "I can see how important this is to you."

"Thank you, Angie." They sat for a while and enjoyed the warmth of the sun. Then Tzippy said, "Let's you and me go downstairs and have some lunch. What do you say?"

Angie smiled and said, "Mrs. B., that sounds like a fine idea."

Chapter 18

Dr. Waterday's office was located in a flat-roofed brick building at the end of a cul-de-sac. After Tzippy's taxi dropped her off, she stood on the hot blacktop for a moment, watching the cars speeding by on the interstate, all of them in a hurry to get somewhere. She wished she could jump in with one of the drivers and say, *Take me with you*, but there was no escaping the fact that for the moment, she was where she was. She put her hand on the doorknob and hesitated again.

It had been nine weeks since the doctor had seen something on her last mammogram, back at the end of January. Tzippy had put off the appointment not only because one thing or another had always been more immediate, more demanding of her attention, but also because she'd never been one to rush after bad news. She pushed the door open and went inside.

It was better that she had come on her own; she'd always preferred to deal with misfortune alone. Stan had gone off to play golf again with Freddie, and Angie was back up in Vero. Angie had promised she'd give the Vero family notice, go up to see Shari, and then return to Bal Harbour in time for the wedding. Tzippy had bought Angie a ticket on Delta and had called Naomi to arrange for her to meet Angie at Bradley International, north of Hartford. And, with Stan's encouragement, she had decided to talk to Jocelyn before the wedding but not to let her go until after the celebration. No need to be short-handed on the big day.

They'd talk to her soon, emphasizing how badly she needed Jocelyn's help with all the preparations while Angie was up north.

Dr. Waterday's reception area was unexpectedly empty. For a moment, Tzippy was disoriented, so used was she to seeing the room filled with expectant mothers. She took a seat and leafed through *People*.

After a while, she checked her watch, rose, and walked to the reception window. "Tzippy Bryer," she said to the woman behind the glass screen. "I have a three o'clock."

"He'll be right with you, Mrs. Bryer."

Tzippy sighed and sat back. Over the past nine weeks, she had dismissed the thought of anything serious; besides, she had done some self-examination and hadn't been able to feel any lumps. But now that she was in the waiting room, she had to control her breathing as fear began to creep up her neck and constrict her chest. She took a deep gulp of air and then exhaled. Why did doctor's offices always make you feel sicker than you were? She started counting silently, told herself to be calm. She slipped a pill, already her second of the day, under her tongue.

She looked at the picture on the wall, willing herself to concentrate on the California poppies and the yellow buttercups. *Such a blaze of color*, she thought. *How beautiful.* Then she had the sinking realization that when she was dead, she wouldn't be able to see buttercups or poppies, and her focus was gone.

The door to the hallway opened, and a nurse appeared, holding a chart. "Mrs. Bryer?"

Tzippy stood up and walked into the hall.

"As you know, Mrs. Bryer," the nurse said kindly, "before Dr. Waterday sees you, he wants to have a second mammogram to double-check. Come this way, please."

Tzippy allowed the nurse to stretch her breasts on the white plate and perform the procedure in the darkened room. The entire process was humiliating, but she endured it. *You'd think they'd have figured out a better way to do this by now,* she thought. The plates were cold, and her breasts hurt when the nurse pinched them into the right position. She held her breath while the technician took the pictures, and then it was over.

Tzippy dressed and waited for the results. When the nurse finally beckoned her into the dark room where the two different X-rays were hanging, Dr. Waterday, in his white jacket, was sitting in a chair in front of them.

Tzippy stood behind him. She didn't say a word.

"Hello there, Tzipora," said Dr. Waterday, one of the few people she knew who used her proper name.

"Hello, Doctor."

"Good news," he said. "It appears we may have a shadow in the first X-ray. The one we took today looks clear. In short, I think there's nothing to worry about."

"Oh," she said. A wave of relief washed over her. She put her hand on the doctor's shoulder to steady herself.

"Now, I don't want us to become complacent. You should come back in three months and have another mammogram. I don't want to take any chances. The benefits of screening outweigh the risks," he said, turning to her for the first time in the darkened room.

"I understand," she said. "Three months."

"This time, don't delay."

"Yes, of course."

"Tzipora, let's keep our eye on this," he said, smiling.

Tzippy smiled back, though she felt like bursting into tears. She had been ready for the worst, she realized, ready to learn that on top of all the other struggles she was experiencing, she would have to worry daily about dying. Now she had been given a reprieve, and it left her feeling weak.

Walking back into the Florida afternoon in a sort of daze, she felt the sun heat her forehead, like a large hand on her skin. In a week, the kids would be coming, and so would Stan's daughter and grandson. Jocelyn and Bella would be busy with the food. Calhoun, the bartender, was going to bring the meatballs and stay to tend the bar. Rabbi Friedman, her old friend, was due to come an hour before the ceremony. Everything would fall into place; she was sure of that now.

PJ was coming to the wedding, too, though she hadn't seen him since the evening with Shari. Also her cousin Goldie and Stan's best friend, Fred. And Rachel Levin. Tzippy lamented that her dear friend Selma Grossman would miss the occasion. She hadn't invited too many people beyond that. It was so much better to have to think about a small wedding than to worry about breast cancer. Thank God—she'd been lucky.

In the cab back to her apartment, Tzippy wondered when her good fortune would run out, but she set the notion aside. There were other ways in which she hadn't been lucky at all—as a mother, for instance. But maybe she could make her own luck from now on.

When Jocelyn asked her how the appointment had gone, she was happy to say it had been just fine. She had a cup of tea and called Mr. Jason and asked him when he was delivering the chuppah.

"Oh, darling, I'll bring it by the end of the week and set it up. Everything will go smoothly."

"I have faith in you. I'm just checking," she said.

That evening, when she and Stan went to Junior's for a corned beef sandwich on rye, she said, "Perhaps we should talk to Jocelyn tomorrow. I don't like hiding things." She felt a new courage since Dr. Waterday's news. No need to overburden poor Stan with any worrisome concerns, she decided. He has enough on his plate already.

"Yeah, let's get it over with," he said, as he took a healthy bite of his oversize sandwich. "God, this is good," he said, wiping mustard off his lips and blinking through his wireless glasses.

Tzippy had ordered a half sandwich and a cup of mushroom-barley soup, one of her favorites. "I don't want to have a scene at the end. You know what I mean?"

"Listen, I'll come over tomorrow, have some of her famous split-pea soup for lunch, and we'll talk." He grabbed a slice of dill pickle and took a bite. "I'll tell her how much she means to both of us, that we really need her to help with the wedding but that Angie is returning and we won't be needing her afterward. Does that sound about right?"

Tzippy put the spoon down on her plate and said, "It sounds good if you say the last part really fast. I'll tell her you're coming for some of her wonderful soup."

After two bowls of split-pea soup the next day, Stan launched into his spiel to Jocelyn Bell, saying, "Tzippy has decided to have Angie return after the wedding." Jocelyn clasped her hands together and closed her eyes. Stan continued, "She's had Angie in her employ for thirty-eight years, and old habits die hard, as they say. This isn't personal, Jocelyn."

"You're taking her back?" Jocelyn asked, "You ain't worried about her stealing again? Mr. Stan, why did you bring me here? So now I get kicked to the curb? I wasn't rowdy, I wasn't loud, but I get the boot?"

"Oh, please, Jocelyn, don't say that," Tzippy said.

"You people have no idea," Jocelyn said. "Mmmmm, mmm." She shook her head, went into the kitchen, and turned up the water, almost wetting her uniform.

"I'll give you a severance check for two weeks' pay," Tzippy said impulsively. After she put the towel down, Jocelyn stopped moving, as if she were in deep thought, and then slapped her face, then again, bringing a flush to her cheeks. Tzippy and Stan stared, aghast.

Stan said, "Why did you hit yourself?"

"Clearing my mind, Mr. Stan. Something my mama used to do."

"My, my," said Tzippy. "Do you feel better now?"

"Yes, I do, Mrs. B." Then she took a deep breath and said, "I was thinking I would like one of those new dresses over at Mrs. Maples'. I heard you bought one for Angie."

"Mrs. Maples' is for plus-size women," Tzippy said, walking forward.

"She's got a section in the back for regulars," Jocelyn said, folding up the dishcloth.

"Well, if you would like a new dress, then we'll go buy one," Tzippy said, walking closer to the sink.

"Thank you, Mrs. B.," Jocelyn said, and moved toward Tzippy, touching her left arm.

Without realizing it, Tzippy's right hand rose up and stroked Jocelyn's flushed cheek.

As the smell of coffee wafted through the apartment, Jocelyn carried the steaming brew into the open dining area. Tzippy put a box of chocolates on the table and took off the lid.

"Let's go out on the deck, Stan, and get some sun," Tzippy suggested.

She watched Stan select a piece of milk chocolate and pop it into his mouth. Tzippy said, "Have a piece of candy, Jocelyn."

Jocelyn's eyes widened as she studied the box of chocolates. "Thank you, Mrs. B. I think I will." She selected one wrapped in gold foil. As she unwrapped it, Jocelyn looked thoughtful. "In case it don't pan out with Angie, you can call me back, Mrs. B. I understand you and Angie got history."

"Yes."

"I hope it works out for you, if that's what you want."

"Women," Stan said, putting his feet up on the hassock. "I never will understand them." He leaned back and puffed on his cigar.

Two days later, Tzippy and Stan looked at a larger apartment in the same building. The superintendent, Sully, took them up to the sixteenth floor and showed them a three-bedroom with three baths, a living room and dining area, a state-of-the-art kitchen, a stacked washer and dryer, and a den that had a built-in bar and was big enough for a pullout couch. There was a long deck off both the living room and the master bedroom, with a view of the pool area like the one Tzippy had, and a large foyer with two big closets.

"Looks about like yours, baby cakes. Everything's just scaled bigger. What do you think?" Stan said, walking around and opening drawers in the kitchen, turning on the bathroom faucets to test the water pressure.

Tzippy could easily picture her furniture in the apartment. She was glad Stan had an extra room for himself, and she smiled to herself as she imagined the new peignoir sets she could buy to surprise her groom at bedtime. "I approve. It's not that much different. You're right," she said.

"The living area is roomier by eight hundred square feet," Sully said. "All new appliances in the kitchen, too."

"We'll need it starting now, the beginning of April," Stan said.

"You don't give a lot of time," Sully said.

"Right," Tzippy said. "Can't you do that? Also, Sully, how about a fresh coat of paint in the master bedroom? We're newlyweds."

"For you, Mrs. Bryer, of course. Mazel tov!"

"How much more for a month?" Stan asked.

"Another seven hundred dollars," Sully said.

Stan looked at Tzippy and nodded.

"Would you arrange the movers after you finish painting?

And a good cleaning, too. Don't forget the windows, inside and out."

"I'll need a deposit," Sully said.

"I'll give you seven hundred right now," Stan said, pulling out a wad of bills. "I'll need a receipt."

"Fine, fine," Sully said, taking his pad from his back pocket. "For Mrs. Bryer, I'm always happy to oblige."

Before Angie left on her mission, Tzippy spoke to her. "Dress warmly," she said. "This time of year can be very damp. Did everything go okay with your employers?"

"They were surprised," Angie said, "but I think they understood."

"I'm glad you have the time to take this trip and come back to help me with my wedding preparations now. Please call after you see Shari. I'm quite worried about how she'll receive the two of you," Tzippy said. "She hates surprises. She may throw the both of you out!"

"Don't worry, Mrs. B. Relax," Angie said, chuckling.

When Angie and Naomi phoned to report that they had arrived in Boston, the temperatures were in the low twenties, the snow was dirty and slippery, and the winds off the Charles River were fierce.

"It's freezing here. Get me back to Florida," Angie told Tzippy.

"I gave her a scarf and a hat, Mom," Naomi chimed in.

They had checked into the Marriott Copley Place, as Tzippy had instructed, and taken a suite.

"What's with Shari?" Tzippy asked, anxious to get news. She pictured Shari's apartment in the brownstone on Beacon Street, with its rickety elevator. The apartment was old, the bathroom dated, but the rent still reasonable. She had two narrow bedrooms and a small kitchen; the living room looked out on the street and had a bay window where Shari put her plants. Tzippy had gone up from New Jersey to help her decorate when she'd first taken the place back in 1980, after her divorce. A few chairs, a picture, a fresh coat of paint, and the apartment had looked better, but Shari had been stubborn and hadn't allowed Tzippy much input beyond that.

In fact, Tzippy had felt wounded when Shari called and reported that she'd picked out new material and had drapes custom-made. They had had an awkward moment on the phone.

"I'm sure they're cute," Tzippy had said.

"Cute?" Shari had said. "What's cute about drapes in a living room? It's not a nursery, Mother."

Why do I feel as if Shari has to include me in everything in the first place? Tzippy had begun to wonder. Shari was a grown woman, yet Tzippy often begrudged her the chance to do for herself.

"We went up to see her, and she looked terrible," Naomi said on the phone now. "She answered the door, but she didn't even have the damn lights on. She just sat there, all curled up, in the dark room. It was eerie. And I think she's lost more weight. No kidding."

"Yeah, she's mighty skinny," Angie said. "I opened up the windows just to let air in and make the apartment smell better. The place needs a good cleaning. And the plants needed water, so I gave 'em some."

"So, did you speak to her?" Tzippy asked.

"Well, we did, finally, but it took some time," Naomi said.

"What happened? How did Shari respond?" Tzippy asked, coughing into her tissues.

"She was angry at first," Naomi said. "She said we shouldn't have made the trip."

"But then we gave her loving," Angie said.

"I took my hands and held her face, put my hands on her cheeks," Naomi said.

"I told her I was sorry about taking the money," Angie added. "Said you and me had made up."

"I told her that we loved her and that things would work out," Naomi said. "I told her to give you another chance to make it right."

"I sat next to her and put my arms around her," Angie said. "I whispered to her that if you could forgive me, you was an upstanding woman."

"Goodness," Tzippy whispered. "How did she respond?"

Naomi said, "She started to weep—real tears of sadness, like a baby—and we took her in our arms and rocked her."

"That child is hurting real bad, Mrs. B. She is one wounded puppy, as they say," Angie said.

"Oh, dear. Now what will you do?" Tzippy asked.

"Well, we're going out to dinner later to talk some more," Naomi said.

"I offered to cook her favorite meal if she wanted me to, but she said no, she wanted to go out," Angie said. "We're going to a seafood place she likes."

"Let me know what happens," Tzippy said. "Don't let her get drunk. Promise me."

"No one's getting drunk with me around," Angie said.

Naomi laughed on the other line. "Except me. I could use a drink."

They called back in thirty-six hours to report on their progress. They had dined out at Legal Seafood, gone to the Museum of Fine Arts, walked in the Commons, and gone to Starbucks on Newbury Street for lattes, twice.

"All this walking is killing me," Angie said. "I'm going on a diet."

"The weather's warmed up, so we're not so cold, at least," Naomi said.

"Just tell me: Are you making any progress?" Tzippy asked.

"She's agreed to come down to Florida and try to work it out with you," Naomi reported. "That's the good news."

"What else?"

"She said she's staying only one month, and then she's going home and that's it," Angie said.

"Does she think this is a thirty-day wonder?" Tzippy asked.

"Mom, take what you can get," Naomi said.

"Yes, you're on the right track, Mrs. B."

"You're right. When will you be here?"

"We have things to do, and Shari has to get a couple of matters in order. We'll be there for the wedding, okay?"

"Okay. Call me from the airport so I know you're leaving. I'll see you at the wedding. God, I'm ready for a drink, too!" Tzippy sighed as she hung up, but she had to admit that her plan seemed to have worked. Getting Shari back to Florida was the main thing, and, as lagniappe, they'd all be there when she and Stan tied the knot.

They called her from the airport. "Shari was impossible at the end, Mom," Naomi said. "She was in a snit, like she was mad about going. Took her suitcase down from the closet, threw in her clothes, went to the bathroom, and got her stuff. Then she took a shower and we waited while she was in there, listening to her moan and talk to herself. We didn't know what to do. She came out and stood there dripping in the doorway."

"Why was she so angry? I thought she'd agreed," Tzippy said.

"Probably 'cause she don't like being told what to do," said Angie.

"She doesn't like cooperating. It's not in her nature," Naomi said.

"God forbid she should listen," Tzippy said.

"When we got to the airport, she ran up the escalator. She was behaving like an untamed animal," Naomi reported. "I tried to slow her down. Poor Angie couldn't run. I couldn't stand the way she was acting, so wound up. I yelled at her to calm down and stop it already. Finally, she did. She breathed in and out, hung her head. She admitted she was being a bitch. Then she leaned on my shoulder. I could tell she was tired."

"Oh, Naomi, I'm sorry to put you through all this. Thank you for getting your sister," Tzippy said.

And now, Tzippy thought, *she's boarding the plane, her thin body folding into a seat. She'll ask the stewardess for a blanket because she's always cold.* In her mind, Tzippy saw Shari buy a drink when they came around with the cart; she saw her talking to the person next to her.

Well, Tzippy thought, *Shari can do whatever she wants on the plane, but once she gets to Florida, we have our work cut out for us.*

Chapter 19

On April 2, the day of the wedding, Tzippy woke up feeling rest-less. She snuck out early and took a walk on the gravel path that fronted the beach. As her mother had said, "Go to the sea and be healed." She needed to calm down before the ceremony.

Children were already squatting by pools of water on the long stretch of sand. As she watched them running in the lacy edges of the surf, Tzippy wished she was young and could jump into the waves, too. She had been a spunky girl and had loved the ocean and the rush of excitement when she dove under the cresting breakers. Now, all she could do was watch the kids and admire their limber bodies.

She thought about Benny and their long marriage and knew this marriage to Stan would be completely different. She loved Stan, but not with the passion of her youth. Indeed, all that pas-sion had engulfed her, trapped her, put her at risk. These nuptials, on the other hand, would be sweet, comforting, and safe. With Stan, she was free and much more at peace. When she'd been young and in love, her whole life before her, she had thought, as everyone does, that nothing bad could befall her. And, after all, beginning a family had been exciting. But it had also been fraught with fears and expectations, and soon the simple events of life had overwhelmed her. She should have known what Benny would turn out to be; she'd seen the way he looked at other women when they were dating. But she'd been smitten.

And after Laura had answered the phone that night in 1965 and Tzippy had learned the truth about Ben's affair, she had realized her entrapment and her world had unraveled.

Only Claude had given her relief. Shari had gotten sick. Malcolm X, Martin Luther King, and the Kennedys had been assassinated. Vietnam had spiraled out of control. Riots had erupted in Newark, Chicago, New York, and Watts. Richard Nixon had been elected. The world had gone crazy, and her family had been left in shambles. In the eyes of the world, she'd had a full life with diamonds, beautiful clothes, and a successful husband. But Tzippy knew the truth. She had failed her own kids, even though they were the most important people to her.

Tzippy dropped her head and kept walking, the sand spreading her toes, until her breath grew heavy and her legs were fatigued. As she skirted the shoreline, she felt the urge to confess it, say out loud, even if the crash of waves drowned out her words. "I have been a frivolous woman," she said. "I have been a thief." She had been greedy. She'd taken and taken, whether she'd needed to or not.

Tzippy wiped the tears from her eyes and walked back slowly toward the swimming pool and her apartment. With great effort, she ascended the staircase to the pool area, clutching the banister on each step.

"Are you all right, Mrs. Bryer?" the lifeguard asked, as he put the cushions out on the chaise lounges. "Maybe you walked too long." He offered her a chair to rest on.

"Thank you," she said, as she settled for a few minutes on the striped cushion and rested her head on the pillows. She knew she had a lot of work to do with Shari, but perhaps she could still set things right. *Be okay,* she coached herself. *You're a tough old bird.* The sun felt so good on her face.

⌒

Jocelyn was in the kitchen, ready for the day.

"I'd love some freshly squeezed orange juice," Tzippy said, feeling like indulging herself.

"My pleasure," said Jocelyn. She was in a better mood since they'd made a trip to Mrs. Maples' and had bought her a pretty dress with poppies splashed all over the fabric. She'd selected a red beret to compliment the dress, and Tzippy had nodded approvingly. Now, however, she was dressed in her usual starched and spotless uniform for her last day of work.

The day went off as planned. Maria performed her magic, trimming Tzippy's hair into a fresh, stylish angle and attaching the hairpiece. After writing a check, Tzippy kissed Maria on the cheek and she left carrying her brown leather tool case.

Rabbi Friedman was the first to arrive. He lived in Miami Beach now that he had retired from Tzippy's former synagogue in New Jersey. He seemed genuinely glad for her. His family had come from Ivia, the same shetl in the old country from which Ben's father, Harry, had come. Both families had escaped the state-sanctioned pogroms. Harry had peddled junk, then industrial waste, then had gone into manufacturing. The rabbi's father had read Yiddish newspapers to his wife and daughters every night after supper. His son, the future rabbi, had gone to Hebrew school, the chider, downstairs from the shul.

Tzippy liked that he was a learned man, and Ben had often asked him for advice. He had relished his relationship with Rabbi Friedman.

After some of the guests arrived, Calhoun, the bartender, poured chilled champagne into tapered flutes. The dining table had a centerpiece of flowers with gold sparkles. Yellow-and-gold mints, with "S" and "T" entwined on the tops, sat in a silver dish. Jocelyn served the hors d'oeuvres at five o'clock to the hungry guests. Stan came late because he'd gotten caught in traffic, but he brought his daughter, Evelene, with her short-cropped hair and sensible shoes, and his bespectacled grandson, Michael.

"Baby cakes," Stan said, "come over here."

Tzippy walked toward her groom, who led her into a corner.

"I just want to tell you how happy I am today and how much I love you," Stan said, squeezing her delicate hand. "You're the love of my life."

"Oh, Stan, thank you. I love you, too, and am thrilled that we're making a new start together. Isn't it exciting?"

"Best decision I ever made."

"You're the finest man I ever knew," Tzippy said, and she kissed him gently on his lips. "Forever."

"Forever," he responded.

Then they joined their guests, laughing with them and accepting all their "mazel tovs."

Stan wore a white dinner jacket with Mr. Jason's boutonniere on the lapel. His tanned, wrinkled face glowed with happiness, and Tzippy basked in his enthusiasm for her. He could have found a younger bride, but no—he'd wanted her. Coming from his tough, poor childhood in Newark, he viewed Tzippy as a woman of style and wealth. Maybe he just wanted Benny's bride, she thought for a moment; the men in his group had always admired Ben. But then, Stan had been Ben's true friend. Hadn't Stan bought him an expensive pair of baby-blue pajamas from Neiman Marcus when he'd been sick in the hospital? Hadn't they talked until the wee hours of the morning?

Anyway, Tzippy decided, Stan just loved her for her. She was Tzippy, full of her own impressive qualities. Why not?

When Brucie arrived with Jill, tall, statuesque, and more beautiful than ever, everyone turned to look. Stunning in a royal blue sheath with crystal beads around her neck, Jill hugged Tzippy and told her she loved her.

"I couldn't miss your wedding, Mom," she said, acting as if she had never run off with the cardiologist.

Tzippy blinked and whispered, "Oh, it's good to see you and have you back with Bruce." However, she wasn't going to pretend as if nothing had happened. Her son had been heartbroken. Tzippy could just see Brucie out there, by the detached garage, in the gathering dark, chopping and splitting firewood with determination and relentless anger. No, Tzippy wouldn't lightly forget Jill's rejection of her son for a doctor with three houses.

She turned her gaze toward her cousin and smiled benevolently at Goldie, who looked lovely. With her bee-stung lips, she kissed Tzippy on the cheek and squeezed her arm. "You got the guy, Cousin," she said, and then added, "I can't believe Jill's back with Brucie."

"I know," Tzippy said. "But this isn't the right time to talk about it," and she moved on to someone else.

And then, as if Brucie's and Jill's entry weren't enough, Naomi, Angie, and Shari walked into the living room. All of the guests stood and stopped talking. Shari looked thin and pale, but she was there, hanging onto her sister's arm. Tzippy didn't know what to say, so she waited to see what Shari would do.

"Mom, I'm here for your wedding," she said.

"Well, I am so glad, sweetheart," Tzippy said. She wrapped her arms around Shari, and tears came to her eyes as she felt her daughter's slim frame. She rocked Shari a little as they renewed their love.

"You look lovely," Shari said, nodding at the beige silk shantung suit and pillbox hat they had purchased together at Neiman's. "Where's my Nicole Miller?" she said, as if it were the most normal request.

Tzippy's lips spread into a gracious smile. "In my closet, sweetheart," she said. "Go put it on."

Shari reappeared a few minutes later in the Nicole Miller

polka-dotted dress, just as PJ happened to walk through the front door. His face lit up, and she smiled back at him.

"Shari, you look great. Love that snappy frock," PJ said.

"Thank you," she said, and spun around, giving him a full view.

Tzippy clapped her hands in approval.

Ike said, "Hey, Mom, you should see our fish stuffed and mounted, hanging over the fireplace in the family room." Naomi kissed her husband, everyone laughed about the prize-winning bluefish, the tension dissipated, and all the guests resumed talking.

During the ceremony, Rabbi Friedman, bearded and gray, gave the blessings and sang the Hebrew prayers while Stan and Tzippy stood erect and serious under the chuppah and their guests sat in folding chairs around them. Tzippy admired the flowers and ivy cascading into elegant folds, framing her and her groom.

When the rabbi pronounced them husband and wife, Stan stepped on the glass, wrapped in a white napkin, broke it into many pieces, causing everyone to clap and call out, "*L'chaim*" for good luck.

I am a married woman again. I have a second husband. I never thought this would happen to me. It feels wonderful, Tzippy thought.

As the guests dispersed for the reception, Angie nodded to Jocelyn Bell and pitched right in serving and cleaning up. The two maids seemed to get along well, based on an exchange in the kitchen that Tzippy overheard.

"I got me a dress over Mrs. Maples', too," Jocelyn said, over the sound of running water.

"What do you mean?" Angie asked.

"Mrs. B. done bought me one. Real nice, with a red hat to match."

Angie said, "You sure are one nervy girl, woman."

Tzippy smiled and sighed with relief.

When Tzippy was alone for a minute, Angie sidled up to her and said, "In the end, Shari was like a lamb, Mrs. B. I think she wanted to come back. She told me she couldn't miss your wedding. Now, go figure . . . what if we hadn't gone and fetched her?"

Naomi saw them talking and came over. "Mom," she added, "she really wasn't doing well. I think we did her a favor by coming to rescue her. Maybe she's worried she'll die in a ditch if she doesn't clean up her act. I think we got to her, don't you, Angie?"

"Yes, I do. She had that fear in her eyes, like she'd seen a ghost," Angie said.

"We got her in the nick of time. God knows what she would have done."

Tzippy shuddered at the thought of suicide but said simply, "Well then, it was the right decision," glad to know that for once she'd done the proper thing for her youngest child.

She looked around for Shari then and saw her having a private moment out on the deck with PJ, standing under the cradle moon. When they returned to the party, they seemed pleased and were arm in arm, Shari in her pretty dress, a glass of gin in her hand. Tzippy held her breath but didn't ask. Stan whispered in her ear, "The lovebirds seem to have reconciled." And then he kissed his bride.

Who knows if it will stick this time? thought Tzippy. *I'm still not sure how I feel.*

Ike proposed a toast in his smooth voice. "To my mother-in-law, Tzippy, and to Stan, a great guy and now part of our crazy family. Welcome, and thank you for having the courage to join this group of strong-minded individuals. You and Tzippy deserve many happy years together. *Mazel tov!*"

After the toasts, they all went out to dinner, except for Rabbi

Friedman. Tzippy stood by her front door as the guests filed out and heard them chatting.

"I wouldn't miss this," Rachel Levin said, hobbling along on a cane while her driver held her handbag.

"I give Stan a great deal of credit," Stan's friend Freddy said. "I'm not sure I could do what he's done. It scares the bejesus out of me."

While Tzippy and Stan—Mr. and Mrs. Fosberg—were away, Shari and PJ went off on his boat, *Sweet Caroline*, to see if they could rekindle their romance. But Shari, it seemed, had learned a thing or two. "I told him I couldn't go out with him if he kept seeing other women," she reported to Tzippy on the phone.

"What did he say?" Tzippy asked.

"He said he's not sure he can make that commitment, but that he likes me a lot. Said he needs some time to think about it."

"So now what?"

"I don't know. Maybe I'll just work on you and me and the eating disorder group stuff and put PJ on hold. No need to get hurt again."

"Good for you," Tzippy said. "That's the most sensible thing I've heard you say in a long time." She smiled into the phone but stopped herself from saying another word.

The new apartment was a bit disorienting at first; the fact that it was just like the old one but also different had Tzippy confused for a day or two. But she soon felt right at home. The other change—Stan and Angie and Shari—would take some getting used to. Stan's toothbrush did indeed hang next to hers now, and she had to make space for his toiletries so he could have his own area in the double-sink master bathroom. But he moved his computer and leather chair into the third bedroom and often spent several hours in there by himself, giving Tzippy her space, and that pleased her. All in all, she was thrilled with how everything had shaken out.

Angie still ran her bath and occasionally massaged her feet at night, but more often Stan took over the task, preferring to take care of his new bride himself. Occasionally, he rubbed the inside of Tzippy's leg, or they kissed and fondled each other. It was a nice arrangement, although they had both started to feel their age. All of a sudden, because of poor circulation in one leg, Stan had begun walking with a cane, which curbed his morning jogging. Angie had to do more of the driving while Tzippy and Stan sat in the back, holding hands. When Tzippy's leg cramps interrupted their sleep, either she or Stan would turn on the porcelain lamp and he'd rub her twisted foot. They'd go into the small kitchen and steep a pot of tea or sit on the yellow sofa and sip some brandy before returning to bed. Sometimes Angie heard them and got up to check on them or fluffed their pillows. Tzippy and Stan would get back under the covers and Tzippy would roll into Stan's arms, kissing him and wishing him, one more time, a sweet good night.

Meanwhile, Shari was sleeping in the den on the couch and waiting for Tzippy's next move. She mostly hovered in the background, sipping her gin, doing sit-ups, and visiting the bathroom. Tzippy gave Angie a concerned look whenever Shari stayed in there too long. But as soon as Tzippy announced, "I'm going to call Pamela Warnick and find out about groups," Shari nodded her consent.

Two weeks after the wedding, after kissing her good night, Stan said, "Well, I married you and got a maid and a daughter, too." Tzippy smiled in the darkness, happy to have been given a second chance in several departments. Her luck hadn't run out yet.

Chapter 20

Tzippy and Shari stood outside, waiting for the valet to pull up in the town car. It was the middle of April. Stan had gone off to play golf with Freddie, Angie was busy with housework, and Tzippy had no idea how long the two of them would be at Lakeville, so she had asked Shari to drive.

When the car came, Shari got in behind the wheel and Tzippy slid delicately into the passenger's seat. Although it was only April, it was over eighty degrees already, and the humidity made it seem even warmer. Tzippy felt a trickle of sweat start its way down her neck from the back of her hairline. Shari opened her window and lit up a cigarette.

"Must you?" Tzippy said.

"Yes, I must, Mother," Shari said.

"Well, keep the window open wide. I need air," Tzippy said. She coughed into her tissues and hoped that the pill she'd taken would kick in soon. Her nerves were on edge.

Shari stopped at a light and blew smoke out the window. She tossed her cigarette out after a few more puffs and then looked at her mother. "Listen," she said. "I don't want anyone ganging up on me over there."

"What are you talking about, Shari?" Tzippy asked.

"I'm talking about another scene like the one we had in the restaurant before your birthday party," Shari said, pressing her foot on the gas pedal. "That's what I'm talking about. I won't be made to feel as if everything is my goddamn fault, while other people act like assholes."

Tzippy jostled in her seat and moved her head a little. "What makes you think that's going to happen?" she asked. "This is an entirely different group of people, folks we've never met, except maybe Pam Warnick." She hugged her Chanel handbag for security.

"I just don't want to feel like the black sheep," Shari said.

"And I don't want to feel like the evil mother," Tzippy said. She took a tissue out of her bag and dabbed her nose. She had hoped they'd get off to a more positive start, but she could see that Shari was already defensive. It could be a long afternoon.

"When Brucie twisted my arm and gave me that Indian burn, not too many people came to my defense. Aren't people responsible for their actions, Mom?"

"Yes, of course they are," Tzippy said, looking inside her bag for a second pill. Perhaps she should wait before taking another so soon, she thought, but some days just required more assistance. When she found it, she slipped it under her tongue. "I can't remember that night, Shari. It was months ago. Can we just concentrate on today? This is a new beginning for us."

"Yes, I suppose you're right," she said. "This is about us. It's just that I'm like an elephant—I can't forget."

It's just that you hold grudges, Tzippy thought. "I'm hoping we'll learn some new things today. Let's just try to stay in a good place, okay, sweetie?" She took Shari's thin hand and gave it a squeeze. She was surprised when Shari squeezed back.

They drove in silence and followed the row of palm trees against the blue sky. The grounds of the center appeared newly mown, and men were watering beds of geraniums. Tzippy was pleased that it looked attractive and hoped Shari wouldn't make any more negative comments. As Shari parked, she lit another cigarette and opened the window all the way.

For a minute, they sat in the car and watched a family walk toward the clinic's side door. The parents led the way; one of the daughters, clearly anorexic, dragged behind reluctantly. Another girl, her age and wearing purple glasses, brought up the rear, dressed in black goth garb. She had a tattoo of a lizard curling around her leg. The anorexic girl was wearing a long-sleeved gray sweater, despite the heat. Tzippy understood why she wore such a heavy garment: either she was cold or she was concealing her skinny arms, or both.

Shari parked the town car and came around the door for Tzippy in an unexpected gesture of kindness. As they walked toward the building, gazing up at the windows and looking around the flowerbeds, Shari turned and said, "Mom, when we get inside, I've got to use the ladies' room." For a brief moment, Tzippy wondered if Shari was going to make herself throw up, but then she didn't want to know. Not now—not minutes before they went into the meeting. What good would it do? She'd get herself more upset. On the other hand, she should know what was going on. It was her responsibility, for God's sake. Wasn't that why they were here?

Tzippy breathed in the cool air-conditioning as they entered Lakeville. Shari went to the ladies' room while Tzippy inquired at the desk about the meeting; then she walked to the restroom as well, gently opening the door to listen. No one was in there but Shari. Tzippy tried not to move. She didn't hear any vomiting, and she didn't smell anything. Perhaps this was a legitimate visit. Tzippy waited to see when Shari would be finished. Finally, when nothing happened, Tzippy went to the door of the stall and knocked.

"Shari, are you okay in there?"

Silence.

"Open the door, sweetie."

With great effort, Tzippy got down on all fours, on her poor bony knees, and tried to see under the bathroom door. Her knees chafed and began to hurt. She wanted to lie on the floor and weep, but instead she stretched her neck until she could see inside the stall. There was Shari, curled up on the floor, looking like a cat taking a nap.

"Shari, what are you doing?"

Spotting Tzippy's face under the door, Shari yelled, "Get away! You're spying on me!"

"Please get up," Tzippy said, raising herself up off the cold linoleum and trying not to slip. Every ache in her body had been rekindled.

The door opened, and Shari came out. "I can't believe you were on your knees. God, Mother, you're going to kill yourself doing that."

"I was worried about you."

"You thought I was barfing, didn't you?"

"Yes."

"Well, I'm just scared. No vomit. It's over. Let's get out of here."

They put their arms around each other and walked out of the ladies' room with their heads touching.

Outside, a door led to a flight of stairs. Tzippy stepped slowly and held on to the banister. She had worn comfortable, low-heeled shoes, but still, it was difficult for her and her legs ached, especially her calves. But she didn't complain. She had to be tough.

Shari turned and asked, "Are you okay?"

"Yes, I'm fine," Tzippy said.

Shari said, "Here, give me that," and took her Chanel bag. "What the hell do you have in here, Mom, the king's jewels?"

Tzippy smiled. "Not even my own jewels." *That was a nice gesture*, she thought.

The meeting room was large, with two arched windows on

either end. There were several dormers on the side, two skylights in the roof, and a slippery polished floor.

An older woman with salt-and-pepper hair and dangling earrings met them. On her simple cotton T-shirt was a badge with her name, Lucy.

"Hello," she said, "and welcome." She took Shari's hand between hers and nodded warmly to Tzippy. "Is this your first meeting at the center?"

Shari stood mutely and glanced at her mother. "Yes," Tzippy said. "Yes, it is. I spoke to Pam Warnick."

Lucy's hair made her look older than she was, thought Tzippy. It was pulled back in a ponytail that reached to her shoulder blades, and wisps of it floated above her delicate, flat ears. Obviously, she didn't believe in makeup or hair dye. Her eyes were clear, and the fine skin underneath them crinkled when she smiled. Her ankle-length skirt was thin cotton, bohemian, and she wore draped around her hips a wide leather belt with a big silver buckle. Around her neck was a necklace of multicolored stones—amber, amethyst, and topaz.

"So glad you're here," Lucy said. "Please take a seat."

The room was cavernous and silent, despite the fact that twelve people were already there. They sat on pillows on the hardwood floor in a haphazard circle, in distinct family groups, like souls cast up on an island. The troubled girls—and they were all girls, though Tzippy knew that boys sometimes suffered from eating disorders as well—were immediately obvious. They sat a bit apart from their parents and siblings.

They were gaunt, unnaturally still, and, despite the heat outside, most of them wore a long jersey or sweatshirt. The girls huddled in their too-large garments, looking cold, withdrawn, and haunted, as though listening to interior voices. Some of them had bought Diet Coke or iced coffee, black, no sugar, which they sipped through straws.

As Tzippy sat reluctantly on the hard floor, she heard a rustling behind her and turned to find Lucy carrying a pale yellow cushion with red flowers embroidered on it from one of the dormers.

"Here," Lucy said. "Perhaps this will help."

"Oh, thank you," Tzippy said. She put the yellow cushion beneath her and slowly, with Shari's help, lowered herself onto it. It was large and soft. Shari sat next to her, looking apprehensive.

"I can't believe we're doing this," Shari whispered. "Why did I ever agree?" She rolled her eyes. Beyond the weight she'd lost in Boston, she'd been eating less in the days before the meeting, Tzippy had noticed. This entire process was pushing Shari back in the direction of her old standbys: cottage cheese, melba toast, and black coffee. There was some kind of competition, Tzippy had heard, among anorexics: Who could be the skinniest? Shari wasn't going to attend this group and not be one of the thinner ones. She had done fifty sit-ups twice daily on the rug of the den. Tzippy hadn't commented, just observed.

The meeting room was beige and cream and had no style except for the pillows, brown, pale yellow, and ivory, all oversize. The one that Lucy had given Tzippy was softer and downier than the others. Perhaps she had sensed that Tzippy, at her advanced age, required more comfortable seating. Tzippy took note and was appreciative. Maybe there were a few benefits to old age—just a few.

Tzippy saw no sign of Pam Warnick, although she'd said she'd be there.

"I really hope this isn't a disaster," Shari said, scowling. Tzippy's heart went out to her—a girl with a history of failed hopes and time running out, who had grown up in suburban comfort, among people who thought she'd been privileged, who never understood what she suffered. And, of course, she'd experienced more than her share of painful personal disappointments, however much she'd contributed to them herself.

"Let's give it a chance," Tzippy said.

Three more people joined the circle—a Hispanic family that included a tall father who looked like a basketball coach, wearing a T-shirt with a high school logo and a baseball cap; his plump wife; and his daughter, a tall, thin teenager—and then Lucy, who lowered herself onto a pillow and started to speak.

"Good afternoon," she said. She gestured to her name tag and smiled, "My name is Lucy. I work here at Lakeville. I'm a licensed social worker with over fifteen years of experience with eating disorders, and I'm here today to try to help you."

No one said a word. Tzippy glanced at the faces, at expressions that conveyed expectations, relief, fear, and anxiety. A woman raised her hand, and Lucy nodded in her direction.

"Are we going to break up into smaller groups, or are we going to stay like this?"

"Like this," Lucy said. "At least for the time being. There's nothing to be afraid of. Why don't we go around the room and introduce ourselves? Just say your first name, please."

She nodded to a woman who said her name was Brenda and then turned to her daughter. The girl looked as though she wanted to disappear, but she whispered, "Anne" and then turned to the person beside her. The names came slowly at first and then more quickly. The skinny ones, the sick ones, whispered their names shyly—all except Shari; she and the basketball coach practically shouted their names, overcompensating for their nervousness with false bravado.

"I'm Bobby K., number two," the coach said, as if his copying Bobby Knight would impress everyone. A couple of people laughed, but no one laughed when Shari shouted her name.

It took a few minutes, but afterward everything seemed better to Tzippy, less tense and hostile. People wiggled around on their pillows, pulled into each other, and the circle got smaller.

To Tzippy's right sat a woman of maybe fifty, very thin, in

white pants. She struggled to get comfortable, seeming unhappy about sitting on the floor. Finally, she stood up and stretched her legs and Tzippy could see that her pants were flat and loose and that she had no definition on her bottom, no flesh. Tzippy was surprised to realize that she was a patient, someone as old as Shari—older. Then she sat down and tried to remain still. She turned to Tzippy and said, "I'm sure we'd both prefer chairs." She smiled, showing her stained teeth.

"You're right about that," Tzippy said.

No one said a word. The fragile sense of common purpose had disappeared.

"I'll start," Lucy said, after a few minutes. "I decided to work on this particular problem because my sister was anorexic, and it badly damaged my family. I'm happy to say she slowly got better, and so did we. So I know it can happen. I'm here because I want to help you deal with the problem in your family."

The plump Hispanic woman next to her pressed her fingertips under her chin, looked with solemn eyes, and said, "I'm Rafaela, and I need help with my daughter's eating disorder. I feel like I'm always walking on eggshells."

"Yes," Lucy said. "Good. Thank you."

The coach next to Rafaela said, "I'm really Joe, Rafaela's husband. I'm angry, and I don't want to be. My daughter throws up her meals. It's unhealthy, it's a waste of money, and it's disgusting."

Lucy nodded encouragingly.

"My girl's a basketball player," Rafaela said. "She also has a job after school. How's she going to do all that, not to mention do her homework, when she's throwing up all the time?" she moaned.

"She's got talent," Joe added. "She could be a star."

Tzippy could see that Joe was both a bad husband and a bad father. How could the women in that family be happy with someone like him?

Then a woman with a French accent began to speak. Beside her sat a dark girl with long, stringy black hair. "My name is Louisette," she said, "and we're from Québec. My daughter has had anorexia, now bulimia. I have learned so much about eating disorders." She waved her arm in the air. "I'm going to a therapist now myself. Peggy has been inpatient, outpatient, and independent, at home."

The daughter lifted her head. She looked at the group through abnormally large brown eyes. "I'm Peggy. I'm twenty-two. I used to starve myself, but now I binge and throw up. I go for a while and I'm fine, and then something gets me crazy again."

"I'm Roland, Peggy's brother." To Tzippy, he looked about fifteen, with a lanky frame.

"What do you think?" Lucy asked Roland.

"Oh, I think this eating thing is stupid. Not to eat good food. My *maman* is a fine cook, but Peggy is an unhappy girl. Maybe because my *papa* isn't home enough, maybe because she doesn't have a boyfriend. I don't really know."

"Thank you both for sharing," Lucy said, nodding toward Shari as well.

Everyone started to speak. Then they stopped because Pam Warnick had appeared.

"Please don't let me interrupt. You sound like you're doing fine," she said.

Lucy glanced at Shari again and nodded. "Why don't you tell us about yourself now?"

Tzippy's heart was beating rapidly, and she started to cough. As she took a tissue from her bag, she wondered if she was going to be ill. *What have I gotten myself into?* she thought.

Shari had worn a simple shirtdress that made her look younger, like a schoolgirl, almost. The buttons down the front of the dress were pearl, the dress beige. She wore a brown leather belt around her waist, and flats. Classic gold hoop earrings. Nothing too sophisticated, but it was clear, when Tzippy compared her with the others, that she seemed to exude a sense of wealth and privilege. Her thin arms poked out of her short sleeves.

"My name is Shari," she started. "I'm here because my mother wanted me to come. She wants us to fix our relationship and for me to get better. I had anorexia as a teenager, and it still comes and goes. Sometimes I binge and purge. My life has been difficult. My mother and I argue." Stopping, she stared at Tzippy. "I'd like what my mother wants," she said, dropping her eyes as if Tzippy were dangerous. "I'm tired of fighting and tired of struggling," she said, looking up again. "I'd like some peace."

Glancing across the room, she gestured toward Roland and his mother and sister. "I feel like I've let too many things go, and now I feel like a failure."

"Thank you," Pam Warnick said. "That was very honest, and yet you're right. Why do you think your relationship with your mom has been troubled?"

Everyone stared at Pam. Then they waited for Shari to answer.

"I didn't live my mother's dream. I didn't marry a urologist and get a stack of credit cards," she said, again looking directly at Tzippy, who began to feel more self-conscious. "I didn't sign on for a house with two acres and boring sex. I didn't have kids and become a soccer mom. No, instead I became broken." Then she paused and raised an arm, indicating there was more. "And I have a problem watching people eat, especially overweight people. It's the truth." She paused. "I'm not proud of it. But I just can't stand watching fat people eat. I want to scream and tell them to stop and ask them why they are stuffing themselves. I want to say, 'don't you see all those folds of flesh on your waist? Don't you care?'"

Tzippy was amazed at her daughter's revelations and wondered, for the first time, if she had been the cause of Shari's revulsion at fat people because she herself had been critical of them. Tzippy knew she had been judgmental of people, but the possibility that her daughter might now reflect this trait shocked her.

"I'm sorry you feel that way," Pam said.

"Why should you be sorry?" Shari said sharply. "Isn't it true?"

"Maybe fat people have disordered eating, too, just like skinny people," Pam said. Shari looked shocked.

"Thank you for sharing," Lucy said.

Then it was Tzippy's turn. She cleared her throat and tried to regain her composure. She had to be brave.

"My name's Tzippy, and I'm eighty years old. Despite what my daughter implied in her remarks, I truly want her to be happy." She smiled thinly. "I may be the oldest mother here," she said, "but I guess I believe it's never too late to change. I'm afraid I've damaged my daughter. I'm haunted by that charge, and I'd like to fix things between us." She lowered her eyes and was quiet.

Pam Warnick said, "That was very courageous, Tzippy, and I applaud you for coming here at this point in your life. I, too, was a mother, but my daughter didn't make it. She died of cardiac arrest when she was sixteen. She was both anorexic and bulimic. This is a terrible illness, and you're smart in coming here. Don't give up. In the words of Winston Churchill, 'never, never, never, never give up.'"

The people in the room began to clap, mildly but consistently, in steady, rhythmic applause. Then the clapping gained momentum and all the people, even the very thin and sick girls, joined in. Joe, the basketball coach, clapped most loudly of all.

Tzippy was so moved to hear them all in unison that she ascended from her pillow. Slowly and stiffly, she rose and led the clapping standing up. Everyone followed her, for surely, she thought, if an eighty-year-old woman could stand up, they could, too. In the end, all the people gathered that afternoon at Lakeville Eating Disorder Center stood and gave a round of approval to Pam Warnick and Winston Churchill's motto of enduring determination.

"I think this is the perfect time to pause," Lucy said, as the clapping subsided. "Let's take a ten-minute break and then reconvene. There's coffee and tea on the bridge table and a restroom downstairs. There are free pamphlets, as well as books to purchase, and a paper for everyone to write their name, phone number, and e-mail address on, in case anyone wants to contact someone. Remember, this is all confidential and only the people here have to know about your attending."

During the break, Shari and Tzippy walked over to the bridge table to get coffee. Tzippy was surprised when the French-Canadian boy ambled over. He nodded to Tzippy but quickly turned his attention fully to Shari.

"You look like you're waiting for this to be over," he said. "Or is that just the way you want to look?" He had a cowlick sticking out of the top of his head.

"I can't decide whether I want to be here or not," she said.

"Maybe because you're older. And cooler."

"I was pretty sick in my teens and twenties, but I'm better now."

Tzippy butted in and said, "We're here to fix our lives. This is Shari's first time."

"Of course," he said. "I shouldn't have said that. My sister struggles, and it affects the whole family. It's frustrating."

He made himself a cup of chocolate with hot water and a packet of powder and started to sip it. "This stuff isn't half bad."

"I think your sister doesn't have a strong enough sense of herself," Shari said. "She seems shy."

"Yeah, she's timid. What about you?"

"Well, I'm not timid. Other than that, who knows? My mother had a plan for me, didn't you?" she said, turning toward Tzippy. "Always telling me not to eat too much, get A's, be perfect."

"Maybe you should talk to the group," Roland said to Shari.

"You're more mature than a lot of the girls and probably have more perspective. It could help them, coming from someone like them. Tell them not to waste their lives staying like this," he said. He looked at Shari and raised his eyebrows, as if daring her.

"Oh, I don't know."

Tzippy said nothing, wondering if Shari would take the bait. Roland had almost taunted her, and Shari wasn't one to back down.

Just then, Lucy spoke up in a loud voice. "Everyone can gather in a circle again. We have a little more to do before the session is done for the day."

Everyone sat back down, and Lucy began, "Let me say that people with eating disorders suffer from a conflicting mind-set. Part of them wants to get better and live a successful, independent life, and another part of them is negative and afraid they will never be able to get healthy and free."

Rafaela said, "But what if they resist our help? You can't force someone. What should we do?"

"And what about reward and punishment?" Joe asked.

"I'm not sure about that," Lucy said. "Too often they're punishing themselves, as well as their parents."

Tzippy asked, "What if your daughter is an adult herself? What if she drinks too much, as well as bingeing and purging?" She hoped she hadn't gone too far, but she had to know.

"Your daughter has to do the work herself," Lucy said. "You can't do it for her. But I'm sure you have work to do as well. Perhaps you should go to an Al-Anon meeting and listen to the other parents, try to be patient. Remember that you cannot make her better, just like you couldn't make her into who you wanted her to be in the first place."

Shari spoke up suddenly. "Wait just a minute. I don't like being talked about while I'm sitting right here. I can speak for myself, if you don't mind."

"Please go ahead," Lucy said.

"I grew up in a bubble, thinking everyone was like us—with two cars in the garage and a black maid. I was sheltered; all my parents' friends were country club members, Jewish philanthropists, businessmen, or retired doctors living in Florida."

Tzippy said nothing and held her breath, fearful of what would come out of her daughter's mouth next.

"Our family tragedy, in my opinion, was that we really didn't like each other. And there were secrets." She stopped and said, "I think I've said enough for the first meeting."

Tzippy expelled a sigh of relief. She closed her eyes and said a small prayer, thanking God that it hadn't been worse. *Secrets*, she thought.

"One more thing," Shari said. "I wanted the truth, but I wasn't allowed to ask questions." She stopped and took a deep breath and stared out at the group.

Roland hooted. "Thanks," he said. "Very cool."

"Yes, that was revealing," Lucy said. "Thank you for sharing."

Pam Warnick cleared her throat and said, "We'll revisit this more at the next meeting, but the hour is just about up. Shari, that was very bold, and I'd like to add my two cents here: Parents, don't be afraid to express physical affection to your child, no matter how old she is. I wish I'd done more cuddling with my daughter. I think I was cold, not demonstrative enough. I was brought up to always be stoic. That's now one of my biggest regrets."

Lucy said, "Also, encourage your daughter to explore her *own* interests, not *your* interests. She's her own person. I cannot emphasize this enough."

Tzippy started coughing and took her tissues out of her bag. She found her pills and slipped one under her tongue. *The third one this afternoon*, she thought. She'd better be careful. Trying to remain composed, she wondered if she was going to be able to endure this entire process with Shari. Perhaps she had bitten off more than she could chew.

Secrets. Like her thefts.

For an instant, she pictured herself off on a deserted island where no one would reach her except by ferry. She'd be free from this pain. Her friend Esther had sent a postcard the other day, reporting that her family had moved her to an old age home because her health was failing. She was too much trouble for them now. In Esther's famous scrawl, written all around the edges, she said that she was surprised to find she was happier away from her family, away from the spoiled grandchildren who were overfed and under disciplined. Now she lived in a room that had a large window with flowered curtains, played Scrabble with the other ladies, and had tea and butter cookies at three o'clock. Even though Esther knew the food was tasteless and she was waiting to die, she was happy to be left alone.

But Tzippy wasn't ready for an old age home. She'd promised herself she would get through this. The anguish and the embarrassment, her mistakes, were all going to be out in the open, weren't they? She sighed and tried to be patient.

Everyone in the room got to their feet and started talking. "Also," Lucy said, "there's a family support group, for family members and loved ones only, on Tuesday night at seven."

Pam Warnick came over and shook Shari's hand. "Your mother is courageous to come at this time in her life," she said. "I hope you and she can work things out, Shari. I've never gotten over losing my daughter, so I feel committed to this cause and I admire your mother's dedication. Anytime you'd like to meet with me personally, or the two of you together, feel free." She smiled, and her eyes crinkled; she still seemed a bit distant and Episcopalian, but Tzippy could tell she was trying to be friendlier than usual.

"Thank you. Perhaps we'll come and see you together another time. I appreciate the offer," Shari said, more cordial than she usually was with strangers.

Tzippy smiled and thanked her as well. "I'll call you," she said to Pam.

On the way down the stairs, Roland saw Shari and said, "I like hearing you talk."

"You're a good brother for coming," Shari said.

"You think? *Merci.* You have a brother?"

"Yes."

"You should call him and talk to him. Brothers do care, you know."

For a brief moment, Shari seemed to consider that idea. "Yeah, maybe you're right. Worth a shot."

"See you next time, *oui?*"

"Yes, *oui!*"

They found their car in the parking lot and rode back silently, sitting next to each other. Shari opened the window halfway and smoked while Tzippy thought ahead to her apartment, her haven. Angie would have everything in order. The beds would be neatly made; Stan would be sitting in front of his computer. Perhaps he'd be tired. Tzippy kept wondering about the boy, Roland, and why Shari had responded to him so well. She'd always been attracted to the odd and the eccentric.

Once they were back in the apartment, Shari retreated to do sit-ups, sip her Tanqueray, and smoke her cigarettes out on the deck. Tzippy found Stan in his office, busy researching golf clubs, courses, and professionals on the Internet. "Hi, baby cakes, how'd it go?" Stan asked, his head in front of the big screen.

"It was different—I can say that. I guess it went okay for the first time. I'll tell you about it at dinner. Right now, I need a tub."

The next morning, Angie brewed the coffee, brought in the daily newspaper, and set it on the dining room table next to Stan's plate.

Then Shari appeared and sat at her place and Angie brought her her usual black coffee and dry toast with cottage cheese.

"How'd it go yesterday?" Stan asked. "You never came to dinner with us; you just conked out."

"I was exhausted," Shari said. "Pretty heavy-duty, but okay, I guess." She sipped her hot coffee and rubbed the sleep out of her eyes.

"Your mom said you had to sit on pillows."

"Yes, and she didn't like that at all, did you, Mom?"

"No, not much," Tzippy confessed. "I think I'll bring my own pillows next time to add to the one they gave me. Maybe I won't be so uncomfortable."

"Can't you get a chair?" Stan asked.

"No, it's okay. I don't want to be difficult. It'll be fine," Tzippy said, deciding not to bring too much focus on herself.

"I think it's great that Mom doesn't want to be difficult and wants to just go along. This is a first." Shari laughed. Then she took her dry toast, spread it with cottage cheese, and took a healthy bite. "I think it's wonderful."

"I heard you gave a little soliloquy about your family life," Stan said.

"Yeah, I got going. There was this kid there who kind of egged me on. Anyway, it was the truth, so what the heck?"

Tzippy started coughing and sipped some water, then said, "I have a feeling we're in for some interesting discussions."

"You asked for it," Shari said. She chewed her toast.

"I did, and I'm not sorry. I think I'll attend the parents' group on Tuesday night. Stan, you're welcome to join me, if you want." Tzippy stared across the table at her husband. She knew that he was accompanying her to court on Monday.

"Baby cakes, I wouldn't miss it for the world."

Chapter 21

The courthouse in Miami sat at the top of a wide row of impos-
ing concrete steps in the center of the government complex.
Its redbrick exterior and white trim, emblazoned with Roman
numerals commemorating the date of its construction, radiated
an aura of importance and majesty. From the aprons of five high,
rectangular windows, large American flags hung vertically and
rippled like wind on water whenever a breeze passed by. Tzippy
walked slowly up the stairs toward the doors, holding tightly to
the arms of PJ and Stan. Today, given what lay ahead, she didn't
feel strong enough to make it up alone. The two men helped her
position herself on each of the white ledges, before she lifted her
legs to the next step. They were patient and polite, and Tzippy
knew they did not want to embarrass her.

They stopped midway up the staircase, and PJ asked, "Are
you okay, Tzippy?"

"Sweetheart, we can rest a minute if you need to," Stan added.

Tzippy took the moment to be still. She said nothing and
stared down at the street from which she'd begun this climb.
Two men were ascending the stairs, one in a plaid shirt, carrying
a portfolio, and one who looked as if he must be a lawyer, in a
dark suit. Across the street was a large sign advertising divorce
mediation. Her legs were tired and her heart felt labored, but
she didn't want to be an impediment. "I'm okay. Just one second while I take a breath." She sucked in the humid Florida air.

"There," she sighed. "I'm fine now. Let's keep going, gentlemen."

When they got to the top of the staircase, Tzippy hesitated again. She didn't want to go inside and face the judge, but PJ had had the court date changed once already, and she and Stan were married now. Shari had scheduled a visit with her college friend, and Angie was busy with her household chores. She had no choice. It might as well be today. She nodded her head resolutely and turned toward the ordeal at hand.

The last time she'd been in court had been years ago, when Brucie was in college and had to pay a fine for having too many unpaid parking tickets. She'd met him at the courthouse. He'd appeared in a wrinkled sport jacket and sheepishly rolled out his wad of cash in front of the court officer. Ben had insisted he pay his own fine.

Now she had to deal with her own crime, as a rich old lady who stole goods she didn't need and could have paid for if she'd wanted to. They wrote books about shoplifting and made jokes about people like her. One police officer had said wealthy older women stole because they were bored. Well, he'd gotten it wrong, as far as she was concerned. Although her humiliation was profound, she stood with her chin raised and said, "Let's go in now."

As she entered the dark, high-ceilinged room, a security person checked her purse. She looked up into the recesses of the dome, which arched away from her, and at the pictures of various local politicians on the walls. PJ informed the clerk they were there and was told the case would be heard in courtroom number 4. The hearing was scheduled to begin in ten minutes. They sat down on one of the hard brown benches circling the room and waited. Tzippy tried to stay calm. She had taken a pill before leaving and hoped she wouldn't have to take another one before the ordeal was over.

She crossed her legs. In her white suit trimmed in navy blue, she felt crisp and ladylike. Today she'd tried to appear even more elegant than usual, even though PJ had advised her to dress conservatively. Around her neck was the gold necklace Stan had given her. She wanted the judge to know who she was—not some shlepper from East Podunk, not some common crook. It was important to her that she made a good, solid impression. Stan was pleased that she had worn his gift, and he smiled at her with pride, despite the fact that they were in court because she'd been arrested.

When they finally entered the courtroom, the three sat in the middle of the room, amid all the other people there for one reason or another. They waited while the judge, a scowling older man of about sixty, got settled. He spoke to a woman who held a yellow legal pad; PJ made notes on a pad of his own. Stan sat still and deadpan, stroking Tzippy's hand for reassurance. It reminded her of a time when they'd just started dating and he'd accompanied her to an MRI. He'd stood at the end of the machine and rubbed her foot—a small but reassuring gesture that had made her feel less nervous and claustrophobic. That morning, before they had left, he had shown her a similar kindness, caressing her and saying, "I'm with you all the way, baby cakes, no matter what the results."

A middle-aged woman was called up on a drunk-driving charge. It was not her first DUI. Disheveled and distraught, she stood before the judge. At first she was still, but before long she began moving around. Tzippy disapproved of how she presented herself. She lifted her arms and tried to explain herself, saying, "I really didn't drink that much," and then, "You have no idea what my life is like, sir." Tzippy watched her from behind and wanted to tell her to tuck her blouse in and comb her hair. Her lawyer was young and inexperienced and kept her neither still nor quiet.

The judge appeared to be a no-nonsense, send-them-away sort. He frightened Tzippy as he ordered the woman to attend an alcohol education class for six weeks and suspended her license for six months.

Next, a Hispanic family came to the front of the court. The boys and the older man sat down in the front seats. A young, dark-haired girl of about ten and her mother, a slim woman in a short, tight skirt with a gold streak in the front of her hair, stood before the judge. The charge was shoplifting. Tzippy's heart leaped into her throat as she bent forward to hear every word. A man and an older woman stood to one side. They owned the convenience store near where the mother and daughter lived. It seemed that one day the mother had complained of needing to dye her hair. The girl told the judge, "I wanted to get my mama the hair dye so she would be happy."

The old woman took the stand and wrapped her shawl around her thin shoulders. Her silver hair was pulled back in a bun. She told the judge how she'd been working at the front of the store when the girl had entered. "The child walked right in and down the aisle to the hair products. She knew just where to go. I'd seen her many times before, when she'd come in for bread or candy, sometimes alone, sometimes with her brothers. I'd opened up a big shipping box of cigarettes and was putting the cartons on the shelf behind the counter. When I looked up, I saw a funny shape under her T-shirt. Then she snatched a carton of cigarettes and hurried out of the store. I tried to stop her. I yelled to her, but she kept walking."

"What did you yell?" the judge asked.

"'Hey, what have you got there under your shirt?'"

Tzippy listened avidly.

"Then I yelled, 'You can't take cigarettes! You're too young.'"

"I gave her some money, but she must have lost it on the way," the mother said. She wore high wedge shoes laced up around her slim ankles.

The judge looked at the young girl and asked her name.

"Maria," she said.

"Did you lose the money that your mother gave you?"

The girl shook her head no.

"Why did you take the hair products without paying?" he asked.

"I didn't have money," the child said. She wore navy-blue shorts and a white T-shirt; her hair was long and dark and she was pretty in a way that, Tzippy knew, would one day make men like her.

"Did your mother tell you to steal the hair dye?"

Maria looked startled. "I thought that was what she wanted me to do."

"Why did you think that? Has she asked you to steal for her before?"

The girl looked uncomfortable, stared at the floor, and sucked in her cheeks.

"Did she tell you to steal the cigarettes as well?"

"I just saw them and took them. They were the kind my mama smokes."

The judge looked at the mother and addressed her sternly. "Mrs. Rodriguez, you seem to be encouraging your daughter to become a thief. I don't like the sound of this at all."

The shop owner, a middle-aged man with a mustache, spoke for the first time. "I don't want the family coming in my store if they're going to take things. My mother's too old to go run after them, Your Honor."

A young, court-appointed female attorney spoke up. "The child, Maria, is a victim and shouldn't be held responsible."

The judge agreed. "Mrs. Rodriguez, you and your family are not to shop in this store anymore. You will have to perform fifty hours of community service as punishment. Your daughter is a juvenile. Go see the court officer in the back after we're finished, and she'll explain what this entails. Don't let me see you here in my courtroom again."

Then he turned to the child and looked down at her. "Maria,

you are a young girl and have a long life ahead of you. Don't get into the habit of stealing. If you continue, you'll end up in jail one day. Stop while you're young, and learn your lesson. Take only what you pay for. You're too young even to buy cigarettes. That is the law, and this is the system we use in the United States of America. Do you understand?"

The child nodded her dark head, and her hair swung on her shoulders.

The entire family walked down the aisle to the back of the courtroom. Tzippy was embarrassed because her case was so different and now she looked even more foolish to herself. She started to take another pill from her pocketbook but stopped herself—she wanted to remain sharp in front of the judge. Stan sat still and said nothing. He'd let go of her hand.

Finally Tzippy's name was called, and she and PJ walked up to the judge. Before she went, Stan patted her arm and said, "You'll be fine."

"Mrs. Bryer, it says here you were caught stealing from Saks Fifth Avenue," the judge said, reading from a piece of paper. The two detectives who'd questioned her stood over to the side.

"Yes," she muttered. She spoke almost in a whisper.

"May I say something, Your Honor?" PJ interrupted in his baritone voice. "Mrs. Bryer is an outstanding citizen who was under a great deal of family stress at the time."

"Oh, is that so?" the judge said. He wrinkled his forehead. "So you think family trouble is sufficient justification to steal from a store, Mrs. Bryer?"

The taller of the two detectives raised his hand and said, "Your Honor, we believe this woman has stolen on other occasions as well."

"Were there arrests? Convictions?" the judge asked.

"No," said the detective.

PJ said, "Objection. Let's stick to the incident at hand.

No need to pile on the accusations just because you see an opportunity."

"Overruled. I'd like to hear from the detective. Please take the witness stand," the judge said.

The detective complied and stated his name, Phillip Buck, and his title. For a minute, Tzippy noted how handsome he looked in his dark suit, until she remembered how foolish it was for her to be thinking such things about a man who had so much control over her fate. He explained how he had noticed Tzippy loitering in front of the jewelry counter. "She kept touching the pins and earrings and turning them over. They were sale items. I watched her and waited to see what she was going to do," he said. Then he described how he had distinctly seen Tzippy take the brooch and slip it in her pocketbook. "She put it in the outside pocket of her quilted bag. Then she started to cough and dug into the pocketbook for tissues."

Adding that he thought that was the moment when she'd transferred the brooch to the inside of her purse, the detective said, "She knew just what she was doing. They come into Saks like they're on a treasure hunt." Detective Buck crossed his legs and sat more upright in the witness chair and said that he'd approached her and told her he wanted her to come into their office.

"She was offended by my suggestion and haughty about the theft. She acted like we shouldn't be questioning her," Detective Buck said, then told the judge how he'd finally retrieved the pin with the Saks Fifth Avenue tag on it. He looked straight at Tzippy as he spoke.

PJ, who had been standing ramrod straight beside Tzippy, said, "Objection, Your Honor. This is psychological conjecture."

"Sustained," the judge said. "Just the facts, Detective."

Detective Buck continued, "The lady said, 'Why, I've purchased many items in this store, young man.'"

Tzippy wanted to run and hide. She felt herself blushing

under her makeup, and perspiration started to trickle down the front of her blouse. She didn't dare turn around to look at Stan, but she hated that he was hearing the detective's words. She hoped PJ had some tricks up his sleeve.

When it was PJ's turn, he spoke eloquently. "First of all, Your Honor, Mrs. Bryer is a year-round member of our community, a good woman with a sense of integrity and responsibility.

"I've known her for many years," PJ went on, "and I want to explain the circumstances under which this unfortunate event occurred. Her adult children had come to town in order to celebrate her eightieth birthday. They'd planned a party in her honor. But then when everyone went out to dinner, they had an argument in the restaurant and her son actually physically assaulted her daughter."

Well, Tzippy thought, *that's not exactly what happened, but if it helps me today, I'm fine with it. Besides, all lawyers exaggerate, don't they?*

"Mrs. Bryer was shocked and mortified by this display of bad manners and loss of control. The argument brought up a good deal of unfinished family business; Mrs. Bryer didn't sleep that night after the altercation, so when she went shopping, she was both exhausted and upset. You can understand this, I am sure, Your Honor. This is an eighty-year-old woman. She was alone, widowed, and not well. I believe it was totally out of character for Mrs. Bryer to take something she clearly could afford to pay for," PJ said. His crisp Harvard accent was tinged with added Southern charm. "Surely, this appearance before the court is punishment enough."

The judge looked at Tzippy. She fervently hoped that what he saw was the picture of elegance and propriety, a small, frail woman with a fine nose and coiffed hair and lined skin who looked like she couldn't harm a fly. In fact, in her white Chanel suit, she hoped she had the aura of a kindly matron who tipped well and grinned at strangers, the type of woman who lunched at Maxim's and went out to the theater. She was someone's loving, wealthy grandmother who smiled with her eyes and gave generously to charities. Yes, she sent her soup back in restaurants if the soup wasn't hot enough, and sometimes she grew impatient when she didn't get waited on quickly enough, but she always thanked the help and made friends with shop girls and salesmen at the finest stores. She was a lady—anyone with any sense could see that.

The judge turned over his papers and pushed his glasses up onto the bridge of his rather wide nose. Tzippy wondered if he had children, a quarrelsome family. He looked tired and overworked. She hoped he didn't come from a poor background and therefore resented her station in life.

"Mrs. Bryer, do you think that stealing from Saks is proper therapy because your children embarrassed you?"

"No, no, Your Honor," Tzippy stammered. "I-I—"

"And you believed you were entitled to that thing you stole just because you'd spent a lot of money at the store? Like a dividend for a stock you'd bought?"

Tzippy was speechless. PJ looked grim. The judge shook his head. "Mrs. Bryer, go home and stop this nonsense. I do not want to see you in my courtroom again. Find another way to release your stress. Next time, I won't be so generous. I'll put an ankle bracelet on you and you'll have to stay home for six months." The judge banged his gavel. "Next case," he said.

Though she felt properly chastened, relief washed over her in a wave, and she swayed on her feet. She wanted to kiss PJ but refrained. Stan smiled at her as she walked out of courtroom number 4.

"Baby cakes, you did great. PJ, you were smooth. And a little luck never hurts," Stan said, as he held the door open.

"Thank you, PJ," Tzippy said. As they descended the courthouse steps, she scanned her surroundings. She spotted the

Hispanic family from the courtroom piling into a pickup truck. She saw an acupuncture place and combination insurance–real estate company with photos of houses in the window. She stared at the large church on the corner, and for a split second she wanted to call up the rabbi in Boca and report to him that she had been honest with Stan and he had supported her.

What a privileged woman I am, she thought. Little Maria was a poor girl with a hard life ahead of her. But then Tzippy realized that she, too, had been a poor girl at one time, growing up as a Jew in a gentile country. Perhaps Maria would be all right. Still, Tzippy had been lucky overall. She had friends, she had fancy clothes, she had money, and she could act the part of the law-abiding citizen. When people looked at her, no one knew that all her life she'd been a thief. Well, no more.

"Are you okay, baby cakes?" Stan said.

"Oh, yes, couldn't be better," she said. PJ smiled at her.

Tzippy said, "You made the difference today, PJ." Then she stopped on the step and bent over and planted a kiss on his clean-shaven cheek, a cheek that smelled like lime. *What a wonderful scent*, she thought.

"How about lunch over at the restaurant on the corner? A lot of attorneys go there after court. It's down the street from the Registry of Deeds," PJ said.

"Great idea. I'm treating. You got my bride off the hook, and I'm a happy man. Let's go toast to our good fortune," Stan said.

Tzippy smiled in agreement, but she kept her eyes on the family driving away in their dented pickup.

Chapter 22

When Tzippy went to the family meeting on Tuesday night, she brought along not only Stan but Angie as well—after all, she was a member of the family, too. Pam Warnick stood by the door and distributed nametags. She greeted Tzippy warmly and welcomed Stan and Angie. The meeting room was filled with troubled parents, confused siblings, and worried grandparents. The anguish on their faces testified to the stress they were under, and most spoke in hushed tones.

Before the meeting started, Roland walked over to Tzippy and said, "I wish Shari was here tonight. She'd liven things up."

Tzippy laughed and said, "Well, she couldn't come because we'll be talking about her." She'd spent some time thinking about how Shari had become the family's designated patient—the Bryer family had been a mess, and it had been left to Shari to act it out for the rest of them. Brucie, despite his only-son troubles, Naomi, despite her tendency to sulk and isolate, her pot smoking and her personality flaws—both had escaped. Perhaps Shari had been more sensitive, more vulnerable, to the household dynamics, or perhaps she'd merely been the youngest.

When Naomi had met Ike, they'd gone to espresso bars and seedy biker joints; she'd ridden on the back of his Harley on dark nights, done all sorts of things that concerned Tzippy and Ben, but had escaped their scorn. Shari, on the other hand, had always tried to please them and failed.

"Yeah, I guess you're right," Roland said. He turned and pointed to a smartly dressed man with graying hair. "That's my *papa*. It's too dark for golf, so he finally came. You folks ought to meet, don't you think?" he said.

"I'd like to," Tzippy said. "By the way, Roland, this is Angie and this is Stan."

Roland put his hand out, and Stan said, "Glad to meet you, Roland. I'll go talk to your *papa*, but not about his golf game." He walked over to where the man was getting himself a cup of coffee and started chatting.

Roland was staring at Angie. Tzippy realized he didn't understand the connection. "Angie's my friend and companion," she told Roland. "She's known Shari a long time."

"I think it's neat that you came," Roland said to Angie. "I bet you know a lot about the family."

"You can say that again," she said, laughing. "I've been working for Mrs. B. for thirty-eight years. Shari was just a little girl when I came."

"Shari was seven—just a bundle of energy, and so happy," Tzippy said sadly, recalling how much her daughter had changed since those early years.

Then Stan walked back over with Roland's parents, Louisette and Pierre, right behind him. "I thought everyone should meet, since we all have a lot in common," Stan said.

Leave it to him to warm things up, Tzippy thought.

"*Bonsoir*, Mrs. Tzippy. Glad to know you," Pierre said, extending his well-manicured hand. "My son told me about you." Tzippy noticed his tailored suit and highly polished shoes.

"It's been a difficult journey, *non?*" Louisette said to Tzippy. Louisette was blond, with sea-blue eyes and lines of weariness around her mouth.

"Yes, it has. This illness goes on and on," Tzippy agreed.

"I have been the guilty one," Pierre said. "I work all the time and am away. Poor Louisette is left with Peggy."

"Unfortunately, that was true when my husband was alive as well, but he's been gone ten years and Shari still isn't right," Tzippy offered.

"I was standing on the fifth green today," Pierre said, "when I started thinking about my daughter and whether she had eaten her breakfast this morning."

"Just like that?" Tzippy said.

"*Oui*, I started to worry about her in a new way. I could hardly finish my game. That is why I am here tonight."

"Maybe our two families should have our own private group and see how that goes. What do you think?" Roland said.

"Isn't Roland the most precocious young man?" Louisette said, smiling proudly.

Tzippy was about to say yes, when someone began clapping sharply. "Everyone, please gather 'round," Lucy said. "Take a seat." All the attendees maneuvered themselves onto the pillows set up on the shiny floor.

When everyone was settled, Pam Warnick started. "Tonight, I'm pleased to have a guest with us. He's an esteemed colleague who is well known in the field of eating disorders. He's written books on the subject and has a practice in New York. May I introduce Dr. Karl Watkins."

She gestured to a tall, bespectacled older man, long and lanky, sitting on one of the pillows. He looked uncomfortable. Had he been standing, Tzippy thought, he would have been several inches over six feet tall. He wore a tweed jacket, a blue button-down shirt, and Sperry Top-Siders—the epitome of Ivy League dress.

The circle gave him a mild round of applause and then fell silent. "Hello," he said. "I'm happy to be here tonight. Pam is a dear friend of mine. I, like Pam, have experienced a personal tragedy with an eating disorder." He stopped and looked around at all the people and then went on. "My niece, my brother's daughter, had bulimia and died from electrolyte damage five years ago. It was devastating for all of us. At the time I was practicing general psychiatry in New York, but after we lost my niece, I studied eating disorders and now I see only patients with anorexia or bulimia." He stopped, took a handkerchief from his pocket, and dabbed his face.

The people in the room nodded and looked genuinely appreciative. A mother with bleached hair raised her hand as if she were in school and needed permission to speak. "My daughter goes in the bathroom, and I know she's throwing up. I stand outside the door and listen. Sometimes I even find old bags of vomit in her bedroom. What can I do?"

Everyone started talking at once, and several people, clearly unnerved, got up and went to a side table to help themselves to food and drinks.

The woman's husband, who was sitting next to her, added, "I don't know what to say to her. Should we barge in?"

Dr. Watkins said, "No, I don't think that would help the situation."

Another man spoke up. "I just got married and discovered that my bride goes into the bathroom after dinner and throws up her dinner. She's an attorney, a smart woman, and she's in there every night."

"When did she start this behavior, do you think?" Dr. Watkins asked.

The husband, a man with black hair and a bushy mustache, said, "She said her stepfather used to take her camping when she was a teenager and fool around with her. He threatened her, made her promise not to say anything. He used to slap her on the bottom and say, 'Don't go get fat on me.' My wife said she used to gorge herself with chocolate bars in defiance and then feel guilty and go throw up. I guess that's how it all began."

"There's always a story," Lucy said. "Does anyone else have a story to share?"

Angie raised her arm, then put it down and looked at Tzippy. Lucy nodded in her direction. "No, no," Angie said. "Never mind."

"Go on, Angie," Tzippy said. "Say what you want. Don't worry about me."

Angie started out slowly, her voice a bit broken and humble, but as she went on she gained in both volume and fluency. "When I started working for Mrs. B. here, Shari was just a kid. I hate to say it, but she was always the driven one." She glanced at Tzippy. "Her parents wanted too much from her. In a good way, I guess. She was pretty, smart, always taking lessons of some kind. Mrs. B. pushed her, and Mr. B. was hardly home. Shari couldn't take it. I once caught her at the refrigerator, tearing apart a roast with her bare hands."

"Did you say anything about it?" Dr. Watkins asked.

Angie shook her head no.

"Why not?"

"Oh, I loved my job and didn't want to start nothing. It was intimate. Mrs. B. and I were close."

Stan interrupted and said, "The girl is all over the place, and can she drink. And she likes the men too much, if you know what I mean. By the way, I'm the new husband," he said with a laugh.

Tzippy listened and decided it was time she spoke up. "I'm here to confess I wasn't a good mother and also to find a way to move on. I have to believe there's a way to mend some of the damage, but I don't know how." She stopped and took a tissue from her bag. "I thought the eating had gotten better, but now I'm not sure. She certainly thinks about food more than she should, always obsessing about getting fat. As far as the drinking is concerned, it's true. Shari passes out every night—it's predictable. It's like she doesn't want to feel."

Dr. Watkins said, "It sounds to me as though she might benefit from psychotherapy. Has she ever had any?"

"She went for a brief time, then stopped," Tzippy answered.

"Do you think she'd be willing to resume therapy now?"

"That's a question you'd have to ask her. She's forty-five years old and speaks up for herself. However, I'll encourage her," Tzippy said, thinking how she'd like Shari to see Dr. Watkins.

Then Pierre cleared his throat and said, "I'm the 'bad' *papa* who worked too hard, too many hours, played golf, and didn't spend enough time with his daughter." He shook his head and opened his hands, adding, "I have no excuse. I am a selfish man but a good provider."

Roland said, "Papa is a good man, but I don't think he understands girls as well as boys."

"Why do you say that?" Dr. Watkins asked.

"Because he never asks my sister any questions about what she does with her days. With me, he wants to know everything."

Dr. Watkins said, "I'm sure some of what you say is true. Some fathers have more difficulty understanding their daughters. Then again, some mothers are too hard on their daughters and often clash. Child rearing isn't easy, and some people are better at it than others. A lot has to do with their background. The society we live in also influences things a great deal. The basis of all health is self-esteem. We cannot be too critical or too lenient, and we must respect individuality. It's a tall order. Some girls are more sensitive. If I had all the answers, I'd be a much wealthier man."

"Let's take a short break," Pam Warnick suggested. "Then we'll talk some more."

Angie and Tzippy struggled to their feet.

"I hope you don't mind my talking so frankly," Angie said.

"That's why we're here. It wouldn't do us any good if we were just polite," Tzippy said.

"I'm glad you said that. I feel better. This is one interesting mix of people here, don't you think, Mrs. B.?"

Tzippy looked around the big room and nodded in agreement. "It's hard doing this, Angie, I must confess. I was inclined to turn on my heel and leave at first, but then I realized I have so much to learn from these people. So I stayed."

"You're doing the right thing," Angie said.

Tzippy turned to Stan and said, "I was thinking Shari could have therapy with Dr. Watkins."

"Do you think he's here much? I thought she said he practices in New York," Stan said. "Isn't Shari staying here for thirty days and then returning to Boston?"

"We could change that. I'm going over to ask him. Excuse me." Tzippy walked over to where Dr. Watkins was standing, talking to Pam.

She waited until there was a lull in the conversation and said, "Forgive me for interrupting, but may I have a word with you, Dr. Watkins?"

"Oh, please, Tzippy, talk to him. He's a wealth of information," Pam said, and started to walk away. "Karl," she said, turning back, "Please listen to this woman. She wants to do something before it's too late."

Dr. Watkins smiled and nodded his head in understanding. He turned to Tzippy. "What can I do for you?"

"My name is Tzipora Bryer, and my daughter . . . well, I don't know for sure. She was anorexic and now may be bulimic, and, as you heard, she drinks too much. She's forty-five; this has been going on since she was fifteen. I want her to be happy. I want to see her steady and established before I die. I can't leave things as they are." Tzippy took out her tissue and patted her nose. "Doctor, do you ever come to Miami and do therapy here?"

"Funny, you should ask. Pam and I were discussing that very thing. I'll be coming down every other weekend for long weekends starting in two weeks, and I plan to see clients right here at Lakeville." He smiled and looked down at Tzippy. "How does that sound to you?"

"Oh, that sounds perfect. Can we make an appointment? I am so anxious to start."

"You'll need to talk to your daughter, of course. The therapy is mainly for her, though I think you and she should come together the first few times. Perhaps you could even come for the first session before I leave town this time. How's tomorrow at noon? I have a flight to New York around six and then won't be back for two weeks. What do you think?"

"I think I'm very happy," Tzippy said, smiling and feeling for the first time as if maybe she had broken some new ground.

"Then it's all settled," he said. "I'm looking forward to meeting your daughter. How old did you say she was?"

"Forty-five."

"Well, we'll have some work to do, won't we?" He smiled a bit grimly and then tapped Tzippy's hand. "Leave it to me. I'm an old-timer like you and don't give up easily. Here, take my card."

Tzippy immediately liked Dr. Watkins and his quick decision making; she was walking over to Stan to report the news to him, when Pam interrupted her. "How did it go?" she asked.

"Oh, Pam, he's going to see Shari and me tomorrow at noon. I'm so pleased. Thank you."

"Isn't he something? He just got remarried to a young thing, and she wants to start spending more time in the sun. Aren't we lucky?"

"Oh, dear. I didn't realize. How young is the young thing?" Tzippy asked.

"Young enough to be his daughter, they say. He's a widower and can do whatever he wants, can't he? Men are all alike," Pam said with a false laugh.

"As long as he knows his stuff, that's all I care about," Tzippy said.

"Oh, he knows plenty. You can count on that."

Tzippy felt very lucky to have met Dr. Watkins and couldn't help talking about her good fortune all the way back to Bal Harbour.

When they returned to the apartment, Tzippy could hear the hiccupping of clothes tumbling in the Whirlpool and then spotted Shari catnapping on the sofa in the den. Was she tired, wondered Tzippy, or had she had too much to drink? She slept with her mouth partly open. Standing in front of her sleeping daughter, Tzippy slipped a pill under her tongue.

Angie went to her bedroom, and Stan settled in front of the computer in his room. While she could, without being caught, Tzippy leafed through Shari's pocketbook, which was sitting next to her on the floor. Feeling a bit ashamed of herself, Tzippy wasn't sure what she was searching for but couldn't stop. Maybe Shari took drugs or was hiding a secret phone number.

And then it struck her. Shari had known the problem all along.

Secrets.

Here she was, looking for Shari's secrets. In secret.

Ben had kept Laura a secret, as Tzippy had with Claude—at least, until the fire at the Waldorf Astoria. Tzippy and Claude were there for a tryst, making love in the large, tufted bed, dancing to a Frank Sinatra CD, and showering together in the well-appointed bathroom. When they had to evacuate in their half-clothed state, a photographer took a random picture of them, which wound up on the second page of the *Daily News*. After that, there was no secret—just embarrassment and Ben's anger.

Shari had kept her problems with food a secret, too, though at the same time she'd been screaming for help. The list of things they never talked about, tried to ignore, went on and on: Brucie and his anger, Naomi and Ike's marital problems, Tzippy's and Ben's affairs. And Tzippy and her thefts—the best-kept secret of the bunch.

The only one who was an open book, a man without secrets, was Stan. For the rest of them, keeping something close, not telling anyone else, was a way to try to stay whole, to have something of their own in the world, in a family that was so . . . so thrusting, intrusive, demanding, pawing. Tzippy could hardly breathe. And here she was, doing it again. Perhaps a bath would help her calm down, help her forget.

She hadn't found anything startling in Shari's pocketbook, except for a candy bar, a Baby Ruth, zipped into a side pocket. Was that her secret treat? She would tell Shari about Dr. Watkins and their appointment in the morning.

Tzippy stared out on the pool and was glad for the sunny day that had been predicted. Shari had reacted poorly when she'd told her about the appointment and had said, "I'm too depressed to go."

"What are you talking about?" Tzippy asked. "We have to go. He's only here now; then he'll be gone for two weeks."

"What's the rush?"

"I don't believe you," Tzippy said. "Time is of the essence." She had little patience for Shari's moods. "I could die tomorrow. Besides, you said your time down here was limited."

"Yes, yes, I know," Shari said, stretching her arms in the air.

"You'll go, then?"

"Okay, okay. That's why I'm here, right?" Shari said. She poured herself a cup of black coffee at her place at the table. "When is the appointment?"

"At noon. We must hurry," Tzippy said, sipping her juice.

"I'm going to shower," Shari said. She got up and started toward the bathroom.

"Stan, I think I'll call Ringo. Angie can stay home and do some cooking."

"And me?" he said.

"Go play golf with Freddie." Tzippy didn't want the distraction. She wanted to be alone with Shari. It would be better that way.

"You're sure?"

"Most definitely."

"Let me call Fred."

"Angie, why don't you make a roast tonight?" Tzippy said, turning toward the small kitchen.

"Double-stuffed potatoes?" Angie asked.

"Coleslaw, too," Tzippy said.

"Are we having company?" Angie asked.

Tzippy laughed. "Maybe I'll invite PJ." Perhaps it was a good idea, she thought. He hadn't been over in a few weeks, and she wanted to see what would happen between him and Shari after their friendly encounter at her wedding. She quickly called into the bathroom and said, "Shari, do you mind if I invite PJ to dinner?"

"No, go ahead. Let's see how he's doing," Shari said through the bathroom door.

Tzippy dressed demurely in a pink summer suit and floral blouse, and just before it was time to leave, Shari appeared, wearing designer jeans and short white boots. Tzippy was disappointed in her outfit. She had hoped Shari would dress more conservatively, as she had to attend the Lakeville meeting, in a shirtwaist or simple black dress, but she said nothing. Shari was capable of canceling the appointment if she was offended.

Ringo's cab pulled up to the front of the building, and the two women were off.

⌒

Dr. Watkins's office was on the first floor of the main building and was the opposite of what Tzippy had expected. Instead of comfortable chairs and pictures on the walls, a bookcase, and a vase of flowers, it was furnished simply, with three high, straight-backed chairs and a stark desk.

"Please, ladies. Sit down," he said, gesturing to the seats. "Shari, I'm Dr. Watkins. I'm very glad you've decided to try this. I'll need any medical records you may have. A history of weight. Have you ever been hospitalized?"

"Actually, no," she said.

"How much do you weigh now?"

"Ninety-two pounds."

"Is that your regular weight?"

"I guess. It goes up and down a little, depending on my mood, if I'm in a relationship, stuff like that."

Tzippy lowered her voice a little, even though there were two doors between Dr. Watkins's office and the vestibule. "I'm very worried about Shari," she began.

Dr. Watkins said, "Of course you are." Then, turning to Shari, he said, "Let me begin by disabusing you of a few notions you might have. Your eating disorder didn't start because of a specific event, or character flaw, or a genetic weakness. It's a combination of many things."

Tzippy breathed a sigh of relief as she learned that no specific, major catastrophe had caused her daughter's illness.

"I'm depressed," Shari said.

"Of course you're depressed, for several reasons—the first of which is that you're not getting enough sustenance, you're depleting yourself, and your body overworks to stay warm, or renew the cells, and recoup."

"Yes, yes," Tzippy said.

"You push yourself with too little. Your body's vitamins and minerals are depleted."

"I'm so glad you're telling her this, Doctor," Tzippy repeated.

Dr. Watkins fastened a smile on Tzippy and said, "Mrs. Bryer, perhaps you could refrain from interjecting your thoughts and feelings so frequently."

Shari said, "She always does that."

"Does she?" Dr. Watkins asked, his voice flat.

"Yes. Mother, I can speak for myself."

"I hope so," Dr. Watkins said.

"Why are we here together?" Shari asked. "Why do I need her in here at all?" She stared at Tzippy.

"I wanted to have a family session the first few times," Dr. Watkins said. "Often this is a family disease, though it fastens on one person."

"I think I took a wrong approach in bringing up Shari," Tzippy began.

"You can say that again," Shari said.

"What do you think you did wrong?" Dr. Watkins asked.

"I was too controlling, but I thought I was giving her the best."

"I need a life I can be proud of," Shari said.

"How can your mother help?" Dr. Watkins asked. "Or can't she?"

Tzippy couldn't believe how quickly things were spiraling out of control. Her nerves were already splintered, and she wanted another pill, but she couldn't slip one into her mouth in front of Dr. Watkins.

"She's made me feel inadequate and unsure of myself all my life, so I'm afraid of trying new things that I may want to do," Shari said.

Tzippy briefly wished she had a cigarette and a drink. "I was too outspoken and should have let her do her thing," she said. "I had to be in charge. I'm truly sorry."

"She ruined me!" Shari shouted. Her face turned red, and her right foot, in its white boot, rocked up and down across her left knee.

"You're a grown woman now. You can make better choices," Dr. Watkins said. "You have to take responsibility for your own recovery."

"I do, I do," Shari said. "I read books, have a responsible job."

"This is all to your credit," Dr. Watkins said.

"Then why do you still obsess about food?" Tzippy asked, feeling braver in front of Dr. Watkins. "And drink too much?"

"These are good questions," Dr. Watkins said.

"I can't get free of it," Shari said. "Bad habits."

"What can your mother do to help you get free?" Dr. Watkins asked.

"Maybe stay out of my way," she said.

"Isn't she trying to already?" Dr. Watkins asked.

"Yes. No." Shari stared at the door. "When she says she wants to fix *things*," she said, "what she means is that she wants to fix *me*."

"I want to help," Tzippy said. "I don't know what to do or not to do, to be honest, Dr. Watkins."

"Shari just suggested that perhaps the best way for you to help is to stay out of her way. Your willingness to help may be all it takes. So perhaps you ought to concentrate now on what *not* to do." Tzippy didn't like to hear those words, but she thought perhaps there was some sense to them.

The doctor looked at Shari and said, "What would you like to tell me?"

Shari squinted at Dr. Watkins. "What do you want to know?"

"Whatever pops into your mind. There aren't any rules, and there's not a proper order."

"Well," Shari said, and she blushed. "I don't know why I've been thinking about this, but . . ." She took a deep breath and looked down at the floor. "When I was a young girl, I used to go through my parents' drawers, looking under stacks of clothes, shuffling through papers," she said. "No one seemed to notice."

Tzippy could hardly believe what she was hearing.

"When I got my period and my underpants got stained, I stuffed them into my drawer and went out and bought new ones at the local store on my mother's charge account. She didn't even notice. No one cared or taught me differently," Shari said, her face growing more flushed. "Why didn't she teach me things about being a woman?"

Shari glared at the doctor and then at her mother. "Why?" she yelled.

Dr. Watkins looked at Shari with concern, and Tzippy watched the concentration on his face. What did he think of a mother who didn't even notice her daughter's bloodstained panties? Tzippy's pulse sped up; she thought she might have a heart attack or pass out. She pulled a pill out of the vial in her purse and slipped it under her tongue, too worked up to care whether the doctor noticed. "Could I have a glass of water?" she asked. She began coughing and took out a tissue.

Dr. Watkins went out into the hall and returned with water in a dripping glass. He sat back down and asked, "Why didn't you explain menstruation to your daughter, Mrs. Bryer?"

"I thought . . . the maid . . . someone," Tzippy stammered, the words all jumbled. "I didn't think . . . I was embarrassed." The quiet of the room sat like a blanket on the straight-backed chairs. "I don't know," she finally said. She hung her head and felt the dryness in her slack mouth. She was having trouble breathing.

"She was embarrassed," Shari repeated. "Yeah, she was embarrassed, all right, when her fuckin' famous comedian brother, Lenny, stayed with us and crept into my room to fondle me!" she yelled, her eyes bulging. "I told her I didn't want to sleep in that room. I told her something was wrong, but I was just a kid. Do you think my mother wanted to know the truth or intended to protect me? No, she did nothing, nothing." Shari's face had turned strawberry red, and the veins in her neck protruded. Tzippy's head spun, and she wanted to crawl under the chair, run away. Shari made her feel like a witch.

Dr. Watkins looked at Tzippy and asked, "Did you realize this was going on, Mrs. Bryer?"

"I wasn't sure. I didn't know what to do. I felt squeezed between my brother and my daughter, paralyzed."

"You want to know what happened, Dr. Watkins?" Shari asked. "I went to bed with a butcher knife, a goddamn butcher knife, and when the dirty old man came into my room, I shook that blade in his face and said, 'If you come near me one more time, I'll stab you.' Uncle Lenny never touched me again." She laughed, but it sounded more like a groan or a noise from an animal, deep and feral. She threw her head back and rolled her eyes. Finally, she straightened up and said, "Mommy dearest didn't do shit."

Tzippy's shame was immense; she wished she'd never called Lakeview, never met Watkins, but it was too late. All her failings were being exposed, and now she looked like the awful person she was—a weak, selfish woman and the worst kind of mother. Rocking in her chair in small, jerky movements, she willed herself to keep from falling apart. She kept telling herself that she could do this. She had to. Soon she would be dead and it wouldn't matter.

"Once, I cheated on a test and got caught," Shari continued. "My father reprimanded me. I don't know why I cheated. I knew the work. Some girl wanted the answer. I should have said no. I don't know why I was so pliable," Shari said.

Tzippy wondered if all this—looking through other people's things, keeping secrets, cheating, stealing, abuse—somehow ran in their family. Feeling embarrassed by these revelations, she tried to compose herself and look normal by keeping her mouth curved upward.

"They sent me to a girls' school," Shari went on. "My mother didn't think the high school was fancy enough. I got fat because at night I ate cheese and crackers while I studied. I was horrified as my weight rose and cried when I reported it to her on the phone after a school weigh-in—a hundred and twenty-seven pounds. How could I be a well-turned-out girl if I was chubby?"

Tzippy listened to this as if for the first time. She remembered how shocked she'd been at the news of Shari's weight. That had been right before the anorexia began.

"I hated school, but I pretended to like it. I wanted to be slim and happy, but now I wasn't. I wanted to please my parents. There were many rules. When the school had mixers, I wasn't allowed to date boys who weren't Jewish. But the catch was that none of the boys were Jewish—not in WASP Land." She bent her head and laughed at her own joke.

Tzippy grimaced and tried not to blush.

"I had to go along, be accepted, study hard, and smile. I was supposed to feel grateful, pert, bubbly, and beautiful. Instead, I felt plump, pimply, dumb, unattractive, and unpopular."

Dr. Watkins said, "Go on."

"My mother got fancier and shopped in better stores. My father was home less. He took a lover."

"How did you know that?" Dr. Watkins asked.

"I overheard my mother telling one of her sisters on the phone. She was crying and sipping scotch. Then there was a picture in the newspaper of my mother with her lover without his shirt on outside the Waldorf Astoria when they were evacuated for a fire. My fancy mother, having an affair with Claude the chauffeur."

Tzippy became more and more uncomfortable as Shari recited their family history. *All the dirty laundry*, she thought. *All the soiled and bloody underpants, the molestation.*

"I was afraid of my father," Shari continued, "though I don't really know why. He was the bad guy in our house, because my mother made him that way and because he liked being the boss. Maybe I'm scared of all men." She looked at Dr. Watkins accusingly.

Then the room fell silent. The clock moved, and Dr. Watkins uncrossed his legs. "Shari," he finally said, "I've changed my mind about the best way to proceed. I want you to come and see me alone next time. During the break, make a list of the careers you would choose if you could. What do you like to do? Teach, write, care for people, sing, design, garden, pray, run things, dance, walk a dog."

"And me? What should I do?" Tzippy asked, leaning forward in his direction.

"Write a list of all the things you're sorry for in regard to Shari," Dr. Watkins said, as he took off his glasses and laid them on his desk. "We'll meet in two weeks, but I'll see Shari alone first and then the two of you together. It will be a double session."

Tzippy glanced at Shari and nodded in agreement, as Shari did the same.

"I'm afraid we're out of time," Dr. Watkins said, standing up. "I have a plane to catch, ladies, so you'll have to excuse me."

Tzippy felt a huge wave of relief. She couldn't have stood another minute of this. All she wanted to do was go home, crawl under her sheets, and fall into a drugged sleep.

When she and Shari went out the double doors of Dr. Watkins's office, they passed a small waiting room where a blonde was sitting on a couch with several large suitcases beside her. *That must be Dr. Watkins's new wife*, Tzippy thought. The young woman was reading a magazine and was casually dressed in a cotton dress, with a small turquoise scarf around her neck. She wore no makeup. She was attractive, thought Tzippy, but not fabulous, more the kind of girl you would see on a college campus with a book bag and an A-line skirt and slightly too-wide hips.

Tzippy wondered whether her unkind, judgmental attitude was a result of anger at Dr. Watkins as she attempted to recover from their session. Sometimes it was better to know nothing about your therapist, so he could seem like a blank piece of paper. But maybe she was always this critical. Maybe that was the problem.

☞

Neither of the women spoke during the cab ride. Even Ringo stayed quiet, probably sensing the tension in the air. The only thing he said was, "Mind if I play a tape—some piano music, no words?" Halfway back to the apartment, Tzippy broke the silence and said, "Ringo, can you take us past Mrs. Maples' store?" She turned to Shari. "I thought I'd like to pick up something for Angie. It's her birthday tomorrow."

"What did you think of the session, Mother?" Shari finally asked, lighting up a third cigarette and opening the window a little wider.

"I don't know. Difficult. A bit much for me. We'll have to trust that Dr. Watkins knows what he's doing."

"He has his own style—I'll say that," Shari said, puffing away.

"Well, sweetheart, you have *your* own style as well."

For the second time that day, Shari threw her head back and laughed, enjoying the compliment. Tzippy hadn't seen her laugh twice in one day in years. Tzippy wondered about the world and why people were so crooked or selfish. She felt no better than Nixon, no smarter than Reagan, no more decent than Kennedy. Why couldn't she have created a lovable, stable, traditional family, not this group of characters, drunks, and moody types?

What had happened? She had to be the best. No overweight farmers for her—only the elite, the elegant. And look what she'd gotten instead. Served her right. Shari, drunk. Brucie being jerked around by his crazy wife. Naomi and her fast-talking, slick husband. Tzippy knew that she and Ben were to blame, but still it bothered her that all her children had taken such paths, made choices she didn't approve of.

No, Tzippy needed to be grateful for her family. What was wrong with her, being so unappreciative? And she had Stan, who was good, truly good, a decent man, the most honest man she had ever known.

Thank goodness Ringo knew his way to Mrs. Maples' so she didn't have to lean forward and direct him. When he stopped in front of the store, she saw a group of women inside.

"Please wait," Tzippy said to Ringo. Then she turned to Shari and said, "I need you to help me find something nice for Angie."

The weather had turned oppressive. Shari acted as if she'd never said the unkind words she'd said in Dr. Watkins's office, and Tzippy pretended there was no tension between them. They walked past the large hot-pink flamingo studded with pink beads, with long, thin, silver wire legs, black beak, and bulging eyes, and into the store. As they entered, the bell rang and cool air swirled around them.

"Oh, it's so nice to be inside," Shari cooed.

A saleswoman with white-blond hair looked up from behind the counter where she stood. "May I help you ladies?" she asked.

Tzippy looked around the room and noticed sale signs everywhere. "Look at all these markdowns," Tzippy said. "What's going on?"

"We're selling the business," the woman said.

"Really?" Shari said.

"Oh, dear," Tzippy said. "That's a shame. This is the only place to go for a certain type of dress."

"Maybe the new owners will carry on," the saleswoman said. "There's quite a large inventory, after all."

"But it's been successful, hasn't it?" Tzippy said.

"Yes, indeed," the woman said. "It's not the bottom line. The owner's wife recently died, and . . . well, I think he's just lost heart. He'd like to travel a bit now, from what he tells me, get away from here for a while."

"I can understand that," Tzippy said. "It was hard when my husband died."

"She has a new husband now," Shari said. "The grass doesn't grow under her feet."

"Shari!" Tzippy said. Shari smiled sweetly, as though she'd meant no harm.

"Anyway, we're shopping for a birthday present for a . . ."

"Generously proportioned friend?" the saleswoman asked.

Tzippy said, "You took the words right out of my mouth."

Shari had already started fingering through a rack of muu-muus, housedresses, and caftans; she had a good eye and knew Angie's tastes.

It didn't take long. "What about this?" Shari asked, taking a caftan from the rack and draping it in front of her.

It had diagonal, colorful stripes popping out from a subtle gray background. "That's perfect!" Tzippy said. "Right off the bat! Good for you."

"Yeah," Shari said. "I do have a talent for retail."

"That's why you're doing so well at the Gap!" Tzippy said brightly, knowing that wasn't exactly true.

"Except for the fact that it's in a mall and part of a chain."

Tzippy said nothing. She took the caftan while Shari turned her back to the rack and ran her knuckles absentmindedly over the row of dresses. "But I could do a lot with a place like this," she said plaintively.

Is she suggesting she take over Mrs. Maples'? *Well*, thought Tzippy, *that's an interesting idea.* She'd have to give it some consideration. After all, she wasn't going to live forever.

Chapter 23

The apartment was filled with glorious smells when they returned. They found PJ and Stan on the deck, having cocktails. The heat had eased some, and a cool sea breeze softened the humidity.

"Go freshen up a bit before he sees you," Tzippy said, unable to refrain from instructing her daughter.

Shari ran and took a quick shower. Tzippy hoped she'd cream her body with the scented Laura Mercier they'd purchased, powder her nose, put on some mascara and bright lipstick, choose some dangling earrings, and throw on something a little revealing—perhaps her scoop-necked aqua cashmere top . . .

She shook her head, reprimanding herself. She knew it wasn't right to think in so much detail like this, but the habit was ingrained.

When Shari emerged, Tzippy saw that she was, for better or for worse, her mother's daughter. It was almost as if she'd read Tzippy's mind. "Sweetheart," she said, "you look wonderful."

Shari said, "Thanks, Mom." Tzippy poured herself a glass of wine and went out onto the deck, where the breeze was delightful. Shari stayed behind in the kitchen with Angie.

"This is the life," Stan said, stretching out his legs on his chaise lounge.

"We've made the adjustment rather well," Tzippy said. "Don't you think, darling?" She smiled at her new husband.

"Baby cakes, we're doing swell."

Shari appeared in the doorway, holding a silver plateful of canapés, which she placed on a small wrought-iron table. As soon as PJ saw her, he went over, took her hand, and led her to the corner of the patio. Tzippy tried to stay close enough to eavesdrop.

"You look lovely," PJ said.

"Thank you," Shari said, lowering her eyes.

"How are we doing?" PJ asked.

Shari said, "I don't want to disappoint you."

"That goes both ways, you know. I was a jerk."

"I drink too much."

Tzippy carried a bowl of mixed nuts to the table where the canapés were and then pretended to pick something off the tile floor.

"I want us to see each other. Can we try?" PJ said.

Shari said, "I'd like that." Then, as Tzippy straightened up, she saw Shari smile and kiss him quickly on the lips.

Angie called, "Dinner's ready," and everyone went inside to gather at the table. As they sat down, Stan asked, "PJ, how's business?" PJ had bought a bouquet of flowers, daffodils, and tulips, and they now sat in the center of the table in a short yellow vase.

"Depends who the clients are, Stan. You don't always get who you want," PJ said.

"I was wondering, do you charge a flat rate or by the hour?" Stan asked, as he carved Angie's roast.

PJ smiled. "You're not shy, are you?"

"Curious. I like to know how things work, that's all. I was always in sales, so we worked on commission."

"First, I get a retainer."

"Your dad was an attorney, too, right?" Stan said.

"Yes, and a damn good one," PJ said. He began to cut the thick slice that Stan had served him.

Tzippy hoped Stan wasn't being too nosy. "Please, have one of Angie's baked stuffed potatoes."

"Thanks," PJ said, lifting one onto his plate. "He brought a lot of skill and vigor to all his cases."

"A wonderful man," Tzippy said. She sipped her wine. "I had the honor of knowing him when I was just Tzippy Finkel, from West Belchertown." She recalled his long, polished desk, his silk shirts, and his Radcliffe bride.

Shari said, "My dad liked your father a lot," and then she smiled. Her dark hair and olive skin looked radiant in the dining room light. Tzippy was glad she'd invited PJ.

As they all dug into Angie's delicious roast beef, smothered in onions, Shari said, much to Tzippy's surprise, "PJ, I wanted you to know my mom and I have started going to support meetings at this eating disorder center."

Tzippy put her fork down on her good china plate.

"No kidding?" PJ said. "When did all that start?"

"A few weeks ago. It's been very interesting; we're going to therapy with this great doctor, Karl Watkins. Ever hear of him?" Shari asked.

"Can't say that I have. We lawyers don't know a lot about the medical field, as a general rule, but I'm sure he's as good as you say."

"And I think I may go into a quit-drinking program that one of the people there told me about," she added, shocking Tzippy further.

Unable to contain herself any longer, Tzippy asked, "Who told you about this?"

"As a matter of fact, Roland told me his *papa* is a recovering drinker and attended the program. I may try it." She smiled at all the people at the table, cut a piece of roast beef, and popped it into her mouth.

Tzippy stared at her daughter and wondered at this new

attitude. She looked over at Stan; he, too, sat shaking his head in disbelief but said nothing to upset the mood. Tzippy was so excited she wanted to get herself a pill to quiet her nerves, but she refrained from rising from the table and instead said, "Angie, this is one delicious dinner."

"I don't remember when I've had such a good meal, Angie," PJ added. "I mean it. This is as fine as any you get at those fancy restaurants."

Angie beamed like a light bulb, and Tzippy smiled.

"You keep cooking like this, Angie, and I'll have to let out my pants," Stan said, loosening his belt at the table.

Tzippy laughed and said, "Oh, darling, you just like to eat. Don't blame poor Angie."

"Yes, you're right. I'm just a glutton for good food and drink," he said. "Excuse me, folks—I need a stroll to burn it off." He rose from the table. "I think I'll go walk down the path while there's a little light left. PJ and Shari can go on the deck and watch the sunset. I'll be back for dessert. There *is* dessert, right?" he said.

"Mr. Stan, I made myself a birthday cake for you all to enjoy," Angie announced. "It's my favorite kind of cake, carrot with cream cheese frosting, so you go on and take a good, brisk walk and hurry on back. I got a nice, steaming cup of coffee to go with it, too."

"Angie, I've died and gone to heaven. You are something else," Stan said, as he grabbed his cane and headed out the door.

Shari and PJ went out on the deck. Tzippy watched as Shari lit her after-dinner cigarette and they stretched their legs out on the chaise lounges; then she went into her bedroom, popped her tranquilizer, and found the birthday card she'd purchased to go with Angie's gift from Mrs. Maples'. *It's been quite a day*, she thought.

When Stan came back from his walk, she was sitting at her writing desk, signing the card. "What's come over Shari?" he asked.

"You know as much as I do," Tzippy said, licking the envelope. "Let's see how long this lasts."

"You're right, of course," he said, putting on a fresh white shirt.

"It's a beginning," Tzippy said.

"That's my girl," Stan said, patting Tzippy's shoulder.

Tzippy lifted the large box wrapped in Mrs. Maples' foil.

"What did you buy?" asked Stan.

"A wonderful caftan," Tzippy said. "Shari picked it out. And by the way, Mrs. Maples' is for sale," she added.

"And that means what?" Stan asked. He looked in the mirror and straightened his hair with his fingers.

Tzippy couldn't help the smile that spread across her face. "I don't know yet, but I've got a hunch."

"Tzippy, you are full of surprises, aren't you?"

"Stan, my mind keeps cooking!"

They walked into the dining room, carrying Angie's gift and card, and laid them on the yellow sofa.

Stan opened the slider and said, "Kids, come in. We're having birthday cake."

Shari and PJ came into the living room from the deck, arm in arm. They were grinning and kissing, and PJ was rubbing Shari's bottom. At one point, Shari even giggled, and for once Tzippy didn't think it was alcohol-related.

They all sat down around the table, and Shari said, "I plan to stop drinking by the end of the month, but tonight I'm having two gin martinis so I can get a good night's sleep." Then she finished her drink and put down the empty glass. "That's number one, in case anyone's counting."

Tzippy looked over at Stan, and he winked his approval.

Angie walked in and set her birthday cake on the table. It was decorated around the edges with little pink rosebuds. Tzippy clapped her hands and said, "It's not every day a person gets to bake her own birthday cake," and everyone laughed.

They lit a candle and sang "Happy Birthday" to Angie while she smiled broadly.

"Sit down and have some, for God's sake," Stan insisted.

"Don't mind if I do," Angie said, and settled into one of the chairs. As she ate, Tzippy gave her the gift from Mrs. Maples'.

"Oh, mercy. What a beautiful dress. Thank you," Angie said, looking genuinely pleased. She stood up, put the caftan across her body, and twirled around. "It's so pretty, Mrs. B. Thanks so much."

"How old are you this year?" Shari asked.

"Fifty-seven," Angie answered, sitting back down in her chair and folding the dress carefully.

"No kidding?"

"Can you believe it?"

"No, not really. Shari was seven when Angie came, and she was nineteen. Do the math," Tzippy said.

"Great cake, Angie," Stan said. Everyone nodded in agreement. "Cream cheese frosting is my favorite. How did you know?"

"Oh, Mr. Stan, I know lots of things about you," Angie teased.

Finally, the table was cleared and Tzippy said, "You are to do nothing tomorrow. Hear me, Angie?"

"Yes, ma'am. I think I'll go to church."

"Good idea."

Shari said, "PJ and I are going next door to have a nightcap."

"I'll leave the lights on," Tzippy said.

"Do you have a key?" Stan asked.

"I'm fine," Shari said. "Got one."

Tzippy had to admit that PJ's positive influence on Shari was causing her to reconsider the pair's relationship. What if Shari really could stop drinking? Maybe it was too much to ask. Tzippy hoped not, but she would wait and see and maybe say a prayer.

⌒

In the morning, Angie went off to church in her powder-blue suit and hat and Stan sat in front of his computer. Tzippy ate breakfast with Shari and couldn't stop herself from asking about PJ.

"We had a good, long talk," Shari said.

"And?" Tzippy squeezed lemon into her tea.

"He wants me to stop the booze," Shari said, breaking a piece of rye toast in half. "It's killing the relationship. I think if I stop . . . well, maybe . . . We'll see," she said. She spread cottage cheese on her toast.

Tzippy said, "You have to stop for yourself."

"I know, but it's a motivator."

"Well, yes, you're right," Tzippy said, moving her small bowl of raspberry jam closer.

"I'm going to try. Booze is bad on so many levels for me," Shari said, looking directly at her mother. "I just have to get past the habit."

Tzippy thought about her own history of drinking and wondered if she'd ever seriously thought of stopping. And then there was her pill taking. As she spread raspberry jam on her own slice of rye toast, she wondered what they talked about at AA meetings. "Well," she said, "if you attend an AA meeting, I'd like to go with you. I'm interested in what goes on there."

"Sure, Mom," Shari said, staring at the cottage cheese and then eyeing the preserves. She smiled at Tzippy and said, "How's that raspberry jam? Pass it over."

When Shari and Tzippy returned for their next appointment with Dr. Watkins, two weeks later, in the middle of May, Shari drove and they each came with their list. They'd been working on them during the hiatus; Tzippy believed Shari was as serious as she was about presenting the doctor with as accurate a picture of who they each were as they could.

"Ladies, how are we doing this week?" Dr. Watkins asked. "Shall we have our joint session first or second?" He looked at both of them. "Do you have a preference?"

"Since we started off together, let's continue this way for now," Shari said, sparing Tzippy the decision. She didn't want to get on Shari's bad side too early in the process.

"Well, since you seem so eager to get along, why don't you share your list, Shari?" Dr. Watkins said, settling into his straight-backed chair.

Shari looked up and smiled. She was wearing a more appropriate outfit today, a simple summer dress with flounce sleeves, scattered with small flowers. She smiled as she took a long yellow piece of lined paper out of her handbag and started to recite.

"A few of the things I wish I could have done are . . ." She stopped and appeared embarrassed. "Oh, hell, I'll just say it. You asked. No comments." She stared at Tzippy. "I'd have liked to be a trial lawyer. I have visions of me trying a case and my mother sitting in the gallery, looking on proudly. I see her watching me. I'm prepared. I'm nervous but confident. Also, I'm dressed in a wonderful, expensive, conservative dark suit with just enough leg showing to be sexy but also proper. I'm brilliant and sharp. That's my first image."

Tzippy and Dr. Watkins smiled and nodded.

"Please don't laugh at this one," she said. "The next career I envision is me as a ballerina. I'm dressed in a lavender tulle skirt, wearing toe shoes with ribbons crisscrossed up the calves. My hair's up on top of my head. I'm beautiful and I'm spinning. One of the male dancers lifts me over his head. It's a dazzling performance."

Dr. Watkins nodded and waved his hand to go on. "This is good, Shari."

Tzippy sat silently in her straight-backed chair and worried that her list wouldn't measure up, was too factual, lacked enough emotion, but it was too late to change it, she thought.

"In my next fantasy, I'm an artist and for some reason am married or living with a man. We live in a Cape house by the marshes. We work every day in separate studios. My room has a big easel, and I do oil paintings. I sit on a stool in an old shirt that I use as a smock. There's a loaf of homemade bread in the kitchen on a wooden breadboard. I baked the bread myself. We eat thick slices of the bread with sweet butter. We have no children. It was a mutual choice because we are into our careers. It's a good life, and occasionally we travel to New York to art galleries or show or sell our work. I love my husband and my life."

Dr. Watkins said, "My oh my, you do have some wonderful, vivid fantasies. I can see you're disappointed. You haven't been able to live out any of those, have you?"

"No," Shari said.

"Why do you think that's so?" he asked.

Tzippy was flabbergasted. Didn't Shari and Watkins know that some of this was a matter of talent? Who knew whether Shari could draw or dance?

"I don't know . . . No follow-through; not sure how to get there . . . I wanted to, but I got sidetracked." Shari shook her head, and tears came to her eyes.

Tzippy hadn't even known about any of Shari's private dreams. Now, she asked her, "Why didn't you tell me? Also, why didn't you write about being an actress? Your father thought you had so much talent." *Even though your drama teacher said not so much,* she added silently to herself.

"Oh, Mom, you know. I just wanted to please you. Yes, I should have written about acting. I didn't know if I could succeed. Some of these ideas were embarrassing. I was confused." Shari wiped tears from her eyes.

"Perhaps she felt too pressured by you, Mrs. Bryer, and didn't have the clarity to think it all through," Dr. Watkins suggested.

Perhaps, Tzippy thought, but there were plenty of kids who

were pressured who went on to do great things. Nevertheless, "pressured" pretty much summed it up. *She wasn't able because of me.* Reaching into her bag, Tzippy craved a pill.

"Hold on," Dr. Watkins said. "How many of those pills do you take in one day?"

Tzippy looked up, scalded with shock. "It depends," she said.

"What kind of medicine is it?" he asked.

"Half a milligram of lorazepam for anxiety, to calm me down."

"How many are you supposed to take?"

"Two a day. Maybe three, if needed."

"And how many do you usually take?"

Tzippy started to squirm in her seat, and Shari looked at her with wide eyes. "I don't keep count. Maybe five, six."

"Perhaps, Mrs. Bryer . . . perhaps you're addicted to prescription medication, just as Shari is addicted to alcohol. Perhaps the two of you should think about what you can do to face these addictions and rid yourselves of them. Rehab. Or AA or NA meetings."

Who does he think he is, comparing me to Shari? thought Tzippy. *She's a drunk; I have a real condition that requires medication—over years of stress from Benny and Shari.* "I can just cut back. I'm sure I can do that without a problem."

"Try to stick to the doctor's suggestion of two or three, tops."

"Yes, of course," Tzippy said, though she thought, *He has some nerve embarrassing me like that.*

"Now your list of things you wish you hadn't done to Shari, Mrs. Bryer. Have you got one?"

"Oh, yes," she laughed. "A long one, I'm afraid." She pulled out her notepad and opened it up. It was wrinkled and covered in her handwriting. "I was too pushy, too critical."

"Could you be more specific, please?" Dr. Watkins said.

"Well, I tried to change Shari into the girl I thought she should be, and I guess I made her feel less good about herself in the process. I felt I needed to do that, not because she didn't have good traits but because I had this ideal girl in mind."

"Yes, and what did this ideal person look like?" he asked.

Tzippy felt very uncomfortable. "She was beautiful and classy and tall and slim and bright and graceful and well-mannered and upper-class." She felt a small piece of satisfaction saying it like that, like divulging a secret. "There—I've admitted it."

"And Shari didn't measure up to this ideal woman?"

"Well, she was lovely. I just wanted to smooth out the edges. Even movie stars need help," Tzippy said, feeling foolish after she'd uttered these words.

"In the process, you made your daughter feel less good about herself. If you didn't refinish her, she'd never measure up," Dr. Watkins said. He crossed his long legs and waited.

Well, Tzippy thought, *I wouldn't have put it that way*. The way he said it made it sound as though she'd thought of Shari as a piece of furniture.

The silence in the room was long and achingly uncomfortable. Tzippy didn't know what to say. But what had struck her most forcefully were the words "upper-class." She hadn't written them down; they'd just tumbled out. Did all this have to do with her own embarrassment and longings, her own shame at her parents' situation?

"I feel like a criminal, like I robbed her of a chance to be happy, but I thought I was doing a good thing . . . Really, at the time, I did," Tzippy stammered.

"Specifics, please," Dr. Watkins said.

Shari jumped up and said, "I'll give you specifics, if you want. My mother was infatuated with her brother's wife, Diana, who was a model and walked with her ass tucked in and her skinny body floating down the street, like this." She planted herself in the middle of the room and started strutting around with her butt tucked under and her shoulders back. "I can just see my mother describing it to me in our kitchen in New Jersey after she met Diana in Manhattan. Diana could do no wrong, even though she was Protestant. No, she was Baptist, the daughter of a Baptist minister. Can you believe this? Of course, no one was supposed to date anyone who wasn't Jewish, but Mom's brother, the pedophile, got the pass because Diana was blond, pug-nosed, pretty, skinny, stylish. Once he captured the thin, photogenic shiksa, that trumped everything in my mother's eyes."

With that, Shari plopped back down in her chair and crossed her legs, one foot bobbing up and down.

Dr. Watkins nodded. "Do any other specifics come to mind?"

Again with the specifics. Tzippy waited and held her breath. What was coming next? She dreaded the answer. Again, Shari stood up and demonstrated. She put her hands on her hips and said, "I was too short-waisted. The girl in the luncheonette had thick ankles. My cousin had fat thighs. No one was as beautiful as Cousin Mindy." Tzippy squirmed in her seat. "The girls in the *New York Times* all went to Seven Sisters schools and got over seven hundred on their SATs." Taking a deep breath, Shari continued, "I couldn't do it. I tried and tried, but I didn't grow longer, smarter, wiser, or better. That's the goddamn truth, in a nutshell." Her breath quickened and her face reddened. "I tried. Damn it, Mother, I tried. I just wasn't ever great enough for you. But you were no Radcliffe movie star yourself. Why did you think I had to be one?"

Tzippy sat silently in her chair and reached for the tissues in her handbag. She had to come clean. Wasn't that the point of this? Wasn't that what she had promised herself—to turn things around, set them straight, right her wrongs before she died?

"I did it all to my daughter, Dr. Watkins," Tzippy began hesitantly. "The truth is, I never felt good about myself because I grew up poor, in an immigrant family. Jealousy simmered inside me all of my childhood. My mother was a washwoman with an apron, taking in boarders. I wore hand-me-downs. I couldn't afford to go to college, and I dreamed of being a fancy lady. After I married Ben and had money, I wanted Shari to go to the best schools and be beautiful like a model or a movie star—brilliant, charming, outstanding. However, I coveted the credit because I was empty inside and needed to be bolstered. I wanted to be the brains of the whole project.

"Where did that leave Shari?" Tzippy asked. She took a deep breath, gained her strength, and continued. "Well, I wasn't a nurturing mother because I was too wrapped up in myself and didn't think about her feelings, her needs, or her interests. Oh, I thought I did, but it was for me. I gave her elocution lessons because I hated her New Jersey accent. I thought she sounded classless with that accent. I was a selfish woman, and I ruined my daughter. Ben said Shari had been damaged, and I knew he meant by me."

Tzippy felt as if she were confessing to a murder. "Now you have the whole dirty, ugly truth." She lowered her head and let the tears stream down her wrinkled face, over her makeup. She felt her mascara running under her eyes before she took a tissue and patted her face dry.

The room was silent with the fog of truth, dense and thick; Tzippy could hear cars moving along the road outside.

"I'm going outside now for a cigarette," Shari said. "You can finish up with my illustrious mother, Dr. Watkins." Her performance over, she left the office and closed the double doors firmly.

Dr. Watkins asked, "How are you doing now, Mrs. Bryer?"

"I haven't lived eighty years without being strong."

"To your credit."

"I'm wondering why you didn't call Shari on her fantasies. You can't be an artist or ballet dancer just by wishing you were. Who knows if she had that talent?"

"She probably didn't," Dr. Watkins said, "but that's not the point here. We're simply trying to get Shari to express her feelings. Later, she can come to understand that perhaps her fantasies were unrealistic. That's when she'll begin to take responsibility for herself.

"I think maybe we've finished for the day," he continued. "Shari and you both seem to have had enough for now. Overloading the old neural circuits is never a good idea. Why don't we meet in two weeks, one more time as a double session? Then we'll go with Shari alone."

Tzippy wrote a check and slipped it over the desktop.

"And the pills . . . You'll cut down, won't you?" Dr. Watkins said.

That's the hardest part, thought Tzippy, but she answered, "Of course. Whatever you say, Doctor."

On the drive home, Tzippy was silent. *How do you resume conversation after you've been attacked? How do you talk after you've confessed to being a sinner?* Each time she tried to speak, the attempt left her feeling nervous and incomplete. She made sounds that were part sighs and part moans. Breathing slowly, closing her eyes, she slowed the fluttering in her chest. Gazing at her daughter, she wondered how she felt. Tzippy said, "Shari, I know I messed up as a mother. I sucked, as you would say."

Shari didn't answer right away, but she did look a bit surprised at Tzippy's choice of words. She kept driving, lit a cigarette, blew the smoke out the window, and nodded her head, as if in agreement. Then she said, "Mom, you didn't suck all the time, not at all. Sometimes you were nice, but you often forgot about my feelings totally."

"Did I make you miserable?"

"You just wanted what you wanted, and that made me miserable."

"But I wanted good things."

"I never got to decide. You directed me, like I was a prop."

"It was that bad?"

Shari let out a howl as they drove down the interstate and didn't let up for a good half a minute, as if she were releasing all the pain and frustration she'd stored for years inside her slim body. Tzippy watched, afraid to say anything, but she thought her heart would explode or she would faint or die of anxiety. Then Shari stopped and everything went silent again.

"Are you finished?" Tzippy asked, once they were off the interstate. They came to an intersection, and Shari took a right turn, then stopped at a red light. As she leaned her head on the steering wheel, Tzippy said, "Please." She reached over and touched Shari's hand. "Please," she repeated.

Shari clutched Tzippy's hand and held it. For a brief moment, Tzippy felt as if they were connected like soldiers on a battlefield, defending each other's lives. Then the light changed and Shari let go. "I'm okay now," Shari said.

They drove in silence again for a while, until Tzippy summoned the courage she thought perhaps she'd lacked. "Listen," she said. "Let's go to Mrs. Maples' again."

"Why?"

"Because last time I saw something there that got me interested."

"What is it?" Shari asked, annoyed. She stopped at another red light.

"When you heard that the store was for sale," Tzippy said, "I could just see it in your face. The idea that maybe, if you had a store like that . . ." Her heart was pounding, afraid that Shari would reject her. "You need something in your life, Shari. What if I bought that business and you ran the store? You could sell fashionable, cute clothes, dress up the inventory, create the window displays, order the merchandise, advertise, have a life as an owner of a cute boutique, and be proud of yourself."

"There you go again," Shari said. "Trying to make me into someone you want me to be." But her voice was far from strident.

"No," Tzippy said. "This is different. This is someone *you* want to be, not someone I want you to be. This was your idea—but you didn't talk about it because you don't have the money. But I do."

"Are you trying to buy my love, Mother?"

"I can't buy your love. I know that. We've been through too much. The damage is done. But I can try to give you a legitimate way to turn your life around. Why not?" she asked again. "Consider it a loan, if you want. Though I'd like it to be a present."

Shari stared ahead, and, try as she might, Tzippy could not read her expression. Was she going to howl again? Get out of the car and walk away, abandoning her mother in the middle of the traffic? Tzippy didn't have a clue. Shari's breathing was slow and steady, and she kept both hands on the wheel. When the light changed, she took her foot off the brake and the car moved forward.

Tzippy knew it was a wonderful idea. She felt it in her bones, and though she knew that part of her desire to repair the damage was selfish—she couldn't die in peace with Shari so upset—she also knew that her desire to give her daughter something she herself wanted, not something Tzippy wanted, was pure and good. She knew this was her last chance.

"Well," Shari said. She smiled. "Maybe it would work."

When they got to Mrs. Maples', they could see women inside, elbows hitting shoulders, hips knocking hips. A mound of clothes was stacked in a corner, and two sale racks were filled with dresses and skirts, shirts and jackets.

Tzippy stared through the front glass, and when Shari walked past the pink flamingo and opened the door, the sound of ringing floated through the air.

The signs that now announced another 20 percent off the original 50 percent discount had the customers crazed. They snatched and grabbed and held items close to their chests. One woman was trying to pry a blouse loose from another woman's hand. They were grunting and groaning.

"My oh my," Tzippy said. She caught Shari's eye, and they looked at each other over the melee.

"There'll be nothing left to sell," Shari said.

"You'll buy all new. Maybe you don't want these *schmattes*," Tzippy said.

Her energy was low from the tension at Dr. Watkins's and the chaos in Mrs. Maples'. She just wanted to get more information about the business and then leave. She searched for the peroxide-blond saleswoman and spotted her. Today she was wearing her hair slicked back, held in place by a large black barrette.

They talked for a few minutes, though Tzippy had to raise her voice over the noise in the shop. The saleswoman left and returned with a manila envelope that she told Tzippy contained a prospectus, facts and figures concerning previous years' grosses, and other business-related papers.

"Is this everything we need?" Tzippy asked. "Who should I call if I'm interested?"

The saleswoman tapped the envelope. "It's all in there," she said. "And sorry for the chaos. It's been crazy all day."

Tzippy and Shari thanked the woman, made their way through elbows and shoulders, opened the door, and scooted out. It was a relief to be back on the street.

"We'll call PJ when we get home," Tzippy said as she climbed into the town car.

"Yes," Shari said. "He's got to look at the figures." She looked happier than she had in days.

Chapter 24

Two weeks later, at the end of May, the day was humid and already Tzippy felt weak, but she didn't want them to miss their scheduled appointment with Dr. Watkins. "Turn up the air-conditioning a little, Shari. God, it's hot today," Tzippy said. She fanned herself with a magazine. "Oh, that's much better. Thank you." She reclined in the leather seat of the town car and enjoyed the cool relief.

"I just wanted you to know . . ." Shari cleared her throat and gripped the steering wheel more tightly.

"Yes?" Tzippy said.

"I mean, just because of Mrs. Maples' . . . that doesn't make everything else go away. I still have memories, feelings."

"I know, sweetie," Tzippy said. "And they'll have to come out." She tried to sound encouraging, but Shari's words made her dread what was coming.

"How are you ladies today?" Dr. Watkins asked when they arrived.

"We're fine—just trying to stay cool," Tzippy said.

"Yes, it's very warm. I have cold water here if you need it," Dr. Watkins said, pointing to a large pitcher on his desk. "How shall we begin? Shari, do you want to start?"

"Yes," Shari said. "I've been thinking of a few things I'd like to discuss."

"Please go ahead, then," he said.

"First of all," Shari said, "I want you to know my mother has done a very good thing. She knows I'm interested in retail but that I wasn't happy at my last job in that industry, so she's proposed that she help me start my own business. I won't go into details now, but the point is, she saw I was interested in something, and she listened and watched, and, regardless of her own interests, she's encouraging me. So that's progress."

"Yes," Dr. Watkins said. "Yes, it is."

"But," Shari said, "there's still a lot of stuff from the past." She stole a look at Tzippy. "What I want to know today," she said, "is why my mother didn't go with me to the dermatologist's office when I was seventeen and had a goddamn bald spot the size of an egg on the back of my head."

She stood up by her straight-backed chair, as if she were about to take flight, as if the energy inside her body was building up and ready to explode. In her straight red skirt, black sleeveless top, and red Jimmy Choo high heels, she looked like a rocket and her eyes never left her mother's face. "Why, Mom?" Shari said. "Why didn't you hold my hand? Why didn't you comfort me and tell me everything would be okay?"

Humiliated by the attack, Tzippy reached into her purse and thought absentmindedly about taking a pill but then realized that her pillbox wasn't in the purse because she'd been trying to cut back, partly in solidarity with Shari, who had indeed quit drinking, as she'd promised. Instead, Tzippy reached for her tissues and blew her nose, although she wanted to stuff the tissues into Shari's mouth and make her stop talking. Instead, she sat stoically, despite the dizzy feeling beginning inside her head.

"No," Shari continued. "You stayed home in your matching outfit with the short bolero jacket and high heels. You went into your dressing room with that textbook-size blue check register, opened and waiting, and paid your goddamn bills."

Tzippy stared at her and tried to recall the day so many years ago. She couldn't remember why she'd stayed home. Had she thought Shari could take care of things herself? Had she been too busy paying bills so Benny wouldn't notice how much she'd spent that month? Had she needed to send money to one of her Finkel relatives who needed extra cash? Perhaps that was it, but she had no real answers.

"You imagined I could drive my little old self over to that nice lady doctor and get a long needle plunged into my head all alone. At seventeen, I was all grown up; I could handle it because I was a big girl," Shari waved her arm dramatically. "I could drive, so why couldn't I go get a needle stuck in my scalp?"

She turned to Dr. Watkins. "She didn't want to watch it. She didn't want to hear the doctor tell me I needed more vitamin B because my skin was dry, and that I should eat more butter and cream and milk." Shari shook her head back and forth. "She didn't want to hear how her daughter was starving herself."

As she sat back down and crossed her legs, her calf swung up and down under her slim skirt. "Mom, I told you all about the appointment when I got home. We stood in the kitchen, and I reported how she took me into a dark room and stuck that long needle into my scalp to make my hair grow back. You stood by the sink while Angie was dicing vegetables and listened. I told you what the doctor said about my diet.

"And what did you do? You said, 'You should have a nice grilled cheese sandwich and a bowl of cream of tomato soup for lunch.' That's what you said. I can remember my mouth salivating, I was so hungry. *Perhaps*, I thought, *my mother will actually make me this delicious-sounding lunch. Now that she's heard what the doctor said, maybe she'll feel sorry for me.* I was starving, and I could taste that cheese sandwich melting in my mouth. Did you tell Angie to cook it? No. Did you cook it? No. Did you think I would cook it? No one cooked the goddamn grilled cheese sandwich.

No one. You just walked back into your dressing room and sat back down in front of your checkbook."

Shari breathed heavily and held her arms around her midsection, hugging herself so she wouldn't fall apart; she swayed and rocked, and the tears streamed down her cheeks. "I was ravenous!" she yelled. "I wanted that goddamn grilled cheese sandwich. I wanted your love. I wanted something!" Then she stared at Tzippy, the wetness of her tears smearing her mascara, making her look raccoon-like.

"You know what I did?" she continued as Tzippy sat, horrified, and Dr. Watkins remained silent. "I walked over to our Coppertone refrigerator and took out a chicken wing from supper the night before and went out and stood by the glass storm door and sucked that chicken wing and chewed it and devoured the marrow inside the bone. I was so hungry, I couldn't get enough."

Tzippy's head spun with shame and guilt. Her body felt warm. What kind of monster had she been? What was wrong with her? She didn't believe the meanness, and yet she knew it was true.

Dr. Watkins said, "Mrs. Bryer, what are you thinking?"

There were no words to defend herself, no explanation. Tzippy lowered her head and said, "I have nothing to say because I can't get over my behavior, Doctor."

Shari got up and said, "I have to go to the ladies' room," and she left Tzippy there alone with Dr. Watkins. "I'm a bad person," Tzippy said, covering her face with her hands. "You heard her."

"Yes, I did. What are you feeling?" Dr. Watkins asked.

"I feel terrible," she said, lowering her hands and placing them in her lap. "Sick to my stomach. You heard her. It's true. I don't know why I didn't go. I should have. Other mothers would have. They'd have driven their daughter to the doctor, held her hand, acted remorseful, but that was who I was. I probably had some personal business to attend to that morning, had to get a check out to my brother or my cousin. I convinced myself Shari would be okay going to the doctor's alone," she said, shaking her head in disbelief. "When I die, they'll say I did all these things wrong. Made so many mistakes. Let my family down."

"Who are 'they'?" Dr. Watkins asked.

"My children, especially Shari."

"That's important, what they think?"

"I'm not a bad person," she said, staring at the doctor. "Not really."

"You're contradicting yourself," Dr. Watkins said.

"I know, I know," Tzippy said, squirming in her chair, criss-crossing her legs, trying to get comfortable. "I'm such a mess." Now that she was reducing the pills, she had more anxiety.

"What do you mean by 'a mess'?"

"I thought I could do this therapy, wanted to do this. But it's too hard for me," she said. "It's too hard to hear all these accusations. I feel bombarded, attacked. I want to crawl under a rock, maybe run away. Really, I can't stand it, Doctor. It's too much for me. I'm too old and too tired."

Then she saw spots before her eyes and started to feel light-headed. "I'm not well," she said in a throaty voice. She started to topple, her thin body bending into a lump and then a small pile on the floor. She saw one of her brown-spotted hands fall forward just as her eyes fluttered shut.

"Mrs. Bryer?" Dr. Watkins said, bending over her. She could dimly see him as he jumped up and dialed his phone. "An elderly woman just fainted in my office. Dr. Karl Watkins. Lakeville Eating Disorder Center. Hurry, please."

"Shari!" he yelled as he opened his double door. "Your mother has fainted."

Shari ran into the office and threw herself down on the floor. "Mom, what's wrong?" She patted Tzippy's face. "Oh my God, I've killed her!" she shrieked.

Dr. Watkins brought Tzippy a cup of water and lifted her head so she could drink. "Mrs. Bryer, have some water." Then he looked at Shari and said, "Please calm down. Get ahold of yourself."

Tzippy raised her head and took a sip; the water was cold and felt good on her lips. "I'll be fine," she said groggily. "What happened?"

"You fainted, Mom," Shari said. "I yelled at you. You got upset."

Tzippy lifted herself up on an elbow. "Please help me up."

"I called 911," Dr. Watkins said.

"No, no. I just got a little light-headed," she said. "I'm hot."

"Let them check you," he said.

In no time, it seemed, the medics were there, wheeling a stretcher.

"It's not necessary," Tzippy said.

A medic took her blood pressure. "It's a little low," he said.

"Better low than high," Tzippy said.

"You got too excited," Dr. Watkins said, sitting back down behind his desk.

"I'm okay now," Tzippy said. She sat down in her straight-backed chair.

The medic said, "You should come to the emergency room and let us check you out, ma'am."

"No, no," Tzippy said. "I'm quite all right."

Shari said. "Are you sure, Mom?"

"I'll come to the hospital after I finish here. Shari will drive me. I promise," Tzippy said. "Let's finish up the session, please."

Dr. Watkins nodded to the medic.

"I'll be right outside," Shari said.

Tzippy sat for a moment and stared at the doctor. His head grew larger and then shrank until it was the proper size. She heard a faint humming in her ears, but after a while it went away.

"I'm not sure we should continue, Mrs. Bryer," Dr. Watkins said.

"Well, *I'm* sure," Tzippy said. "So please . . ." She gestured at him, and he sat back in his chair. "No time like the present." Annoyance suddenly swept over her. Without the pills, she was irritated more easily. "Oh, for God's sake, stop looking at me like I'm some sort of bug."

"Why did you think you could do this, Mrs. Bryer?" Dr. Watkins asked.

"What choice do I have?" Tzippy asked. "I wanted to set things right. But maybe it's too late to make forty years right." She grabbed a tissue and wiped her tears. She patted her cheeks. A few minutes passed, and then she stopped crying.

"Do you feel better?" he asked.

"A little."

"What happens now, do you think?" he asked.

Tzippy shrugged.

"Do you ever pray?" Dr. Watkins inquired. "Did you ever?"

"When I was a young girl," Tzippy said, smiling in recollection, "I loved to go to the synagogue and hear all the chanting. At night I prayed in my bed. Alone, I asked God for help. I always needed help from God."

"Always?"

"Yes, I struggled."

"How?"

"I wanted to improve my situation, even then, as a youngster. Sometimes I did things I shouldn't." She looked away, ashamed.

"Like what?"

Tzippy squirmed. "Took things, hid them, made up stories."

"What did you take?"

"An ivory hand once, when I was at an antique show with my father. It was my first theft. I wanted it because it was so beautiful. It spoke to me in some strange way," she said, looking into the distance. "I hid it under my mattress. Then I took other things: a pretty hanky, a ribbon, a lipstick."

"Did it make you feel better?"

"Yes and no."

"Do you still take things?" Dr. Watkins asked.

"Why are you asking me?" Tzippy stared at him curiously.

"You know."

"I stole from Saks a few months ago; I took a brooch on sale. It was awful because I got caught." She wanted a pill so badly. "That was the last time."

"What are you going to do now, Mrs. Bryer?" Dr. Atkins asked. He took his glasses off, wiped them with a soft cloth, and then returned them to the bridge of his nose.

"I'm going to see it through to the end," Tzippy said, lifting her chin up. "That was my intention when I came here, and that's my intention now. It hasn't changed. Even though I just complained," she said.

"Do you feel cooler and less upset now?"

"Yes," Tzippy said, crossing her legs. "As a matter of fact, I do. I guess I needed to vent." She smiled, proud of her resiliency.

"I give you great credit," Dt. Watkins said. "However, I don't want you to get sick from the therapy sessions."

"I'll maintain. Shari plays rough. We'll fix things as best we can," Tzippy said. She was a realist. She hoped Shari wouldn't kill her with her anger.

For a minute, Tzippy wondered at her situation. Here she was, sitting with Dr. Karl Watkins in a small, spare office, the elderly WASPy doctor and she, the even older Jewish lady, working together and looking at each other. Both of them had seen a lot of life, she suspected, and both knew families could be extremely difficult. His niece had died of bulimia; his first wife was dead. *God knows what else*, she thought. Did he have children? Did they give him *tsuris*? Fate could throw curveballs and hit you in the stomach. They also both knew life was filled with many innings and chapters and that, with diligence, a person could turn things around.

"Please go to the emergency room and get checked out before you drive home," Dr. Watkins said.

"Yes, I will," Tzippy, said. "At eighty, I don't have many more chances."

Mrs. Maples' was the next item on Tzippy's agenda, and so she scheduled a meeting with Shari and PJ at PJ's Palm Beach office for Thursday, June 29. PJ, Tzippy, Shari, and the owner of Mrs. Maples' met while the palm trees bent gracefully in the breeze outside. Mr. Stern was a short, stocky man. Though he stood with his chin tucked in, extra skin overlapped his buttoned shirt collar. He wore a gray suit and tan loafers and was polite. Reaching for Mr. Stern's wide hand, Tzippy noticed his college ring, gold, with a large red stone in the center. After she shook his hand, she asked, "What school did you go to, Mr. Stern?"

"Boston University," he said.

"My husband went there as well. What a funny coincidence. I wish he were here now so you could review old times. Boston's a great college town."

"Yes, yes, I wish my wife were here as well. Unfortunately, she just passed away," he said.

"I heard that, and I'm very sorry," Tzippy said.

"Thank you. I'm glad she's past her suffering—though, after forty-nine years with the same partner, I'm finding the adjustment difficult. I can tell you that I'm anxious to consummate this deal. The incident on the store's closing day did it for me," he said, as he sat down.

"What happened, Mr. Stern?" PJ asked.

"Oh, God, a woman collapsed with a pulmonary embolism

while she was holding a stack of marked-down items. The clothes got thrown all over the floor, and the poor woman nearly died in my shop. Fortunately, an ambulance came quickly. All the other ladies in the store were screaming like crazy people and fled in a panic. It was not a proper ending after twenty-five years in business." He took a handkerchief from his pocket and dabbed his full face, though the air-conditioning was on in PJ's office.

"What a sad story," Shari said. She sat in the chair to the side of PJ's desk, looking lovely in a navy blue Theory suit and a white blouse. "Did the woman recover?"

"She's in intensive care over at Mount Sinai," Mr. Stern said.

"Well, I'm sorry," PJ said. "A terrible conclusion to a long era of hard work. However, everything appears to be in order." He held the contract up. "Here's a list of the fixtures Mr. Stern is leaving behind. Ladies, take a look." PJ gave each of them a copy. "Does either of you have any questions?"

"When can I actually take over?" Shari asked, clearly excited.

"We'll need a final walk-through before the last check is drawn," PJ said.

"Fine, fine. I have no problem with that. It's all procedural," Mr. Stern said.

"Where are you traveling to first?" Tzippy asked, after glancing at the list. She wanted Shari to be the one who made the practical decisions.

"My daughter and I are going to Israel," he said.

"That's wonderful," Tzippy said. "I'm going to Paris for my eighty-first birthday."

"Very nice, Mrs. Bryer. You don't look a day over seventy."

And so the deal was done and on November 1, 2000, Shari moved into Mrs. Maples', which she renamed Shari's Closet Boutique. Brucie and Naomi sent flowers, telegrams, and baskets of fruit. Shari ordered new clothes from trendy vendors, gave deep thought to how to decorate the front windows, and stayed up late, tagging and sorting her inventory as the boxes arrived. Angie came and helped her sort and stack and got to take home any extra-large dresses left behind.

When the cash register arrived, Stan took her across the street and opened up a business account at East Coast Ocean Bank, where Shari got a night deposit bag and a large gold key. She set up a ledger to keep track of all pertinent information regarding sales taxes, wrapping supplies, advertisements, payroll, and each category of sales. She would sell dresses, handbags, jewelry, tops, skirts, and hats.

"Hats complete an outfit," Tzippy said. "You'll probably add even more categories as you go along."

"She's got a good head on her," Stan said. "As long as she keeps off the booze, she'll be all right."

Shari continued seeing PJ, and Tzippy went with her to AA meetings, where the two of them sat in stunned silence as they listened to the recovering alcoholics share their stories. In time, Tzippy realized anyone could be a pill popper or a problem drinker. Who knew what happened behind closed doors? Benny used to say that you really didn't know what went on between a husband and wife unless you were in bed with them. How right he was. *Oh, dear, if Benny could see us now*, she thought, as she took a dollar from her wallet and dropped it into the straw donation basket being passed around.

In mid-August, during a break in the meeting, while Shari was outside smoking, Tzippy spoke to the well-coiffed lady at the end of the row.

"Hi. My name is Tzippy," she said.

"I'm Irene," the woman said, as she kept knitting.

"Nice sweater. For your grandchild?" Tzippy asked.

"No, my great-grandchild."

"Really?"

"Yes, I was a real child bride," Irene said, and laughed. "I was fifteen."

"Wow, that *is* young."

"Well, I got pregnant and there was no choice back then. My mother was horrified, even had my brother jump on my stomach to abort the baby, but nothing happened. So I married the fellow."

"Wonderful that you're knitting." Tzippy changed the subject to avoid sounding shocked at the story. "I'm trying to give up prescription pills."

"That's a hard one."

"My daughter's an alcoholic," Tzippy said, attempting to be as open as Irene, then realized she was trying to shove it off on Shari again. "And . . . and I'm a bit of a drinker myself—or was."

"So you come together?" Irene asked, her eyebrows rising in surprise.

"Yes."

"My kids said I had to come here and stop drinking," Irene confessed. She put down her needles and squeezed Tzippy's hand. "They wouldn't let me see the new baby if I didn't stop drinking. I was hiding the booze in my dresser."

"How long have you been sober?" Tzippy asked.

"Two years, six months, twenty-four days," Irene said, giving her a big grin. Her teeth were stained from smoking.

"You're doing great," Tzippy said.

"I'm trying. What about you?"

"I'm working on breaking old habits from long ago," Tzippy said.

"Here we are. Never too late. If you ever want to talk, here's my phone number," Irene said, scribbling on a piece of scrap paper. "I mean it."

"Thank you." Tzippy smiled. Clutching the information in her palm, she went back to where Shari had taken a seat.

"I've made a new friend," Tzippy reported. "That lady at the end, the one knitting. She gave me her phone number." Tzippy showed Shari the scrap of paper.

"Good for you, Mom. I just keep meeting men who want to pick me up."

When it was time for Shari to speak, she got up in front of the group and said, "Hello, my name is Shari and I'm an alcoholic."

Tzippy sat still, waiting to hear what her daughter would say.

"To begin, I've had a messy life. I started drinking at thirteen and got sick after every time I was drunk, but that didn't stop me from continuing. I drank because I didn't feel good about myself. My mother put a lot of pressure on me, and I had low self-esteem. She gave me all kinds of lessons—piano, dance, elocution, art, Hebrew school, you name it." People in the audience laughed. "I starved myself for the same reason. Fear of being fat drove my adolescence. I couldn't please her, and I felt rotten about myself. I had sex with boys because I wanted love. I guess I was a bit of a slut." Tzippy squirmed in her seat. "When I went to college, I weighed eighty-three pounds—a real beauty." Again, the crowd laughed. "I stole food from the girls' dorm and thought I was going to be sent to a funny farm." More laughter. "I called my mother and told her I needed to see a doctor. She didn't ask what kind of doctor. We both knew. I went to a shrink and just wanted to be normal. Instead, I eloped with a guy after dating him six weeks. That was a big hit." Laughter again.

"I got married to an alcoholic, and every night we drank rye and ginger ales. I had various jobs—retail, secretarial, real estate—but nothing stuck. I tried to make a baby but had miscarriages, maybe because of my diet, or lack of diet. My husband cheated on me, and I spent a lot of time going through the trash, looking for receipts to prove his infidelity. Why didn't I leave him, you might ask?" Shari said. She had the crowd in her hands, and Tzippy was suddenly sure she'd missed her profession as an actress. "Well, I'd rather go through the trash and get drunk, that's why. Smart girl!" The crowd laughed harder. "Then I got divorced after he left me for some chick ten years younger. I felt like an old shoe that had been tossed away. And that gave me a reason to drink even more. Beaujolais Villages was my favorite wine. Every week, I threw away a garbage bag of empty bottles. Lillian Roth had nothing on me."

Tittering and nodding. "Then I switched to vodka so no one could smell the alcohol. My habit grew and grew, until I was a full-fledged boozer. Tanqueray on the rocks lured me. Every day I wanted it. You know the routine."

Shari tried to sound casual, but Tzippy could tell she was embarrassed. Tzippy was amazed at her daughter's honesty. She wasn't ready to get up and speak in front of a crowd, but she understood blocking out the bad feelings. She knew it well. She remembered Benny and Laura and how miserable she had felt. *Why is life so difficult?* she wondered.

"I got sober, finally, a little while ago. It's been a struggle, but I'm doing it. Now my head is clearer and I don't embarrass myself. My mom and I are in therapy together, and I also go myself. I have a boyfriend who's glad I've stopped drinking. There is hope. I have hope. And I am turning the page. Thank you."

When Shari sat down, Tzippy squeezed her hand and whispered, "You were very brave." There were tears in Shari's eyes, and after the meeting many women came up to her and told her they understood. Some gave her their home number, and one invited her to a women's meeting on Friday night, held right there in the church.

"It's a real good meeting. Great bunch of gals. You ought to come. You'd fit right in. I promise," said the young woman, a bleached blond with a small tattoo on her shoulder. "We've all been through shit, believe me."

A week later, in preparation for opening her shop, Shari flew to Boston, got out of her lease, and gave her next-door neighbor her winter coat and heavy sweaters. Upon her return several weeks later, she took a small apartment downstairs from Tzippy in the same building and the two of them continued their AA meetings and therapy sessions with Dr. Watkins.

Stan was happy about Shari's living downstairs so he could have some private time with his bride.

"I was hoping we could fool around on the yellow couch," he said on one of Angie's days off.

"Oh, sweetheart, we'll have to put a large bath towel on it," Tzippy said. She was still embarrassed but was trying to be a good sport.

Stan spread a turquoise terry-cloth towel across the two seat cushions. It was shocking how men had no color sense. Tzippy slipped on a peignoir and lowered the lights while Stan turned on Frank Sinatra.

"Have I told you how much I love you?" Stan asked. He dropped his pants next to the cocktail table.

Tzippy lay down on the yellow sofa. "Sweetheart, I think I know, but you can tell me again," she said, as her black peignoir opened, exposing her breasts.

And he did, and he did.

Shari's Closet Boutique opened on December 1, in time for the holiday season. Naomi and Bruce sent poinsettias to congratulate Shari, and the shop was bursting with color and little twinkling lights. The shelves were stuffed with gift ideas—zany pocketbooks, perfume, artsy silk scarves, and hats with matching gloves. The bell rang frequently, every time a customer entered, and outside the pink flamingo had a string of white lights draped around its neck. There was even a little Hanukkah tree right by the front door. It was hung with blue glass ornaments and had a Jewish star on top and gifts scattered all around it.

Stan told Tzippy that after the year the two of them had just had, it was time for them to kick up their heels as well, and he insisted they celebrate New Year's in Paris, getting a jump on her eighty-first birthday. Who was she to argue with an offer like that?

When Tzippy and Stan were overseas, Naomi called to report that she and Ike had paid a surprise visit to Shari's shop. She described how Shari had stood behind the counter, ringing in a sale, while her assistant had wrapped a Christmas gift.

"Oh, I'm sure your daughter will love this," Shari had said to the woman as she wrote up the sales slip. There were racks of dresses sorted by color. A wall of shoes covered the back—high heels, kitten heels, slingbacks, and booties. Some had buckles, bling, and bows. Christmas songs played, and Elvis Presley's voice put the customers in a good mood.

A gal came to the counter with a handful of lace bikini underpants. "I need these for stocking stuffers for my sisters," she said.

"Great idea," Shari said. She wore a red Santa hat slanted sideways, with bright red lipstick and a matching red dress. "I have these little mesh bags we can put each one in."

"Perfect," the woman said.

"She's full of clever ideas," Naomi told Tzippy. Shari had decorated her front windows with an artistic display of career dresses, each mannequin sporting a Santa hat as it held an adding-machine tape that draped around a filing cabinet and into the next mannequin's hand. The tape created its own design around the figures' legs and arms. The next window had a sign that said "yummy!" And the mannequins each wore an evening dress in a primary color while they held ice-cream cones filled with ruby-like gems, instead of cherries. The glass stones were also scattered on the floor around the mannequins' evening shoes.

"Mom, she's doing just great. Ike and I were so impressed," Naomi gushed.

At her hotel, Tzippy received pictures of both display windows, as well as one of Shari behind the front counter. She had sent postcards to Shari, and Naomi reported having seen them on her bulletin board. Mona Lisa's half-smile was on the front. Underneath, Tzippy had written, *Dear Shari, I hope the shop is buzzing with holiday business. We love gay Paris. I am so proud of you! I knew you could do it! Love, Mom.*

Naomi said that Shari smiled at the customers and wished each one of them happy holidays. While they were there, the phone rang, and when Shari answered it, it was PJ.

"Shari's Closet Boutique. May I help you?"

Shari smiled. "I can manage eight p.m. It'll give me time to close up, do the deposit, and get to a meeting on 79th Street," she said. She put her hand on her hip and posed like a mannequin. "Well, it's pretty hard not to make sales at this time of year," Shari said. "Christmas is major in the retail business."

Shari laughed and hung up the phone and told Naomi and Ike that PJ had said she was a natural.

Naomi's glowing report put Tzippy in a wonderful mood for the rest of her time in Paris. She drank wonderful coffee and tried not to eat too many pastries. She and Stan strolled the boulevards and stopped at small cafés. He was the dearest husband, and his steadiness was helping her live without popping a pill every time she had a nervous attack. While they were away, they had given Angie a paid month off and told her to go visit her family.

Brucie and Jill were back together, but Tzippy knew that the reunion had been fragile and might splinter at any moment. Naomi and Ike were overextended financially, as Ike was opening up a new shopping mall somewhere near a college. Now, for the first time, Shari appeared more stable than the other two children, Tzippy thought. Perhaps she really had helped her youngest, most damaged offspring.

The best news was Shari. A new, sober life. With God's help, Tzippy hoped, things would keep improving. With God's help, she wouldn't steal anymore. With God's help, she would live a little longer, and, who knew, maybe Shari and PJ would tie the knot. *A mother can dream. Especially a Jewish mother*, she thought.

Chapter 25

The weather turned warmer, and the snowbirds returned to their northern homes. Tzippy preferred the quieter life after many of the visitors and the three-monthers retreated to New England and their other lives. The beaches were less crowded, the restaurants easier to get into, the ocean warmer and more swimmable. With Stan's strong arm to steady her, she liked to walk just a bit into the surf and let the waves splash her legs. Sometimes she would sit and get completely soaked, just to remind herself of her lost youth and the days when she'd enjoyed jumping into the waves and getting her heart pumping fast.

When her old friend Lillian Stone had been diagnosed with inoperable cancer the year before, Lillian had taken out the old, thick-tired bike stored in her garage and ridden around the streets of Boca Raton. She had gone over to Mizner Park, where all the shops and restaurants were located, and up and down the residential streets, her thin white hair flying and her shirttails flapping in the breeze. "Just one more time, I want to feel the wind in my hair; just one more time, I want to feel like a kid again," she'd said with crinkling eyes and pallid skin when Tzippy had questioned her. She'd died two months later, and Tzippy and Stan had sat together in the Unitarian church while Lillian's granddaughter, a divinity student from Harvard, conducted the service. They had passed out little mesh bags filled with seashells and candy to each mourner—gifts from Lillian.

She'd always been a rare bird, that one. Tzippy admired her originality. She had studied at RISD and had been full of artistic notions. *What a loss*, thought Tzippy, as she squeezed Stan's hand during the eulogy. *Lillian had the right idea.* She had lived her life in her own, original way and hadn't cared what other people thought.

When Tzippy first returned to her apartment after the Paris trip, she felt rested and renewed. She signed up for a course in conversational French so that when they went back, she'd at least be able to converse with the shop owners and waiters. Visiting the antiques and the exquisite paintings in the museums had reinvigorated her interest in the arts. *Oh, such beauty. How poor Papa would have loved Paris*, she thought. And then she remembered how she'd stolen the ivory hand, and she was ashamed of herself all over again.

One morning when she and Angie were alone in the apartment while Stan was out golfing, Tzippy sat with her tea and rye toast and said, "Remember how I told you about getting caught by a detective in Saks?"

Angie stopped what she was doing and came over to where Tzippy was sitting. "I remember, Mrs. B."

"Well, I did steal something, and I went to court. Stan was with me. The judge let me off, but I'll never forget his face."

"Oh, Mrs. B., I'll never forget how bad I felt for betraying you when I took your money. I'm just grateful you gave me a second chance."

"Me, too," Tzippy said. "I've been given a second chance as well. A do-over for my whole life, practically."

Angie laughed and patted her arm.

Tzippy wondered what might have happened if they'd never taken things. It was a silly thought, a foolish waste of time, because that wasn't their story, was it?

"Have you ever taken any other things from people?" Tzippy asked.

"Do you mind if I sit?" Angie asked.

"No, please. I want to talk."

Angie sat down at the table and clasped her large hands. "I once took a candy bar from a store when I was a girl. I wanted that candy bar so bad I could taste it. We kids were always hungry."

"Did you ever steal anything as an adult?" Tzippy asked, as she sipped her tea.

"Other than your money, only one other time. I stole that pink pashmina from a shop, but then God saw fit for it to be lost, so I never got to wear it."

She looked at Tzippy, and Tzippy recalled how she had stuffed the cashmere shawl down the incinerator, resentful that Angie had such an expensive item. Tzippy closed her eyes in disbelief at her own meanness and smallness. She spread some jam on her rye toast, which had grown cold, and took a little bite in order to give herself time to absorb the absurdity of the pashmina saga.

"Well," she finally said, "we'll just have to get you a new one and pay for it properly this time." She smiled at Angie. "I took things in my life, Angie, and now I'm in therapy because I want to understand why and I want to stop."

"That's a fine thing, Mrs. B."

"We're kind of alike, you and I, aren't we?"

"Yeah, I guess in some ways we are." Angie rose from the table and started to clean up the crumbs with the dish towel draped over her shoulder. "Except you're the rich lady and I'm the help."

Tzippy laughed. "Angie, one of the things I love about you is that you always speak the truth. But remember, I may be the rich lady, but you're my friend. When I die, I want you to have a year's pay and my town car. I'm going to put that in my will."

Angie's face perked up. "Why, that's very nice of you, Mrs. B., but you ain't dying so fast."

"Well, I can't live forever, can I?"

"Let's not talk about that depressing stuff. What are we doing today?"

"Let's go down and see how Shari's making out in her store. She told me they got in some new merchandise and she was changing the window displays. That girl has a wonderful artistic bent, don't you think?"

"I think that child has turned over a new leaf and you should feel terrific about all the work you did on that subject."

Tzippy rose from the table and started toward her bedroom. "I need a tub, and then we'll go. Angie, I love you. I couldn't have done any of this without you."

"Go on and take your tub, and don't be slipping. Call me if you need me." Angie turned and went back into the kitchen.

Tzippy shook her head in wonderment and smiled to herself as she went to turn on the water. How she loved Angie.

How she loved her bath and her toilette every morning.

How she loved her life.

Acknowledgments

I have many people to thank. As I wrote this book, I had a wonderful editor, Steven Bauer, from Hollow Tree Press in Bath, Indiana, who guided me, taught me, and helped me get *Tzippy the Thief* ready for publication. I then worked with Annie Tucker, from She Writes Press, who was instrumental in helping me tighten up the story.

My son-in-law, David Jacobs, was my first reader, and he gave me confidence to go on. My daughter, Danielle Jacobs, read my manuscript and wanted to show the book to her book group. My partner, Manny Sieradzki, helped me with computer issues, my website, and all business matters.

I thank my publisher, Brooke Warner, for her help and instruction, and my publicist, Victor Gulotta, for marketing my novel and showing me the way to bookstores, signings, and other media outlets.

This is a work of love, and I hope no one sees himself or herself in the book, because each character is a composite of my imagination, with bits of real folks thrown together. This is what a writer does. Plus, I am a clinical social worker and have heard many stories, which occasionally I used or rearranged to add drama to my novel. It is all part of the process of creating.

I hope you enjoy *Tzippy*!

About the Author

Patricia Rohner was born in New York, New York, where her mother spent New Year's Eve in the Doctors Hospital. She first lived in an apartment in Forest Hills, New York, and then moved to a home in South Orange, New Jersey, where she spent her childhood. She attended a Hebrew day school, a public junior high school, and then Kimberley Academy, an all-girls high school in Montclair, New Jersey. She loved to paint and write and was in the drama club. Rohner spent her summers at Camp Lown in Maine. At fifteen, she went to Europe and Israel for six weeks with relatives and returned to the United States on the *Queen Mary*.

Rohner graduated from Brandeis University, where she majored in theater arts, and later received a certificate in communications and a master's in social work, both from Simmons College in Boston. She worked as a clinical social worker, owned and ran a gourmet kitchen shop in Newburyport, Massachusetts, and sold real estate. Rohner has published seven short stories in literary journals and won first prize in a poetry-reading contest, as well as first prize in an art show for her sculpture of a female head.

Rohner has four wonderful children, a daughter and three sons, and twelve grandchildren, all of whom are a source of great pleasure for her. She also golfs and loves the Boston Red Sox. She lives half the year in West Newbury, Massachusetts, and the other half in Boca Raton, Florida.

SELECTED TITLES FROM SHE WRITES PRESS

She Writes Press is an independent publishing company
founded to serve women writers everywhere.
Visit us at www.shewritespress.com.

*A Tight Grip: A Novel about Golf, Love Affairs, and Women of a
Certain Age* by Kay Rae Chomic. $16.95, 978-1-938314-76-6. As
forty-six-year-old golfer Jane "Par" Parker prepares for her next
tournament, she experiences a chain of events that force her to
reevaluate her life.

Hysterical: Anna Freud's Story by Rebecca Coffey. $18.95, 978-1-
938314-42-1. An irreverent, fictionalized exploration of the seemingly
contradictory life of Anna Freud—told from her point of view.

How to Grow an Addict by J.A. Wright. $16.95, 978-1-63152-991-7.
Raised by an abusive father, a detached mother, and a loving aunt
and uncle, Randall Grange is built for addiction. By twenty-three,
she knows that together, pills and booze have the power to cure just
about any problem she could possibly have . . . right?

Wishful Thinking by Kamy Wicoff. $16.95, 978-1-63152-976-4. A
divorced mother of two gets an app on her phone that lets her be in
more than one place at the same time, and quickly goes from zero to
hero in her personal and professional life—but at what cost?

Just the Facts by Ellen Sherman. $16.95, 978-1-63152-993-1. The
seventies come alive in this poignant and humorous story of a fearful
rookie reporter at a small-town newspaper who uncovers a big-time
scandal.

Royal Entertainment by Marni Fechter. $16.95, 978-1-938314-52-0.
After being fired from her job for blowing the whistle on her boss,
social worker Melody Frank has to adapt to her new life as the assistant to an elite New York party planner.